LOGGING ON

Bass sat entranced, his fingers limp on the obsolete keyboard, his thoughts a thousand miles from the small, dank room. A black blot formed in the haze before his unfocused eyes. First wavering, stretching, becoming diffuse, it eventually followed his mental command, and became a disk, a shrinking dot, and finally a point.

It split. *Two*, he subvocalized. *Two* dots, *two* chickens, *two* psatla. *Two.* Haze coalesced into a line connecting the points. *Line. Geometry. Two points define a line.* Bass reviewed the first three theorems he could remember. *Three* theorems. His mind rocked with the impact of quasiphysical forces shaking his synapses, triggering bursts of unconnected thought, memories, erotica, numbers, concepts . . .

At last it stopped. Haze coalesced again: [MOD2 OPSYS 3.32]. Bass sighed. The brain-mapping was through; he was past the threshold that drove men insane.

A PLAGUE
OF CHANGE

L. Warren Douglas

A Del Rey Book

BALLANTINE BOOKS • NEW YORK

A Del Rey Book
Published by Ballantine Books

Copyright © 1992 by L. Warren Douglas

All rights reserved under International and Pan-American Copyright Conventions. Published in the United States of America by Ballantine Books, a division of Random House, Inc., New York, and simultaneously in Canada by Random House of Canada Limited, Toronto.

Library of Congress Catalog Card Number: 92-90156

ISBN 0-345-37828-8

Manufactured in the United States of America

First Edition: September 1992

To the mentor I have never met, who set the standards and the goals, the man who brought all the colors and textures of the mind to the worlds of science fiction: Jack Vance.

PROLOGUE

The trader resisted an urge to wrinkle his nose at the stinking, alien air. No telling whether the wormbags could read human mannerisms and be offended. He couldn't afford negative reactions—he needed what they had to sell; his world had to have it or it would die.

"Thessse we will take," hissed a chorus of alien mouths. Pale, sinuous "arms" indicated a cluster of potted trees and an accompanying stack of vacuum-packed seed canisters. A snake-like appendage wrapped itself around the slim trunk of a sugar maple. "Isss thissss one native to your colony world?" The sibilant, nonhuman pronunciation issued from a score of tiny worm mouths, one to each pseudotentacle. Quivering, speaking spaghetti, the trader thought, repressing a shudder. Bleached grass snakes bundled together in a sheaf, covered with chitinous beetle wings. It was hard to remain rational in the presence of psatla even though he was not, by nature, a xenophobe. No trader could be. Was it the pheromones? Some chemical component of the creatures' reeking air? They're colonial intelligences, he told himself, not single beings at all. They look like worms because they *are* worms. But we need them, he reminded himself. The blight spreads. Without their tailored viruses to combat it, every vascular plant on my world will be dead in five years, and the colony with them. Mastering his repulsion, the trader replied. "It's a maple. A native of my species' homeworld."

"Ssso I sssuspected," mused the shapeless ugliness before him. A single ashen strand writhed from beneath protective chitin and snapped off a leaf, curled around it, crushed it methodically, and drew it into the pulsing shadows beneath overlapping chitin plates. "It tassstesss like the fffungusss that plaguesss your planet."

1

"Earth?" the trader exclaimed. "The blight is an Earth disease?"

"Earthhh . . . dirt, sssoil. Ahhh, yesss. Dirt world, homeworld. Like treesss, your roots remain in earth, on Earth. Isss it not ssso?"

Humor? Can a synergy of semisentient worms make a joke? The trader forced a smile—not that the creature would recognize it as such. "So we call it," he replied through clenched teeth. Had the being, the psatla, "tasted" the genetic structure of the leaf so easily, and recognized the scattered chainings of nucleotides that fungus blight and maple trees held in common, the genes of Earth? The trader fought against distraction. "You have chosen. Do we have a trade?"

"A bargain? Yesss," the psatla responded. "These ssssufffice. Your world'sss sssurvival fffor oursss."

The trader's curiosity was piqued. "Your survival?" he asked, bolder now that agreement was reached.

"Not thessse treesss alone," the psatla whispered. "But, with many othersss, thisss bare world will sssomeday sssusssstain usss." The trader understood, then. From orbit, he had seen bare rock and empty ocean, continents dusted with lichens and brown moss. Only the temperate and tropic coasts had been green, the green of dense forest, of deep, humus-rich soils. Terraforming. With only biologicals to work with, the wormbags were trying to transform a world. Even with their inborn ability to read and manipulate genes, it was a millennial task, for psatla manufactured nothing. They had no ships, and couldn't fly them if they had, so they were dependent on human trade for everything they couldn't grow. Theirs was a desperate, tenuous situation. "I wish you success," he said, a trace of pity in his tone. "I hope you're given the time for it."

"*Given* time?" The worm mouths sighed. "Isss time a giffft, or a given?"

The creature *is* playing with words, the trader realized. Just how smart is it? He had to remind himself again that psatla, ragtag composites of worm brains and worm mouths though they might be, were sentient beings. *Different* intelligences, but not necessarily *lesser* ones. "You may not have thousands of years for your task," he answered. "You may not even have fifty."

"That isss a ssserious contention," the psatla hissed quietly. "You have wisssdom we lack? Will you tell usss your thoughtsss?" It motioned with a cluster of chitin-wrapped white strands, a humanlike gesture.

I'm being invited inside. I'm not sure I want to see how these creatures live. Would the stink of them be even more intense, within the rambling structure of vines and branches and bark they called home? The trader doubted there would be lace tablecloths and a silver tea service.

"We offer you refreshment," his host said, as if sensing his thoughts. "Cofffee from the berry bushesss of your ssspecies-home, and tobacco, if you desssire it. Humansss who have tried them sssay they are excsssellent." There was no choice. The trader ducked his head into the dim, open doorway . . .

The ship rose silently at first. Then, as its increasing speed warred with the friction of thinning air, it howled distantly, left a faint contrail, and disappeared into the brightness of the morning. Pungent scents rose in the humid air around the two psatla. Translated into the human tongue, the shifting odors may have meant something like this:

Human-ships are the blood of the starlanes. An acrid scent, the ozone of discharging fuel cells and the reek of hot steel, was followed by the richer iron tang of human body fluid overlaid with frosty cold and the vacuum of a scent-numbing enzyme. *If human culture fails, all transReef and much beyond will die with them. Phastillan itself will not survive.* The odors of fiberglass, of raisins and sweat, of oil, cheap perfume, and many other scents no human would think to associate with "culture" were succeeded by death stench and wet rust, then supplanted by scents of growing things from a dozen worlds and their final decomposition by-products: interstellar decay. Finally, the scents of the very planet itself dried, desiccated, and blew away on dead, empty winds.

The seed is planted. A wet-earth scent, accompanied by a subtle puff of growth hormone felt rather than scented. This from the larger of the two beings, whose chitin plates were bright as new-minted gold. *Will it flourish?* A brief gust of "anxious."

Time . . . the gift, if given . . . and the winds and rains of the trader's far world, will allow the fruiting tree. A wafted mélange of seasonal odors in rapid sequence with the odd, cold flavor of rain on far-distant slopes, then the tang of ripeness, of rich juices flowing, from the trader's counterpart, green-chitined with a touch of bronze.

Will new seed return here? How will that be? Maple-leaf scent, faint, then grown heavy, followed by the volatile hormone "curious wonder."

Like the spinning maple-tree seeds, green-bronze assured his superior in words of crushed-leaf scent, *many will scatter, but one, surely, will blow even this far on the ship-winds between the stars.* The latter was machine oil and ozone, then a cold scent-absorbing-all-scents, a sensory void.

It is well. Warm sunlight on black soil. *We will wait for it. We will live, and our effort will continue.* Roots and humus, and a waft of mating pheromones that caused both psatla to spread their chitin plates wide, savoring it.

Bronze-and-green ''spoke'' aloud then, a drawn-out rush of air that would have sounded, to human ears, like a sigh.

CHAPTER
ONE

Five hundred years out from Earth, Man is still Man. Across two thousand parsecs of drifted stars and immense black voids, boys are still boys. Vassily James Cannon was no exception. He stood stiffly at attention before Captain Sotheny and prepared for the worst.

''Congratulations, Cadet. You've successfully completed your self-assigned mission: you've attained the bridge of the *Stella M. Carrington*. Some facets of your academy training have been demonstrated. Evasion, infiltration, and a good knowledge of the ducts and systems of a Class C freighter. Oh, yes. And computer break-in as well.'' The captain's voice was soft, mellifluous—and heavy with sarcasm. Vassily ''Bass'' Cannon had heard such voices before, and never had they meant him well.

''Yes, sir!'' he said crisply, in good academy form with no superfluous muscle movement.

''Then let me test another area of your training: law. Were you of my crew, what would prevent me from spacing you this instant? What rights would you, an invader of my sovereign territory, have?''

''Nothing, sir! None, sir.''

"Admirably precise, Cadet. Correct. I could have you spaced or flogged. But you're a passenger, and thus my charge; and you're a minor as well, so not legally responsible. Those things give me a certain latitude in dealing with your 'crime.'" The captain leaned back in his flight couch; whining servomotors adjusted it to his shifted weight. He pressed his thumbs together and steepled his long fingers. "Demonstrate further, Cadet. Cite each infraction and crime you have indulged in, its appropriate Uniform Disciplinary Code punishment, and your academy's indubitably milder variant thereof. Be specific."

"Sir! Removal of a ventilator grille: unauthorized modification of ship's life-support equipment. Maximum disciplinary action: ten lashes and/or ten days' incarceration or confinement to quarters.

"Crawling through the ventilation and service duct so accessed, and use of restricted service corridors: unauthorized entry. Maximum action: ten lashes and/or ten days.

"Use of an unauthorized computer interface to reprogram seven corridor locks in order to gain entrance: sabotage of ship's operating systems while under way. Maximum peacetime penalty: fifty lashes, incarceration for the duration of the voyage, and permanent grounding at the next port of call."

"And your academy's version?"

"Sir, the Crowe Academy code is the same, but substitutes expulsion from the academy for grounding where the offense is sabotage."

"You're harsh on yourself, Cadet. You made no attempt to claim a lesser offense where you might. The exact punishment is, however, at my discretion, and I'm not a harsh man, so I'll give you your choice: seventy lashes, as specified, to be given ten per day, then incarceration in the *Carrington*'s brig until we land on Cannon's Orb three weeks from now. That's your first choice. The second is perhaps milder, as you're technically a passenger on this vessel: if I am satisfied that she is in no further danger from the exercise of your ingenuity, you may continue as a passenger. In that case, though, I'll recommend your immediate expulsion from Crowe Academy, and you'll be blacklisted from here to Earth—be assured that as an officer in the TransReef Merchant Service, my word carries the weight to accomplish it. Your choice, Cadet?"

"Sir! The first choice, if you please."

* * *

"Wasn't that harsh? The choice you gave him?" The *Carrington*'s second officer—also the captain's wife and the mother of his three sons—shook her head slowly, not raising her gaze from the chart holoscope.

"Not too. I've scanned his records from Crowe. They're all on his vita card in the purser's safe. I know who—and what—he is. His cleverness with the ship's computers is only a side effect of his real talents. At Crowe, he was right off their test scales in so many areas that they're downright afraid of him."

"What's to be afraid of? He's only a boy."

"Yes, but a boy who may grow into one of the most brilliant military, political, and economic strategists that the galaxy has ever produced . . .

"And did you hear him—'use of an unauthorized interface . . .' A hat! The kid used a homemade, functioning, bloody-be-damned hat to link with our comp! And he doesn't even know how special that makes him."

"Neither do I," Second Officer Sotheny responded. "Just what is a 'hat'?"

"A bioelectronic interface. That, and the software to run it. A headset creates a three-dimensional field, a fifth-force reticulum that 'reads' his directed thoughts and translates them into machine code. In reverse, the computer manipulates the field forces to jog his brain. Information is *right there* in his head when he needs it. Some users can 'see' colors, pictures . . . anything that can be broken down into code in the first place."

Lady Sotheny shook her head and made a rueful moue. "Fine. Now I know what a hat *is*—that glorified hairnet you took away from him. But I don't see what the fuss is all about."

The captain sighed, his face a mask of bitter resentment. "Every officer candidate gets tested on the hat. In all the time I was in Service, not one man passed the test. I didn't see them, but I heard that two otherwise fine and stable cadets washed out afterward—both Section Eights, mental defectives. Just from *trying* that damned hat. One in gods only know how many billion people can use a hat. Can you imagine it? The power you'd have with all that knowledge right there in your head? All the information in a data base like the *Carrington*'s even closer than your fingertips? Can you imagine it?" Sotheny shook his head.

"I can't. And neither can you," she replied dryly. "If we could, then we'd be like him, wouldn't we? We never imagine anything really alien to us." She leaned back in her seat. "Those stories about nonhuman aliens—written before we actually encountered any—had all sorts of exotic speculations about strange societies and biologies, but ultimately the aliens were us in disguise. Not all of us, just parts. There were aliens who had no emotion or were all emotion; kind ones who loved, and warlike ones who had no word for peace. Facets of us, all of them.'' She breathed deeply, assured by her husband's intent silence that she would be allowed her entire say.

"Can we explain the real aliens we trade with in human terms? Gelenites *act* almost human, when they're around us. No matter they're radially symmetrical and 'see' only electric fields. They even *sound* human. They sing, recite poetry . . . but when they're by themselves, they eat feces to get acquainted with each other, and pith their own infants' brains to make biological serving robots.

"And armoths? They like music, human music. But an odd sound, a particular voice or machine rattle, can trigger a killing rage . . . there, see? I said rage. But do I *know* that? What I mean is, they *act* as a human might, if he were enraged, that's all. For all I really know, an enraged armoth might be wishing me happy birthday.

"The other alien races are even worse. Only our computers can talk with engstroms. Even their name belongs to the man who discovered them. Those wormbags, whatever they're called—''

"The pissants? Psatla, I think.''

"Yes, them. They stink. And they talk with smells, or phero-mones. What does my—forgive my crudeness—what does my crotch say to a wormbag? Nothing I'd *intend* it to say, I'm sure:''

She drew in a deep breath, and let it out. "Aliens. We just deal with them empirically, without a scintilla of real understanding. We trade with a hundred species, Earthward of the Reef, and only two others have starships—or want to. The rest are too well adapted to their solitary worlds, or they can't even conceptualize the rest of the universe.

"And young Bass Cannon?'' she wondered aloud. "Are the academy's manipulations of him just as empirical? Do they know what they're dealing with? Is there as little common ground?''

"At least he's human,'' Sotheny mused. "His mother wanted an exceptional son for her husband's sake, and that's what she got: an administrator extraordinaire to take over the Cannon empire. Only it might not be just Jack Cannon's fiefs he inherits, you see. The Panaikos Council has feared the inevitability of economic and political chaos in transReef space—we're mineral-poor and vastly overextended—and they knew they'd need generals of his potential caliber. They've been cultivating them—talented cadets, especially from key families like his. It's established policy. But the Cannon boy mustn't know—not yet, at any rate.

"You see," he went on, responding to her unasked question, "I'm only following Crowe's recommended treatment of him." The captain smiled. "That's how I know he hasn't cracked his vita card's codes. He would have changed those recommendations for sure."

"But why be so rough on him?"

"He's arrogant, irresponsible, and selfish," the captain said with a sly grin. "A boy, in other words. But of all boys, he's got to be trained and disciplined before he discovers what he is. Personally, I think he'll survive it—he's got more than a streak of his father in him, I can tell."

"He made the right choice, then." It wasn't a question. "And if he'd chosen expulsion instead?"

"It would have been a less responsible choice. He knew he could still have had a plush life on the Orb, being who he is. But he chose a man's punishment, not a boy's."

"And if he hadn't?" she persisted.

"Then he'd never have gotten off Cannon's Orb again. Not even dead."

Sotheny's second officer sat still for a long moment, staring into her instruments. Finally, she looked her husband in the eyes. "Perhaps he knew that. Could he? What if he chose the right alternative for all the wrong reasons?"

"I don't think there are any wrong reasons. He chose rightly, and that's what matters. The pain will pass, but he'll remember the lesson of it." Captain Sotheny shook his head thoughtfully. "I don't think we've heard the last of him. Oh, yes—I 'forgot' to confiscate his illegal hat."

CHAPTER

TWO

Cannon's Orb. A silly, pretentious name. All the lovely, evocative ones had been taken long ago: Windswept, Thalassa, Winter. The trite ones had been reiterated in every fashion, too: Heaven, Eden, Valhalla, Journey's End. Bass Cannon shrugged. His father might have done worse. The lovely blue-green and buff world could have been "Jack's Planet."

From low orbit, the Orb displayed an intricate weave of submerged mountain chains. Even the equatorial peaks showed signs of glaciation: toothy arêtes, round-bottomed valleys chained with azure lakes and fjords. Short, fast rivers tumbled from high valleys in hundred-meter cascades, then separated into braided deltas.

The dominant life-forms of the planets were trees. The thirty thousand identified species were only those that were economic resources. Metalvein, violet-heart, and mountain redfern were beautiful; sooder and sweet nellie were aromatic, intoxicating; feathervane, redspalt, and rock-ivory were dense and strong. Trees and timber were the wooden backbone of the colony. Each man, woman, and child knew the feel of sawdust, the smells of wood growing and wood being cut.

Earth grasses introduced in the Barrens and on the coasts converted loess plains and dust basins to rich range land. Some trace elements were missing from the Orb's soil, but they were easily traded for. Jack Cannon's colonists enjoyed a diet rich in red meat.

The Orb was a product of rare circumstances: twenty thousand years earlier its sun, Mirasol, was within the Caprian Reef, a jumble of opaque dust, supernova remnants, and detritus. Mirasol, formed in an older region of the galactic arm, had entered the Reef with its fourth planet already rich in life. For a million years collisions with Reef substance roiled its atmosphere and muted Mirasol's sustaining warmth. Glaciers increased the world's albedo, reflecting back the star's diminished light. They cut, ground, and pushed the planet's surface into new and contorted forms, and cleared the land of all but scattered life.

The Caprian Reef was dense enough to absorb light, so it looked like a rift in the star fields to casual observers. Seen from the Earthward worlds, it was just one of many "empty" patches of sky that hid the glorious jeweled crown of the galactic core from view. But it was more, much more, as the first star voyagers to approach it discovered to their dismay. The Reef extended farther than the black cloak of its visible portion had indicated. As near as could be estimated, it stretched most of the length of one galactic arm, an irregular spiral reaching far beyond the maximum range of human ships. Toward the galactic zenith and nadir, too, the Caprian reach stretched farther than ships could reach in a lifetime or ten. There was no way around it—only through it.

Most of the Reef was invisible, composed of quirks and accidents of gravitation that separated vagrant motes and particles of antimatter from a galaxy hostile to them. Perhaps there had been an antimatter world, once, or a star, that wandered in from above the galactic plane only to be destroyed in its first contact with the "normal" stuff of interstellar dust and protocometary ices. Whatever its origin, the Reef fabric was a twisted lamination of matter and antimatter indistinguishable until contact was made, and contact was deadly.

Ships could plow through ordinary matter as dense as the Reef's invisible fringes, and elsewhere they did so. But the first ships to thread the Reef's voids had to travel slowly, at a small fraction of light's velocity. Ahead, they flung scattergun pellets of dust that spread into clouds, testing each obstructing haze for the annihilating blaze that signified antimatter. They had to map their every move to the limits of their instruments' accuracy, and then hope that the tugs of not-quite-random gravitation upon slow-swirling Reef substance did not close their trail behind them.

The starlanes through the Reef were now wide and clear, by those early explorers' standards. Ships threaded their tortuous routes in six months or a year, subjective time. Those paths were few, though, and bought with thousands of lives, and more ships than starfarers wished to contemplate. The Reef trails were the caravan routes of space, the long, dry desert passages where danger and death stalked the traveler who strayed from the proven route, and where even care and caution could not always prevent an encounter with a lurking enemy, a stray unmapped wisp of hostile substance.

Nineteen thousand years before the first human landed on the Orb, Mirasol emerged from the dark-matter core of the Reef, and tiny patches of brown and green crept out across the face of the fourth planet.

Five thousand years after that, the glaciers were only dirty gray traces in the high ranges and at the poles. Every patch of soil deep enough to hold a root grew a tree. A million species or more spread from protected valleys and propagated by root, rhizome, seed, and spore.

Fishlike creatures swam in lakes and oceans, and catlike, omnivorous "grabbits" dominated the land, abounding in this area, starving in that. No predators existed.

A hundred and twenty-five short years ago, a worn, antique spacecraft of Earthly origin had assumed a wobbly orbit around the Orb. The lone young man on board studied the planet with old, well-maintained instruments. He mapped, plotted, and analyzed; then he landed. Kneeling in tall feathery ferns amid the crackling and chirping hymns of a myriad unseen insects, he raised his face skyward to his god, and he prayed. Taking samples of soil, air, and vegetation, he hopped from one continent to another, collecting and studying, and after several months he began his long journey back to Earth.

In spite of his elation, it was no pleasure to return to the Earthward worlds. Sparse and lonely transReef might be, but it was clean and uncrowded, unmarked by the tensions of populations pressed elbow to elbow on overused, dirty worlds. It was unsoiled by the decadence and perversions of a culture turned inward on itself, a society stratified and ossified, where men like Jack Cannon were viewed as dangerous upstarts, as threats to the vast interlinkages of wealth and power that prevailed.

The first colonies among the transReef stars had formed the Panaikos Council: Pan-aikos, "of all our houses." Council ships patrolled the transReef passages and council pilots guided ships through. Pilot fees, fines, and duties funded other council functions, among them the registration and licensing of new transReef colonies and the approval of colonial planetary constitutions. By Council policy, such documents had to address the maintenance of basic human rights; but the forms of colonial government, from essentially anarchic contract systems to hereditary monarchies, were left to the licencees.

In thirty years, planetary time, Jack returned, having aged only five years. He brought with him the Panaikos Council's license to colonize the world now officially named "Cannon's Orb" and an approved constitution that defined the contract system by which he would govern it. Since crimes like rape, kidnapping, and murder fell within the Panaikos Council's jurisdiction, Orb law had only to deal with lesser crimes, most of which could be treated as breach of contract. Under Orb law even assault was so considered, for the eschewal of such violence was part of each colonist's basic contract. Even children, upon coming of age, had the choice to sign or emigrate.

This time Jack came in a larger ship with a five-man crew, bringing half a thousand hopeful settlers under contract to him. His prime contractor was Elias Cotter, for whom the Orb's initial settlement was named: Cotterville. Still young, Jack Cannon stayed for a few years until he was sure that Cotterville was a going concern. Five hundred colonists—he had chosen them carefully. The first roof under which they had all slept, together, was a great timbered hall, a church.

When lights glowed in two hundred wooden houses along several muddy streets, and when the first five million board feet of exotic logs were loaded in his hold, Jack Cannon departed. With that cargo alone he could have stayed on Earth as a rich man, but that wasn't even a consideration, so thirty planetary years later he returned to Cannon's Orb.

This time he had aged only four years, for interstellar travel was unpredictable. Over the same route, tiny variations in a ship's drive potentials and changes in the web of forces that united the galaxy changed simple relativistic time dilation. Aboard a ship, time was less constant than the mountain winds on Jack's world.

Five thousand contractors and subcontractors disembarked: equipment, seeds, animals were off-loaded and distributed to new townsites, leaseholds, and camps. Three great cargo vessels were filled with the choicest woods the planet could offer. A thousand species were represented, each more lovely than the one before it. Jack went back to Earth again on the third ship, after five years on the Orb.

Before he left, his parting words to his colonists were delivered from a low dais at the head of the Cotterville church. It was a sermon and a good-bye: words to last for a generation. The godly men he'd chosen vowed then and there that when Jack returned to the Orb, their unborn sons would know his parting phrases by heart.

Those men aged thirty-two years while Jack trod metal decks

and viewed distorted stars through portholes. Returning, Jack Cannon's biological age was only forty-two. He felt no regret that the fleshpots, the forced-labor camps spanning whole planets, and the psychic pressure of uncalculated billions of trapped, restricted souls was behind him at last and forever. He stayed in Cotterville while his future home, High Manse, was built near the site of his initial landing. From that time on he meticulously guided the progress of his world, the world to which his son Bass now returned.

The jolt of retrofire jarred Bass from his reverie. The *Carrington* was decelerating. He would soon be off the damn ship for good, and it couldn't be soon enough for him. During his final weeks on the *Carrington* he hadn't caught the slightest hint of Captain or Second Officer Sotheny's well-masked sympathy. He could, however, finally shrug without pain. The nerve-whip left no physical signs of its seventy passes across his back. The muscle spasms had lost their grip over the last two weeks, until only painful memory remained. He was still a cadet at Crowe Academy, the best Spacers' Guild school beyond the Caprian Reef, and he still had his pride: not one whimper had escaped his tight lips during the week of hell he'd endured. Old Sotheny had been disappointed, he was sure.

Someday when I inherit the family holdings, he thought in a spurt of compressed rage, he'll return to the Orb, with an empty hold, and he'll leave with a cargo of air, too! Let him explain that to the *Carrington*'s owners. Bass comforted himself with such unworthy thoughts during the ship's thirty-minute descent, but felt no better for them.

As the ship's levelers sighed and settled firmly on the ground, Bass gave his freshly pressed uniform a final inspection before joining his waiting family. Jack and Raquel Cannon pressed forward in the small crowd. Jack's quiet way was such that the ordinary citizens of "his" planet hardly knew his face, but Bass saw him immediately, for Jack Cannon still towered over most people. Seventy years had bowed him only slightly, and his shock of silver hair added inches. Raquel possessed a spare, angular grace that well fitted the "queen" of a lovely, provincial world. Bass met them at the base of the rollaway stairs.

"Merry Christmas, son. Welcome home."

"Hi, Dad. Mom, what's for dinner?" His mother's throaty laugh rewarded his old joke.

"*Plus ça change* . . . but you've changed, Bass!" She held him at arm's length, her slim hands on her tall son's broadened shoulders. "Academy life must not be too hard on you. You're taller." Bass flung his arms over both his parents' shoulders as they walked from the field. Dad's not as tall as I am, he realized. Have I grown that much since last Christmas? A rush of confusing notions tumbled one over the other inside him: smug satisfaction with his emerging manhood shaded into wistful regret for the childhood he'd given up. He'd played his last prank as a child, and had paid for it, seventy times, as an adult.

"Where're the girls?" he asked. "I thought they'd all be here to welcome me home."

Raquel wasn't sure exactly which girls he meant. Before his acceptance by Crowe Academy, Bass had cut quite a swath through the unmarried daughters of his father's contractors and other landowners. Even at fourteen . . . especially at fourteen . . . he'd been viewed as a threat to morality and their daughters' virginity. Jack and Raquel had been relieved to see him off for his first year, hoping the academy would provide outlets for a healthy fourteen-year-old's libido, ones that wouldn't damage his family's staid reputation. When he came home for the summer, their anxiety turned in a different direction . . . but no one talked about that, not willingly. Bass had several sisters, and his mother purposefully assumed they were the "girls" he meant. "Tonight's chapel night, you remember. The choir will be performing excerpts from Deladius's *Kyraito sil Lixen*. Your sisters are rehearsing." She sounded proud, urbane.

"Incredible!" Bass blurted. "The masterwork of a pagan, nonhuman offworlder? Here, in the heart of God's own realm?" The warmth of his tone took the worst sting from his sarcasm, but he still felt his father's shoulders stiffen. "Hey! I'm sorry! I'm happy things are loosening up a bit, that's all. I think we should temper our devout little lives with a bit of whimsy."

"Deladius wasn't human, true." Jack's voice was slow and deep, as threatening as the distant rumble of violet-streaked storm clouds that were even now building in the lime-green sky over the Estvold hills. "He was an alien, but he died in the Faith, and the Synod has approved his works for informal services. The works and the being who wrote them."

Bass's laugh was sarcastic. "What a shame! If they'd banned it instead, I'd suspect it might be worth hearing. In fact, I wouldn't miss it!"

"Bass, drop it!" His mother cut him off. "You're here, and it's Christmas. Won't you come, just this once, without an argument? The estate managers and their families will attend tonight's services, and many contractors, too. We will all be there, as befits our family's position on this world, so I'll hear no more of it.''

"Sorry, Mom," he said mildly. "You know how I feel. But I'll be there. For the family." *Other worlds have holiday orgies, games, great, glittering pageants and festivals,* he thought. *What do I get to do on leave? Sing hymns with log farmers and their prick-teasing daughters.*

There were no customs formalities for the Cannons of Cannon's Orb. The saloon 'car awaited them at the edge of the landing apron. The 'car was obviously not new; its thick, maroon finish had that swirling luster only age and many coats of pigment lovingly rubbed out can give. It was a Stollivant, the estate model made in limited numbers for the well-to-do, and its design had not changed in over a century: a central coach pod like an elongated egg, half-metal and half-transparent, with three banks of seats. Four repulsor pods melded with the main body at the places a land vehicle would have had wheels. A brassy rail ran its circumference where glassine and metal joined and doors folded out as ramps for graceful entry. The interior exuded odors of faint perfume, tobacco smoke, and old leather.

"May I fly us?" Bass inquired. "I've got my all-class license." He hated sounding like a child. *How easily the old habits returned. I should just have opened the passenger door for them, and gotten in front,* he realized. *The key's always there.*

Jack smiled tolerantly. "Take her away, son. Easy on the combat maneuvers, though. I want to keep my lunch."

Waves of diffuse warmth ran through Bass. *The old camaraderie was still there! I do love the old man. Why can't he just accept me? Accept that I'll never be like him or believe as he does? Maybe,* he thought hopefully, *we can get away for a day's fishing in the Jumbles, forget about everything else.*

Bass took the car up smoothly. Its turbine generators whined evenly and the repulsors pushed them swiftly up to the heavy craft's hundred-meter limit without apparent effort.

"The right-quadrant repulsor's been replaced, hasn't it?" A year earlier, it had clattered and pulsed annoyingly under load. Bass's sensitive ear had heard it long before anyone else, and his judgments of machinery were uncannily accurate. Jack had obviously heeded his warning. "I'll bet there's not a chunk of original gear left on the old bus, Dad. Aren't you ever going to get a new one?"

"There's a shop in Fallen Rocks that's making a few light-duty floaters now. Perhaps in a few years they'll be set up for larger craft, but we're still basically a timber-producing world. Perhaps if the whole transReef wasn't so shy of heavy elements, if we could mine our own metals economically, then we could industrialize, but . . .'' Jack's voice faded dreamily. "Besides, the old beast isn't worn out yet, and a new one would have identical components.''

"I suppose so. Sometimes a change is nice, though, for its own sake. Hey! What's that down there?'' Bass banked the aircar to allow his father a better view from the side window. Raw ground spread out alongside the lumber trace which wound below them. Geometric excavations pocked the blue and russet expanse of shaggy grass and second-growth bloodbushes. Yellow excavating machines were parked helter-skelter.

"Hmmph. A change, I think.'' Jack Cannon smiled quietly while his dry witticism sunk in. "That's Orb Industries' new dimensioning mill. We'll be shipping sawn and graded timber by next year, and a bit more money will stay here on the Orb where it belongs. The way freight and fuel costs have been going up every month, we can hardly afford to ship logs anymore.''

"Isn't it a bit far from the timber operations? You'll need a railroad.''

"The market's changing, son. We have to change, too. Some clear-cut timber will still go by rail to the port, but this plant will handle top-grade metalvein and violet-heart, and some mountain redfern in the summer. We'll select-cut each log and fly it here.''

"Can you show me the plans? You must have them on the house com.'' Jack affirmed that he did, and Bass swung back on course for High Manse.

When Jack had returned from his last space voyage, he had brought Raquel, then eighteen. The great stone and timber lodge, set into a southerly ridge, had been home to them and their children ever since.

Children. Peggy, Ariane, and Elspeth had come along at regular two-year intervals, but when Raquel despaired of giving Jack the son he craved, the interval between babies shortened. Barbara, Sally, and Joyce had only a year and a half between them.

As soon as baby Joyce weaned herself, Raquel decided to endure the six-month voyage Earthward through the Reef, then home to the Orb. Her excuse was obscure, even to Jack, having to do with inheritances and an unwritten family code of honor. It was just the right deception for a man of Jack's upstanding, somewhat rigid nature. Raquel felt guilty for her trickery, and she was terrified of the dangers and ugliness a woman alone would have to face on Earthward ships and on humankind's home planet itself, but it was her love of Jack that drove her.

Recent developments in starship technology allowed passengers on new and retrofitted ships to keep a one-to-one chronological relationship with their departure points, even at superluminary speeds, so when she returned she was only a half year older. Bass was born almost exactly eight months after that. Raquel never knew that the lab gave her son more than she'd paid for.

If there was gossip about Raquel's questionable journey among the devout ladies of church, town, and forest preserve, it never reached Raquel's ears. No discussion of "unnatural manipulation" took place in the Deacon's Council, either. Jack Cannon had worked harder than anyone, and had taken less reward than he allotted his contractors and managers, so if his wife was willing to take sin on her own soul to give him a son, then damned if anyone would make it harder still for her.

The saloon car crested a final dark copper ridge and was over the estate. High Manse seemed small to outsiders, because it nestled into the rough hillside like a natural formation, exposing only slated roof and hewn granite wall to view. Its flues were shaped to resemble natural crags. Inside, even the public rooms were on a human scale, built more for living than for show. "Intimate" groups of ten to fifty guests that felt just right at the Manse would be lost and forlorn in the high halls of more pretentious estates.

Bass dropped the aircar to the apron in front of the main house. "I think I'll ride down to Five Corners, see if Rob's around. We always used to meet there."

"Bass?" His mother's forehead wrinkled with tension.

"Uh-huh?"

"You don't expect to see . . . anyone in particular?"

"What? I mean, who?" His blank look gave way to dawning comprehension. "Oh, Mom! I know Lorraine isn't there anymore. I wasn't even thinking of her." He forced a reassuring grin. "She's not on the Orb, anyway."

"No, she's not." Raquel's words dropped like stones into mud. "She left last year, after you did. Rumor said she'd followed you . . ."

"Mom, you worry about everything! I haven't seen her—and I don't want to. It's over. Besides, I've rediscovered girls my own age, so now you can worry about that."

Raquel rewarded him with a smile as bright as Mirasol's rays. Relief colored her words. "I'm glad you're over her, Bass. It wasn't just that she . . ."—Raquel made a conscious effort not to let that one word, "she," sound like "that woman"—"that she was so much older than you. You hurt so, and you were so young . . ."

"Yeah. It was pretty rough on me. Right from the beginning." It still is. It always will be. Lorraine . . .

She had been thirty-five or even forty-five—Bass didn't have any idea, really—and he'd been fifteen. She hadn't intended to seduce him, despite what people said later. It just happened. He remembered, mostly, her room and her bed, passion, and an agony of the spirit that pervaded their time together. That first night, when he snuck up to her room and hid there on a dare from Ollie and Rob, he'd had no thought of love, only curiosity about the lone woman from off-planet who had taken a room there in Five Corners. If she had been old—or even looked her age—none of the boys would have given her a thought, but she was dark, mysterious, and quite pretty.

He knew now that if she hadn't been drunk and running from something, someone, she would have sent him away, but . . . In the course of that one short night he was stripped of his youth and his fantasies. Love. Is it a rigorous new position? A proud endurance record won with aching arms and battered groin? Or going home alone in the small hours each night, vowing that it's over? What he felt during the hot, sweaty hours lying stiffly in his solitary bed, fighting the urge to get dressed and go to her—that hadn't been love, nor was the excitement that tightened his gut and groin at the thought of taking the two-track road to Five Corners one more time. One more time . . .

Lorraine hadn't been good for him. He knew that now, just as Raquel had known it all along. No boy, no matter how virile, how driven, could have lived up to Lorraine. But God, it had been good sometimes!

Raquel must have read something of his thoughts in his face, for her worry lines returned. "How did you know she was gone, Bass?"

"Mom," he explained patiently, "you aren't the only one who writes letters. Rob wrote, too . . . Hey! It's almost four. He'll probably be at the Corners already. Gotta go, Mom."

"Why don't you come in and change first, Bass?" his mother asked. "You can keep your uniform neat and have it pressed for tonight."

He vetoed the suggestion brusquely. No way am I going down there looking like a hick timberman, he thought. I earned my bars, and I'm wearing them.

His father looked long and hard at him. "I'd not want you to give yourself airs, Bass. It's not our way."

Bass shrugged acquiescence and walked with his parents to the house. Airs? Was that what they thought? He had *earned* the right to wear that uniform, earned it by hard work, study, and recently by pain and humiliation. No one, no one at all, was going to deny him the satisfaction of showing his friends what he had become, what he had accomplished. Less than an hour later, when he slipped out to the aircar, he was still wearing his proud academy colors.

CHAPTER
THREE

Five Corners: nine unpainted wood buildings, single-story except for the New Paradise Café, which had rentable rooms upstairs. Bass's eyes quickly turned from those curtained windows back to the aircar's instruments. Lorraine's windows, and her curtains left behind. He imagined movement—a heavy drape pulled slightly aside. Lorraine. Waiting for him. Angrily, he jerked the 'car's prow around.

The five roads into the Corners seemed to trail off in the near distance, to vanish as if they went nowhere, existing only to give the cluster of sheds and defunct vehicles a reason for being. The northeast road was no more than an extended driveway to High Manse, an old construction trail. The others had enough traffic to keep the slow-growing native ground covers from obscuring them, no more.

Bass recognized two of the aircars parked at the Old Saw Tavern, so he brought the Stollivant down between them. One was a utility vehicle belonging to the Magnusson Company, one of his father's prime timber contractors. The other, even more ancient than the Stollivant and showing every year of it, was the proud personal property of Rob Santiago, Bass's closest childhood friend. Alighting, he thumped its scored and dented cowl as he walked up to the tavern. With Rob, he reminisced, he had probably lifted every component in and out of the clapped-out vehicle at least once. Only skill and considerable attention kept the old bird flying.

The tavern was dark. Mirasol's light was whiter than Sol standard; everyone wore ultraviolet-screened contacts indoors and out, and even the lightest summer clothing was full-covering and reflective. Windows were shaded and baffled to keep out the carcinogenic light. Thus the tavern's occupants recognized Bass well before his own eyes had adjusted to the gloom.

"Hey, Bass! When did you get back?" Rob jumped up to throw an arm around his shoulder and pummeled his back. "Whoo-ee! Cadet Captain Cannon!" he said when he noticed the bright silver bars on Bass's collar. "Here, stand back, you guys. Let's get a good look at him."

The others hadn't crowded all that closely. Actually, they had stayed clustered nearer their table than to Bass, who recognized Ollie Nickerson's plump form first, and then Alexei Dovstran's pale blond hair. The squat, broad-shouldered silhouette behind them was Stef Myers. Wayne T'song was still sitting at the round table. "Ten-hut! Let's have a little respect for our returning hero," he said, all too laconically.

"Hi, Wayne," Bass said equally diffidently. "Can I buy you guys a beer?" He looked from one of them to the next, but saw only cold rejection and a resentment so strong it shocked him. Much had changed, he realized. These hard-faced young men weren't the boys he had chummed with. The old games of just-pretend were gone, and in their place were hopes, agendas for their lives, with no open slots in either for Bass Cannon to fill. *They* were companions, comrades. *He* was what? An enemy? Perhaps. Certainly no longer a friend. His uniform and boots felt tight, and his collar bit into the hot flesh of his neck.

"Nah. Lunch break," Stef said. "Can't be drinkin' until after hours. We work for a living, now." Stef was truculent even at the best of times, so Bass ignored the jibe and sat down. Dad was right, he realized. I should have changed first. I should have listened to Dad. He tried to tell me, in his way. I'm a Cannon. My family rules this world, and these guys know it. And the uniform . . . it's the last straw. Now they're all convinced I'm a snob. He changed the subject. "Are you all working on the same job? What are you doing?"

"Clear-cutting on Sarpint Ridge. Tomorrow we'll be forming up for the last caravan to Cotterville," Ollie explained in his usual level tones. "We're eight days ahead of schedule, so there's a bonus due us."

"Great! Maybe I can help, eh?"

Bass's reply engendered a stiff silence. Stupid. Stupid, he thought. Everything I say makes things worse. There is no common ground here at all. These people are . . . alien . . . to me.

"Look, Bass," Wayne said cautiously, thinking out each word before speaking it. "It's all very well for you to come down here in your fancy uniform, but this job is no kid game. We've been sweating it out on the Ridge for six months now, and it's our own operation, not your father's."

"Yeah!" Stef cut in. "No need for you to get sawdust on your fancy spaceman suit—we're not cutting you in on what we've earned anyway. You kin go back up on the hill and polish your boots."

"Sorree!" Bass spat. "I guess I've been away too long! I thought we were friends. I don't want any of your money, I just wanted to help."

"We don't need no help from you," Stef insisted. "We been doing just fine. Let Daddy find you a nice office job, huh?"

Bass was taken aback by Stef's bitterness, by the sting of rejection, and worse by Stef's condescension. The uniform that represented pride, accomplishment, and manhood to Bass was to Stef a little boy's playsuit, for dress-up and pretend. He couldn't understand the cost of earning it. To Stef and the others, pride was callused palms, accomplishment was a stack of graded timber, and manhood was . . . Bass's face flushed with a mix of anger and undeserved shame. His gut tightened and adrenaline overrode the remnants of his common sense. He struck back without thinking: "Got your little niche cut out, eh, Stef? A contract with Magnusson? Ever think who holds *his* contract?"

Bass knew he was overreacting. Stef, the bully, his childhood nemesis, had ruined his glorious entrance. He was embarrassed now, and he lashed out to cover it. Sucking in a rough breath, Bass spat out, "Did he hire your old man, too? Or is *your* daddy too busy pouring booze down his gullet?" Bass's angry singsong cut through the dim tavern like sharp blades. "Why don't you sign him on yourself? He'll never get a contract from anyone else!"

Myers said nothing, though the flush darkening his face was visible even in the dimness. Stef's father was unable to hold even the least responsible of jobs. Booted off a spaceship he'd been crewing on, he had landed on Cannon's Orb with nothing but a thirst. One of the whores in Cotterville gave him Stef, and had supported father and son for ten years, until a customer slit her throat. After that, they lived from day to day on odd jobs and charity.

Stef didn't reply. He reddened and half rose in his seat. Bass almost wished Stef would fight him, but the other boy sank back in place. That was the real indictment, Bass knew: *You're a Cannon, and I'm nothing. If I fight you, I lose no matter what. Beat me, and you win. If I beat you, a Cannon, then what will happen to me, later? Contracts? There won't be any. I'll never do any better than my dad. Cannon influence will see to it.* The internal struggle Stef hosted prevented speech, and though Ollie and the others had heard everything, they, too, remained ominously silent. Bass immediately regretted everything he'd said, but it was beyond recall.

Bass's insults were two-pronged: Jack Cannon had chartered the Orb under a contract system that allowed him to issue prime contracts to settlers, who in turn issued their own. Delegation was complete, and accountability linear, so Jack could spend the necessary years off-planet building up trade and recruiting settlers.

No subcontractor—technically—owed anything to Jack Cannon. Each man answered to the one holding his own contract, and was responsible only for those whose contracts he, in turn, held. Only those specific three-tiered relationships were acknowledged, and a certain rough egalitarianism prevailed. The religion of Jack's selected colonists and the lingering traces of the colony's primitive early days meant that older women held marital contracts only, though that was rapidly changing. What remained unchanged was that few men or women were outside the contract system entirely. Stef's father was one of them: uncontracted and uncontractable.

Even a subtle reference to his father's status could have been construed as an insult by Stef, and Bass's angry remarks were the kind grown men sometimes died over.

Alexei and Wayne peered silently into their glasses, and only Rob continued to recognize Bass's presence. He tried to ignore the electric tension in the air. "Are you using the family monster?" he asked awkwardly. "The Stollivant?" He nodded in the direction of the door.

Bass looked around. None of the others would meet his gaze except Stef, who stared at him with inarticulate hatred. "Yeah. I am," Bass said. "Come with me?"

"Uh-huh. We've got to talk."

"Good idea, Spaceman," Stef grated. "Don't hurry back."

Rob jerked Bass out the door before he could make another unthinking reply. "Blight, Bass! That was really dumb," he exclaimed as the door shut behind them.

"What was? Coming here? I guess it was, wasn't it?"

"You know what I mean."

"Yeah, I know. But what was I supposed to do? Just stand there and take it from him? He didn't have to start right in on me, either."

"He's been trying to get ahead. You really hit him hard. Damn it, Bass! You haven't been here! Stef's been doing really well. You blew it this time! You don't know what it's like, either, working and living with those guys day and night. We're a team, now. All for one, you know? Even me, Bass. I mean, we've been best friends forever, and I don't think that's changed, but this is different. You have Crowe Academy, and a real place on the Orb when you graduate. We have to *make* a place for ourselves—and especially Stef." Bass didn't reply. What could he say? He knew he'd been a fool, but even now the adrenaline lingering in his blood wouldn't let him admit it.

They climbed into the Stollivant, and with the resiliency of youth, their talk turned to the military craft Bass was learning to fly. But the conversation felt forced and unnatural, and they soon gave up. They flew over the Shadney River's towering stands of larch and sooder, then followed the river for several minutes in silence.

"Better drop me back at Five Corners, Bass. Maybe I can smooth things out. Besides, I have to go home and clean up for chapel tonight."

"Yeah, me, too. I wish I could skip the whole thing, but the Queen requires my presence."

"My ma, too. It's not so bad, though. The Mallin twins'll be there. You remember them? The brunettes?"

"Uh-huh. Nice." Bass's low-key reply belied the sharp twinge in his groin that even the memory of the twins brought. He'd spent more than one long summer evening with the twins—one or both of them: evenings of groping, clutching, giggling adolescent passion that, always unconsummated, had left him light-headed and aching. After Lorraine, though, he hadn't resumed such frustrating pastimes. "Picked one for yourself yet?" he joked.

"Hah! If I could tell them apart, I might. If I contract with old man Mallin next year, maybe I can find out how closely they match."

"Better be careful," Bass warned him. "Deacon Mallin'll nail your hide to his barn if he catches you."

"I suppose you'd know about that, wouldn't you?" Rob teased him.

By the direct route, they were over the Corners in minutes. "See you tonight, Rob. If you don't go down in smoke first."

"There's always a first time, eh? See you." The Corners were empty of craft other than Rob's and the Stollivant. They'd gone back to work, Bass supposed. He pointed the old 'car toward High Manse. Even Mirasol's brilliant glare failed to penetrate his depression. It was starting out to be a really great vacation!

CHAPTER

FOUR

Chapel was . . . well, it was chapel. A bit more crowded than an ordinary service, a little brighter with all the extra candles. Christmas. Perhaps I should stay at Crowe next year, with the "orphans," Bass thought. Chase downside girls who aren't afraid to drink and dance—and more. I should have done it this year.

He estimated that eighty aircars clustered around the plain stone building. It looks like third shift at a finish mill, he told himself. Indeed, the chapel had no distinguishing ornamentation, no architectural flairs or follies. Its ashlar walls were bland taupe stone, its wood fasciae carefully painted to match. Its curtained windows were small and multipaned like small-time factory windows on any industrial world. The First Dharmic Church of Christ, Reincarnate, had placed no ban on the use of stained glass, statuary and carvings, or other distracting frills, but neither did it encourage them. Jack's austere nature, one that had tolerated years of loneliness in a barren scoutship, had no use for them either.

Bass went in at his mother's side, feeling conspicuous without a group of older, taller, sisters to shield him. He smiled and nodded at neighbors and acquaintances in the close-pressed mass of faces.

Jack sat on a stiff-backed, spindled chair facing the congregation, raised only a few inches above them on a roughly finished wooden platform. It was exactly high enough for him to lock eyes with those in the back row, over the heads of the others—and not an inch higher. Jack had planned it that way: the First Dharmic Church didn't encourage its ministers giving themselves airs, either.

Ollie's parents were in their usual seats, as were Wayne's. Neither of the boys was present, and Bass was sure that his father, from his vantage point, had noticed the vacancies in their family pews. There would be wondering, perhaps questions, later.

The service went along at its usual pace, and Bass was no more bored than on numerous other occasions. One good lesson of the military life was how to survive being bored. At least he didn't have to stand at attention.

Giving his father due credit, it could have been worse. Jack Cannon was an excellent speaker. Though his voice was becoming airy with age, some of its mature resonance remained, and it had lost no volume at all. It filled the crowded room to the rearmost corners, not allowing the sleepiest, nodding head a moment's rest.

The subject of his sermon that night was, predictably, the meaning of Christmas. The subject had less scope for charismatic harangue than Jack's favorites, for which Bass was grateful. He half listened, becoming fully aware of Jack's words only when they diverged from what he had heard before.

"... The man Jesus said nothing about the souls of nonhuman sapients. Why should he have? There were no gelenites in Galilee, no armoths in Samaria, not even a lone psatla in Rome, the greatest city of His time. In an earlier incarnation, six hundred years before, he had even less reason to speak of such—his fellow humans, separated from each other by language and extremes of custom, were alien enough. But even then, his Hindu people knew that even beasts of burden were more than Godless flesh; nothing indicates that the Buddha rejected that belief.

"Our own Church, first among many that will surely follow, has addressed the question of alien souls with more than words.

An armoth, taking the honored name of Saint Deladius for his own, was gathered to the Church only months before his Passing On. The choral celebration you will hear shortly is his final tribute to the Church, to you, to all of us who share his adopted Faith: the *Kyraito sil Lixen*. In Armotha, that means 'My Soul Has Wandered.' Some have remarked the similarity of the title to a Song we have all heard: *Kyrie Eleison*.

"The Church's decision to accept Deladius has been hotly debated. Perhaps, for all of us, his music will give answers no words can provide . . ."

Bass listened intently despite his earlier disparagements, for the small choir was quite good, and Deladius's masterwork deserved the high praise it usually got. When the choir's last echoes died, the benches in neat rows across the floor were moved aside and stacked equally neatly. Coffee was served—real Earth coffee, not the locally grown, acidic brew. There were small snacks, too, but Bass couldn't force himself to eat; his stomach was still twisted with unspent anger and frustration. Rob pushed through bunched families to get to Bass.

"The twins're over there by the door, Bass. Come with me before Mallin drags them away, all right?"

"I don't know, Rob. I'm leaving in a week and it'd probably take two just to get a kiss. Don't let me stop you, though."

Rob was crestfallen at first, but then he gave Bass a long, penetrating look. "That bad, huh? Have you decided what you're going to do about Stef?"

"I think so. Not today, though. Have fun with the twins, will you? Squeeze one for me?"

"Not much chance of that! Not yet, anyway. Well, good luck, Bass. I hope you straighten things out."

"Thanks, Rob. See you." Rob made his way back across the room. Bass mixed politely with the older folk who surrounded his parents, answering their repetitious questions about academy life and how good it must be to be home. He never initiated a conversation, and went into no greater detail than direct questions demanded. He was relieved when he saw people working their way to the door, when they came to say good-bye instead of to pass the time in idle chitchat.

On the way out to the Stollivant he didn't talk, and he hardly heard his parents' murmured conversation as he steered the aircar through the darkness. At the Manse he avoided their curious, concerned looks and, pleading a headache, went directly to his room.

His old, comfortable bed was too soft now, and he tossed and sweated in it, wishing for his firm foam pad in Barracks Seven-B. Finally, he tossed a blanket and pillow on the floor and fell asleep in seconds.

The kitchen terrace was pleasantly cool, its dark slaty flags still sheltered from Mirasol's morning glare. Later in the day, it would be a furnace. "Where's Mom?" Bass asked as he poured himself a glass of sailfruit juice from the thermal pitcher.

"Com center. It's a workday for her, Christmas or not. She'll be back by noon, though." Jack Cannon's cheery voice rang falsely on his son's ears. "Do you have plans today?"

"Ah . . . I thought I'd do a little hunting down in the Wallow. Rob told me the grabbits are overbreeding, getting into the fields."

"You're not going alone, are you? You know how I feel about that. Can't you get someone to go with you? Wayne or Ollie, maybe?"

Here it comes, Bass thought. *By the way, I didn't see . . .*

"By the way, I didn't see them in chapel. I understand they have a contract with Magnusson. He's working near enough for them to have come."

I won't crawl. He'll find out what happened anyway. "We had a quarrel yesterday. Stef Myers and I. They're boycotting me, not the Church. I'm sure they'll be back after I've gone."

"Anything I should know about? I don't like resentments to fester. If any ruffled feathers need smoothing, son . . ."

He's treating me as an adult, Bass realized. Damn. This is going to be even harder than I thought. Bass knew then that he was going to tell his father exactly what had happened. As an adult, he would have to do more than slink offworld until time muted the nastiness of his words. A formal apology was due. Ollie and Wayne would accept it matter-of-factly. Alexei would shrug it off and smile—but Stef? Stef would gloat.

On the Orb, children were usually exempt from rigid adult codes of behavior. But they did learn the forms: *My words have given offense. I humbly apologize for having said them, and I wish to make reparation. I await your considered suggestion of how that might be done.* Stef wouldn't make it easy for him.

"What did you say, Bass?"

"It was my fault, Dad," he blurted. "I asked if I could work with them, and they brushed me off. Stef was pretty mean about it. I lost my temper and said some stupid things . . . about his father." Haltingly, Bass described events as they had transpired.

When he finished, Jack was silent. Bass had seen his neck and cheeks redden, saw the cold glitter of his narrowed eyes, the wrinkling of his weathered forehead that deepened as Bass spoke, but he returned his father's gaze steadily, face on. He saw Jack's visible effort to quell his ire before he spoke. *As I should have done yesterday,* Bass realized.

"You are my son and heir," Jack said at last, "and whether or not you choose to return permanently to the Orb when you graduate, to take the reins of power from me, you'll still be richer and more powerful than most men dream of being. Unless you throw it away, that is—and what you did today was a step in that direction.

"I didn't choose the contract structure only because it was simple to administrate. I chose it because it veiled the extent of my own interests. The flaunting of power breeds resentment and, ultimately, revolution. The Orb was my discovery, and how I chartered it was my decision alone. I could have been a king, pope, even called myself God had I wished, and only the caliber of the colonists I recruited would have suffered. Only a weak ego needs such trappings, and you're not weak."

Jack raised his hand, palm outward. He hadn't finished, merely paused to weigh his next words. "That is the situation. The structure now exists, unchangeable except by the Panaikos Council, and the Orb will remain a contract world. Do you wish I had decided otherwise, Bass?"

"I don't think so. I've only experienced one other system— Crowe democracy. Our system seems to work well enough." Bass's tone was thoughtful and serious, with no trace of childish servility or adolescent pique. Jack clearly sensed that his agreement reflected honest opinion.

"Here, it does. Some contract worlds are ill-disguised hells— like Hematite and Dagnabbit." He leaned forward as if he were about to impart a precious secret to his son, a preacher's mannerism. "A light hand makes the difference. A careful balance between ostentation and reticence. A humble demeanor, a willingness to delegate all but essential decisions, an open ear to contractors at all levels." Jack couldn't help sounding like a preacher, but Bass was used to that.

"Illusion and willing self-delusion are my machine's lubricants. Every man wants to believe he is a free agent, with only simple and clear-cut obligations, and Stef Myers is no different. Disregarding your cheap shots about his father, your worst act, in my view, was to 'put him in his place.' You broke the hard-gained illusion that, since he holds no contract with you, he is your equal in all respects. You threw sand in the works. Now I expect you to clean it out.''

"I plan to, Dad. A public apology—reparation, too, though I don't know what he'll ask for." He stifled the urge to throw his troubles upon his father's still-broad shoulders, to let the older man take the burden from him and to be, once again, a child.

"Will any of your friends act as arbiter? Or will you have to submit to a professional?"

"They're all involved. A professional, I guess." Professional arbiters were Jack's own innovation. The Orb had no judicial system, as such, and there were few crimes not definable as breach of contract. Refusal of private arbitration by either party to a dispute caused it to default to the Guild, and refusal of Guild arbitration resolved the issue in favor of the other party. It was simple enough, and it worked.

Bass hoped that Myers would choose to accept his simple apology without reparation, but Stef's mind was a dark, unpredictable place. Bass wasn't optimistic.

Jack nodded. "This has to be resolved immediately. Guild arbitration could hold you here, and you'd miss school. When will you see him?"

"They're taking a load of timber down from Sarpint's Ridge tomorrow—I'll try to get up there before they leave," Bass said glumly. For the second time in a month, he'd committed himself to an adult penalty for childish acts. It was no auspicious beginning for the balance of his life.

From his son's expression and posture, Jack understood the tenor of his thoughts, and squeezed Bass's shoulder. "You have to come up against yourself sometime, Bass. Now's better than later, when you really have something to lose. Get it over with so we can take a couple days off for fishing, eh?"

They hugged. His father didn't feel so slight right then, even though Bass had to bend his knees for the embrace.

CHAPTER

FIVE

Bass flew a utility floater out to the timber camp the next morning. The flight took him over a series of ridges that had escaped the worst ravages of past glaciation. Blackleaf thorn trees filled the valleys like thick, matted moss. It would never do to be forced down there—no man without a 'dozer or a flame gun could hope to cut his way out of the tangled, spiky mass. The ridges were covered with friendlier growth: mayberry and greasewood, sugarroot and conifers. There would be sodafruit in the understory if the grabbits hadn't gotten it all.

Bass looked for signs of occupation: smoke columns, sawdust haze on the fickle ridge-and-valley winds, the snaking course of a fresh trail. There—a road! Yellow earth gnawed by heavy equipment led under a canopy of beersap. Where were the floaters and the cargo lifts? Bass dropped his own floater to the ground under the trees, where dull brown rectangles of matted fern and old leaves marked the locations of tents now struck. He had the right place—but the timber and the men who had cut it were gone.

"Bass Cannon! Is that you?" A booming voice from a copse of beersap startled him. The speaker was smaller than his lungs presupposed. He wore cruising clothes, lighter and cooler than those worn in open country, but less effective against the sun: blue trousers bloused over webwork boots, and a plain cotton shirt. His face was a mass of wrinkles like a dried snowberry.

"I kinda thought you'd show up. Good thing you took your time."

"Hi, Albee. I'm surprised you're still here. Is everyone else gone?"

"Yep. Magnusson sent out extra lifts, took everything in one haul. They're in Cotterville by now, probably half-drunk already."

"Why's it good that I took my time?"

"You'd know that better'n me. That Myers boy's been talkin' fierce. Don't know how you riled him so, but he's out fer you, sure thing."

Bass's heart sunk. A formal apology, even reparation, was one thing, but if Stef had spent the past day and night brooding, things could get nasty. Stef would ponder the wrongs done him and hold them close, but once he started talking big to the others, he'd feel committed to go for blood—Bass hoped only figuratively.

"I've got to apologize to him. I lost my temper and said . . . things."

"You might want t' wait a day'r so, let him wind down a mite. Maybe Ollie and Wayne can calm him, if you give 'em time."

"Aw, Albee—I want to get it over with. Besides, it's only Stef. You know how he is, always mad about something. Anyway, I've got to see him—I'm leaving next week. Back to school." And there's Dad. I can't face him until this is settled. I won't.

Albee shrugged. "Good luck, Bass. Give my hello to yer old man, eh?"

"Sure, Albee. See you next time." Bass took the floater up to maximum altitude. The wind was behind him across the mountains and down the outwash plain, and he made good time. He had little to think about except his coming encounter with Stef. In spite of the confidence he'd expressed to Albee, Bass was worried. Stef was tough, and a good enough scrapper to give Bass a few bruises. That would be like Stef, to prefer a fight over a grown-up settlement.

He reached Cotterville by late afternoon. The Meadows came first: the Orb's only true slum. Rows of unpainted wood buildings, none over three stories high, were separated by muddy furrows laid out as streets. Most were clogged with refuse, animal pens, and decrepit floaters.

Beyond were higher buildings surrounding the port and the Orb's ever-growing commercial district. Between lay unpretentious shops, with taverns and restaurants on the ground floors and dwellings above. Open, tree-lined squares were kept clear for floaters and aircars.

Bass tried the port first. If the cargo hadn't been turned over to its buyer, he'd only have to find a ship surrounded by orange Magnusson craft.

There were three ships in. One was a small, private craft. The others were typical transReef vessels, cargo ships with minimal accommodation for passengers—ships much like the *Carrington*.

One was shiny and well painted. Large timber bunks were stacked around it and its hatches were all open. The other looked like it had taken no cargo, and seeing its scored, battered exterior, Bass wondered if it was in shape to lift at all.

No Magnusson machinery was in evidence around any of them, so Bass swung around the port, trying to second-guess his—erstwhile?—friends. He wasn't going to get home by dark.

He quartered the town, flying diagonally and earning glares from other fliers, but saw no orange vehicles. Had they left immediately instead of hanging around the port? Perhaps Magnusson's older contractees, family men, had—but the others? They must have gone to one of the Meadows dives, where, according to local tradition, drinks were strong and every barmaid was a part-time whore. Those places could be as rough as big-time spaceport bars, and people got killed sometimes. There weren't any MPs or shore patrols on the Orb. Under normal circumstances, he wouldn't go there, but . . .

Though Bass had spent little time in the Meadows, he flew over them every trip in to the port, and he'd seen the crude signs whitewashed on blackened roof shakes:

NANCY'S LOUNGE
girls + Girls + GIRLS

AL PEREDISIO
Always Open

SEMBER'S Dine-n-dance

He found their Magnusson craft on his first circuit, at Nancy's. The place was quiet that late afternoon. A wide apron and parking area, and the great sweep of the roof itself, covering almost a half acre, indicated that the placidity was only temporary.

Bass made his way inside and waited in the lobby to let his eyes adapt—he felt enough at a disadvantage without the additional handicap of partial blindness. It wasn't hard to find them. The bar was an island of light in the dim expanse of tables and upside-down chairs. The only patrons were Rob, Ollie, Alex, and Wayne. Where was Stef? They watched him approach without greeting him. Flesh tightened across the back of his neck. It wasn't getting easier.

He'd walked into a spaceman's bar once. Cadet uniforms weren't exactly welcome there. The patrons had all watched him like that, staring and silent. He'd ordered a drink, downed it quickly, and had been allowed to leave. This wasn't going to be so easy. Even Rob was silent. Only a quick, nervous grin showed he knew Bass at all.

"I've got to talk with Stef. Is he here?"

"Out back," the bartender growled. "Watcha want with him?"

"Will you call him for me?" Bass countered. "We have to talk."

"Get 'im yerself. Through there." He gestured with a spatulate thumb to a door behind the bar. Had Bass met him before? There was something elusively familiar about him. He was short, with thinning hair neither blond nor brown, a stocky build and a truculent, abrasive manner. Two scars crossed on his left cheek, one old and white, the other still tinged with pink and only narrowly missing his eye. Knife scars, Bass thought. Who was he?

"I'll get him for you." Rob had slipped off his stool and was halfway around the bar to the rear when the bartender spoke.

"Siddown, kid! You're not his gofer. He wants my son, he kin go hisself." Stef's father, of course. With a job. That made Bass's insults worse.

"Sir, it would be better if you called him out here. What I have to say calls for witnesses." Bass tried to keep his voice calm and level.

"He's right, Mr. Myers," Rob said placatingly. "I think this concerns all of us, in a way. I'll go get Stef and . . ."

"You siddown, like I said. This rich ninny 'n his fam'ly's pushed us around long enough. If he wants Stef, he can damn well get him hisself."

The last thing Bass wanted was to confront Stef alone. He wasn't afraid of what the other boy might do to him, but a violent confrontation would create complications. He wanted to end the quarrel, not further it. Besides, without witnesses, any apology he might make would have no weight and would have to be repeated again later. He shrugged. He could go to the door, call Stef, and wait there.

Shouldering past the stout man, he pushed the double swinging door wide. "Stef! Stef Myers! I need to talk with you."

Musty silence greeted him. He had stepped into a storeroom lined with cases of empty bottles. Gray light fought its way through the dirty glass of a loading door and fell on stacked spun-aluminum kegs. A yellow glow streamed past a half-open door farther on. An office? Why didn't Stef answer him?

With a sound like a shot, the door behind him slammed shut. He heard its iron bolt clack home. He drew breath to call out again, but expelled it sharply as something massive struck him across the shoulder. His forehead struck the door's edge and he stumbled, dazed. Pain spread like fire up his neck and down his arms. He felt the grinding of broken bones.

Combat mode! Now! Echoes of a drill instructor's voice penetrated the mist. *You, Cannon! Does it hurt? It's gonna hurt more, so get with it! Defense posture. Now!* Obediently, Bass's body moved, assuming a protective stance. He spun toward the source of the impact, forearm angled across his face, eyes leading movement by a fraction of a second, ears tuned for the lightest sound.

Yellowish light reflected from Stef's pasty face, caught in an expression of surprise. The heavy pipe in his hand had hurt Bass, and Stef hadn't expected a counterattack. He slid back as stiffened fingers darted for his eyes. He couldn't move fast enough! As in slow motion, he saw light hairs on the back of the hand that reached toward his face, saw a bit of dirt under Bass's fingernail.

The blow never landed. As Bass's arm reached its fullest extension, he felt something give inside. He grunted in pain as his shoulder buckled, as bone fragments grated and muscles twisted in agonizing spasms.

Cannon! Your arm's broken! Forget it! Use your feet, Cadet, your feet! Bass automatically turned his leftover impetus into a pivot, knee rising up, good arm drawing in the other one: an ice skater's move, or an orbital pilot's. Linear motion became circular, speeding up until the kick landed.

Stef's grunt, and the impact of Bass's heel on ribbed muscle and bone, told Bass he had injured him. Broken ribs for sure. Bass attempted a follow-through, but his injury threw him off and he stumbled badly. He would have been killed right there if Stef had been trained to fight, if his body too, had been an integral weapon. He would have moved in with hands and feet. He didn't, but he still had the heavy bar. He took the extra time to ready it, and swung powerfully at Bass's head.

Hearing the swish of air, Bass twisted, and the heavy pipe glanced off his skull instead of crushing it. There was a flash of meaningless, disconnected agony, and then nothing at all.

"If you kill him, you'll have to kill me, too." Rob was adamant, though he was ready to break into tears. "He was coming here to apologize. What more do you need? We should be getting him to a medic, not standing around."

They had dragged Bass out into the tavern. The yellowish light couldn't disguise his unnatural pallor, but worse injuries were beneath his skin. The blood trickling down the side of his head looked black.

"You're in this, too, kid," Henry Myers growled. "Any rap, any trouble, Stef's not going to take it alone. I'll swear you all beat on Cannon, see? Maybe you'll get off, but you won't wanta live on this shitpile planet anymore."

"I don't care, don't you see? I just don't want him to die." Rob was desperately frightened, and torn two ways. Bass had been a fool. He'd asked for what Stef gave him, almost. But thoughtless and cruel as Stef had been, these were Rob's teammates and partners now—even Stef. Even Stef, who nobody really liked, or *could* like. But death? He shook his head in silent negation.

"He won't die from that tap," Stef interjected. "And that's the problem. This is Cannon's Orb, see? Like in Jack Cannon . . . or Bass Cannon. Nobody says it's *Myers'* Orb, now do they? The high-muck Cannons only let my dad stay now 'cause he don't cause no trouble. My ma getting herself kilt almost got us throwed off the Orb, and I was only a kid, even. You guys might walk away from this, but me? My pa? Hah! The arbiters'd have us stripped and packed like frozen fish on the next ship."

"That's not true!" Rob protested. "Bass wouldn't do that. He came here to apologize to you, not to hurt anyone. Besides, you have *some* rights here. An arbitrator wouldn't ignore them completely."

"You think his father'll feel that way, too?" the elder Myers asked dryly. "Big Jack Cannon, up there in his fancy house? Him'n his kind been tryin' for years to get me throwed off the Orb. He kin *buy* arbitrators. You think there's anyone ain't scared of Big Jack?"

"You didn't do anything, Mr. Myers. We'll all swear to that. It's between Stef and Bass. Bass *knows* he was wrong, that he said fighting words. He really was going to apologize to Stef. I know Bass. I can talk with him, get him to call it even. But we've got to decide now, or he'll die!"

Ollie spoke up for the first time. "Look, Rob. Be practical for once. What will Bass do, anyway, when he graduates from his soldier-boy school? He'll come back here and take over from his father in a few years. You think we'll get any good contracts if *he's* running things? After this? But if Bass just disappears, then Jack's got to turn to someone else, doesn't he? And who better than *us*, his son's best friends? Look, this is our *future* we're deciding here." Rob was sickened by Ollie's cold analysis, his "practical" plan to use Bass and Stef's stupid fight for advantage. He looked to Wayne for support, but Wayne and Alex both averted their eyes. Rob knew he was beaten. "No killing," he croaked. "You have to find another way."

Henry Myers grunted and motioned his son to him. They went aside and spoke in low tones. A decision was reached, and with identical determination displayed on their square, stolid faces they turned to the others. Hank spoke for both of them.

"Okay, here's how it's gonna be. We got two choices." He raised a thick forefinger, tapping on it with the other one. "We *could* kill him here 'n now, ditch him and his floater—he must have one out front—'fore anyone else even knows he been here. We're all each other's alibi, see?" Henry Myers sounded as if the situation wasn't new to him. Rob half stood to protest, and Myers pushed his chest. "Siddown and shudup. Yer in this too. Stef'n I'll swear it. So will Ollie. He knows what side of the plate you eat off.

"Now then, we crash th' floater with him in it. That's easy enough. If that's not okay with the rich kid's butt buddy here—" He put a thick hand on Rob's shoulder, squeezing it until the boy winced, "then the two of 'em kin go together.

"Otherwise, like I said, we got one other choice. I got a friend out at the port. A shipowner. We put the kid on his ship 'n their medic looks at him. Then they brig him until lift-off, and no harm's done. Besides," Myers said with a crooked grin, "it's what he's schooled for, isn't it? We're just upping his graduation a bit. We kin still crash the floater, see, only without the kid in it."

Ollie, always the pragmatist, shook his head dubiously. "He'll come back, sooner or later. Then what will we do?"

"That ship won't come back here. It's got old engines, time-stretchers. The kid ever comes home, we'll be long gone, me 'n Stef. Then you four kin say whatever you want."

"There'll be questions," Ollie said, nodding. "But without Bass, there'll be nothing anyone can prove." He had obviously decided what was to be done—for all of them. "But what about the aircar? If there's no body in the wreck . . ."

"We take it out over the ocean," Myers replied, "and leave it on the water, with his uniform all folded neat-like, and let it float back in. They find it, why, he just dropped down for a swim, got cramps and drowned. Simple, see?"

CHAPTER

SIX

Muffled metallic sounds: the clatter of a frenetic winch pawl, clanging hatches, the squeal of ill-maintained heavy machinery. Then: a shrill double tone, each note so close, so almost-tuned, that it caused the very air to throb. It reached down from the upper limits of audibility and tickled deep inside his ears. Bass knew, in the most general of terms, where he was. For a moment, he thought he was still aboard the *Carrington*, that the days past had been only a dream, but the return of awareness brought pain: throbbing soreness across his temple and by his right ear. Sharper pain concentrated under his right arm, shooting along his ribs and spine whenever he shifted his weight. His hands and feet refused to answer his mind's commands.

He was lying on his back. There was light somewhere overhead, but his eyes were crusted shut. He struggled without success to take control of the dead hulk that was his body, but all he could do was make things hurt. The effort exhausted him, and he fell back into a dull, dreamless sleep.

On the Orb, Jack Cannon raged. Raquel withdrew from her work for three days, emerging from her room for her son's memorial service. After that, she was seen only rarely, usually by com, not in person. A month after Bass's disappearance, she quietly slipped aboard a fast, unscheduled freighter, bringing only clothing, a few books, and in her womb a female embryo only a few days old. Her delegation of the many tasks she had performed was thorough and complete; no one missed her. Not even servants' gossip hinted to the outside world that she was gone.

Raquel knew what was in store for her and for the cells growing inside her; this was her second visit to the genetic clinic on distant

Earth. The embryo would be extracted, its genes mapped and compared with hers and with the record of Jack's, on file from the last time. The learned doctors would again comment on the odd viral damage to Jack's genes. As the damage seemed to have no negative consequences, they would shrug and get on with their task: the modification of embryonic sex chromosomes from phenotypic female to phenotypic male. Then the cells would be force-grown to their proper age and reinserted.

Under simple magnification, the sex chromosomes of Raquel's latest offspring would still be XX, female, but the child she bore would be as vigorously male as a proud father could desire.

Just before Christmas, she returned, pale and wan from her secret ordeal and her advanced pregnancy. Basil Benjamin Cannon was born at High Manse just in time to be viewed by the primes and their wives when all drew together for the holiday. Jack no longer raged. One of the primes who had contact with him in the months following the tragedy summed up the new Jack Cannon: "He's pleased with his new son, but he's become an old man, just marking time. It's business as usual, but his heart's not in it." Little Ben kindled a certain light in Jack's eyes, it was true, but the baby boy was still almost eighteen years shy of being the vital young son Jack had lost.

Raquel had proudly chosen Ben's proper name, Basil, just as she had picked Vassily for Bass. Both, she claimed, were family names. No other Orber, not even Jack, had benefited from a classical education, so none knew the real significance of the names—that both were rooted in *basileus*, which once meant *king*. "False pride," Jack would have said had he known. Etymology was of little importance on a colony world, and, further obscuring the common origin, even in the birthing-room Jack chose to call his new son Ben.

In May, less than half a year after Bass's disappearance and "drowning," Henry Myers was found dead in a Meadows trash heap. Reeking muck filled his mouth and eyes. His throat had been slit. No investigation was made, no arbitration required, for he had neither friends nor relatives to mourn him. Stef had disappeared a month earlier without informing anyone of his plans. There had been an unregistered armed trader in port at the time, the kind that sometimes indulged in honest trade between piracies and smuggling runs. Perhaps his father had known where he had gone.

Aboard the *Sally B. Halpern*, Bass Cannon mended slowly.

His broken ribs healed cleanly. His cracked skull left no chips or splinters to press on his brain, but his shattered zygoma welded itself in a lumpy mass through which his jaw muscle ran painfully. He was subject to massive temporal-muscle spasms and consequent headaches which drove him to his bunk for hours or sometimes days at a time. Pain shaped his life: he avoided chewy foods, shunned tension and conflict for the jaw-clenching they brought on, and worked quietly and efficiently at the tasks assigned him.

He wasn't a slave, but the effect was the same. He had been signed onto the *Sally B.* while unconscious. No money had changed hands, but his medical care had been expensive. The *Sally B.*'s captain, Alois Battersea, planned to recoup his loss when he transferred Bass's contract on some out-of-the-way world downReef. Functionally, though, Bass was a ship's officer. Merchant vessels like the *Sally B.*, undermanned and running high-risk routes on limited budgets, couldn't afford to waste talent, so once Battersea realized that his shanghaied crewman wasn't going to sabotage the ship or attempt violent revenge he made good use of Bass's training.

Bass rose rapidly from sweeping and cleaning on the lower decks to a third officer's post on the bridge. Pain conditioned his thoughts as well as his outward actions; it wasn't long before he was actually content to be aboard the *Sally B.*, to be an efficiently functioning member of her crew.

And more than one of *Sally*'s female crew members had noted him with approval once his bandages were off. Following his rise from deck-sweeper, they found ways to demonstrate that approval. So many ways. Though he still slept in his own bunk in the officers quarters, hardly a night passed without a warm, anonymous feminine shape slipping quietly beneath his sheets, without the sweetness of hardened nipples brushing his chest and smooth thighs clutching his own. Some nights he had more than one visitor, but he never failed to satisfy his silent benefactresses.

Not yet eighteen, he saw nothing unusual about his opportunities—shipboard life was like no other, and crews made their own rules—and didn't consider his stamina unusual. He happily, greedily awaited his off-shifts, his "nights." It was so easy—no one demanded anything, it just seemed to happen. On those rare occasions when he was too tired to want companionship, he had only to say so, and a quiet, unrecognizable voice would say, "Tomorrow, then." He laughed a lot, and his partners laughed with him. Daytimes, he tried to say funny things, to elicit a familiar, quiet laugh, but it didn't work—bedtime giggles had a special quality never heard in the galley or on the bridge. Nonetheless, he eventually figured out who was who, but never let on. It would have spoiled things.

Battersea was quick to recognize Bass's adaptation, and soon allowed him almost unlimited access to the ship's computers in his off-watch hours, a decision he never regretted. Bass modified several of the ship's programs, improving her drive efficiency by several percent. Still, the aging engines performed at only thirty percent of their rated efficiency.

Bass knew that more improvements could be made, but having established his own credentials, he was content to wait for the right opportunity to take his next step toward freedom. A step. Not blind reaching out, not mere favor-currying survival. He had grown up. Perhaps the feedback cycle of anger-pain-anger had effected the change; he was forced to think, not merely react. Pleasant thoughts allayed agony. Positive ones, concrete plans of action, brought satisfaction. He worked and reworked his strategy, his contingency plans, against the day when conditions were right.

Sally's first port of call was Arbuckle's Station. Arbuckle, whoever he had been, was long gone, but his trading post was still going strong and his salvage yards were a mecca for the run-down, neglected, and out-of-date ships that serviced the boondock worlds of far transReef. Near-orbital space around Arbuckle's Station was cluttered with dead and decommissioned ships. It was a junkyard. The planetary surface, not large as planets go, was the same. Too small to retain an atmosphere, it was a perfect place to store ships that could land under their own power. A thousand of them sprawled across the featureless plain beyond the spaceport domes—antiques for the most part, but there were a few newer models, accidental casualties whose owners had found it cheaper to abandon them than to pay Arbuckle's exorbitant repair rates.

Alois Battersea came not to sell, but to buy. Only a few crates of miscellaneous cargo were offloaded. Battersea made his habitual check of the salvage yards, and he came back to the ship swearing and shaking his head.

"Someday *Sally*'s goddamn drives'll blow and we'll never see port again. Everybody's got engines, but never the ones I need."

"That's because she's so old, isn't it?" Bass asked, fighting to keep his voice level and casual. His racing heart drummed and blood rushed in his ears. Conscious effort and thinking of his strategy for freedom helped quiet his runaway reactions and still the throbbing pain always lurking only a thought away. "Can't you refit her with a newer type?"

"I could, if I had the programs to run them. Nothing on the old girl's compatible with anything else this side of the Reef."

"If you can get engines to fit her, I can make them work."

"Oh? And where did you learn that skill? Did your academy teach you that, too?" The captain's skepticism was only half-sincere. Bass had been careful to understate his abilities, and had continually surprised him with results exceeding his stated goals.

"In a way, sir. They taught us how to repair battle-damaged drives, the newer kinds—reprogramming them so they'd interface with jury-rigged control systems. I could do the same for *Sally*'s controls. Can you get the engines?"

"We'll see. What else would you need?"

He was caught! Bass hid his elation behind a pensive stare at the gray metal bulkhead above. "If the salvage yards have engines, they should have the proper drive-field emulators, too. I can use those to change the control parameters and test them. If it works with the emulators, it'll work with the new drives."

"And what will you want for all this? More than a pat on the back, I'd guess." Battersea peered cautiously beneath half-shuttered eyelids, his immobile face cracked only by the slightest smile.

"I want my contract signed over, and back wages on account." Bass let his triumph show, knowing that his requirements were going to be met. "And," he added spontaneously, "regular third officer's pay from now until I find a ship going back home."

Battersea smiled broadly. "That's all? No punitive damages? And you'd trust me to keep my word?"

"Will you trust me not to write some sort of time bomb into the operating programs?"

The captain's smile dropped momentarily, then returned with even greater intensity. "You're a sharp one all right. Stinky Myers didn't lie about that. I'll trust you to give me the codes to disarm your bomb once you're safely off the *Sally B*. Shall we drink to it?" Bass wasn't a whiskey-drinker, though he'd slugged his share of rotgut liquor with his fellow cadets. The fine, pale stuff that Captain Battersea poured was a different thing entirely. Calversham's Vat, Bass read on the blue-and-gold label.

Bass's subsequent progress on the drive programs was as smooth as the whiskey. The emulators were set up in two days, and by the end of two weeks, when two heavy floaters arrived with the *Sally B.*'s almost-new engine units, he had the controls working smoothly.

Installation took longer. By the end of their second month on the backwater planet, Battersea was in sorry shape, mumbling his conviction that his poor excuse for a ship would never lift again, that the portside butchers who'd hacked her apart would never find all the pieces.

To judge by his gloomy mood, he seemed convinced that *Sally* would be forever lost the first time he turned on the drives. He cursed the Reef whose narrow starlanes passed only vital goods, prohibiting the transport of massive, brand-new engines except in massive, brand-new ships. He called himself twice a fool for allowing his ship's junk engines to be replaced with newer junk engines.

Bass avoided contact with him when he could. He seldom suffered his headaches when he was working with the ship's computers, but Battersea's lack of confidence was stressful. Bass knew the *Sally B.* would function as promised.

When the new units had whined up and down their vibrating scales countless times, when the installers were done checking their work, Battersea called Bass up to the bridge. "Well, Third, do you want to be up here for the proof of your work?"

"I'd like that, sir."

"Good. I want you here if we come off drive in the center of a star."

"Everything's in fine shape, sir."

"So you say, so you say. I hope you're right."

The *Sally B. Halpern* pushed out of atmosphere on a new, smooth note, and assumed temporary orbit, where Bass and the other officers made a final series of checks under Battersea's baleful eye. When she broke orbit for the second leg of Bass's journey, her drives hummed more smoothly than ever before in the captain's memory, and his mood lightened considerably.

Arriving in their destination system after several weeks under way, they calibrated the ship's clock. Though time dilation during Bass's first transit on the *Sally B.* had been on the order of one to eleven, this last time it had been a neat one to one. The days had passed simultaneously on board her and on the worlds and star systems they had threaded between.

In spite of his success, Bass was profoundly depressed. He was only eighteen—a birthday had passed unnoticed—but the ship's calendar read CE 2473. Ten years had elapsed on the Orb. His father would be truly old, now—if he was alive at all. His mother?

Ten years stolen. His depression was aggravated by the new engines; now, when it was already too late, the *Sally B. Halpern* could travel the high roads of space.

Captain Alois Battersea was an ugly man, cast in the same mold as his erstwhile crewman, Henry "Stinky" Myers, with a pock-marked face, shambling gait, and grating voice—but the resemblance stopped there. Myers had been cruel; Battersea was merely tolerant of the rougher aspects of his chosen life, where the safety and profit of his ship was concerned.

The new engines would pay for themselves, and from now on there'd be no need to squeeze each credit so tightly—no need for marginally profitable sidelines like the shanghaied-labor trade. Battersea felt good about that.

He felt good about Bass, too. A strange, distant youngster, but damned determined. A good officer. The captain knew Bass wouldn't stay on. Battersea would have let him go even if there weren't a time bomb in the ship's programming. Still, he owed it to *Sally* to try.

"There are strange things happening out there, Bass. Too many ships disappearing along the Reef. You might be safer with us than heading back again. Why not wait for a better time—even a year or so?"

"I've read the reports and log dumps, sir," Bass replied with a slow shake of his head. "Whatever is happening back there, you're best out of it. But the further I go, the harder it's going to be to get home at all. Will you put me off on the next world where I can earn passage money?"

"I won't be able to change your mind, will I? Very well. You pick it, you've got it. With your wage, you'll have over three thousand credits to start with. I'd make it more if I could afford it. The drive modifications are going to pay for themselves, but not soon enough for you to share in those profits."

"I'm grateful for my wage, sir."

After that encounter, Bass spent even more time at *Sally*'s main console. His research was no longer mechanical or abstract; he needed a destination, a world where he could make enough money to pay his way home. He studied all the possibilities, rated them, and weeded them out. Dates and figures scrolled up his screen faster than most people's eyes could have read them. Even without a hat he was a sponge, absorbing the masses of data he was afloat in.

Gradually, as if knowledge seeped in without active seeking, he became aware of trends no one else had remarked upon: trails of phenomena that, taken together, summed up the Panaikos Council's most ominous predictions of chaos and despair, and amplified them. The hat would have made things clearer. With it, Bass could have translated figures from data bases into visual cues, categorized and manipulated them like chess pieces, seen them like a spaceport traffic controller sees ships and satellites and planets in his holochamber. Bass could have walked those unseen worlds in his mind, then weighed the significance of production, transport, and trade like pebbles in his hands.

Even without the lost hat things stood out from the gray background of commerce and industry like particles traces in an antique cloud chamber. They intersected, merged, and went their separate ways again, and Bass couldn't have explained why or how he was aware of them, only that their effect upon his thinking was magnified with his exposure to ever more extensive data.

Shipping was decreasing, and shipping was vital to all transReef. As a side note to his military-history classes, he remembered an important point: militarism had characterized the ancient Roman Empire, but *trade* had made it live. Denarii, solidi, livres, pounds sterling, dollars, and credits, accepted and freely traded, maintained empires. When confidence in currency fell, empires did also, for barter could not finance armies, universities, or princes.

Even on the Orb, the signs had been there. Jack traded lumber not for credits, but for metals, machinery, and other goods. It was no way to run an economy.

Rome fell. Vandals, Visigoths, Huns, Alans, and a score of peoples flourished in its place, albeit on a smaller scale. For the average man, the Dark Ages were no darker than before. Crops still grew, and babes were born. But transReef wasn't Dalmatia, a few days' sail from a Roman shore. The Reef was no Adriatic Sea. And no transReef world shared the perfect mix of elements that was Earth's. Perfect, because humans had evolved to use what was there, and had no need of what wasn't.

Without trade, transReef crops *would* die for lack of trace elements like zinc and selenium. Without trade, babies *would* be stillborn or deformed, retarded or insane. Only trade kept transReef alive. And trade itself was dying.

Bass didn't know what to do with his insights. Who could he approach with the certainty, undocumented as it was, that the coming unrest would be far greater than anyone had imagined, that the coming decades were an intersection at which humanity—

on the transReef worlds and even across the Reef to the Old Worlds and Earth itself—would be forced to choose among innumerable branching paths into the future?

Who could he, Bass Cannon, convince that, of all those paths, only a handful would lead to a future in which humanity would stand out like a supernova among the already bright stars of the galaxy, among the hundreds of other races and species already strewn wide across it?

Thousands of paths led elsewhere. Those Bass imagined vividly, his images drawn from inward sources whose existence he'd never imagined. He saw mankind scattered, a subject species on a half-million alien worlds: workers and petitioners, cattle. Worse of all were his visions of worlds upon worlds, the Orb among them, whose cities were abandoned monuments, crumbling blemishes in landscapes dominated by inhuman, alien forms.

Intuitively, without a hat to help him visualize the apelike faces of prehuman ancestors, he nonetheless understood the nature of the human failure, the failure that was sometimes damaging but never fatal—on Earth.

Humans had evolved first as social apes, with ape culture—such as it was—and ape behavior. The demands of technology, of increasing complexity, led to a unique nonbiological culture, to constraints on humanity's raw nature that permitted the building of pyramids and starships. On Earth, when cultural control failed—when war, charismatic leaders, or new religions swept old ways aside—humans still survived. Genes still flowed even to isolated tribes; babes nursed and grew.

For transReef, lawlessness, anarchy, and the failure of cultural controls meant more than a time for withdrawal to the woods or to isolated mountain valleys, a time to abandon cities and palaces for the safety of rural anonymity. Ancient, biologically programmed behaviors meant death in isolation, not salvation. Stripped of common conventions, means of exchange, rules and rulemakers like the Panaikos Council, the ape-men would run free for a time, and then die.

Worse still, Bass saw, there had never been a true "transReef culture," only a scattering of individual, individualistic worlds, each going its own way, self-absorbed and self-congratulatory, linked only by the annoying necessity of . . . trade.

Why was he vouchsafed these insights? Who was he, to be so sure of the course of universe-twisting events? Why didn't he even consider that they might be paranoid aberrations? Could others see what he saw? He didn't think so. But someone must! The councillors and sociodynamicists? Increasingly, as data flowed, as paths clarified in his mind, he began to compartmentalize them and isolate them from his daily life and thoughts. There was nothing he could do about them anyway.

As he studied the worlds ahead of him on *Sally*'s route, a conviction grew until it approached certainty: one—and only one—of those worlds was pivotal to him and to the "historic flow" he perceived. It seemed unlikely that the two were related—after all, that would mean that he had some place in the resolution of his species' fate. And who was he?

His more immediate problem was that he didn't know the name of that pivotal world. Coris, a local trade center and *étape*? Aphane, with its noted university? Or Caddon, which was the breadbasket for half a sector? All were significant worlds, influential ones where a talented individual could work to earn passage money and more, but still, something felt subtly wrong. Something was missing from his analyses—hidden, perhaps, because he placed too much emphasis on each planet's obvious assets.

Each time he rose from the console, he shrugged off his indecision. There was still time. He could wait until *Sally* was ready to break orbit before it was too late to leave her.

When the answer came to him, it arrived not as a flash of insight but as a creeping suspicion that gradually became a dead certainty. At first he resisted it, because the world he focused on was such an unlikely one. When he informed Captain Battersea of his choice, the captain was totally unimpressed.

"Phastillan!" he exclaimed. "That's not a human world, it's a pissant colony."

"Psatla," Bass corrected him. "They're really not insects. More like armored crustaceans, I think. Have you ever seen a squid?"

"The things with tentacles? The ones that eat ships?" Battersea's grimace gave his opinion of such creatures.

"No—that was only a story," Bass replied with an indulgent chuckle. "Real squids are only about this big—" Bass spread his arms a halfmeter. "People eat *them*, not the other way around. Anyway, psatla are all tentacles, with protective chitin over them. The chitin's the only reason they look a little like fat bugs. And they're not hive creatures—they have an elaborate caste system, and they communicate with odors."

"Just so," Battersea replied, unimpressed with Bass's xenological knowledge, "but there aren't more than a hundred human beings in Phastillan's whole solar system—I read the reports, too.

What'll you do for company? Besides, there's something else that's funny about pissants—nothing that gets in the reports, you understand, but people who work for them get . . . strange . . . and never talk about the planet.''

"Whatever it is," Bass said with a confident grin, "I can handle it. They've bought five million credits' worth of salvage computer hardware that's junk unless they can hire someone like me to set it up and run it. The company that sold it to them went bankrupt.''

"What do they need the stuff for, anyway? Pissants aren't supposed to be able to use machinery.''

"They don't use much. They're almost instinctive bioscientists, and they terraform their planets with specially bred bioforms—everything from bacteria to full-sized grazers. They were trying to computerize their operation on Phastillan, and now they're stuck with a warehouse full of junk. They're offering five thousand credits a year for a qualified programmer. I could be on my way home in two years if I take the job.''

"I see what you mean. If you can take two years with no company but pissants, the money makes sense.''

"I'll survive," Bass assured him.

CHAPTER
SEVEN

VoiceLog 3.24(r), Shipsoft Corporation, Tacoma, S3
Timecode 772.403.9621

>Shipowner de Witte has assumed personal control of the ship's log. From now on its entries may reflect only tangential reality. As acting captain of *Reef Runner IV*, I will maintain this subfile as long as I am able.
>Using parallel circuitry built into the ship when my father owned her, flightlog data will be dumped sequentially into an-

other masked subfile. These files are accessible only with my
personal code or the registered shipbuilder's.

> This morning we unlocked from Longaway Station with six
"passengers." Owner de Witte has not revealed our destination, but Longaway's proximity to the Caprian Reef suggests
an Earthward journey. Also, the six poor things we took aboard
are only children, young, comely, and brain-damped. There is
no market for luxury slaves on transReef worlds. *Reef Runner*
was built for smuggling, but this insults her too much. I have
talked with Mark, and he agrees. We have no plan, as yet.

> Alta Van Voort, acting captain, *Reef Runner IV*.

By the time *Sally* swung into a lazy orbit around the blue-oceaned,
tawny-and-green-flecked globe that was Phastillan, Bass had dug
more information from several unfiled data blocks in the ship's
archives.

Psatla concern for the delicate state of their planetary equilibrium would force *Sally* to remain in orbit. They feared vacuum-
resistant bacteria clinging to hulls, disease organisms that might
find new hosts among Phastillan's beasts, and atmospheric disruption caused by even the most delicate landings and takeoffs.

Human settlers rated planetary biotas and resources by their
commercial value. Psatla rated them on similarity to their original
homeworld. Few worlds measured up, so psatla colonies were
few and far apart, a chain of worlds five or even ten thousand
light-years long. Phastillan was the colony of a colony many times
removed from its source.

Psatla modified suitable worlds to approximate that faraway
prototype. Whole genera of plants and animals were extermi-
nated, ecosystems changed beyond recognition. Native species
that could be modified to resemble homeworld forms and to function similarly were nurtured and mutated. Psatla genetic skills
were unsurpassed, but were narrowly channeled toward the goal
of similitude.

Mechanically, psatla were dolts—without outside help they
could never have left their planet of origin, for they built neither
ships nor factories, and refined only a few ores and chemicals
using tailored bacteria that ate rock or wastes and excreted aluminum, oils, or fertilizers. But they were an old race. The first
forgotten starship to set down on their homeworld belonged to a
race now extinct. Psatla, unable to travel faster than wind, let
alone light, still realized the potential of it. Their visitors thought

of the convenience of having such expert biomanipulators nearby, safely trapped on a planetary surface, and offered a few adventurous psatla a ride. The first psatla colony flourished. Millennia later, other starfaring races called on them, and again, psatla hitched rides.

Psatla communicated among themselves with scent, not sound. Over millennia of dealing with other races, they evolved a spoken tongue—first a pidgin, later an integral part of their own culture. How else would they express hard, scentless concepts like "windmill," "dragline," and "map"?

But psatla's path from world to world grew no smoother with time. Every species had a narrow range of temperatures they and their commensals could tolerate, a narrow band of stellar radiation they required. Psatla needs were specific, their tolerance slight. Eighty thousand years before humans left Earth, they ran out of worlds that could be changed with biological arts alone.

Desperate psatla hitchhikers, with no funds to seek further, contracted with a shipmaster who threatened to put them off at his next planetfall. There was a world where psatla could survive . . . If one narrow isthmus was channeled out, tropical currents would warm an island chain where they could live. And they would be grateful, and generously so, to the benefactor who made it possible. "Clean" industrial atomics launched from orbit carved the channel, and months later psatla disembarked on their newest world. The starfarer never regretted the expense of establishing that psatla colony. The vaccines and pharmaceuticals he received in return made him rich.

The precedent was remembered, and transmitted by other psatla hitchhikers and other star captains. Worlds farther and farther from the psatla ideal could be transformed with the help of alien technologies as well as psatla ones.

Phastillan had been colonized by the Reis sept, a young shoot on the ancient psatla tree. The current Reis *sfalek*, or leader, Phaniik Reis, was a radical innovator. One innovation was his attempt to computerize the modification of his marginal planet. Had political and economic conditions remained stable he might have succeeded, but variables like bankruptcies, lost cargoes, even human cheating, hadn't been considered. He and his people were saddled with hardware that had cost years' worth of their offworld exchange, and it didn't work. Bass, still fresh from his victory with *Sally B.*'s drive modifications, contracted by ship's radio to put it all together for them . . .

Before he shuttled down to Phastillan, *Sally*'s crew had a party

for him. Battersea broke open a fresh case of Calversham's whiskey for the occasion. "That's the nicest thing about boughten
cargo," he commented. "I own it, so I can drink it—and what
we don't finish off tonight goes down with you, Bass. I don't know
what those bugs drink, do you?"

"No idea, sir. I'll be glad for a few bottles of Vat. They'll last
me a long time." More than anything Battersea could have said,
that gift told him that he was, indeed, more than just another
departing crewman. It was the captain's way of remembering Bass:
there was no way his store could be replaced, not unless *Sally*'s
route took her back to the obscure planet where it was made. It
was as if he were saying, "When I reach for a bottle, and it isn't
there, I'll remember another loss, too." Bass felt the same way.
He would miss the gruff old man.

"I'll drink only in remembrance of you," Bass said. Then,
feeling foolishly intimate, he looked around him and added, "All
of you."

Bass dared drink only moderately; a mild hangover could set
off a chain reaction leaving him more dead than alive. At the party,
he nursed a four-ounce glass through most of the evening. Everyone else made up for it by drinking their fill. Bass felt a bit drunk,
though he knew he was only relaxed, in the company of friends
at last. Friends. Not the "best buddy" kind like he and Rob had
been, but still friends. People he'd worked side by side with, eaten
his meals with, who accepted him.

While conversation skirted around him, he looked at each of
his friends in turn, putting names to faces, remembering snatches
of small talk and things shared. He knew that the memories he
was trying to fix forever in his mind would still fade, that in two
years or ten their faces would blend with the visages of strangers
yet unmet. Only Battersea's face, he suspected, would remain
photographically clear.

He thrust melancholy thoughts aside—someone was asking him
to leave portside messages that might eventually reach *Sally*
through the passing of log dumps from ship to port to ship. Then,
after a flurry of final toasts and well-wishes, he made his way to
his bunk for the last time.

Battersea himself helped Bass snug down the joints of his evette, the one-time-only space suit that would later be ejected from
Phastillan's shuttle. Heavier suits, evas, were fitted for specific
crew members, but Bass had never had one. Holding the evette's
helmet under one arm, Battersea asked, "When you're down on

the surface, will you radio me?'' Bass raised a quizzical eyebrow. "The time bomb," Battersea elucidated. "Remember?''

"Oh, that!'' Bass replied with a wide grin. "There isn't one. There never was, so you can still snatch me back, if you want to.'' His grin stiffened, then. "I'm not even sure I'd mind.''

"Don't tempt me, Bass. I'll miss you.'' He was grinning, too. Two fools standing around with their teeth bared at each other, the captain thought, when they'd both rather cry. "I didn't really think there was a bomb,'' he said.

Bass only kept grinning. Words wouldn't come. Silently, he took the thin, flexible helmet and lifted it onto his head. Battersea checked the seals.

The psatla shuttle hung off in orbit while Bass rode a cable to its airlock. As soon as atmosphere was restored to the lock chamber, a very human voice addressed him.

"Take off zhe suit. Zhe air iss wiz a medication to keel off zhe zhairms on you. Eet steenks, bot no 'arm weel come to you, okay?'' The accent might once have been of earthly French origin, but now it was only one more variation on the standard English that had spread from world to world along the Reef.

Bass complied. The air stank of disinfectant. "All set in here,'' he said. The inner door slid open soundlessly, allowing him to enter the shuttle itself. There was nothing alien about the craft; it was a standard type, mass-produced on a dozen worlds. Even the pilot was as human as he sounded, a slender dark-haired man not much older than Bass.

"Welcom' to zhe soil of Phaniik Reis, *sfalek-thes tei Phastillan*—zhe beeg boss, zat ees. I am called Zhems Reis, *psaalek-ni thsaan tei psaalek Thesakan.*''

"Great!'' Bass said sarcastically. "What does all that mean?''

The shuttle pilot laughed. "Eet means zat I am Zhems—J-A-M-E-S—Reis, zhe chef peelo—pie-lot—an' zat I work for zhe being called Thesakan. You weel lairn soon enough zhe speech. Now seet. We go down.''

Bass sat. Though the shuttle used its chemical-fueled engines for takeoff, landings were unpowered. It was a rough way to come down, hammered and tossed in the solid-seeming air like a stone skipping over pond water, and when they came to rest Bass was thoroughly shaken. Such landings would have been part of his academy training in the school year he was even now missing. Even now? He laughed silently, bitterly. Only the last few legs of his travels had been one-to-one. That school year was ten years in his absolute past.

"Come," James beckoned. "I tak' you where you weel live."
Outside, Bass could feel the heat radiating from the shuttle as he
walked across damp, dew-laden sod. It seemed to be moss, not
grass. A low ground fog swirled about his legs and lower body.
He wondered if all Phastillan was this damp.

The shuttle's heat created a cloud of ion scent around it, and
hot metal and pyroceramics had inundated his sense of smell, but
when he was far enough from the shuttle the planet's own odors
reached him. He was overwhelmed. The Orb had been highly
scented by its aromatic flora, and Bass had always reacted strongly
to it on returning from offworld, but Phastillan . . . a thousand
distinct traces assaulted him. They didn't blend into one characteristic scent but maintained their individual identities, piquing
his nostrils one after the other in an olfactory symphony.

Spicy, sharp tickling alternated with heavy sweetness, while
waves of cloying fermentation advanced, ebbed, and swept over
him again. His head spinning, feeling a persistent itch deep behind his eye sockets, Bass tried to breathe through his mouth
alone. Can I possibly get used to this? he wondered. Or will I go
crazy? James doesn't seem affected. I suppose the impact will
fade, with time. I'll get numb to it, and I won't even notice.

The odors weren't unpleasant. He liked fresh-baked bread,
good red wine, even ripe cheese. He was usually refreshed by the
rich scent of fresh-turned sod, lulled by the methane tang of wet
lowlands. He had often savored the air rising from old wooden
boats, sun-warmed: wet wood, yesterday's fish scales, and seaweed pulled up by the anchor. But this was too much. Seaweed
sandwiches vied with gingery breadcrusts and pine-resin cheese,
accompanied by cinnamon wine.

It was synesthetic; odors lapped over his other senses. He could
almost *see* the violet cloud of cattle-manure-and-fresh-mown-grass
that billowed over him only to be replaced by skin-tickling, insect-
crawling burnt pepper, hot oil, and honey, and the plucked-violin
staccato beat of pinched rosebuds and sour cream, of . . .

He pulled out of his trance. James called the high, wood-
wheeled vehicle that awaited them a "trap": it was drawn by an
animal. Bass had seen pictures of horse-drawn carts, of course,
but that creature was no horse. It had no distinct legs, consisting
only of ropes of corded muscle covered with irregular plates of
rough chitin. Underneath it, extensions of white flesh writhed
across the mossy ground like so many snakes. It was a crude doll
made from bunches of twine coated with dried, cracked mud. Its
head was a shapeless lump set athwart the middle of its "spine."

Its most distinctive features were three large, sad blue eyes that rotated in no apparent concert. He was torn between a laugh and a shudder. Its particular odor signature was sun-heated grass, crushed lemon balm, and vinegar. "A *beteph*," James called it. "A psatla horse."

The wagon's driver was a psatla, and however prepared Bass had thought himself, he was still shocked by its appearance. There had been no holographs of psatla in *Sally B.*'s data. It smelled of rotting wood, of musty, abandoned barns. Its face, when it turned to face him, was antlike in a way. But "ants" on the Orb had been tiny brown creatures with six, eight, or ten legs and hard bodies.

The psatla, standing in the front of the wagon, was as tall as Bass. Hard chitin sheathed its head like a helmet drawn up in three transverse crests from front to top. Each crest shrouded a forward-facing eye like a putty ball with a pencil-sized hole. Its analogues of head and shoulders were overlapping chitinous rings, which verged into odd-shaped plates further down. A pair of plated arms, jointed much like human ones, drooped from gaps in the shoulder-rings. The psatla's lower body was draped in a skirt that hinted that its chitin plates might not continue to ground level. Under the creature's horny armor writhed inch-thick ropes of creamy white muscle, twists and coils and bunches in constant motion like snakes or tentacles. Bass suppressed an atavistic shudder. He let his eyes go slightly out of focus and concentrated only on the being's vaguely humanoid silhouette, not its strange anatomical details.

"You spoke to . . . ah . . . him," Bass said to James. "Is their speech hard to learn?"

"Not hard to lairn, jus' hard to spik well. Zhere ees a grammair—a book an' some tapes."

The trap moved smoothly along a mossy roadway between slender, broad-leaved trees. Flowering vines clung to their trunks, displaying mauve, violet, and deep purple blooms the size of dinner plates. Were they native to Phastillan, or imports? They looked suspiciously like "real" flowers—Earth stock, like the Orb's. Vegetal perfumes shifted in rough sequence as they progressed: crushed mint, the stink of a frightened garden snake, geraniums, bee balm, and petunias. Some scents were sweet, others acrid or painfully bitter. Small, noisy life-forms thrashed and chittered overhead, releasing showers of dew and captured raindrops, mercifully water-scented and clear.

Ahead, geometric shadows resolved into wing after wing of a

rambling building. A house? It blended gracefully with the forest. Intricate wood shingles covered irregular roofs from swayed ridges to wide, upswept eaves. Below, walls existed, or did not, in whimsical fashion. Poles, seldom straight, often branching, held the structure up. Between them, irregular panels of mossy fieldstone and daubed wicker blended in pleasant confusion with unsilled openings that hardly distinguished inside from out.

"Eet ees zhe house of *Pralasek-thes* Swadeth, your new boss. You weel live zhere."

A wave of panicky loneliness swept over Bass. "Do you live there, too?" he asked hopefully. Here he was after only an hour on Phastillan's surface, having seen only one member of the planet's dominant race, and he already felt like he hadn't seen another human in years.

"Me? No vay! I leev at zhe port. Wizh zhe ozzer humans." Bass felt even worse. There were no other humans out here. In spite of his brave words aboard the *Sally B.*, he was overcome with doubt. Could he really handle two years of this?

The trap pulled up at the "house"—the *asaph*, James called it. Was that the front door? The rear? A path of mossy stepping-stones, too close together for human tread, led through a casual opening and curved out of sight in roof-shadow. Bass climbed from the wagon.

"Do I just walk in?"

"Somebody weel be 'long. Zhey expect you. Find a place to seet. Maybe I see you sometime, eh?"

"You can count on that! Hey! I forgot to ask. Are there any girls on Phastillan? Human ones, I mean?" James's laughter echoed in his ears long minutes after the trap had pulled out of sight, leaving Bass alone, more than a little afraid, and puzzled as well.

He found a tree stump under the roof of an alcove. It was worn smooth as if from sitting, and its upper surface was shallowly dished. Though its edge cut into his thighs as he sat, it was better than the ground, which, even under the sheltering roof, was still beaded with late dew.

CHAPTER

EIGHT

Psatla had a penchant for natural, unregulated forms, Bass observed. Their joinery was exquisite: irregular roof poles and wall
plates were mortised perfectly, their shoulders cut so precisely
that a hair couldn't have fit in the gaps. Shingles woven in place
with split withe and roots formed patterns close up, but seemed
naturally irregular from only a few feet away.

It was very beautiful, and not alien at all, the beauty of vines
twining about hedgerow trees, of water cascading over jumbled
rocks, artifice grown like natural things. He wondered where in
this strange, lovely place he would be lodged, in what sort of bed
he would sleep.

The overwhelming odors of Phastillan's life-forms muted as
his brain's censors filtered them. He reviewed his first experience
of Phastillan. Besides the odors' intensity, there was a qualitative
difference from any other planetfall in his limited experience.
Like connecting into a data net with his hat, he had sensed an
interrelatedness, a content, that he associated not with scent, but
with sound, light, and electrical impulses. Could he recapture
that sense? Would he someday be able to "shut off" the defensive
insensibility his brain had imposed, and "read" those volatile
messages?

A wicker panel slid aside on silent runners, and a psatla moved
smoothly forward from the shadows. This one, too, was almost
as tall as Bass. Otherwise, it was only superficially like the one
who had driven him here. Its shiny chitin plates gleamed with
iridescent patches of midday sun, not mud-colored, but a green-
gold that swirled like dragonfly wings. Motionless now, peering
at Bass from impenetrable pinhole pupils, it exuded . . . power.
Power and threat. Threat and . . . concern? How could that be?
Was his imagination running away with him?

"Welcome, Vassily James Cannon. I am Swadeth, one low on the first branching of Reis. Has your waiting been long enough?" Its voice was smooth and only slightly accented with a sibilant, nonhuman resonance. Words issued not from a single mouth, but from hundreds of tiny ones at the ends of its smooth, white "tentacles," a chorus of voices. What did the question mean? Bass suspected Swadeth wasn't apologizing for having kept him waiting. He deliberated before he replied. "I have had time to appreciate your *asaph*'s beauty. I'm glad I was given that opportunity."

Could an alien being speak warmly? Swadeth's voice conveyed that impression even though its tones emanated from the slightly open gaps in its carapace, resonant and sighing at once. "It is good. You will flower well in the Reis garden, Vassily James Cannon. Come. I will show you where you may rest and renew yourself." He turned silently back into the house. Bass followed, leaving the wicker door open.

Irregular triangular openings were set in the joinings of roofs and walls. Cool, diffuse light penetrated the complex beam structures above, and fell like deep-forest sunbeams on the small plants and mosses covering the floors.

The psatla slid ahead of him on a mass of tentacular muscles beneath its lowest chitin plates. It wore no garment, so Bass was able to observe its progress—as smooth as if it were on wheels. The soft, green floor was undisturbed by its passage. Bass's own narrow, booted feet left heel-shaped depressions as he walked.

"Swadeth?" he said tentatively. The being stopped and rotated to face him. "May I remove my boots? I'm afraid they'll chew up the moss."

"Indeed, Vassily James Cannon, you exceed my hopes for you. Remove them. I am well pleased."

It had been the right thing to do. The moss felt good to his bare feet: cool, not chill. They passed through room after room. There were few corridors, just a labyrinth of superficially similar chambers. Hundreds of them, Bass estimated, each with its own subtle details of wood, withe, and mood. How many psatla lived here?

Swadeth stopped before a door woven of round twigs and bark-covered vines grown to the shape of the opening, then stood aside.

"Here?" Bass asked. "Shall I enter?"

"Here, if you are suited to it. There are others, also." Ambiguous. Not "If it suits you." Bass felt that his reactions were being scrutinized and analyzed. He slid the door panel aside and entered a chamber brighter than the others. A translucent plastic membrane was stretched over a withe window frame. A metal cot supported a stuffed tick and neatly folded blankets.

The closed window trapped an odd acrid-yet-sweet odor whose origin eluded him until he saw what was stored under the cot. The space beneath was stuffed with labeled boxes and plastic-wrapped packages of human-manufactured toilet paper.

Well, why not? He laughed silently. *I wonder how psatla shit?* Would I have noticed such a prosaic smell earlier? All his life he'd lived with that cheap, manufactured perfume. Toilet paper. A flower scent so abstracted from its natural prototype that it was identical even from world to world. It had taken exposure to a truly alien environment to bring it to his conscious awareness.

The floor was dry and brown, exposing hard-packed dirt. Wrongness pervaded the room. Bass stood wiggling his toes on the moss, feeling its stiff dryness. He turned to his host.

"Did this room belong to the human I'm replacing? It's different from the others."

"The *saf-thsaan-ni* Michael Devoro slept here," the psatla replied tonelessly.

"Swadeth, I have no wish to offend—may I ask questions without fear of angering you?"

"Questions are no cause for anger." The hard, alien face was unreadable. Swadeth's eyes were black pinholes in their rounded, wrinkled-mud protuberances.

"Michael Devoro didn't like it here, did he?"

"I suspect he did not."

"Are there other windows like that?"

"No."

"Will the moss recover? Or is it dead?"

"It will live again, with love."

"Would it recover faster if the window was open to the outside?"

"Yes."

Bass thought hard. "I'm as human as Devoro," he said, "and my ways are probably much like his. I'm ignorant of rooms where everything is alive." Swadeth remained silent—no question had been asked. Bass doggedly persevered. "I might, through ignorance, destroy something of value, as he destroyed this moss with his boots and his closed window. Perhaps I should stay in this room just so I don't do further damage, but . . . I don't want to. I don't think I could . . . love . . . this room."

"It is enough. I will take you to another." Swadeth turned—a curious, smooth about-face as if he spun on bearings—and moved to another doorway. Bass followed. That room was open to the forest; its moss was glossy blue-green. Dry fern fronds were piled neatly on a bed of washed gravel in a corner. The fern scent was muted and comfortable, reminiscent of lazy fall days in the dappled sunlight of his homeworld groves.

The brush pile: a sleeping place? There were no blankets, but the outside air flowing through the room was warm. Bass suspected it might always be so. *Is there no need for the elaborate shelter from environment that I take for granted? Is my own range of tolerance close enough to psatlas' that I can live here on their terms, in their manner?* He decided to chance it.

"Yes, this room feels better. May I use it?"

"You will live here. I will leave you to contemplate. One will come for you later, to bring you to food." Swadeth spun about, slid away from the doorway, and passed out of sight. Bass's shoulders slumped as tension drained. *Contemplate?*

He peered past the twisted poles of his doorframe. Swadeth was gone. He was alone. He set his boots down by the door and examined his new home. One side was entirely open. Ferns and light brush grew up among the trees, and there was no sign of a trail, no indication that he would not be as private in his three-walled room as Michael Devoro had been next door. He left the wicker door to his room open.

There were two other doors, one on each wall, opening into adjacent rooms. He went to the northernmost one, opposite Devoro's, and listened, hearing nothing but the faint soughing of the breeze outside, the drip of water droplets from leaf to leaf to ground.

He knelt by the low bed of fronds, pushed on them with both hands. They were soft to his touch, springy, and they smelled faintly spicy, like verbena, or coriander, or . . . like Phastillan fern fronds. He edged onto the "bed." It absorbed his weight easily, guiding him to the center. Lying on his side, he ruffled the exposed frond ends, examining its structure. It wasn't just a haphazard pile of chopped vegetation. The lowest layer was coarse and twiggy, with progressively softer layers atop it, stems outward, in bundles tied with twists of long grass. The topmost surface was feathery-soft, the periphery stiff, and the center resilient. He wouldn't roll out of bed.

Bass turned onto his back and stared at the ceiling. His stomach rumbled noisily. He was long overdue for lunch. Ah, well, he would get on schedule, he would adapt. Thoughts of home conspired with the mandala patternings of the intricately woven shingles, and he dozed.

Nightfall came quickly. Asaph Swadethan was near Phastillan's equator. *Pralasek-thes* Swadeth felt . . . what did a psatla "feel"? Perhaps one could say that his *ksta*—his many components, each with its own tiny brain fragment—agreed that the new human was truly different from the others. Perhaps, having thus agreed, they flooded their common bloodstream with complex, hormonelike chemicals which made Swadeth content.

Bass Cannon knew no more than any *fsa-psatla* outsider, but he saw much, and drew correct conclusions. *Ksta* writhed in avid, hungry anticipation: the presence of Bass conflicted with *psalaat-thes*, the Great Plan for Phastillan. It was Phaniik Reis's Plan, not Swadeth's.

Phastillan's humans were disaffected, unmotivated, and lost. Psatla chemosensory organs spotted such types by their glandular "signatures." They "smelled" losers. Devoro had been one, and the pilot, James, was another. All losers, except Bass.

Travelers expected preimmigration blood sampling, but psatla cared less about microorganisms than they let on. They sampled for other things: motivation, intelligence. How? A blood sample was decanted. Psatla dipped white, tentaclelike "fingers" in the red-brown fluid. "Good," they said, or "Not that one. He is wrong for us." *Taste. Smell.* Human words for rudimentary chemosenses. Psatla "words" were analogues of the substances they sensed: chemical traces synthesized on the spot, transmitted by touch or a puff of air, and "heard" not by ears, but by the recipient's chemosensors, like "tasting" the original.

Bass was not rejected. He should have been. He was too smart, too motivated. A sensitive psatla could taste such things, so Swadeth had tasted Bass's sample himself, and his *ksta* savored risk and potential. The coded records Captain Sotheny had read on the *Carrington*, the foil and plastic vita card now lovingly packed away by Bass's mother, told much the same story Swadeth intuited from one small glass tubule of blood.

Given correct stimuli, Bass Cannon would do more than build a computer system from Phastillan's junk. He would shake the world, and on those tremors Swadeth would rise to greater *gadesh* than he now savored. Alternatively, he might fall in a crevasse the shaking opened. It served no purpose to dwell on it, for the gamble had already begun.

Swadeth spread his carapaces, exposing delicate white *ksta* to cool night air, a rare, vulnerable gesture reflecting utter confidence. The wormlike *ksta* beneath his head shell closed their hypertrophied eyes, and the newly exposed *ksta* that formed Swadeth's body viewed stars in the soft night sky with their own sharp, tiny orbs.

Bass wasn't immediately required to work. Psatla expected newcomers to contemplate, to explore their surroundings, so he spent his first two weeks learning the *asaph*'s layout. Its dim, interconnecting rooms—the maze of Knossos re-created in wood and withe—became as familiar as the *Sally B.*'s corridors. He lost his conscious awareness of odors, but on a basic level they were his guides. If a room was empty, he knew before his hand touched its sliding door panel. If a chamber's occupants were busy, he knew. If they wanted the momentary diversion his passage would afford, he knew that, too. A whiff of cinnamon, burnt motor oil, or sweetened coffee would tell him, though he was seldom aware of the messages.

Apartment house, office complex, factory, and village: Asaph Swadethan was all those and more. Light work was done in individual rooms, and joint tasks in roomy common areas or courtyards open to leaf-scattered sunlight.

In his own room were a table which folded from the wall, a human-manufactured stool, storage nooks, and an oil lamp that burned cleanly and smelled like cloves.

At the center of the rambling structure was a chamber built of concrete block and steel beams. It was the largest room in the *asaph*, the size of a small gymnasium. Fluorescent tubes lit it harshly. Psatla avoided its ugly severity, where ozone competed with phenol to overpower psatla smells. The odors of electricity and human machinery were a silent roar, white noise that created olfactory silence, informational void. The computer center was a communications nexus, the still-dormant brain of Phastillan. It housed the systems that Bass was expected to get up and running.

Why had the facility been placed at the *asaph*? So many disruptive changes had been made to accommodate it. Generated power had been wired all the way from the port. Concrete and block had been lugged in on *beteph*-drawn carts. It struck Bass as odd. Psatla, as he was growing to know them, were usually conscious of the utility of their efforts. Perhaps the project's importance to Swadeth made it necessary for it to be close at hand, but the *pralasek-thes* never visited, satisfied to receive Bass's periodic progress reports.

Bass gained the impression that he himself was of more interest to Swadeth than the computer system. He observed that he was seldom alone. Unobtrusively, psatla watched him. Even when he slept his watchers weren't far away. On several occasions he had awakened from vivid dreams and found unreadable psatla faces hovering over him, quick-moving eyes and gingery tang indicating concern. That Swadeth knew of those nighttime disturbances was made clear when they met and talked.

"Dreams interest me," Swadeth stated during one meeting. "Among us, an analogous phenomenon occurs when our subunits—our *ksta*—seek to reconcile their differing realities. But if you have no *ksta*, as we know them, then who speaks with whom in your dreams?"

"I'm no bioscientist," Bass said, "but I've read that human brains are divided bilaterally. Perhaps one side speaks with the other. I don't really know." He vaguely understood such concepts, but mankind's interest in its own internal workings had flagged during the transReef expansion. There had been too much to do, too far to go. Bass's education reflected that neglect, and though Swadeth pounced on his statements at first, when he realized the limited scope of Bass's knowledge he became impatient and returned to his other business, whatever it was.

Bass began learning the spoken psatla vernacular. He could already pass the time of day with his housemates and dinner companions. Those numbered almost two hundred. He met fifty or sixty psatla during his thrice-daily visits to the communal refectory. All were members of the *Pralasek-thes* Swadeth's "branch," or work unit, and all were dedicated to the computerization of Phastillan. Thus all were, until Bass got things under way, out of work.

That was to Bass's advantage. With time on their hands, the *asaph*'s dwellers, especially the low-ranking *tsfeneke*, lingered over meals. Three of them—Flesteh, Kesseth, and Enaaseh—had arrived, via devious and peculiarly psatla reasoning, at the conclusion that spending extended lunch hours with *Thsaan* Bass would enhance their *gadesh*, or status. At least that was how Bass interpreted their attentions. He would have liked to think he'd made friends with them, but he hadn't discovered a psatla word for friendship. Where no word existed, could the concept be understood?

Mealtime brought other revelations. He discovered that psatla were composite beings—each of the white ropes that ran beneath their exuded chitin plates was a subbeing, a wormlike, unintelli-

gent *ksta* that linked with others to become a sentient being. Each
worm element could feed singly or through osmotic contact with
designated feeder elements usually located, for convenience, in
the psatla ''hand.''

Psatla ate by soaking these worm fingers in the soup, or—if
they were unusually hungry—by judiciously unravelled parts
of themselves to get even more fingers in the pie. Bass wasn't
especially squeamish. After his initial shock, he enthusiastically
pushed a whittled wooden spoon among those feeding fingers in
search of scattered solid morsels that were, to psatla, inconven-
iences. He didn't ask what went into the psatla soup.

Had he asked, his meal habits might have suffered change.
Psatla were efficient nutrient-converters, but they did not need
every molecule they ingested. Some surplus they stored in temporarily specialized *ksta* for later distribution; plant nutrients
might be saved for a particular plant whose yellowed leaves demonstrated need. Toxins were either denatured, then excreted
through the cloacae of foot *ksta* into the soil or saved internally
to be spat or injected into some animal to be collected for exam-
ination. Unneeded nutrients suitable for psatla or human consumption were excreted directly into the most convenient place:
right back into the soup.

Bass was the object of curious investigation by his *asaph*-mates,
who never lost their amazement at his clumsy, mechanical eating
habits. Young psatla, recently integrated, didn't hesitate to explore his feeding apparatus, especially his teeth. After once being
nearly gagged by a curious finger, Bass set firm limits to such
explorations.

Despite regular importunement he refused to demonstrate his
excretory rituals for them. He maintained a discreet privy a short
distance out in the woods near his room, and was quite grateful
for Michael Devoro's parting gift.

More difficult than the language was the system of ranks and
titles that defined every individual's place in the ''branch'' and in
the Reis ''tree.'' There were five major divisions of *gadesh*, or
rank. *Sfalek* was first. *Sfalek*, the stem. Titles could be modified
by *-thes* or *-ni*, ''low'' or ''high''; *-thes* might indicate variously
''most influential,'' ''wisest,'' ''furthest seeing,'' or rarely ''most
dominant.'' Even as Bass came slowly to an intuitive understanding of *-ni* and *-thes*, he would have been hard put to define them
aloud other than as least and most significant. Phaniik Reis was
Sfalek-thes, the base of the stem, the support upon which all Reis
depended.

A *pralasek*, plural *pralasekt*, the first branching, was equivalent to a staff officer. On Phastillan, a relatively new colony, there were four branchings, totalling twelve individuals.

Next were *psaalekt*, "branches." To Bass, they were managers, sergeants, or foremen. Swadeth claimed eight such branches, each one with three individuals: *psaalek-thes*, *psaalek*, and *psaalek-ni*. Low, middle, and high.

The general populace were *tsfeneke*, "twigs," otherwise unranked. Status among them fluctuated with temporary alliances and task orientation. Each *tsfeneke* answered to his own *psaalek* and none other. Bass wondered how they ever managed to get anything done.

A final category was Bass's own: *thsaan*, "flower." Flowers on the Reis "tree" could bloom on trunk, branch or twig. Most *thsaan* were outsiders, humans, who didn't fit but had to be acknowledged and sometimes obeyed. Psatla temporarily attached to an *asaph* not their own were also called *thsaan*. The status and authority of a *thsaan* was one step lower than the individual to whom he attached; thus Bass, *thsaan* of a *pralasek-thes*, had for all practical purposes the rank of *pralasek*, high status indeed.

Then there was *gadesh*: Bass first interpreted it as rank or status. Gradually he realized that, like most psatla words, it had multiple meanings based on context and mood, and upon the status—*gadesh*, of course—of the speaker. Literally, it seemed to mean "correct service," proficiency at making right judgments concerning Reis welfare, but there were subtle overtones of intrigue and honor, too, of great power given, of disgrace and banishment, death and danger. Bass resolved wholeheartedly to avoid all *gadesh*-related matters.

CHAPTER

NINE

> >LOGFUNCTN:420.091.9411 COMMENT:
Lifted ship from Pocasa. No fuel there. No life. It looked like a plague of some kind, but I suppose starvation was at the root of it. According to the ship's log and my officers' announcements, I am mildly concerned that *Matteo* may have to breach her reserves if we don't find fuel at the next Class B or better port. Unofficially, I'm concerned we may never see a functional port again.

There is a madness loose among the stars. TransReef cannot survive without trade, without ships like *Matteo*. I remember when our arrival meant festival time on some worlds. Now, wherever we turn, we are beset by greedy men who would destroy us. The fine citizens of Mer would have stripped us of our remaining fuel, and for what? To power up their idle municipal generators, to light their city streets a little while longer and pretend that the greater darkness had been vanquished. Better they had filled our hold with drums of nutrient-rich fish oils and commissioned us to trade for the tidal generators they really need. Did their portmaster really believe I would honor his holding seals on my landing struts, with my ship at stake?

I will continue to operate *Matteo* for her designed purpose, and seek trade. If, as I fear, there will be no more trade among these stars, I will set her down for good. I will not turn buccaneer, even to save my ship.

Jacomo Pirel, captain, *Matteo d'Ajoba*

Getting the mainframe running was no easy task. Michael Devoro had been incompetent. Control blocks had been switched with data modules, buses had been rerouted and cut as if the man had no idea of what he was doing. It took Bass a month to get the diagnostic programs to boot up. Two more weeks elapsed before he traced the last misplaced connection. After that, the real difficulties began.

The unit was a hundred years out of date and built only for data handling. At its best it would be stiff and inflexible. The problem wasn't design or construction, but basic architecture: it was one of the last sublight computers to be manufactured. Newer models incorporated elements like microscopic starship drives to "think" at translight speeds. Electric impulses, or—as with Phastillan's mainframe—molecular-optic ones, were slow.

The bottleneck of light speed had been foreseen as early as the twentieth century, five hundred years before, for speed had ever been the cyberneticist's goal. From the beginning, computer development had been a race between faster machines and increasingly complex, time-consuming tasks. "Fast" magnetic disks replaced tapes, then superconducting circuitry was built,.then laser optics replaced wires and printed circuits. Finally, light itself seemed too slow.

Phastillan's computer represented the peak of development for sublight machines. Each block of circuitry and memory was a single macromolecular crystal, "grown" with optical paths and microscopic lasers to drive signals. As fast as it was, twenty-five years after its introduction programmers were already chafing at the limitation of C, the velocity of light. For three centuries they had cursed that seemingly insuperable barrier, just as Bass did every day.

Setting up any cybernetic system was a cut-and-fit process. Despite rigorous manufacturing controls and rechecking programs, glitches occurred. Bass grumbled that the first words taught a budding programmer had to be, "Why is it doing that?" or "Where did that come from—I didn't put it in there."

He wrote dozens of patch programs, checked the output generated by millions, even billions, of data bits from the manufacturer's test files. At first he was satisfied to get consistent responses, even if they were nonsensical. Later, he began tracing down thousands of individual errors flagged by his own tests.

Interfacing the peripheral units was almost simple, though he suspected the agency that had sold the system had known that they wouldn't be doing business transReef for long. The incompatible equipment they'd supplied was little more than warehouse gleanings, junk. Nothing fit on the first or second try.

He finally discarded the entire area-network plan, programming and hardwiring around it in favor of a slower, centralized arrangement that routed everything through the mainframe. The geosynchronous satellites that would carry the signals from terminal to terminal would have to work hard to manage the doubled traffic that would result, but those had been supplied by a different agent, and they were more than adequate.

The system was primitive even by transReef's frontier standards: no holographic imagery, just flat screens; no verbal interfaces, either—everything had to be input from keyboards. That wasn't an oversight—psatla speech didn't lend itself to being machine-coded. Its logic was too difficult for human programmers, so speech circuitry had been omitted.

What Bass missed most was his hat—the brain-scanning I/O device that allowed him to become one with the machine, to swim within its data currents instead of being a spectator forever alongside the stream. But a hat would have done psatla no good at all—it had taken millions of man-hours to create programs that "thought" in the imagery of an English-speaking mind. There were no programs for other languages that he knew of—it was easier to teach users English. Besides, psatla didn't even have a centralized brain to interface with; their thinking was scattered among their composite parts, their *ksta*.

Nonetheless, Bass planned to build his own hat, if he could beg, borrow or buy the parts for it. Perhaps he could prevail upon some sympathetic ship's comp officer to sell him bootleg interfacing programs. If not, he'd write them himself.

The best Bass could say for the system was that it worked. Three months after he'd started, ranks of terminal units were set out on ten tables, twenty to a table. All functioned. Bass could go to any one of them and access the mainframe or another terminal.

For the moment, he resisted the temptation to sit down and explore, to merge with the data streams pent within the great machine. It would have been pure self-indulgence, he told himself, psychocybernetic masturbation; there was nothing in the data banks but old news, years out of date. There would be time later to make that plunge, when real information was flowing through the system's electronic vessels and nerves, when he'd built his hat and programmed it.

The night he finished the hardware phase of his contract, he went to *Pralasek-thes* Swadeth's room. Swadeth wasn't in sight, so he sat on a root and pondered. It was a room just like—and just as unlike—any other. Wood, moss, and stone combined in subtle harmonies to make statements of attitude, mood, and *gadesh*. Scents of balsam and old wool overlaid a base tone of dew-damp granite. The comfortable, familiar childhood odors could have been created for his benefit, to put him at ease. Psatla odors were communication, though he still had no idea of their scope and much went on around him that he missed. His senses just weren't attuned or sensitive enough, even though he had never used any of the sense-numbing alkaloids. Perhaps he could learn, though; chefs and wine tasters trained their senses to impressive extremes.

Bass realized that he hadn't even touched his gift from Captain Battersea. Had he been too busy even to relax with an occasional nightcap? Ah, well, there was no ice at Asaph Swadethan, and he hated warm whiskey.

Remembering the whiskey led his thoughts along another path: Captain Battersea . . . the *Sally B.* . . . human companionship . . . then sex. Sex? When was the last time he'd even thought about sex? Weeks ago? Months? Incipient panic nibbled at his guts. What was wrong with him? He should have been climbing the walls by now! He hadn't even had a wet dream—nor had he fulfilled his promise to visit James, to meet some of Phastillan's women. Girls . . . sex . . . the thoughts didn't cause the slightest stirring in his groin.

Bass emerged from his uneasy cogitations, hearing sounds from a door beyond. Pushing his self-concern aside for the time, he peered into the next room.

Bass was attuned to the details of Reis life now, and he discerned several visual statements he'd missed before: Swadeth's room spoke of strength with its heavy scantlings, of stability with the smooth-burnished rocks that bordered it inside and out. It spoke of complex thought patterns through elaborately knotted withe and wickerwork, of subtlety and concealment through its hidden storage nooks and veiled openings. And there was no door on the house-side wall, only an opening that announced to all the state of Swadeth's *gadesh*: that room of strength, stability, and complex mystery was open, always. Bass stepped in unannounced.

"*Thsaan* Bass. Your task progresses?" Swadeth spoke in Psatla.

Swadeth's household had adopted the abbreviated honorific and nickname. *Thsaan-ni sta Pralasek-thes Swadeth te Vassily James Cannon Reis* was ridiculous. The humble abbreviation, combined with Bass's single-minded work habits, gave him an air of considerable dedication: *gadesh*.

"The *sfalek-* and *psaalek-*machines now speak to each other through the small worlds above," Bass answered in the same tongue. "They are ready. When will those-who-learn come?" Such paraphrase was necessary in Psatla, which had no words for computer, terminal, or relay satellite.

"How many must come?" Swadeth asked him in English. "Will you teach two or twenty?"

"I think ten at a time. That's manageable. If everything goes well, training will be finished in a year, and I'll still be able to oversee operations for a few months before my contract is up."

"I will arrange it. They will come. And you? You integrate well with my *asaaphan*, my household, and you gather much *gadesh*, I am told."

"I'm learning to speak your language a bit—as you can hear. I've found psatla who accept me." Bass paused and thought for a moment. "Of *gadesh* I know only what I am told. I haven't sought it—if *gadesh* accrues to me, it's the result of my accomplishments alone."

"You must understand *gadesh*, Bass—it is everything. When you choose a task, *gadesh* is proposed; when you succeed, it is gained. When you eat lightly, you promote the feeding of *tsfeneke* and others, and *gadesh* is created. But when you feast, it is not lost. I fear for you, *Thsaan* Bass. *Gadesh* raises you high in my esteem and my own *psalaat-ni*, my path, is widened as well, but understand that there are other *pralasekt* and *pralasekt-ni* who have paths of their own, who do not celebrate my elevation through you."

"Politics!" Bass spat in English. Swadeth's English, though sometimes stilted, was excellent, and he could not have helped hearing the resentment and frustration in that one word.

"I'm trying to understand your ways," Bass said more calmly, "especially *gadesh*—but it's too confusing. I'm doing the job I was hired to do and I'm not causing anyone trouble. All I want is to get your people trained, get paid, and go home. Isn't that enough?"

"It may not be. I will do what I can to protect you—my *psalaat-ni* requires it—but you must protect the *gadesh* you gain also. Understanding is required for that."

"Then won't you help me to understand? Will you explain *gadesh* to me instead of just hinting and beating around the bush?"

"What is 'beating around the bush'?" Swadeth asked.

Bass tried to explain the idiom, choosing the memory of a children's cartoon—a fox and a rabbit—to illustrate.

When he finished, the psatla's body was doing something very strange. His chitinous covering, normally tight against him, was fanning out in separate plates. Bass tried politely not to stare, but it was impossible—for Swadeth looked like nothing so much as a greenish-gold pinecone. And those . . . things . . . peering out from under each lifted scale? White, soft, wiggling *ksta* . . . like worms!

Bass shuddered. For a moment, he had had the impression that Swadeth was coming apart right before his eyes. But as quickly as it had happened, the psatla regained his normal configuration. The white "buds" retracted and their protective sheaths drew tightly down. Once again, Swadeth was smooth, glittery and insectlike.

"Excuse my . . . lapse," he said. "Your idiom stimulated strange thoughts among my *ksta*. You imply that I, Swadeth, am thus a predator and you are my prey? Or is it the opposite? Together we circle the plant without coming together, without satisfaction or safety. It is very . . . funny." The last word was spoken as if Swadeth had dredged it up from a file of human expressions hitherto labeled irrelevant. What, Bass wondered, did psatla consider humorous?

"Gadesh," Bass reminded him. "Am I in actual, physical danger from these others?"

"I will try to explain. All psatla follow one *psalaat*, one path. New 'families' like the Reis are created, new worlds made proper for them. You understand?"

"Go on."

"The ancestor of Phaniik Reis was *sfalek* on another world. His *gadesh* was such that he was too . . . too good . . . for that world. His *psalaat-ni* had become *psalaat-thes*, the Great Plan: to make proper another psatla world."

"Kicked upstairs," Bass mumbled. Then aloud: "He could rise no higher without becoming *sfalek-thes* on his own new planet?"

"He could no longer promote the Great Plan without creating a new psatla domain and family or forcing the *sfalek-thes* to do so. The ancestor of Phaniik Reis didn't win, you see. He lost his battle, and thus Phastillan became a psatla world. Do you see now?"

"I think so . . . . I don't know. But Swadeth, I'll never be a true Reis. If I try, I'll go crazy. All I can promise you is that I'll fulfill my contract, collect my pay, and go home. Will I be allowed to do that?''

"I hope so, *Thsaan* Bass. Only remain aware that other paths diverge, they wax and wane inversely with mine. When doubt arises, when things are not what they seem, come speak with me. Will you do that?''

"If I smell a rat, come tell you about it. Sure, I'll do that.''

"Then tomorrow I will choose ten *psaalek* to learn of the terminals. Teach them data-input and button-pushing, no more. Do not strengthen their *psalaat-ni*, their minor ambitions, with deep understanding, lest your *gadesh* and mine be shown false.''

"I'll keep them in their place. Never teach the slaves to read, eh?''

"Exactly.''

"Are we finished, then?''

"We are finished. Good night, Bass.''

"Good night, Swadeth.''

The training began. Bass explained data gathering and retrieval to high-ranking Reis. He showed them what input was required, and what output they could, eventually, expect. That output would depend on their own efforts, Bass told them. Currently, the massive mainframe was an empty shell, a collection of operating programs without data to work with. Only when they had taught their own underlings to use the remote terminals would it come alive. Like a hungry hatchling it would ingest everything fed to it: Phastillan's weather, oceanography, and geology, catalogues of bioforms from the great trees down to the lowliest insects and bacteria.

Only then, when the voids in its frame were filled with glistening, crystal data blocks, would it glow from within as data was shuttled about, sorted and correlated at light speed along its jeweled internal pathways. That glow would increase with time and input until the fluorescent lights of the facility were needed only to illuminate the darkest corners of the great room.

Eventually, all Reis financial data would be in the data base also, for the maintenance of offworld exchange was vital to the purchase of chemicals, machinery, and human mechanical expertise.

Life, geology, weather, tides—every minute aspect of Phastillan would be definable. It would be possible to predict the results of the tiniest manipulations.

History would be included: not the history of psatla and their acts, human-style, but the history of species, from the homeworld and every psatla planet on the long, outward route of their colonization. It would include the descriptions of mutations, adaptations, exterminations, on a hundred worlds, and it would take years of continuous psatla work.

Less than a week after the first group of trainees had departed—taking ten of the two hundred terminals with them—Bass verified that sizable chunks of data were already being filed.

Upon Swadeth's recommendation, Bass "hired" three psatla of *psaalek* rank, members of Swadeth's "first branch." Initially, their duties were limited to the duplication of backup file blocks, which were taken to a stable-atmosphere cave elsewhere on the continent. Swadeth was vague and elusive about the cave's location. Protecting his *gadesh*, Bass thought. Keeping an ace up his sleeve.

The three assistants, *Psaalek-thes* Tsestra, *Psaalek* Klent, and *Psaalek-ni* Gisseth, were soon burdened with more work than they could handle as terminals were distributed and busy psatla fingers fed the data stream. They, in turn, enlisted the aid of a dozen, then two dozen *tsfeneke*.

Bass hardly noticed the days and weeks slipping by. He didn't care. Work was everything. His spirits rose and fell with his students' progress, with the sparkling activity growing inside the bright, old-fashioned monomolecules. No outside circumstances intervened. He knew no one on Phastillan, so no one called him or visited.

His students, now scattered across the planet, didn't live by Asaph Swadethan's clock, so he was on call twenty-five hours a day. He snatched sleep during momentary lulls, and never took a day off.

Even Bass's body failed to distract him. When he awoke with a full bladder, his erections were mere inconvenience, curiosities he took no pleasure in. A lengthy piss outside his room drained even residual sexuality.

Once, mildly curious, he attempted to masturbate. He managed to tease himself erect—but there it ended. There was no reward, hardly a twinge of feeling. He felt ridiculous, lying on his back and watching his useless pole standing before him. His hand fell away and he dropped into deep, dreamless sleep. The strangest thing about it was that he couldn't have cared less.

Work went on. The computer room could barely handle the activity. Its dehumidifiers and air conditioners strained under the load of respiration and the gusts of wet outside air that came in each time one of the four doors was opened. Bass had three doors sealed and the row of rooms around the facility emptied, forming a peripheral "hallway" and work area. The remaining door was given an airsealed vestibule. He encouraged psatla to work in their own rooms.

Just as humidity crept into the computer area, ozone, phenol, and hot-copper odors insinuated their way into every room of the *asaph*. Bass suspected that the odors were, for psatla, like the clatter of a factory in a quiet residential block.

Bass missed Christmas and the New Year without knowing it. Three months along in the training he saw his first human face.

James Reis—Bass didn't know his surname—entered the room properly barefoot. "Allo, Bass," he said cheerily. "My *gadesh* jus' jomped seex notches, I tseenk. Swadeth stole me from Thesakan. Now I work for you, eh? At leas' when zhere's no shottle flights."

"James! It's good to see you." With conscious effort, Bass refrained from hugging him. Forgotten emotions surged. "You—work for me? You mean flying the backups to the cave?"

"Zhat, an' later I fly you aroun' to zhe ozzer places, to zhe terminals."

Bass was reacting in a strange way. He couldn't take his eyes off James's soft, flexible human face, his dark, glistening human eyes and the profusion of uncut brown hair that swirled like feather-fern about his face and ears. With avid eyes, he caressed James's firm, jointed legs, savoring their humanness.

His reactions shocked him. Three months? No, more than that. How long? He'd been immersed in his task, had become obsessed. He had become *Thsaan* Bass in all but his body, had forgotten even to think of visiting the port again, of seeing his fellow men—and women.

His mind numb, he stared at James, who regarded him quizzically, one eyebrow raised. Bass had an erection. Blushing furiously, he stalled, not standing up to greet his visitor. What was wrong with him? "Over there. Sit down, James. Wha . . . what are you doing here?" he stammered, aware that the other had noticed his embarrassment and its cause. What would he think? Bass wanted to shrink into the cool, mossy floor, to disappear. He wanted James to leave, to never see another human. What was happening to him? The erection wouldn't go away.

"Eh, you're een bad shape, *ami*. You even seen anozzer human een zhese seex months? You been to zhe port for zhe girls?"

"I . . . I've been busy. The computers . . . I don't know anybody on Phastillan except psatla."

"Ees zhe phairomones—an' you got zhem bad. I seenk I take you to see Betsy, or maybe Sorayan."

"Pheromones? Is that what's happening to me? I'm not going crazy or weird?"

"Not any more zhan any of us on zhis crazy world," James said with a shake of his head and a bitter gaze.

CHAPTER
TEN

VoiceLog 3.24(r), Shipsoft Corporation, Tacoma, S3
Timecode 772.608.1284

> Dingenes de Witte sold the slaves to a Luna Personnel agent yesterday, and cargo crates were laded today. Tonight, Owner de W. was drunk again. I assumed the con at 21:23. My husband Mark (acting first officer) checked our cargo while Owner de Witte was indisposed. Manifest and log record a cargo of telescoping coring pipes, but Mark's ThruScan revealed 85 Jovia Model 22C space-to-space missiles, the newest FTL drive-frames from Ceres/Krupp.

> No destination has been declared yet, but de Witte had *RR*'s antimatter-ablation blanket restored in Luna Dock. I suspect we're going to smuggle the missiles through the Reef.

> So near. I always wanted to see Earth. It's quite pretty, from Lunar orbit. I'm not so sure I'd want to get closer. Dingenes went down, of course. He was born there.

> Alta Van Voort, acting captain, *Reef Runner IV*.

An "isolation syndrome." Of course! In his discomfiture, he clung to the knowledge that there was an explanation. Academy cadets were taught the dangers of alien body chemistries. Not diseases, because their bacteria and viruses were less dangerous than mutated earthly ones. Plagues that eradicated colonies between one shipfall and the next were always human ones, and no microbiotic tragedy ever spread between the stars. Traffic was sparse, voyages long, and diseases incubated, flowered, and died en route. Perhaps a few missing ships resulted, but that was all.

Pheromones were another matter: volatile hormones exuded by one member of a species and absorbed by another, with direct physiological or behavioral results. They were insidious, and subtle, because they couldn't be tasted or smelled, yet they slipped past the blood-brain barrier via the unsheathed olfactory nerve. Higher brain functions weren't invoked by such vapors; they only served to rationalize effects after the fact . . .

A human male meets an attractive, desirable, and willing female, but is inexplicably unmoved. Later, even in the course of one evening, he encounters another female who is dowdy, socially unacceptable, and not even interested in him, but who causes a strong sexual response. Rut. Chemistry. Musk. Pheromones. Magic.

Merchants, diplomats, and negotiators conduct affairs in person with great success but, when confined to letters, 'phones, even full-semblance holovision, they fail as often as they succeed. Personality. Presence. Pheromones.

Politicians shake hands, slap backs, speak, mingle, and breathe common air with constituents and influence-wielders. Some have it, some don't. Conviction. Impact. Personality. Charisma. Pheromones.

A man speaks before a tight-packed crowd unmoved by his eloquence. Another speaks, and the crowd becomes a mob. They run, they smash, they burn and kill. An atavistic survival program: the chain-reaction response of ancestral apes, antedating reasoned response by a million years. Mass insanity. Mob psychology. Pheromones.

Two men are alone in a tiny shack. Snow is roof-deep outside. For weeks they breathe common air, mix body oils left on playing cards and hatchet handles. Their movements stir flaked-off skin cells and loose hairs. Tension builds. Flee, their bodies tell them. Take a walk, get away for a while. But snow continues to fall for another week, and only one man emerges into sparkling sunlight.

The other lies inside with the hatchet buried in his head. Isolation. Cabin fever. Pheromones.

Population pressures create odd behavior in men, caged monkeys, and rats: mass murder, bizarre aberrations, maternal neglect and infanticide are only a few. From ancient Sodom and San Francisco to the Marble Rock Mine and the Asteroid War, concentration and density have triggered primordial mammalian reflexes. Atavisms. Decadence. Pheromones.

Even human appearance has been altered down through the millennia by the subtle chemicals of behavior, for what function is served by such oddities as beards and patchy body hair but the improved transmission of such essences? Surface area; evaporation; communication.

Alien races have chemical signals, too, based on their needs and ancestral genes. Such quick and simple communication is too effective not to be used. Though the "fit" of such alien molecules to human receptor-sites is usually incomplete, humans have become violent, hysterical, or paranoid in alien presences. Pheromones.

"I guess I've become a bit strange," Bass mused apologetically. "I learned about such things at school, but here—it never crossed my mind. By the way, who's Betsy?"

"She ees a mechanic. Also a whore."

"Ummh. And the other? Soraya?"

"Sorayan. Zhe same, but where Betsy ees beeg," he cupped his hands meaningfully on his chest, "Sorayan ees sleem. Zhey're bot' young, zhough, an' not too *cher*—expensive."

"And you think that's what will put me right again? Sex? I've gone for all this time without even thinking about it."

"Zhat's what Phastillan does. You forget, bot when you get wiz zhe woman—e'es like zhe eart'quake, you know? For bot' of you."

"I'm not a believer yet—but let's go anyway. We can have a drink or two, and I can look around."

James smiled knowingly. He gestured to the doorway. The trap awaited them. Its driver was the same Reis who had met them at the shuttle half a year earlier, but now Bass saw him with new eyes. The psatla was no longer a strange, exotic, even fearsome being, but an individual with a face, features, and his own uniqueness. The wet-wood smell that lingered about him was clearly his own—Bass's nostrils had become sophisticated enough to separate the actual odors of wagon, psatla, and the ungainly *bephest*—

and Bass perceived him as dour and unhappy, a *tsfeneke* whose
age had bought little *gadesh*. Thereafter Bass ignored him.

Once they were under way, James again brought up the isolation syndrome. "You knew you were seek? You saw zhe signs uff
eet?"

"Not until you came. I felt okay, I think. What signs do you
mean?"

"Zhe desires, zhe dreams, zhey all go away."

"Yeah, that happened to me. But I thought it was . . . I don't
know what I thought. But James . . . I'm pretty normal, usually."

James brushed Bass's lingering embarrassment aside and explained how the syndrome manifested itself on Phastillan. That
required a lengthy divergence into the psatla reproductive process, which James understood only vaguely. Bass's own knowledge allowed him to fill in the blanks.

He learned that psatla had two sexes. Females were egg-layers,
and unintelligent: large, pale worms like the preunion males. Only
their function as holders-of-eggs qualified them as females, and
there all resemblance to human sexuality ended. With life spans
equal to the males', they lived in the forest humus, feeding on
roots, stumps, and the punky, rotten wood of downed trees.
The female life-style explained the psatla urge to re-create their
homeworld: half of their species required damp soil and forest
shadows to survive.

Throughout their intelligent phase, males remained neuter, but
when senescence overtook them they went into the forests. Chitin
plates fell; cellular, chemical, and nervous bonds between their
ropelike "muscles" dissolved. They literally fell apart. Pale, unintelligent male snakes slithered off under the leaf mold in search
of female counterparts. They mated, then they died. Or did they?
It was said that *ksta*—essence, soul, intelligence—remained. Psatla claimed to remember things from past lives, even from other
worlds.

Eggs hatched. Tiny beige creatures—legless and eyeless, male
and female—ate and grew, and exuded. Drawn by chemical messages, the fat male worms gathered. Repulsed by them, females
dug deep and fled. Males entwined, coalesced, and specialized.
Eye patches became eyes, simple worms became tubes of muscle,
guts and hearts and brains. Tiny mouths secreted chitin. Fragments of memory, personality, and scattered ego united and concentrated. New psatla males, bark-stained and mud-crusted,
staggered from the forest, drawn by the silent call of the *asaph*,
a wafted organic-molecule beacon.

Psatla pheromones were not like human ones—not exactly. Even in a universe of unlimited possibilities, exact matches seldom occurred. But in a universe where species of many origins mingled, partial matches did.

A lone human, isolated from his own kind and plunged into the stew of foreign hormones, adapted to them, accepted them. His sexual urges attenuated, his dreams became placid. He substituted intense activity, concentration, for the divergent pulls of his own kind. He became, in effect, a psatla. So James believed, reciting the common lore of Phastillan's humans. Bass didn't have much confidence in James's biochemistry, but his own wasn't that much better. TransReef schools taught practical things, and graduated tractor mechanics, miners, and starship pilots. Few perceived the need for "frills."

Humans, unlike psatla, were neither wholly male nor wholly female. They balanced between the two. Chemical shifts caused one embryo to become male, another female. Too close a balance, and an androgyne was born—a joke, neither male nor female, or both.

Our lone male, perilously adapted to his psatla environment, would someday reunite with another member of his own species. A male? What matter? Male and female, his kind were walking pheromone factories. Once he was awash in the subtle perfumes of his own kind, ill-fitted psatla molecules sloughed off, James claimed, replaced by the perfect joinings of human essences.

He reacts: his body rapidly runs through its entire repertoire of urge and emotion. He sweats, he shakes, he feels fear and exultation. His cells dehydrate, engorge, and confuse themselves. He is aroused, enraged, or ecstatic—and violently, painfully human.

So far, James observed, Bass's reaction seemed mild. One old man died when he was reunited with his own kind. Heart failure, the autopsy determined. But then, he had been old. Bass needn't fear anything so severe, James assured him. The quick cure was simple: reexposure to his own kind. The more intense his reunion, the better. He must saturate himself in the essences of his fellow humans, female ones. James would introduce him to Phastillan's angels of mercy, Betsy and Sorayan, and his "cure," already under way, would be completed.

"Why didn't they warn me? Wouldn't Swadeth have known what was happening?"

"You bat he knew. I ask you zhis: Did you work harder an' concentrate batter zhan evair before? Deed you do more een seex months zhan you t'ought posseeble? Did zhe Reis not get zhere money's wort'?''

''They used me, you mean.'' Bass's already-strained emotional balance underwent additional changes. His face suffused with blood, his hands clenched, trembled with the urge to strike out. He felt shame, disgust. He suddenly hated the *asaph* and all the pissants in it. He condemned himself for a sucker.

''Hey! Ees okay now! Now you know! From now on, you come to zhe port every week, no? You see me, zhe girls. Zhe work slows down—so what? Psatla maybe shrog zhere shouldairs, bot zhey still pay you. Zhen you go home a reech man, eh?''

The port seemed farther away than it had six months before. He was glad. Perhaps it was only his imagination, but he felt better as they rode, as if his system was steadily sloughing off alien influences, giving them to the fresh, damp air. He was eager for female companionship, too, though he had no intention of buying his way into anyone's bed, pheromones or not.

The port was as he had seen it before, a cluster of human-style buildings at the edge of the shuttle field: dull concrete blocks stacked by a careless child, then abandoned. Their driver pulled up at a building.

''Zhis ees zhe bar. Ees probably not so busy now, wizh everyone working. Later, zhey all come 'ere.''

Attempts had been made to turn the block warehouse into a real tavern. A dark-painted bar was nailed together from packing crates, with shelves of liquors and a large, dirty mirror behind it. Stale beer, fresh plastic-and-fabric odors, and the tang of cheap whiskey all hit him at once. There was even a bartender, the only other person in the place.

''Hi, James. Who's your friend? Oh! You must be the computer fellow. Surprised I haven't seen you before.''

The speaker was short and plump. His sparse dark hair was slick with sweat and too little washing. His round face was jovial, though. A bartender's face.

''E's been out at Swadeth's *asaph*. Been working hees ass off seex months now, so I save heem.''

The bartender thrust a meaty hand over the bar. ''Aha. I'm Zvigno Anson. Ziggy, that is.''

''Hi. Bass Cannon.'' Bass reluctantly put forth his own hand.

''Haven't seen Sora today,'' Ziggy said, his voice abruptly oily and insinuating. ''Betsy's out back. You might want to take a walk out there.'' He raised an eyebrow at Bass. ''Six months? Man, you must be half-crazy by now.''

"I don't think so," Bass said hesitantly. "I felt funny a while back, but I'm fine now." It was true. He felt normal. Was there any point to all this? He had an uncomfortable inkling that he was being pushed into something—like the time a half-dozen second-year cadets had taken him on a joyride that ended at a whorehouse. He'd been horny, sure. What fourteen-year-old wasn't? But he hadn't been in control. He'd performed for others' benefit, not his own. He felt that way now—awaiting another rite of passage. Acceptance by the tribe would follow.

He ordered a drink—Scotch whiskey, unlabeled but smooth—and asked Ziggy about himself. Not a bartender by trade, he'd taken the task on as much as a favor to the other Phastillan humans, he claimed, as for the small percentage he made on drinks. The building was free. Theoretically still a warehouse, no Reis cared how the port was run as long as shipments arrived intact, were stored, and were available when requisitioned. Ziggy managed it all—port, warehouses, and "hotel." Others, he explained, maintained rooms here and arranged their time so they'd be in port on "weekends." By consensus, two days had been designated Saturday and Sunday. Tomorrow, Bass was told, was Saturday. Sunday didn't sound at all like Sunday on the Orb. The way Ziggy described it, it was just another Saturday, but with a hangover.

Bass felt a surge of homesickness for Orb Sundays. They hadn't been all that bad, once services were over. Quiet days. Reading, thinking, even fishing, when he could sneak off . . .

Ziggy microwaved frozen meat loaf steaks and heated a mess of frozen "beans," a local legume. When he slid the plates across the bar to the young men, the familiar meat smell intensified Bass's nostalgia. Were his confusing emotions real, or part of this "sickness"? He felt like crying for his lost home, for Crowe Academy, even for the battered *Sally B. Halpern*. He wasn't horny. Not the least bit.

Bass switched from whiskey to light ale while the three of them talked of their travels, and of the circumstances that had led them to this backwater planet. Ziggy's account was vague—disconnected anecdotes with reasons and motivations excised. He was from Cassembre, Earthward of Phastillan, and he'd worked a dozen minor ports transReef. Now he was here. "Not every exciting," he admitted, "but the pay's good. Only there's not much to spend it on."

James has been born James Aubasson, on Aix de la Recife. Aix had been settled from Laterre, itself originally populated by dissidents from France, on Earth. Before Phastillan, James flew orbital craft for three companies, and had been fired by each for laziness, nonconformity, or peculation—though to hear him tell it, his work had been superior and his dismissals arbitrary. "Zhey nevair fin' anyone batter. Me, zhey know. Zhe new ones zhey hire only fin' new ways to steal. Sheet! Zhe hones' ones stayed Eart'side, eh?'' Perhaps James is right, Bass reflected. Wanderers, flotsam, that's what we all are, tossed ashore by accident, recklessness, and unwise decisions.

Bass told his own story flatly, unexpurgated. Ziggy listened politely, and said little, but James's eyes lit when Bass told of life on the Orb. He pressed for details, but it was too hard to talk about. It still hurt. Bass brushed James's questions off abruptly and asked about the rest of Phastillan's human population.

The others, the fifty-odd humans Bass hadn't met yet? Contract-breakers, erstwhile smugglers, risk-takers who'd taken one too many—all had fallen upon Phastillan in desperation or dejection. As long as they could function at all, psatla didn't care who or what they were. Human weaknesses didn't matter, only performance.

There were no other alien races represented on Phastillan. Only humans. None of the Earthward species expressed the human need for continual expansion, and the transReef stars were thus mostly a human domain. The long, oft-broken chain of psatla worlds stretched across light-millennia in a different direction, through the territories of other starfaring species never seen by man.

Bass noticed a battery-run wall clock and realized he wasn't going to get back when he'd expected, so James led him to the newly installed computer terminal in Ziggy's office. The *psaalek* Thesakan was the terminal's nominal user, but neither he nor his *pralasek*, Sfel, had been trained, so its immediate operation had devolved on Zvigno Anson, port- and quartermaster.

Bass typed coded phrases on the psatla-adapted keyboard. The keys were identified in English, black on beige, and in psatla characters in blue on white, the two separated along the keys' diagonal. A simple toggle determined the operating language. Bass had, in his half year's isolation, learned to use both, and he typed in the psatla mode, to show off. James was suitably impressed, watching intently as sinuous characters marched across the screen.

"There. I've left a message for my students. If anyone else

needs me, I've patched into the 'phone, too. Can I take this along?'' He hefted Ziggy's portable com.

"You are zhe conscientious type, eh? Nevair leave work?" James sounded faintly scornful.

"Look, the psatla may have screwed me," Bass replied intensely, "but that system is still mine. I'm not going to spend one extra day on this mudball because somebody screws up when I'm not around. Understand?"

"Sure, Bass," James agreed, holding up his hands as if to fend off a blow. "Now we go back to zhe bar?"

"Yeah. Back to the bar. Do you still think I need to take your 'cure'?" In spite of his earlier resolve, the idea didn't sound so bad right then.

CHAPTER
ELEVEN

KEYBOARD FILECODE XXXX1 [SIMULATED]
> >[CLOSE] [ERASE] [TRANSLATE]
> TRANSLATE
> >[TARGET LANGUAGE?]
> ENGLISH VAR 3 LITERAL
ENT 1.3 > > >This is the time for men of my kind. Worlds lie open to me, for the taking. My ancestors were desert men, raiders on fat caravans. I, too, now take up the sword. My blade is this ship. I reject its papers, its trivial name, sounding like an Italian ice cream cone. It is the flagship of my fleet-to-be.[DATECODE MISSING]

In their absence the bar had filled. Three men in coveralls played poker, seated on fiberglass packing boxes at a plastic wire-spool table. Others leaned on the bar. Four competed at darts—real ones with metal points, not servo-images. The target folded out from a wall cabinet.

"All zhe comforts uff 'ome, eh, Bass? An' look zhere! Zhe lovely Betsy ees all alone." Bass's gaze followed James's nod, across the room.

Bass was suddenly, powerfully aware that Betsy was the first woman he'd seen in six months. Soft hair haloed her face, giving off a scent of heavy commercial musk he could smell even across the room. There was an evanescent trace of something else, too, something at once subtle and infinitely persuasive. Bass couldn't explain how he knew Betsy was the source of both, among all the other effluvia. Her skin was pale and smooth. Light blue shorts cut tightly into her rounded upper thighs. He could almost see the steamy, estrous vapors rising from her, penetrating him, changing him.

Lorraine! The other woman's name rose unbidden from the crannies of his mind. Lorraine. Why think of her now, after all this time? This girl's nothing like her. She's cheap, a whore. No, there were few similarities—only femaleness and Bass's own growing, surging desire. Again, he felt unable to stop. He stepped forward with the same eager reluctance with which he'd trod the path from High Manse to Five Corners. He was fourteen again. He burned. He was afraid. Only two things were missing: childish guilt and the weight of sin.

Now he knew he wasn't cured, that he had a long way to go, that the odd feelings he'd experienced until then were nothing, mere twinges next to this turmoil in his body and brain. Betsy's shorts outlined plump labia beneath slick, constricting cloth. Wrenching his eyes from the coarsely enticing display, he forced them to travel upward toward her eyes, but they got no farther than her navel—a deeply cupped mystery—and her pleated tube top, a semitransparent token over magnificent breasts, hiding nothing. Nipples stood proud and slightly downturned, their puckered areolae showing darkly pink through white diaphane.

James tugged him across the room and pushed him down onto a lumpy couch padded with worn shock-wrapping. The pilot introduced Betsy breezily, and she dropped casually to the seat next to Bass. James then went off for fresh drinks.

"Hi, Bass," she said. Her voice was low and breathy. Mint-scented vapor wafted across his face, into his nostrils. It penetrated moist internal membranes and unsheathed olfactory nerves and was carried on, willy-nilly, by tumbling blood cells. In seconds, complex organic molecules reached his glands, delivering their overriding messages and forcing production of his own, intensely human, hormones. Long seconds later, long after his body's surging, throbbing reaction to them, the chemical messages reached his brain.

"Hi, Betsy," he croaked weakly. "James wanted me to meet you, I guess." How stupid he sounded! Was that really his voice? Her cool blue eyes flashed askance to James at the bar, and Bass saw the understanding that appeared in them. He missed seeing James's emphatic nod, saw only the glistening brightness of Betsy's gaze. She stood up abruptly. The almost-palpable gauze of heavy-laden air surrounding her was stirred into tumbling activity.

"C'mon. Let's get out of here." She took his arm, and called loudly, "See you, James! Warn me next time, okay?" Bass clumsily got to his feet.

There was a doorway next to the couch; no need to push through the clutter of strange faces. A hallway lay beyond. "Hurry up, Bass." Her voice was urgent, impatient. A heavy door thudded shut behind him, impelled by Betsy's heel.

A bare light-globe illuminated a steel-tube cot with wrinkled white sheets and a heap of gray ship's-issue blankets. Condensate dripped from a leaky air conditioner in a rust-stained concrete wall. Bass stood dazed and numb in the center of the room, seeing only vague outlines, hearing only the rush of his own blood.

"Damn, you've got it bad, kid. I've got it bad!" Her soft fingers trembled as she skillfully unfastened his shirt, his trousers, peeling them from his rigid body. She pushed him roughly at the cot. His booted ankles tangled in his pants and he fell backward across it. Her own shorts fell, torn at a seam in her eagerness.

There were no preliminaries, no niceties. She mounted him avidly and plunged down on him, guiding him inside her. Long moments of thrusting, pounding confusion swept by as he lay sweat-soaked and stiff, arms flapping over the cot's edge like dead, forgotten things. His fists clenched and unclenched spastically. His eyes stared blindly. His brain registered no more than a pale, hammering blur of motion, a haze of yellow-blond hair. His body shook and tingled. Sensations spread through him, unfocused, diffuse.

Then sudden heat coursed over him, and perception contracted from his uncontrolled limbs, leaving him cold except for a burning in his groin as Betsy rode him, as excruciating, unendurable pain shot through his genitals like electric shocks. Corrosive, acid semen shot from him: living cells like tiny drops of molten iron, like microbes with teeth and raking claws. He screamed.

High-pitched echoes beat his eardrums. Echoes? No, it was

her: the behemoth, the great bludgeoning beast who covered him
was shrieking her own orgasmic agony.

A black cloak of frightening heaviness fell across his face. He
fought for breath, each gasp a muffled scream. Thick velvet darkness shaded into the swirled red of backlit blood in his tightly
closed eyelids. The light-globe was a bright orange sun behind
crimson cloud-haze. He felt sharp-nailed hands tugging his arm,
jerking, pulling him upright.

"Get up! My room's down the hall. Hurry, damn you! Before
someone comes."

"This . . . it's not your room?" he mumbled thickly.

"God, no! First door I came to. Come on! I want it again.
Here, hold your pants up." With shaky hands, she thrust a wad
of fabric between his fingers and squeezed them shut over it. His
still-erect penis felt wet and cool where it projected past his hand.
She led him, uncomprehending, from the room.

Another door closed. Another bed rose up to meet his naked
back and buttocks. Again a mad thing mounted him, rode him
mercilessly to a white-hot, agonizing release. Again, the dark
cloak of semiconsciousness muffled her soprano echoes of his
animal sounds. When they finished, he slept as if drugged.

Awakening was a cherry-petal daydream of cool silks, fresh
spring-scented air, and mists of water plashing on rounded stones.
He lingered there, basking in that sunlit glade within his head.

Half-awake, he remembered feeling like this before, an age
ago, it seemed . . . He'd felt drained. As dry as old bones. Only
fourteen, then, he'd made love four times—or had it been five?—
there in the tiny room over the New Paradise Café. The first times
in his young life.

Lorraine. She'd been every boy's fantasy—the beautiful older
woman who taught him everything. Had he been her fantasy, too?
A wiry fourteen-year-old whose cock always came back up, no
matter how tired he was, no matter how his shaft ached and
burned? Had she known that? Had she known he'd wanted to stop,
to give in to the waves of black sleep that washed over him? He
hadn't dared.

He'd thought about sneaking away, that time. Where had she
gone? The other room? Downstairs to the bar? He could have
been on his way up the trail to the Manse, but it wouldn't have
mattered. He'd have been back the next night, and the next—as
long as she wanted him.

Questing fingers of reason and curiosity tugged tentatively at the veil over his mind. Questioning, wondering, they drew it aside. He opened rheum-encrusted eyes.

Pink-petaled wall hangings concealed the raw concrete walls he knew were there. A pale, peach globe of bent withe and paper muted the ceiling light's glare. Cool satin sheets patterned with mauve old-Earth roses slid under his hands. Betsy's room. Her tiny island of human sanity in the alien rain forest, the cement-and-steel port. Quintessential femininity: a stereotype in fluff and fabric, a stage setting where the waterfall was only Betsy showering beyond the frosted glass door. Bass picked grit from the corners of his eyes with a fingernail. The shower sounds stopped.

"Are you awake?" Her voice had a rough edge. Had she really screamed so loudly? Had he? His throat felt raw when he answered.

"Yes. Ah, hi, Betsy."

"Hi, Bass. Do me a big favor and shut your eyes, will you, when I come out? I'm going to go turn out the light." She sounded tense and unsure.

"How come? I want to see you."

"No! I mean, not yet. Will you?"

"Sure. They're shut." A shy whore? I guess that's no stranger than anything else. God! I never thought sex could be so terrifyingly intense—not even with Lorraine. Did I really call her name? Or did I only imagine it? Betsy. Lorraine. Betsy . . . what's happening to me? Can anyone save up six months' lust and use it all in one mad spasm?

He heard bare feet slapping the floor. Concrete? He'd have thought she would have found a rug, a peach or pink or long-piled grassy-green one. There was a scratchy clack of corroded switch contacts, and then darkness. Her slapping footsteps became a muffled padding; there was a rug by the bed. A wave pushed Bass up as the water-mattress moved beneath him. He rolled sideways, reaching for her.

"No. Wait." She held his wrist in a firm grip. He couldn't see her at all in the faint glow from behind the frosted bathroom door. "You stink. Go take a shower, okay?"

He flushed. Now that she'd said it, he noticed his soupy aroma and his oily skin. "I do! Sorry."

"Don't be. It happens, when you're like that." Like what? Six months behind? Her jocular tone sounded wrong, insincere. And the darkness? Betsy hadn't seemed body-shy in the bar, not dressed as she'd been. He was confused. She was like no whore in his limited experience.

He stayed in the shower long after his skin and hair were cleansed, letting the warm water ease his muscles and soothe his pubic bruises. No amount of pondering shed any light on Betsy's behavior.

His eyes adjusted to the orange glow of the low-turned light, but when he returned to the bed, Betsy was under the covers; he saw only a shadow and a wisp of golden hair.

"Mmm. You're nice and clean now." She tossed back the sheet, reached for him and ran her fingers over his chest. "Hair. I like that. I didn't even notice it the other times. I think I'll have you again—right away." Bass felt a cold twinge at the base of his spine. Now she's sounding like a whore, he thought. Or am I being oversensitive? Is that her idea of bed-talk, coquetry? *I think I'll have you* sounds like *I think I'll have a beer*. Her statement was flat, assumptive, an intent expressed without emotion, as if Bass's own desires—even his capacity to respond—were of no import.

"I don't know if I can," he said in a joking tone. "I think I've given my all." He didn't want to find out if that was true. He'd had enough. Too much. He shouldn't have come back to the bed at all.

"Oh, you can! You will, too!" A vicious undertone in her voice grated on his ears. "You aren't cured yet. Shall I prove it to you? Here." The bed sloshed beneath him as she rose to her knees and crawled forward over him, pinning his arms at his sides as she advanced. He waited passively, determined now to defy her, sure that her arrogance had driven off any remaining shreds of desire he might still have felt for her. Betsy put her hands on the headboard and pressed her belly against his face. Stubbornly, he shut his eyes and refused to breathe the scent of her, but she reached behind herself and struck him with her fist, hard, in the stomach. He drew in an involuntary gasp, and with that single breath, he was lost again.

His head spun, he felt dizzy and nauseous, hot and then chilled. She shifted, moved above him, and he responded avidly. Ears muffled between her thighs, he still heard her smug voice. "See? It's all chemistry. I've got you a while longer, yet." He didn't pause in what he was doing to her, only cupped her buttocks to pull her closer. Scant minutes later, she reached back and, finding him erect, backed up clumsily and enveloped him for the third time.

Inwardly he raged, calling her bitch, slut, and whore. Outside, he was a stiffly jerking doll, a clockwork mechanical man thrusting up with his hips to meet her, bruising himself further, unable to stop or even to moderate the painful impacts of thinly fleshed bone. As before, their joining culminated in ecstasy and pain; as before, she cried aloud; as before, he slept.

When he awoke he tottered to the bath and splashed ice-cold water over his face and head. Betsy slept. Returning for his clothes, he discovered a small bedside lamp. He twisted its vernier a quarter turn and dressed quickly, feeling purged of alien pheromones and human sexual desire. His loins were numb, dead to all but the chafe of fabric on his oversensitized skin.

Bass regarded Betsy's sleeping form long and closely. Inspected through clear, dispassionate eyes, she was no longer a lust-inducing houri. She was at least ten years older than he, perhaps thirty or so. The skin by her eyes was crinkled, and becoming inflexible. Her large breasts sagged sideways toward her arms as she sprawled before him, and the skin of her thighs was dimpled with excess flesh. Her belly was permanently seamed across her navel and light stretch marks matched those at her plump hips and the sides of her breasts. Bass was neither overly fastidious nor critical by nature, but he couldn't help marveling wryly at the perceptual distortions his imbalance had caused.

What now? Pulling on his boots, he walked toward the door. Did she expect to be paid for the night's work? He had no money, only growing credit on his account, to be paid in gold when his contract terminated. Never mind, he'd ask James what to do.

"Bass? Please wait." Her voice was little-girl plaintive. "I'm sorry," she said. He hesitated with his hand on the latch, torn between curiosity and his urge to bolt out the door into relative normalcy. He shrugged, sat on the edge of the bed, and looked at her, waiting for her to speak.

"I am sorry. I guess I went a little crazy, Bass. I didn't mean it to be that way."

"I guess I'm pretty stupid," he said bitterly. "I'm not even sure what you're apologizing for. Using me for a sex-slave, or gloating about it?" He shook his head abruptly. "I think I'll stay out in the boondocks if this is what it's going to be like every time. I don't have much self-esteem left, you know."

"You really don't understand, do you? How could you spend six months on this planet and still be so dumb?"

"So tell me," he challenged. "Make me understand."

"You're all bent around because you got screwed, aren't you? Because I screwed you instead of the other way around, right?"

"I suppose so," Bass conceded reluctantly. "Among other

things.'' He couldn't have explained about Lorraine, about the other feelings he'd had. Not that he wanted to—not to her.

"You couldn't help yourself, could you? I'll bet you were so far gone you probably thought you'd die each time, right?"

"That's one way of putting it.''

"So what do you think your pissant hormones were doing to me all that time?'' Hot anger laced her low voice. "God! All that stuff you were throwing into the air! If you bottled it, you'd be the richest gigolo in the galaxy. I was off the top of the yardstick. I don't like losing control like that either. That bastard James could have warned me.'' She smiled then, only a tiny twist of her full lips. "But, like I said, I'm sorry.''

"I accept that. But why was it like that? Why didn't James tell me? He acted like I was going to a picnic.''

"James!'' She sniffed scornfully. "For him, that's just what it would have been. He's an insensitive ass.'' She spoke from obvious personal experience, Bass realized. Why should that bother me so—jealousy? he wondered incredulously. How can I be jealous of a whore's tricks? A whore who—he told himself—he didn't even like? Whom he could easily hate?

"Besides,'' Betsy continued, "I don't think he knew how far gone you were—I know I didn't. Not right away, anyhow. At least you didn't run amok, or something—like jumping somebody right there in the bar.''

"I wouldn't have done that anyway. I couldn't.''

"Don't be too sure of yourself. Worse things have happened.''

"Like what?'' he asked skeptically.

"Well, one man died of it.''

"Shit! That was a heart attack. James told me about him . . . but I suppose you're right,'' Bass said. "It could have been worse.''

"Are you still angry?'' That plaintive tone. He looked in her eyes, and saw no teasing or coquetry.

"No, not any more,'' he sighed.

"Favor, then?''

"What?''

"Come back to bed—just for a while?''

He raised an eyebrow at her, smiling crookedly. "I don't know if I dare. I don't want a heart attack.''

"Not that. Just hold me. Pretend it's all for real, just for now.''

His smile straightened, broadened. "Can I stay the night? It's a long walk back to Swadeth's.''

* * *

They slept immediately. In the morning, Betsy fixed a hot-plate breakfast of reconstituted eggs and tinned bacon. The coffee was real. For Bass, it had been a long time between cups—since the *Sally B*. Later, Betsy took him for a walk out past the port area. It was not yet noon, so the trees were still dripping morning raindrops and dew, and though the air was far from cool, it wasn't sticky-hot yet.

Betsy showed him a favorite path under the forest canopy. It was hers alone, she said, and Bass didn't doubt it. Paths were unpsatla. Their planetary hosts pointedly avoided following the same exact tracks through their forests. Trodden-down soil was inhospitable to their strange other sex and their young.

They talked as they wandered. Actually, she talked. He listened, inserting occasional comments and affirmatives, encouraging her to continue.

"It was never any good, for me," she said as she ducked under a low-hanging branch. "I'd given up blaming it on my husband, on men, even before the divorce. I even tried it with women but it wasn't any better.

"I took an off-planet contract just to get away, to run away, I suppose. I knocked around for a few years on a mining colony, and when I heard about Phastillan it sounded pretty good—all new machinery, breathable air, no underground work—so I signed on for a year.

"When I got here, everything seemed pretty normal until I met my first man just back from the 'bush.' After that, when I discovered what sex could be like for me, I went a bit crazy. I thought I'd been cured. I must have had every man on the planet that first year—and not just once. There weren't so many then, but I was still pretty busy. I started hanging around the port waiting for them to come in." Betsy turned her head and looked back at Bass frequently as she spoke, reassuring herself of his attentiveness. "I didn't like myself very much, but once I'd started being the town slut it was hard to quit. I tried, God knows, but the longer I hid out, working the polar stations, mostly, the worse off I was when I came back."

They emerged from the forest onto a riverbank. The water was acid-brown with decayed vegetation, slow-moving, and the sun was warm on their faces. They were tired of walking. Betsy found a sunny spot where the moss was dry, and she motioned him to sit. He lay back with his hands under his head and stared up at motionless white cumulus clouds. The sky beyond them was bluer than the Orb's, shading into grayed summer-mauve low on a horizon masked with humid haze.

"Go on," he prompted. Why, he wondered silently, do I care?

"What? Oh. You're sure I'm not boring you—or disgusting you—with all this?"

"You're not. I like listening to you."

She was satisfied. "Well, I got over feeling dirty and guilty after a while. I just took what came my way. In a way," she said wistfully, "I felt special—just as fat as I am now, but those men still came to me. I had what I'd been missing before, and I thought it was enough. I wasn't looking back, or ahead."

"You're not fat. Plump, maybe."

"Fat. I'm not unhealthy, not obese, but I'm still fat. Anyway, when my contract was up, I didn't renew. I didn't know about pheromones yet—no one did, back then.

"Once I was off Phastillan, I worked my way along the Reef assembling crated tractors. It was a decent living, and I saw a lot of real estate, but it was an old-style ship, and I lost a lot of years along the way. I'd probably be about eighty back home.

"It took three years before I was ready to admit that everything had gone sour. I still had sex with a lot of men, and somewhere along there I'd started accepting 'presents'—money, too—but it was never any good. No fireworks for Betsy.

"I suppose I would have been smarter to have settled down somewhere and married some nice farmer—I had plenty of offers. But I couldn't think straight about sex, and the longer I stayed frigid, the better Phastillan seemed. I'd figured it out by then—it was something about the planet, not me, so I came back. It took me four more years and every penny I'd saved, so when I walked into the bar here, I was flat broke and without a contract. I still don't have one, did you know?"

Bass could guess the rest by then. Still, he sensed her need to spill it all to him. He wasn't angry anymore, and for reasons he couldn't have explained, he wanted to know about her. "And then?" he prompted.

"The pissants don't care one way or another. I suppose I'm a necessary evil. They don't have to pay me, so why should they care? Even mechanic's work, I do on time and materials.

"Anyway, the first man I was with had been out for a month, and I stayed with him for three days, until he was normal again. Then *pssst!* Nothing. He paid me. No 'present,' just cold cash. I opened an account with Ziggy, started saving again. I'm probably the richest human on the planet by now. But there's not much to spend it on, not on Phastillan.

"For a while, it looked like the pissants were encouraging humans to settle here—they really need tech-types—but the head Reis was afraid that they'd tromp too many worm-beds or something, so they only allowed limited contracts—and me.

"So here I am, fat Betsy and her forty-five men, on the only planet in the universe where a whore doesn't have to fake it. Now that you know all about me, can you still like me?" Her belligerent tone made the question a challenge.

"I like you more than ever. I think I understand now—why things happened the way they did, I mean. But it doesn't have to be like that all the time, does it? Come here." Bass pulled her over to him. They kissed: he, avidly; she, wistfully, almost sadly, at least at first.

Their passion mounted: normal, human passion, it was—two people making love on a mossy riverbank, two naked, sunlight-dappled bodies joined for a brief time. Several times, Bass almost came, barely managing to stop himself. He was on top of her, and his arms were getting numb, so he rolled over, pulling her up on top of him as she'd been the other times. Again, caressing her back, her heavy, bouncing breasts and rounded belly just above him, he fought to keep from coming. Looking down into his eyes, she saw his struggle.

"Don't fight it, Bass. Let it happen." Her words released him and he burst forth inside her, then slumped quickly back onto the moss. His arms still trembled with fatigue. For several minutes he remained quiescent inside her. She ran her hands over his chest, smiling. But there was sadness behind her curved lips.

"See?" she said minutes later, lying beside him. "The magic's gone. You're normal again." Salt and acid tainted her words. When next she spoke, she turned aside as if speaking to a third, imaginary person. It was an impromptu stage show with an audience of one.

"Hey, fella, you're next! How long've you been out? A week? No good—go soak up some more of that pissant magic, then come see l'il Bet, okay?" Bass cringed inwardly at the bitterness and self-pity underlying her monologue. Unheeding, she continued: "You want it anyway? Double the money? Triple? What do I need your goddamned money for anyway! Get out of here." Tears like almost-vanished dew glistened on her cheeks. Bass pulled her to him and held her tightly while she wept.

Those tears had been pent inside for a long time. He sensed

that. He grasped her anguish and despair, and knew them to be much like his own. Only . . . he had a goal, however far away: the Orb. Home. He caressed her soft, nude body, gently brushing away bits of dry moss and old, crushed leaves.

When her weeping was done, he still held her against him, and when he again felt the dull ache of his member rising, he entered her gently. They lay side by side, spoon fashion, hardly moving at all. It wasn't sex, not even sensual, then—only close, as close as two humans could ever be.

Cast aside by the cold, starry universe beyond Phastillan, they lingered, entwined, until the sun's warmth had moved beyond their patch of moss, until the air grew chill.

It seemed like hours had passed. They finally got up to dress, and walked back in silence. There was a shortcut, and Betsy left Bass in front of the bar. A truck, or perhaps a 'dozer, had stalled somewhere up north—a clogged fuel line, most likely—and she'd promised to get it fixed today.

"Bye, Bass. See you again sometime?" Her eyes only briefly met his. She had not said too much for Bass, but he saw that she had made herself vulnerable in her own eyes. He wondered what it would be like the next time he saw her. "You Bet you will," he punned. She smiled wanly. He should only have said yes. She had heard his poor pun a thousand times.

James wasn't in the bar. Neither was Ziggy, but the bare floor had been mopped and was still damp. Bass went to the port office to return the 'phone he'd borrowed. Ziggy was at his desk, using the new terminal. He tapped several keys, clearing the screen of whatever he was doing.

"Afternoon, Bass. I wondered if you'd be by. Are you going to show me how to use this thing?" Ziggy patted the gray metal case.

"Sure, Zig. What do you want to know?"

Bass stayed with him for almost two hours. The computer's operating system was pretty standard from a user's point of view, but neither the two-language capability nor the changes Bass had made jibed with the English-language manual the manufacturer had supplied.

When Ziggy said it was time to open the bar, Bass begged off. Ziggy told him where to find the taxi and its driver. Not until he was several miles from the port did Bass realize he hadn't paid Betsy, or even asked Ziggy about it. His thoughts shied away from the thought of payment. Sex and suffering; they'd shared both. He couldn't think of her as a whore.

It was night when he got home, and he circumnavigated the sprawling building to get to his own outside portal, avoiding the interconnected rooms where he might have disturbed sleeping psatla. He fell into bed and slept soundly, waking up only once, to pull off his boots. In the morning his temples ached from jaw-clenching and his fingers only reluctantly opened up from fists. It was his first headache in six months, he realized with surprise.

CHAPTER
TWELVE

"I wish you had explained it to me," Bass told *Pralasek-thes* Swadeth. "You misused my trust." He spoke in English because there was no psatla word for "trust." Would Swadeth really comprehend, even in English?

Swadeth was a green-gold shadow in the diffuse light of the *asaph*. His body plates were tight against him—his appendages, too—a posture Bass had come to associate with tension and uncommunicative withdrawal. But Swadeth had not withdrawn.

"Do not 'trust,' Bass," he said. "Trust is believing your own wishes. You have gained *gadesh* by my silence. You are *pralasek* in all but name. Such brings its own rewards, and a kind of security, too.

"Think of this: On Phastillan, at this moment, are two million nine hundred and forty-nine thousand three hundred and sixty-seven sapient beings. Of them all, only *pralasek-ni* can challenge your *gadesh*. An ambitious *psaalek-thes*—there are over two thousand—must first become *pralasek-ni*. Of *pralasek-ni* there are three. Thus you need fear diminution of your *gadesh* from only three sources. Of greater *gadesh* are *pralasek-thes* and *sfalek*: in all, seven beings, of whom I am one. Do the mists of morning now clear from your path?"

"You're saying that you've put me—no, 'helped' me to put myself—in a position of great *gadesh*, of relative security, where I don't have to look over my shoulder. Why should I have to, anyway? I'm just a contractee. Do you expect me to be grateful?"

"You misunderstand. If you swing on a weak branch with your feet near the ground, you risk little, and thus fear not. Were the same branch high on the tree, then would you fear? What reward would you demand for such high swinging? That is *gadesh*."

"The more I hear, the less I understand." Bass was exasperated. Was he in danger? Was that what Swadeth was saying? "The concept of *gadesh* expands continually: status, service, risk, power. How can I ever understand something so loose?"

"You must understand it. *Gadesh* is all of those things, and much more."

"And if I don't? If I muddle my way through the next eighteen months, then collect my pay and leave? What of all my *gadesh* then? Can I spend it on Faraway or Kablent? Anywhere else, all the *gadesh* in the universe won't buy me a beer."

"On Phastillan, you need only demand your beer. *Gadesh* is not exchange. Here, drinking your beer does not diminish it."

"Swadeth, I am trying—and thanks for your concern for me. But next time you want to do me a favor, will you tell me first?"

"I am not 'concerned' for you, *Thsaan* Bass. There are no 'favors.' There is only *gadesh*."

"Yeah, only *gadesh*." Bass bade the *pralasek-thes* a sullen farewell, but foreboding followed him out of the room and through the passageways and interlinked chambers. Always *gadesh*. Damn.

What was the psatla telling him? He knew Swadeth didn't speak except on matters of significance—small talk was foreign to him. *I am not concerned for you,* he had said. Did that mean that he, Bass, had no cause for concern? Did it mean that he was no threat to Swadeth, perhaps? Or did it mean that Swadeth didn't give a damn one way or the other? Or none of those? Or all?

How had he gained *gadesh* anyway? Hard work? Or was it successful work? Had he made a contribution to *psalaat*, the path, or was it just because he was, in a sense, Swadeth's protégé?

I resolve, Bass told himself, to keep my nose to the grindstone, to get all the *psaalekt* trained. to get the data bases inputted and the analysis and projection programs on line, and to get off this crazy planet. As a major footnote to his resolution, he added: And to get thoroughly fucked once a week until I leave.

* * *

His next batch of students included one Pralasek-ni Kstala. One of the three I've got to watch out for, Bass cautioned himself. He stands to gain by my failure. He's crawling up my leg so he can slit my throat. Somehow that didn't seem right.

Innately, irrationally, Bass wanted to trust Kstala. Perhaps it was his atypical appearance. Most psatla were quite uniform in size, while Kstala was as small as a ten-year-old human child. Too, he seemed slimmer than others of his race, and he moved more quickly, but with no loss of that characteristic psatla grace and smoothness.

And Kstala was green. Very green. He was the color of duckweed on quiet, sunlit water, and quite without mottling. No shadows of olive or tanbark marred his pure, verdant shade. Rarely, when the light was just right, Bass thought he could see in him a tiny hint of gold. Most *tsfeneke* were brown, verging into olive. Those *pralasekt* Bass had seen visiting Swadeth ranged between copper and brass, with liberal spottings of verdigris where their plates overlapped. A *sfalek*, Bass was told, was a pure, metallic gold, and shone as if polished. Kstala was small and oddly colored, said Gisseth, Bass's aide, because his *ksta* were not all male. Through a rare mixup in hormonal signals, several female *ksta* had been incorporated in him at his joining.

"Kstala," Gisseth added, "will be *pralasek* soon, though he is young. His sort move quickly in all things. They must, for they do not live very long."

Perhaps that's why I sense a oneness with him, Bass thought. Humans, too, carry both sexes within them. And like Kstala, my life will always be too short for what I might accomplish. It was an odd thought. Bass hadn't considered his life lately, nor anything beyond his immediate work. What happened to my visions? I was once so convinced that Phastillan was a pivotal world. I cared what was happening out there. Will it all come back, now?

For the first time in seeming aeons, Bass wondered how chaos had progressed. How many colonies had been abandoned already? How many worlds had just died, quietly, when no more ships came? How many were clinging to life, perhaps turning to raiding others for vital sustenance or fuel metals? But his was a flat, insipid curiosity. He could generate little emotion about the fate of whole worlds, and even his images of death and disintegration were as colorless as pencil sketches, and as lacking in detail. It was much easier to relax, to yield to his apathy about outside events and to concentrate on those things that made him feel good: his problems and successes with the computer work and with his students.

Contrary to Swadeth's warnings, Kstala proved a model student who learned exactly what Bass chose to teach him. Others had been curious about the system, how it worked, what precautions had been taken to prevent extraction of secured data and guard against false inputs—all the questions a curious, and potentially dishonest, human might have asked. But not Kstala. He was aloof from it all.

Training the latest batch took two weeks. On the intermediate Friday afternoon Bass declared a holiday. He would not be available for questions. He used his master terminal to ask Anson, the portmaster, to send transportation for him. The same wagon and driver took him to the port. It was hot and humid, and he dozed on the way, awakening only when the vehicle stopped in front of the tavern. He stood outside for several minutes to slough off the aftereffects of his nap, then went in and found a seat at the bar.

Ziggy Anson was behind the counter. "Where's Betsy?" Bass asked him.

Ziggy answered without meeting his eyes. "Not this weekend, Bass. I suppose she's out at one of the remote camps—or up in the shuttle with James. She likes it, you know." He sniggered. "Weightlessness, I mean. Sorayan's here, though. She's expecting you."

Anger flared. Bass tossed off his drink and clutched his glass tightly. Damn them all! Ziggy, Swadeth, even the whore. Do they all have the right to meddle, to arrange everything without even asking me? Sorayan's entrance put a temporary stop to his inward rage. She knew immediately who he was. Not so unusual, he reflected as she approached him. I'm one face among only fifty-odd others. I wonder if she's talked with Betsy? Maybe Bet is too embarrassed by confiding in me to be here. I'll have to ask about her.

When Sorayan took his hand, when the breath of her greeting passed over his face, he became intensely aware of his reason for being there, and hers. His knees were trembling and he felt building pressure in his loins before he even got a good look at her. Only one week, and I'm in rut already. He was still angry over the way people were manipulating him, and angrier still over his own body's betrayal. He wanted her. She nodded toward the side door, and then went through it. He caught it before it had closed halfway.

Sex with Sorayan was different than with Betsy. Or was it only his own lowered level of need? After the first time, after pain and ecstasy, there was time for easier play, for the assumption of a half-dozen coital positions, for kissing and caressing, getting to know each other's bodies. Bodies. And that's all, Bass swore silently. This time, it's just business, and I'm going to make sure it stays that way.

Sorayan was, he decided, younger than Betsy, more nearly his own age—definitely not over twenty-two. Where Betsy had been soft, emotional, volatile, Sorayan was intense and single-minded. Too, she was athletic, agile, and precise. Where Betsy's passion had beaten upon him, subjugated him, Sorayan played him like a concert instrument in the hands of a skilled—but uninspired—soloist.

He entered her four times that afternoon and night, each time of longer duration and lessening intensity. The fourth time, when he had been in her for what seemed hours, she drove her wetted finger into his anus and massaged him there, bringing him to rapid, fluttering release. Her own orgasm was weak: three stiffened thrusts of her hips accompanied by uninspired grunts and a breathy sigh. It could have been feigned entirely. After that, Bass kissed her good-bye lightly, politely, and slipped out the door, back to the bar.

"Here, Bass. Sign this, will you?"

Bass took the palm-sized sheet of paper from the barkeep's hand and scanned it briefly. "What is it?" he asked.

"Credit transfer from you to Sorayan. I keep the books for the girls, deduct it from your payoff."

"A half gram of gold? She's not cheap, is she?"

"You got your money's worth, didn't you?" Ziggy was annoyed.

Does he get a percentage? Bass wondered. "Sorry," he said aloud, "I'm not complaining. I'm sorry I missed Betsy, though. By the way, what about last week? I didn't sign one of those."

"Are you kidding?" Ziggy's laugh was high and old-womanish, and Bass hated it immediately. "You were pretty hot stuff, I'd say." He chortled. "Bet said it was on the house. She doesn't need the money, anyway."

Bass was embarrassed. He wasn't used to such casual talk and, whatever Betsy had said or hadn't said to the bartender, one word would have been too much. "Will she be back next week? I don't want to miss her."

"Look, Bass—this is just a helpful, impartial word from your friendly bartender, okay? Stick with Sora for a while. Let Bet have a chance to pull herself together.'' His words were jovial, but his eyes glittered fiercely, with an intensity that brooked no questioning, only assent. ''Saturday's your night, see? Not Friday. Just so things run smooth.'' Bass only nodded. Finishing his drink, he excused himself and left the bar. His ''taxi'' was nowhere to be found. It was a long walk home, and he arrived only just before dawn, his thoughts and emotions still in disarray.

Weeks went by in stiff symmetry: graduate a group of students, screw with Sorayan, start another group, screw with Sorayan, graduate a group, screw Sorayan again . . . Bass was unaware of exactly when he had stopped ''screwing with'' and started ''screwing.''

It wasn't Sorayan's fault. She was just as athletic as ever. Physically, she gave him all she could; emotionally, she could give him little, and he could accept even less. He approached her with all the passion his seesawing chemistry demanded, but with no more love or caring than he might give a bottle of foul-tasting pills. Once back on the shelf, he never thought of his ''medicine'' until it was time for the next dose.

Betsy, though—she was a different matter entirely. Even on Sunday mornings when he slept in until noon, he dreamed of her. When he was with Sorayan he tried—unsuccessfully—to pretend that he was with her.

Why? he asked himself over and over. Am I obsessed with her? I only had her once, when I was all jacked out of shape. It was miserable—well, mostly so. Besides, she's domineering, probably half again my age, her libido is as twisted as a corkscrew, and she's fat to boot. Fat! I lied to her. She's more than plump, she's a cow. Why, then, did he dream of those round thighs enveloping him, those udders bouncing rhythmically in front of his panting face, and those clear sky-blue eyes looking down at him?

Not able to see her, obviously rejected by her—for whatever reasons—he tried to forget her. When he failed abysmally at that, he tried to remember her as having been fatter than he knew her to be, to remember her stretch marks instead of her eyes, to think of her life's story as a ludicrous comedy instead of the poor tragedy it was. But in all those attempts, he failed. He still looked for her every Saturday night.

What did he really know about Betsy? At first, not even her last name. And was she Betsy, or Elizabeth, or some odd backplanet variation? He didn't want to ask Zig or Sorayan.

Instead, he joined a card game at a bar table, and only when the conversation had—inevitably—drifted to "Zig's girls" did he make any discreet inquiries.

Elizabeth something Scot. One *t* in Scot. "Something" stood for Marie or Mary. Not Maria. One of the cardplayers had a sister, Maria, and he would have remembered. Was Scot her parents' name or her ex-husband's? How old was she? Who cared? Old enough, and not too damned old, eh? "Whatta you care, Bass?" one cardplayer asked. "You ain't fuckin' her anyway. Just deal the cards."

One weekend he changed his routine, purportedly for work-related reasons, but actually in the hope that he might catch Betsy on duty and have a chance to talk with her. He walked into the bar on Friday night.

Ziggy slammed a drink down in front of him and wordlessly retreated to the other end of the bar. Bass sipped in silence, staring into his glass. Several minutes must have passed, unnoticed. When Bass looked up, the bartender was slipping back in through the door by the sofa.

Had Ziggy gone to speak with her? Was Betsy there, beyond that door and concrete-block wall? Bass imagined himself pushing Ziggy aside, kicking the door open, and storming down the hall to find her. But when he tried to think of what he would say to her, his imagination failed him.

He stayed at the bar. No women came in during the hour that he sat nursing his warm ale. He imagined that he heard a shrill scream, muffled by walls and overridden by cheery, taped music. A passionate scream. Sorayan seldom made much noise during their couplings.

He didn't come back the following night. The next week, he was weak-kneed and trembling when Sorayan took his hand and led him to her room. Her first orgasm was as intense as his own, and her low moans sounded real.

Bass tried skipping alternate weekends, but when he did, he suffered recurring nightmares of estrous felines howling like crying babies, of fluff-tailed behinds raised at him, and of his own deadly, barbed organ like a stiff, thorny branch. One night he awakened with the sound of his own screams echoing in his ears, to see a score of anxious psatla peering down at him, crowding his room. He had raked his belly with his fingernails and had drawn blood. After that, he rigorously adhered to his "medication" schedule, and with only two exceptions, much later on, he never missed a trip to the "clinic."

CHAPTER
THIRTEEN

VoiceLog 3.24(r), Shipsoft Corporation, Tacoma, S3
Timecode 772.625.1929

> Mark and I have discussed suicide, and murder. Strange as it sounds, it's an ethical matter. When Dad lost *RR*'s ownership to de Witte's megacorp sharks, the only concessions he kept were the captain's and first officer's seats, and title to revert to Mark and me when Phelps/deNooye/Kok fully depreciated her. Mark and I thought we could hold up under the strain of conning a company ship, so we stayed on when the P/deN/K heir apparent became owner-aboard.

> Dad was a smuggler, but he'd never have run guns or slaves. Mark and I have delivered six transReef children into slavery on the most decadent planet of all, Earth. Now we're carrying devastation back home with us. Who'll buy these missiles? Pirates. How many more innocent lives will we be accountable for?

> Too bad de Witte changed the key to the arms locker. We could pirate *RR*. But Dad's mods to the standard con will allow us to take control from the owners' suite substation. With luck, once we're deep in the Reef, we can steer *RR* into an antimatter overload before de Witte or the Reef pilot can stop us. With luck we'll have ten minutes before they see what's happening, find us, and burn through the door.

> Alta Van Voort, acting captain, *Reef Runner IV*.

The training phase was completed. Bass reported only eleven suspiciously curious students to Swadeth. None of them were of the *pralasek-thes*'s own branch, which seemed to please him.

Seven, of whom one was Kstala, were from the *asaph* of Lesthef. Three were from Phthaas's house, and one from Sfel's. Bass made much of the disparity of numbers between the three, but Swadeth suggested that such simple inferences were less than useless, and he used the opportunity to again discourse on *gadesh*, to press upon Bass the necessity for understanding—with no more positive results than before.

The growth rate of primary and subsidiary data bases increased as each group of trained operators left Swadeth's *asaph*, every student with a terminal under his arm or carried tenderly before him. Across the face of Phastillan, students became teachers, and input rates soon approached the maximum that the system could handle. Terminal-use indicators on the master display board were lit round the clock.

The supply of blank, backup memory blocks dwindled and was augmented by new purchases from off-planet. Such clear, crystalline blocks were standard articles of trade. Even the rare tramp merchants that still put in at Phastillan carried them, and luckily so, for regular shipping had entirely ceased. Piracy and increases in unexplained ship losses along the periphery of transReef were blamed.

Bass decided that enough raw data were on hand already, in multiple categories. He ran preliminary projections of all the accumulating files, and a cybernetic picture of Phastillan emerged. Sketchy, little better than the cartoon for a final painting, it was already useful. Organized data was being sent to the terminals as well as from them. Weather and climate studies accounted for most data retrieval.

Bass set aside a file to record user times for utility programs in memory, and terminal identifiers. From that file, he could obtain rough ideas of who was doing what. Curious about the uses his students made of the ponderous analytic machine he'd set running, Bass followed their progress via the user file as another person might follow a serialized holodrama. The time thus spent was his daily treat, his addiction. Only on-line did he forget his circumstances and stop counting the credits and days until he could, at last, go home.

On-line . . . a goal he hadn't really reached yet. Phastillan's data base was still too small, and though he had accumulated most of the components he would need to build another hat, he hadn't done it. I'm too busy right now, he told himself. Later, when the system is running itself. But there was more to it. He feared that, with a hat, he'd do nothing else at all, so the components sat in a nook in his room, unassembled. Its operating system and inter-facing programs remained in mainframe memory in a locked file.

The terminal units' design made component failure a remote possibility. They weren't designed specifically for Phastillan, but they might as well have been. Internally, the gray, metal boxes held only four circuit boards sealed within a block of clear, im-pervious resin against the moist Phastillan air.

Other components were of similar construction, and could be plugged in place within a vacuum chamber and sealed against heat, cold, and corrosion. Even keyboards were so connected, activated by keys sensitive to heat, pressure, and electric poten-tial. Sophisticated programs decided which key had been pressed under any combination of phenomena. Terminals interfaced with the mainframe by triply redundant satellite links.

Only human—or psatla—elements were without designed pro-tection. Carelessly placed units were still bumped, jostled, knocked over, and hammered upon by frustrated users, for though psatla thought processes worked in an entirely different manner than did human ones, both differed absolutely from machine thought.

Furthermore, neither the psatla grammar nor lexicon correlated well with the English of the machines' designers—ambiguities, even outright contradictions, occurred with predictable regularity, causing confusion and software-related breakdowns. For all the differences in species, both expressed their frustration with the machines in the same manner. They hit them. Bass repaired them. He cleared them of endless loops, too—the neophyte program-mer's nightmare. He gave impromptu one-on-one lessons. He was very busy.

Between occasional intensive periods of reprogramming and debugging at Asaph Swadethan, Saturday nights with Sorayan, and flights over the whole of Phastillan, Bass's contract time shrank rapidly. Almost a whole year had dropped away, and he had hardly noted its passing. It was a downhill run: four more months. Then, the pissants could find a new fixer. There was nothing left to be done that any fast-fingered hack couldn't man-age. Bass stored his modification specs, plain-language versions of his utility and patch programs, and his monitoring routines in a private file that he would turn over to the new man.

He saw James almost daily now. The pilot made shuttle flights when ships arrived in the system, but those occasions had become more and more sporadic as the months went by. Between times,

James became an aircar pilot. He flew data blocks to the cave storage site for Swadeth, and ferried Bass back and forth between terminal locations for trouble shooting. Though perfectly capable of flying himself, Bass was glad for James's company and for the opportunity to sleep on board the aircar, thus freeing his waking hours for his work.

His understanding of the odd symbiosis between psatla and their human hangers-on expanded as he traveled and observed. Sometimes it even made him laugh. Near the port, on a patch of that "dead" ground that psatla abhorred, an instrument repair-man named Holke kept a weed-infested truck garden. Near the garden was a rusty windmill that pumped water for a small tank. Psatla with business at the port—which they kept to a minimum—refreshed themselves there, showering in a sun-warmed cascade.

The windmill's pump arm had slipped loose. It rose and fell with the wind, unconnected to the pump shaft, and the tank level was low. Green algae plugged its drain screen. A psatla stood foolishly beneath, expecting water that would not flow.

Holke, hoeing his garden, stopped to wipe his brow and saw the psatla. He ambled over, and asked brokenly what was amiss. "Loud butterfly drinks not," Bass heard the psatla say. "Small pool flows not. I am dry." Bass realized the problem. There was no organic connection between the well, the windmill, and the tank, and the psatla couldn't visualize how the reciprocating power arm related to the "butterfly" above, the now-silent pump piston below, and the water tank between. Holke took one look and slid the errant arm over the crank pin without even braking the blades. He primed the cylinder with a cup of green-scummed water, and water gushed cold and fresh from the earth.

Holke climbed to the plank catwalk over the open tank. The psatla followed clumsily, *ksta* reaching for grips on the human-made ladder, slithering. Together, they observed. Curious, Bass joined them. Holke reached in the tank and removed the filter screen from the shower pipe. The psatla watched, amazed, as he scraped green-brown, stringy algae away and replaced the screen. Descending, the gardener pulled the valve cord, and water sprayed freely, splashing his boots.

Bobbing and whistling to itself, the psatla departed. Later, when Holke was gone, Bass saw it return with a curled leaf in its *ksta*-fingers. It climbed to the tank and emptied the leaf, then left again. Bass peered in the tank. Water-skimmer insects darted over the surface, eating algae. The next time he checked the tank, it was clear and fresh. The insects hung dormant on its sides, await-ing fresh growth to feed on.

Weeks later, Holke's garden was clean and weedless. "You must be putting a lot of sweat into it," Bass commented.

"Not anymore," he replied. "That psatla, Athklet, who put the bugs in the tank, fixed my corn for me."

"Fixed what?"

"You know how they are—he took some seed, and looked like he ate it. He spit it up, then planted it between my rows. It grew fast. The weeds hate the new stuff. They don't grow anywhere near it."

Bass pondered his words. "And the pump arm. Does he fix it himself, now?"

"Damnedest thing, Bass. He still hasn't figured that out. Some ways, psatla are really dumb. But not about gardens."

With all his overflights and visits across the planet, Bass was beginning to find Phastillan comprehensible as a world as well as a system of information. From a psatla point of view, it was far from an ideal place for a colony, measured by the sheer immensity of their effort to change it. Whole continents had been selectively denuded and replanted according to a complex plan; crags and arêtes were toppled and leveled using purchased atomics, opening dry, idle land to the warm, wet winds psatla forests required. Great riprap causeways diverted offshore currents in new direc-tions. Even so, the band of psatla habitation was narrow. The tropics were warm enough for them, but the pale, blind females couldn't survive in the leached, lateritic soils, nor could they bur-row in the harsh, thin ground of the central continents. Only where rainfall, temperature, and vegetation produced deep, mycelia-rich humus could they flourish. Most such areas were coastal. Bass, on his flights, was exposed to areas most psatla never saw.

On one such flight, when James had prudently turned far inland to avoid a towering thunderstorm, Bass got a hint that not all efforts on Phastillan were directed to the furtherance of *psalaat-thes*, the "big picture" that Phaniik Reis painted, that his assis-tants, like Swadeth, detailed with brushes and tools like bombs, bulldozers, and Bass's computer.

That first trace seemed innocuous at first. "Hey, James! Look down there—in the creek bed between those rocks—yeah, that one. What is it?"

"Settling pond, eet looks like. For zhe runoff." James obvi-ously saw nothing strange about the artifact.

"But we're two hundred miles inland. Why would anyone care about runoff out here?"

"Eet could be for zhe minerals, zhe trace elements. Such ponds look like zhat—zhe water ees dirty, an' zhey have a side channel for diversion."

"That's right—bacterial separation. I'd forgotten psatla use life-forms to mine for them. Log its location, will you? I'll find out later what it's for."

"What does eet matter? Psatla have many such t'eengs."

"I don't know. Idle curiosity, I suppose. Log it anyway." Bass watched silently as James keyed in their location coordinates with his left hand. He missed an eight, striking the nine instead. Bass didn't say anything about it, because James was obviously too busy flying the craft to correct it then, but he memorized the proper coordinate to adjust later.

"Did you notice that there was no shelter there?" he asked James. "I thought they always had humidomes for this climate." The impoundment was far astern, but Bass's curiosity was undiminished. "And there weren't any vehicle tracks or landing apron, either. How do they check up on it?"

"Ees prob'ly someseeng zhey're done wizh." James shrugged, bored with the subject, so Bass gave up. But he did not forget. The installation was anomalous, and that bothered him. It was data that didn't fit. He thought about it, speculated about its function, all the way home.

CHAPTER

FOURTEEN

Asaph Swadethan was in turmoil. Sharp scents of agitated psatla flooded the computer facility: burnt rye bread and gun oil, crushed marigolds, dill weed and hot wax. The whole computer system had crashed. Terminals didn't function, and the mainframe was going mad. Where it was usually lit from within with coursing light-flow, it was dark. Deep in its crystalline-brick structure, tiny aimless sparks lit and died without order or sequence. Only one data path was lit, glowing brightly and illuminating the room with harsh reddish light, a jagged path that wove through systems and memory like arcing lightning. Bass had never seen anything like it. He was frightened.

The mainframe's diagnostics were intact. Bass connected a terminal directly to a secondary interface, and began asking questions. From psatla accounts and diagnostic routines, he got a rough idea of the disaster's nature.

Three terminals assigned to *Pralasek* Phthaas—mining and resource acquisition—and one used by Thesakan—logistics—were locked into a complex loop. A single signal was flashing from terminal to terminal by way of the relay satellites. They didn't respond to keyboard input. Communication capabilities were tied up, too. Only the satellites' limited ability to accept data at that rapid rate saved the system from a total lockup fixable only by dumping everything and reinputting from backups. It would have taken weeks to fly in the stored backups and reinstall them.

It was quite a puzzle. Bass would have expected a loop to break when one erring terminal was shut down, but he couldn't even get a command through. Spurious code was shunted from satellite to terminal to satellite, passing through the mainframe like a short circuit.

The only solution was to fly to each terminal site and pull their plugs. James offered to handle it. Bass showed him what had to be done, and the pilot departed immediately, eager to be away from the confusion that reigned at Asaph Swadethan.

Bass dozed intermittently at the mainframe's console while James was in flight. He awakened each time a psatla informed him that James was on site at a terminal. As each terminal was shut down—which wiped its programs, data, and operating systems—Bass got another surprise: the loop continued, its path unbroken. When the last terminal had been dumped, the pernicious code was still beaming from satellite to satellite in a tight round-robin, impervious to input from the ground.

The satellites, too, would have to be reset. It couldn't be done from the ground. James couldn't do it alone. Bass would have to go up there with him. He estimated that he and James would have to spend twelve days in orbit, at least forty hours of it in space-suits, to straighten the mess out.

It couldn't be done right then, of course. He was exhausted, and so was the pilot. James had to program their flight, and Bass had to collect diagnostic programs and replacement components. Those were probably gathering dust in one of the port warehouses. Morning would be the soonest he could look for them.

Late the next day, the shuttle roared and shuddered up through Phastillan's atmosphere. Bass breathed crisp, mechanically dried air for the first time in almost two years. He savored the silence and weightlessness of free-fall when the engines finally ceased their battering thrust.

Their initial orbit was elliptical, requiring correction to bring them in line with the first satellite. Bass could have calculated more efficient maneuvers in his head than James managed with his on-board computer, but he kept silent and let the pilot do his job.

Finally, the personnel hatch cycled open. Pumps whined, and the outer hatch swung free. He gazed upon the stars of transReef. The satellite was fifty meters away. It was big—a twenty-by-twenty meter hexagonal prism of gold-plated aluminum. Azure oceans lay below, swept with cloud masses and summer cyclonic storms. Green coastlines edged inland everywhere except near the poles, and elsewhere the planet was golden tan, brown, and rust-red: lichen colors. He marveled at how large Phastillan was, and how small the psatla domain. The magnitude of psatla determination to change it impressed and frightened him at once.

He refocused on the task at hand. The access hatches were bolted shut, and it took forty minutes to get one free. He was sweating when he slipped into the dark opening. A bulkhead blocked the cylinder near its middle. Bass could go only halfway. The modification hadn't been shown in the planetside files; Bass suspected it was one of a pair of bulkheads with a meter or two of add-on components packed between them. Considering the hodgepodge systems groundside, he wasn't surprised.

The access panels he needed to reach were the ones with the bright scratches around the screw heads. Their components must have been installed when the computer was delivered, not when the satellite was orbited years earlier. He slid the offending modules out and ferried them to the shuttle. His air tasted foul. Once he was inside, James helped him out of his suit. "Zhe t'eengs you brought back—can you feex 'em?"

"I won't know until I get into it. Probably. But I'll have to go back later for some other stuff." As soon as the covers were off, he saw the problem: current overloads had caused laser drivers to flash, slagging areas of memory and control. He replaced them and fed memory from backups, then tested them until he was sure they would work as intended. He fetched the other modules. He ate. He slept. He repaired. He slept again. Altogether, he spent five days on the first satellite. It didn't bode well for the rest of them.

It took a whole day to get to the second one. Silently, he cursed James's piloting. He could have gotten there in half the time, by the seat of his pants. Again, four trips out and four back. It only took four days, that time. The third bird was a rerun, but at speed. Bass had it up and running in three days. Between trips over and back, he ate and slept, dreaming of Phastillan, of almost-cool rain, of a shower and clean clothes.

He'd missed two Saturday nights with Sorayan. His system was purged of the psatla hormones that had controlled him for almost two years. He'd breathed canned air and eaten food put up light-years from Phastillan. Still, so deep was his conditioning, he sweated and his hands twitched as he walked from the shuttle to the drab, clustered buildings of the port. It was Saturday evening. Sorayan.

He showered while he waited for her, then took his "medi-cine" expeditiously, as he'd prepared to do. Without Phastillan's chemicals flooding his bloodstream, it was a new experience.

Sorayan's methodicity seemed more mechanical than ever, her agility reduced to frantic effort to hurry his ejaculation and be rid of him. Her mouth, her tongue, her busy hands all teased and tickled him, but penetration required a tube of cold, insipid cream she dug from a drawer, dusty and lint-specked from long neglect. On Phastillan, it was rarely needed.

Even then, pumping energetically, he failed to relieve himself, and only after Sorayan toweled him clean and knelt to take him orally did he finally come. Only then, as she spat his seed on the floor, did he fully understand his own deep disgust with her—no, with his *need* of her. For the first time, he was free of the help-lessness and degradation she symbolized, and their relationship was truly that of a whore and her customer. He didn't say good night when he left. Neither did she.

CHAPTER
FIFTEEN

> >LOGFUNCTN:420.103.5251 COMMENT:

I am depressed and dismayed. Common sense tells me that trade is the only way transReef worlds can meet their varying needs. Yet wherever I turn, men seek simpler, stupid solutions.

On Bellissima, corporate bosses tried to smuggle thugs aboard in dried-fruit crates. They wanted *Matteo*, to outfit her for a small-time ''viking'' expedition against the ConWorld Mines operation on Stibnite, to extort tin and iron. Why? Why, when CWM would surely trade tin for foodstuffs?

Sometimes I suspect we humans were never meant to leave our world of origin. With all our high-flown ideals, our saints and lawmakers, we have learned nothing. We revert to grasping monkeys with our hands stuck in coconut-shell traps, too foolish to let go of the morsels within in order to free our greedy fingers.

Matteo has fuel enough for a two-legged journey. I have plotted our course for New Detroit. With their mixed economy of agriculture and manufacturing, they must be coping well, even though the spacelanes are abandoned by all except vikings, pirates, and refugees.

Jacomo Pirel, captain, *Matteo d'Ajoba*

The computer system needed protection from future crashes. Bass needed to know exactly what had happened. It was no fluke; someone, somewhere, had been experimenting. The looping terminals had all been involved. They had been in use for several hours before the crash, but not one had called for any of the mainframe's subroutines, so they'd been running programs based in on-board memory. But why would anyone risk losing everything in volatile memory, without making backups? There was only one possible reason: secrecy.

Unfortunately, the information in the terminals was lost. Only the errant signal gave a clue to its function. Someone—four someones—had set up a multiterminal operation independent of the central facility. Someone with secret motives. But who? The terminal's nominal users were *pralasekt-thes* Phthaas and Thesakan.

Bass told Swadeth his suspicions, but the psatla merely asked Bass to apprise him of future developments. Bass doubted he'd find out more unless the culprits repeated their experiment. Against that contingency, he modified his terminal-use log to cause terminals to dump their memories to Bass's private file after ten minutes of questionable activity. The user would never know his secrets were being stolen from beneath his very *ksta*tips.

To put the culprits at ease, Bass issued a mild warning against experimentation, a statement any human hack would interpret as license to do as he pleased. His net was cast; now he would wait.

Bass felt a cloud over him, a presentiment of disaster to come. He attributed it to fatigue, burnout from the stress of the past fortnight. As the week progressed, he told himself it was a result of his distasteful coupling with Sorayan and the awareness that Saturday night was almost upon him again. The only way he would feel entirely right would be to get off Phastillan once and for all.

His forebodings of dire events proved out. He was with Sorayan in her windowless room, so he missed seeing the night sky light up like bright, false day. He heard the hubbub in the bar, but wasn't moved to investigate. When he emerged from the bedroom, there was nothing to see but a line of red and gold sparks stretching from one horizon to the other. Questioning others who lingered outside, they heard that a spaceship had entered the system with its drives on full thrust. It had looped so close to the sun that it burnt off its sensors, and had tried to land blind and mute, vaporizing in the upper atmosphere, as the dying sparks testified.

For the fifty-odd humans on Phastillan it was an event, on a world that seemed to shun events of all sorts. For psatla, it was a catastrophe. Jet stream currents were askew, and heat balances awry; atmospheric pressure waves even now sloshed like bathwater. The energy released by several thousand tons of vaporizing spaceship was incalculable.

Bass found James at the shuttle and dragged him, protesting, to the aircar. "The mess isn't up there," he said to the pilot, glancing briefly at the dark sky. "Get me to Swadeth's now or I'll fly myself."

Hot gun solvent, crushed, sour flowers—marigolds? geraniums?—pickles, and burnt bread: a familiar reek. The chaos at the com center was nothing new, either; after the disaster so recently past, Bass felt right at home.

But this crash hadn't stopped the computer. It radiated like a stack of white-hot ingots shot through with red and yellow and flame-orange fire, sometimes sinuous, sometimes lightning-jagged. The ancient beast's really working now, he thought affectionately. It's operating at its orgasmic peak. Slipping into the swivel seat at the main console, he got to work immediately.

In the aftermath of the ship's descent, the computer facility paid for itself several times over. Accurate analyses of changes and countermeasures were needed, and supplied. Bass slept in snatches. Psatla slipped in with food and drink for him and for Gisseth, Klent, and Tsestra, his aides.

All gained *gadesh* in those busy days when the fate of the Reis *psalaat* was in their grasps. Crisis was averted: the plan would continue as before.

Gadesh created changes in the structure of Reis. Gisseth, Klent, and Tsestra were elevated. A *tsfeneke*, Phathut, became *psaalek-ni* under Gisseth; Klent added -*thes* to his name-title; Tsestra became *pralasek* of a new branch, whose specialty was information, an area hitherto considered diffuse.

For his foresight in his instigation of the computerization program, Swadeth was elevated to *sfalek-ni*. The service he had rendered the Reis was unquestionable. Had he wished, he might have challenged Phaniik Reis himself; as it occurred, the displaced *sfalek-ni*—Ghisk—considered himself inadequate to challenge the *sfalek* Khestaat and opted instead to take passage on an outgoing ship. Carrying a case packed tightly with small bars of biorefined gold and another, self-cooled and aerated, containing psatla females, perhaps he would survive long enough to find another modifiable world. But the universe was large, widespread, and such worlds were few. Bass felt sorry for him.

Bass's own position was uncomfortable. As Swadeth explained, his *gadesh* was impressive. "You have gained *gadeh-fes*, the product of great effort; it is advantage without impetus," Swadeth told him, fanning his thin chest plates wide. The gesture often preceded the sharing of intimate thoughts. "You have done, but not moved; saved, but not created. There are other ways . . ."

"*Gadeh-psaa,*" Bass interrupted impatiently. "Creation and innovation that widens the path of all Reis. And that path is . . . what? Ecological domination of Phastillan, pure and simple?"

"Harmony. The balance when changes damp out like wave and counterwave, when opposing ripples create not larger waves, but ever-tinier patterns on the surface of things, and ultimately none at all."

"It sounds like chaos—thermodynamic chaos."

"The heat death? No, Bass. *Psalaat* is no friend of entropy. Look at the surface of my pond. Are the wavelets entropic, gas bubbling from stagnant mud, or are they products of intense order, the busy patterns of many small lives all functioning to similar ends? From your vantage, can you tell?"

"My comment was ill thought out, I think. Sorry, Swadeth—but sometimes things poles apart come to seem similar. The regularities of no organization and the sameness of total control—both leave me cold."

"I suspect you overrate psatla efficiency, Bass." Swadeth moved his plated head in uncanny mimicry of human negation.

That was some trick, for with his body chitin still open, Swadeth looked like a brass-plated pinecone. His contact with Bass had expanded his repertoire of human gestures, but sometimes Bass wondered if he had other sources as well.

Now, for example: Swadeth aped the mannerisms of an aging professor—the premeditated motion of hands, the pensive gaze. Swadeth had neither eyebrows nor a pipe, but Bass could almost see one there, an aging briar whose yellow stem was pointer and baton, punctuating Swadeth's ever-more-correct speech. "Harmony isn't uniformity," he said. "Much diversity is allowed within the shape and direction of *psalaat.*" Swadeth's chitin rattled dryly. "There is *gadeh-ksta* also," he said, "which is influence beyond life, the passage of a plan or ideal through the soil to new generations. The paths to immortality are many and varied."

"*Gadeh-ksta,*" Bass repeated. "Humans think that's a myth. Can you actually transmit memories from one generation to another?"

"What is your human 'soul,' Bass? Isn't it a memory of life before now?"

"My father would make greater claims for it," Bass admitted, "but I'm not sure souls exist at all. But if you psatla could prove memory from past lives . . . if there was a biological explanation for it . . ."

"There are 'empty' sections of DNA in psatla cells," Swadeth informed him, "equivalent to billions of bytes of computer memory. Not truly empty, they are coded for no physical function. Humans have them, too. There is a certain gene your scientists call a homeobox, that we call *psalaat*."

"*Psalaat*? But that's—"

"A path. A way-sign gene that points to others, and tells them when to act."

"Like the pointer in a data stack," Bass volunteered.

"Like that. It calls event-memory and protein-memory alike. Protein-memory carried by the genes, the exons, and event-memory by the introns, between. Humans believe those introns are trash, relics and fragments of ancient genes. If you could read them, what might they say?"

"You probably know more about human genetics than we humans do. It's been pretty much a dead field since the transReef expansion. I guess we've been moving too fast to look within."

"Psatla knowledge of your race is vested in few of us—most dislike your 'taste,' and there has been no need to know you well. But *ksta* . . ." Swadeth "shrugged," creating the motion of shoulders where none were. "Documentation has never been needed. Must you examine your eyes in a mirror to know that you can see?"

Bass expected no clearer answer, but he had other questions. "Is *ksta* 'remembered' in proportion to *gadesh*? Is *gadeh-ksta* something deliberately sought for immortality's sake?"

"*Gadesh* is *gadesh*. One might wish to discorporate at the time of his greatest influence, but do you sense the conflict in that choice?"

"Humans say that only money makes money," Bass reflected, "As *gadesh* seems to create *gadesh*. Discorporation would end that."

"Exactly," Swadeth said. "Choosing the path through the soil is self-seeking. *Gadesh* is lost. The Reis gain nothing. Or is that so? Can one truly weigh the value of *ksta* to the future against utility in the present?"

Again, Bass realized he would get no better answer. If he stayed on Phastillan, saturated himself in psatla ways, raising such questions and absorbing uncritically their oblique answers, everything would fall into place someday. But that would never be. Even two years on Phastillan was too long—he wanted to go home.

But until then, what? As Bass saw it, his only option was as *thsaan* to the *sfalek-ni* Swadeth. His duties would be minimal. He would advise Tsestra and bide his time for the three months that remained on his contract.

He put off further consideration for Sunday morning. After his impending appointment with Sorayan, he could make a human decision—unaltered by hormones, uncolored by *psalaat*.

Fragments of rosy evening sky fluttered through gaps in the foliage above. Swadeth recognized the cries and chatter of several species of nocturnal creatures. One was a *zethal*, a tree dweller. As Athklet had "tasted" the seed in Holke's garden, so Swadeth had savored *zethalt*; his white, snakelike *ksta* had once sipped *zethal* blood.

Within *ksta*, enzymes dissolved cell membranes and cytoplasm, cilia invaded nuclei, and tiny, clever molecules aligned with *zethal* DNA. Enzymes like DNA polymerase split *zethal* heredity lengthwise and transcribed it into chains of nucleosides that Swadeth could "taste" and know. How could he read the *zethal*'s genes? How could Holke read the pump's structure and function, or Bass Cannon the drive patterns of the *Sally B. Halpern*? How did a bird know to fly north in springtime? The reading and manipulation of heredity was as intrinsic to psatla as flying north was to birds, or fiddling and tinkering to monkeys and men. Swadeth had created a retrovirus out of his own nucleotides and infected *zethalt* with it. The virus spread, and soon all *zethalt* carried it. Dormant, it became, itself, a gene, utilizing each cell's reproduction to increase itself. It was a simple gene, for a simple allergy.

Now, during the rainy season, *zethalt*, no longer immune, were driven from their arboreal habitats by biting, bark-dwelling arthropods. Carrying fertile nuts from the deep forest, they buried them nearer the timber's edge. Driven farther, they dug up some nuts, forgetting others. At the forest's edge, they collected borderland seeds and planted them among savannah mosses, and eventually, before their long trek back to the forest, their defecations spread savannah seeds onto the wide mosslands beyond.

Zethalt were vital to the growth of the forest habitats psatla desired. And it was Swadeth's minor modification to their antiallergen production that made them so, as they were driven outward by insects previously harmless.

Swadeth's elegant use of *zethalt* had created *gadesh*, raising him above other *tsfeneke* who had emerged from humus with him.

Now he listened complacently to *zethal* chatter, and pondered a quite dissimilar experimental animal.

Swadeth pondered. The holographic organization of human thought was as far divorced from the "discussions" held among psatla *ksta* as it was from the stiff "trees" of Bass Cannon's data bases, which proceeded precisely from greater to lesser abstraction, from lesser to greater detail. For Swadeth, *ksta* spoke with *ksta*.

Without *ksta* the humans were only *psalaat-thes-tak*, environment, like *zethalt*. The answer existed in the coiled molecules of their heredity, in vast chains of untranslated codes. If ancestral memory, *ksta*, could be found in them, they would be psatla, of a kind, to be cherished and changed. Yes. Changed just as the forces of *psalaat-thes* changed psatla. There would be pain in the changing. They would not take kindly to it.

CHAPTER
SIXTEEN

VoiceLog 3.24(r), Shipsoft Corporation, Tacoma, S3
Timecode 772.626.9542

> Dingenes is smart, like a wharf rat. He suspected we might try something. Mark and I are confined to quarters under con autolock. It looks like the missiles will be delivered after all. I'm ashamed to admit it, but I'm glad I'm still alive. We tried.

> Alta Van Voort, acting captain, *Reef Runner IV*.

Saturday night came and went. Returning Sunday morning to the *asaph*, Bass surveyed his room with an eye to packing. There was surprisingly little he wished to take: toilet articles; a delicate wood carving given him by a diffident *tsfeneke*, mud-brown and silent, who watered his moss and relaid his bedding; a few binders of notes and printouts. He'd pack later, he decided, when he had chosen a path.

He reached into a niche beside his bed and withdrew a miniature memory block, dull now, with no power applied to it. Even powered up, it would look like a small machine controller—something to run a dishwasher or hand 'phone. One side, no larger than an ID card, was a five-gigabyte molecular connector, the kind that snapped onto any standard interface plate. Opposite that dangled taped-together, hair-fine wires—each a thousand-strand cable of linear monomolecular crystals. When finished, they would branch again and again into a hairnetlike mesh. A hat. The hard part's done, Bass thought as he snapped his shirt pocket shut. I wouldn't want to leave this behind.

At breakfast in the *asaph*'s refectory a clear picture of the spaceship near-disaster was emerging. Psatla workers, agog and aflutter, detailed it while he ate. Words sighed from *ksta* mouths while other *ksta* remained in the soup, taking up nutrients. Such was psatla agitation that some forgot not to speak through the submerged *ksta*, causing fine skeins of bubbles to rise from the pots.

Bass heard more details at the com center. The ship had been a trader, its in-system plunge an attempt to dodge an attacker lurking in orbit around Phastillan's sun. Perhaps the pirate was gone, now. If not, there was no way to tell, and no way to warn subsequent arrivals in-system.

Bass wanted to build a warning beacon to caution incoming ships of the threat, but James quickly convinced him that even among the tons of spares and oddments at the port there were no proper parts to put one together. Besides, the pilot pointed out, such a beacon would warn off ships that were their lifeline to humanity.

The whole affair served to remind Bass of his longtime isolation from human events transReef. He resolved no longer to ignore the news: he'd be going out there soon.

Standard procedure called for all ships to dump their logs to local port computers. Most first officers subscribed to intersystem news services, and as a courtesy their latest updates were usually dumped, too. On Phastillan, such dumps were made to the antique computer James used on the shuttle for flight calculations. A rack of old-style data cubes in the hangar office held five years' accumulation of them, and James said there were boxes of older cubes somewhere.

Bass found the newer cubes right away. On the shuttle, he

pushed one into the computer's receptacle, scrolled through a synopsis, then zeroed in on Missing Ships. On the *Sally B. Halpern* he had noted a rise in "missing" reports. Now he realized the situation had worsened: one ship out of two hundred never made port.

He couldn't get more detailed analyses without mainframe capabilities, and the old computer wasn't linked into the net, so he walked to Ziggy's office, chatted a bit, then borrowed a spare 'phone. In the hangar, he removed its cover and ran leads to the computer's output pins.

He made contact with the mainframe and, once the two computers established "handshaking," transferred the data to a mainframe file. The recent cubes took an hour to transfer: push in a cube, wait for a bleep, pull it out and insert another.

He sorted his information. One-half percent of departing ships never arrived. *Sally* had made twenty planetfalls while Bass had served on her. Assuming that his route home would be the reverse of it, his chances of turning up missing at any one port were one in two hundred, but with twenty landings, there was a ten percent chance he would never make it home. He refigured, using only the data from worlds Sally had visited: of scheduled ships, 0.73 percent never arrived. Of tramps, the figure was 0.28 percent. That made grim sense: scheduled runs were easy prey. Not surprisingly, scheduled runs were becoming rare. Next-port-only flight plans were now deposited in time vaults, to be opened after departure, when interception was difficult. Old-fashioned time-stretcher ships ceased to file plans entirely. How could he choose a ship?

There was information unrelated to his travel problems, too, patterns to be discerned. Bass could almost feel the vast changes occurring along the Reef and beyond. He fondled the incomplete hat through his shirt fabric, regretting that he hadn't finished it.

Bass awoke early. It was Monday. Heating a pot of coffee infusion in the shuttle's minuscule galley, he brought it to the hangar office. He wanted further insight into the ominous patterns of political, social, and economic change that underlay the disappearances, changes that were almost palpable to him via the data streams even without a hat, changes that were taking place across the whole of human-occupied space.

But first, he intended to examine the anomalous check-dam and pond he'd seen earlier. Had it really been two weeks ago? The time had flown. He searched construction records: nothing.

He searched through flood control, water management, mineral refining, and a dozen other file blocks: nothing. He was convinced something wasn't right. There should have been traces.

Bass spent two hours checking possibilities, time which resulted only in greater familiarity with Phastillan's inventory of offworld purchases. Where could he go from here? Was it worth pursuing? If there were irregularities, he doubted that he could be called to account for them. Anyway, he'd be leaving soon, going home to the Orb.

What if he was delayed? If he chickened out? One chance in ten that he wouldn't make it. Bass wasn't a gambler by nature, and he didn't like the odds. He might have a long wait on Phastillan. If he was going to be stuck here awhile, he decided, he would have to follow up on the pond mystery. He wanted no loose ends. Tomorrow morning he'd have James fly him to the mysterious dam. He would get a close look, take a few samples, and report it to Swadeth.

Bass decided to stick with Swadeth until he left Phastillan. The computer system was functioning; he'd fulfilled the terms of his contract. Bass Cannon, human, did not aspire to be a *pralasek*. His *gadesh*, so important to psatla, only confused and threatened him. He had known what he was going to do from the moment he had surveyed his room in the *asaph* and considered packing. He'd inform Swadeth tomorrow.

At the tavern he ate well: a sandwich of tinned offworld "steak," *sechan* root from Holke's plot glazed with sweet-sour sauce, followed by a tart, sliced apple from Ziggy's own imported hoard and pie made with a local berry, seedy and sweet.

"Have you seen James?" he asked the bartender. "I want him to fly me to Ksafaa sector tomorrow."

"He was in earlier. If I see him, I'll tell him to pick you up at the *asaph* in the morning."

"Ask him to meet me here instead."

"You planning on staying? Why?" Ziggy's bright gaze was ophidian—a snake about to strike.

"Not right here. I'm going to sleep out on the shuttle," Bass replied without thinking, immediately regretting it. "The *asaph* is in confusion," he lied. "Because of the transition, you know. I'm sacking out at the hangar.

"Look," Bass continued quickly, observing Ziggy's dark scrutiny. "I know you don't want me around here except Saturday nights. I don't quite understand, but I'm not asking for answers, and I won't hang around where I'm not welcome. As soon as I finish this drink, I'm going out to the shuttle, all right?''

Ziggy seemed to relent. "Yeah, okay. Look, Bass. It's not your fault. That time with Betsy—it upset her, see? She just doesn't want to see you—at all. She's a nice girl, a real jewel, like my own kid except when . . .''

He shrugged sheepishly. Bass knew what he had been about to say. Ziggy was a man, with ordinary needs. Bass was troubled by the thought of him and Betsy together. "Anyway," Ziggy concluded, "just play by the rules, huh?''

"I will—for now," Bass said aloud. But someday, he vowed, before I leave this crazy planet, I'm going to see her again, even just to say good-bye. Bass went back to the hangar, no less troubled or confounded than before.

He remembered one more thing he hadn't checked: his computer spy file. As the screen lit, fatigue fled. The area he'd set aside was full! He had allotted enough memory for forty terminal-sized dumps. I must have made some stupid programming error, he thought. I can't have collected that much real data. He checked to see what kind of garbage he'd collected.

But it wasn't garbage. Forty terminals weren't involved, only four—the same four that had caused the great crash. The data that had accumulated was coded, but through his mainframe patch it took Bass a mere half hour to break it—the clever psatla he was dealing with still had a lot to learn about computers, he thought with grim amusement. The first dump, from one of *Pralasek* Phthaas's terminals, was an operating system and a communication protocol, little more than a data relay. Where had he seen something like it? He studied it for an hour before it hit him: he had never seen the program itself, but it was exactly the sort of thing he had visualized as causing the crash. He examined the next three dumps: two from Phthaas's other terminals and one from Thesakan's. Bioseparation data. Heavy-metal and radioactive-ore processing. Uranium- and thorium-refining figures. The last terminal held a software CPU mimic and logic cribbed from the terminals' hardwired routines. How in hell did they pull that out of ROM? Bass wondered. It's all machine code. No terminal user should even know that stuff's there. It contained mainframe utilities, too—statistics and math.

Now Bass knew what he was seeing: a discrete computer within the system. Though crude, inefficient, comparable to a twenty-first-century relic, it had one unique—and to Bass, sinister—characteristic: the whole construct was totally isolated, intended to be inaccessible and secret as well. That it was neither was no fault of its designers; Bass hadn't shown his students everything. He silently thanked Swadeth for his warnings.

He wanted to call Swadeth and wash his own hands of it. He left a message at the *asaph*. Swadeth was off-continent—he could locate him in the morning. He knew now what he would find at the impoundment site, but he still intended to go, to tie up the last loose end. Back at the shuttle, he heated a flask of cocoa to relax. He plugged one of James's music cubes into the pilot's portable sound system and, in spite of his still-racing mind, was soon asleep.

CHAPTER
SEVENTEEN

"Allo! Bass? You in zhere?" Bass rubbed sleep from his eyes and mumbled an answer. James flicked the light control to its brightest setting. "Ziggy tol' me you were sleepeng 'ere. 'E says you want to go to Ksafaa region, bot I t'ink he mistake what you say."

"It's no mistake. I want you to fly me out to that impoundment we saw from the air."

"W'at one ees zhat? Oh! Zhe abandoned dam." James looked out through the shuttle's forward viewports, bored and disinterested. Bass knew that James was no outdoorsman, that he disliked even the feel of open country beneath him, and that he got little satisfaction from flying atmospheric craft at all, but the one time Bass had suggested that James could stay behind and let him go alone on a short flight, the pilot had become quite agitated, fearing he'd be fired if he didn't seem busy. "Why not wait onteel later? E'ees not goeeng anywhere. Zere ees a sheep coming een soon, I t'ink. I mus' be zhere to meet eet. I weel tak' you up zhere nex' week, okay?"

"Sorry, James. I know you hate these little side trips, but this can't wait. There's something funny going on. I'm going to find out exactly what.''

James's interest roused at the mention of intrigue. Bass elaborated. ''Someone had been building dams, secret ones, to process radioactive ores.''

''Bot zhere are many such t'ings, Bass. E'ees no beeg secret. Zhe radioactives, zhey are sold to buy zhe computers, zhe aircars. You waste your time, to go zhere.''

''Not this time. This is no ordinary processing pond. Someone's doctored the records to hide it. Only I kept a few secrets myself—about the computer system. I've barely started to dig.''

''I see. Eef you fin' out who zhey are, you gain more *gadesh* yourself, eh?''

''Shit! I'm not a psatla, James! I don't give a damn about *gadesh*. I just want to keep things honest until I leave this moldy planet.''

''Zhen maybe we better keep our mout's shut, eh? I don' want to gat een any trouble. E'ees you who can go home, not me!''

''James, if you're really scared to get involved, then just forget I told you anything at all. I'll fly myself out there, all right?''

Before James could reply, Bass held up a hand and continued. ''The computer system crashed because they messed with it. Do you know what might have happened to us—to Phastillan and our jobs—if the computers had crashed at the same time that trader did? It's too dangerous to let them continue—and the crash didn't stop them, I know that. At the least, the *sfalekt* may decide that since it's my responsibility to secure the system, I haven't fulfilled my contract, see? I've got to stop them.''

James agreed that Bass was in a most uncomfortable position, and reluctantly agreed to fly the aircar for him. Privately, Bass believed James's fear for his job was exaggerated, but then, James had nowhere else to go. He had the right to be cautious.

''Eef you know who zhey are, why not jus' tell Swadeth an let heem take care uff zhem?''

''Swadeth's gone. I tried to reach him. Anyway, I don't have proof until I get some samples from the pond.''

''Okay, zhen. I weel gat zhe aircar. You can wait 'ere.''

''I want to get something to eat for along the way. Is Ziggy in the bar?''

''E'ees possible. I weel gat somet'ing for you while you gat raddy.''

''Thanks. I'll be along in a few minutes.''

Survey gear was stored in a building nearby. Like all buildings on Phastillan, it was unlocked. What could be done with stolen goods? Bass found a radiation counter, canvas sample bags, and a padded case of glass vials. He tossed a set of tongs and a reflec-suit into a sack.

Thus loaded down, he crossed morning-damp moss to the air-car. James hadn't returned, so he tossed his gear inside and went to find him. The bar was unoccupied. He made himself a sand-wich, stuck a bottle of ale in his pocket, then met James and Ziggy outside.

"I grabbed something to eat, and a bottle of ale. Hope you don't mind."

"No problem," Ziggy replied without meeting Bass's gaze. "I'll put it on your tab."

Bass ate his sandwich an hour after they were in the air. The ale was already warm, and he grimaced as he washed down his bread crusts. There was nothing for him to do then, and the terrain near the port was boringly familiar. He put his feet up on the instrument cluster and relaxed, then dozed. It was a three-hour flight. James only awakened him when they were over the dam.

"Zhere eet ees." He set the craft down a fair distance from the pond. "I don' want to gat too close to zhe radiation," he said. "You gat zhe samples you want, an' we poot zhem far een zhe back, okay?"

"Sure, James." Bass grinned. "You don't have to worry, though. This case is lead-lined." He climbed out of the craft and made straight for the embankment.

As he mounted the slope to the pond, he heard the aircar's drivepods vibrate shrilly under maximum power. He spun around to see the aircar already at altitude and diminishing with increas-ing distance. He stared after the 'car until it was a minuscule dot wavering in heat waves off the sere continental plain that stretched to the horizon. It finally winked out entirely.

What's the fool thinking of? I'll have his ass for this, Bass raged. The son of a bitch is so scared of getting involved, huh? So afraid of losing his piddling second-rate job on this miserable, torn-up planet? I'll have him on the first ship out of here, without a stinking damned credit in his pocket!

Hot childish rage dwindled to glowing embers as his pain-conditioning took effect, and he remembered why he was there. He switched the meter on and was rewarded with a low whistle. There was plenty of radiation.

He dug the reflec-suit from his sack and shook it out, put it on. As he topped the embankment the whistle rose shrilly and green numerals flashed upward. He dipped red-gray sludge from the pond bottom. The radiation counter whistled up through another octave, and he retreated quickly with his full vial. That stuff was hot!

Back below the dam face, he wiped the vial with dead moss and placed it carefully in its container. He walked downstream until the meter registered normal background radiation, then removed his suit and left it on the ground. Farther on, he sat on a patch of dry moss and stared at the empty sky.

As tension from working in the sleeting radiation ebbed from his muscles, Bass's curiosity returned: curiosity that, as he answered his own questions one by one, turned to fear.

Why had James left so precipitately? Because he was afraid. Of what? He could have James fired for leaving him like that. James fled because he was already involved, a part of the plot.

Evidence? It was all there. He stood and surveyed the expanse of unbroken moss and lichens. He looked downslope, then up to the hills behind the dam.

The separation pond is functioning, he noted to himself, but there are no tracks, no signs of equipment. It's as if whoever runs the operation just drops down out of the sky, pumps a million credits' worth of salts and oxides of vanadium, uranium, and lead, and then leaves.

Walking around the uphill side of the dam, not too near the deadly slush, he confirmed his suspicion. Three depressions marked the turf—marks left by the tripodal landing gear of a small but very heavy spaceship.

Who on Phastillan was best placed to deal with outside traders in secret? A shuttle pilot could meet with them in orbit, converse with directional radio, even share a cup of coffee with them without anyone below being the wiser.

A forgotten memory surfaced: tiny bright-metal scratches on the screw heads of satellite inspection panels. Bass knew, now, who'd put them there, who had modified components and, indirectly, caused the computer to crash. Who, besides the *sfalekt*, with their own aircars and pilots, could fly anywhere on Phastillan? Only James.

Bass shook his head. Why had he assumed it was strictly a psatla affair? Of course, there had to be psatla involved. Phthaas and Thesakan, for starters: minerals and transport. *Gadesh* was at stake, *gadesh* that required illicit offworld exchange. Why had he failed to realize that any such plot would require at least one human intermediary like James Aubasson?

What now? His own possibilities were limited. He could wait until he was missed, and hope that a search was made. A slim chance, that. No one knew where he might be. Phastillan was big—he would starve first. Ziggy? He wouldn't miss Bass before Saturday. Neither would Sorayan.

He decided his best bet was to walk to the coast. How far was it? Two hundred miles? He took inventory, sorting through his pockets, finding nothing of any use. He could carry water in the sample vials, though. Upstream of the dam, he found water issuing from a cleft in the rock. It tested radiation-free, so he filled his containers.

He walked in the almost-dry creek bed, only leaving its level gravel for an occasional sight-check of his direction. The stream maintained its coastward course. At least it's all downhill, he jested bitterly.

Why had James left him alive? Was his sudden departure part of some plan, or just panic? He must have known Bass could reach the coast in a week, living off the land.

At dusk, after walking steadily for several hours, he gathered grassy vegetation and piled a makeshift cushion. Its scent reminded him of his bed in the *asaph*. There were few other odors in the crisp air; Phastillan's perfumes seemed confined to the psatla habitats. He settled down with a wistful sigh.

CHAPTER
EIGHTEEN

KEYBOARD FILECODE XXXXX [SIMULATED]
> >[CLOSE] [ERASE] [TRANSLATE]
>TRANSLATE
> >[TARGET LANGUAGE?]
>ENGLISH VAR 3 LITERAL
ENT 1.4> > >On Jerusalem we took a hundred slaves. I am not religious. The old ways were dead in my grandfather's time,

but would not *his* father have praised God for what my sword has wrought? My grandfather's grandfather drove the Israeli usurpers into the sea, fulfilling the Promise, but it was a sea of space, not salt water. We were deceived by the Jews yet another time, and we met them again on this transReef shore.

Now vengeance is complete. All are dead, save these slaves. Even here in my cabin, I hear the Hebrew bitches weep for their kin, all gone at last, all slain.[DATECODE MISSING]

"Human fffemale." Thesakan's English was barely understandable. Her scent is *fsa-psalaat*, unpredictable. What scent is that? What human madness? What does it say?

"*Pralasek* Thesakan." She bowed slightly, stiffly from the waist—a human gesture, with subtle inferences of status in its depth, its precision. Psatla also bowed, after a fashion: a recognition among equals.

A whiff of winy vapor escaped. He inclined his head carapace slightly in her direction. His articulated surfaces were stiff, grating as he moved.

"You are in great danger," she continued without preliminaries. "I've come to warn you, to ask you to change your course."

Sweat ran in cold runnels beneath Betsy's shirt. Thesakan had to be approached carefully, led to believe what she wanted. She feared him. He was black. As black as coal, the only psatla she'd seen like that. No *ksta* white broke through that unreadable blackness. A devil, she thought irrationally, a terrible, hunched-down, black bug.

Have psatla ever killed humans? There had been disappearances. Internal synthesis of quick-acting poisons? Secreted enzymes that break a human down into soup . . . Can he smell my fear? Will the perfume cover it?

The odor of cheap musk, a product of some transReef chemical plant, stung her eyes. She'd never used the awful stuff except when she was with Zig—he'd given it to her. Her nose wrinkled, both from the perfume and the thought of him in her bed. He stank of sour beer and sweat. His own nose was definitely dead.

"Exssplain. Undersssstanding isss not. What?" Thesakan rumbled. "Exssplain danger, warning."

"Your plan—*psalaat*—is about to be exposed. Phaniik Reis, Swadeth—all will know it. Do you want that?"

"*Psalaat*-mine. Knowledge? More wordsss. Sssay."

"I know everything James and Ziggy have been doing." A lie. She knew so little, but would Thesakan dare call her bluff? "And it's all recorded elsewhere. If I'm not kept safe and free, my knowledge will go to the *sfalek*." There! She'd said it.

Thesakan sought an appropriate human word. "Blackmail," he said after a lengthy silence. Her perfume annoyed him greatly. He was blinded as if by bright, harsh light. "How? Sssourcesss? Why?"

"Men boast—in bed and out. They make promises, too. I know about your heavy-metal refining, your offworld accounts. I also know you've been conned. It's all useless to you. It has been for a long time."

She shook her head, blond hair swaying, her expression almost sad. "Poor Thesakan. For all your clever plotting, two amateurs took you in. It may have been a good plan once, but transReef's in chaos. Your offworld accounts, if they really exist, are frozen. The credit's no good. Only the metals themselves are worth anything, and they're gone, aren't they?"

"Fsa-kneth tes theh," the psatla hissed cryptically. "Exssplain."

Betsy did. Without transportation and communication, assets everywhere transReef were frozen. Accounts could only be collected personally. Could Thesakan risk going offworld? Could he make his wants known if he did? Could he trust James and Ziggy not to disappear with his credit? No, no, and no. It was over, she stated flatly. Thesakan could only hope to keep news of his peculations quiet. She reminded him that she was prepared to spread that very news unless . . .

"Conditionsss?" the psatla sibilated. "What?"

"Bass Cannon must live. That's all."

"No undersssstanding 'all.' "

"No other conditions. James and Ziggy are going to kill him. I want them stopped."

Thesakan had not risen to *pralasek* by being slow to decide. His *gadeh-psaa* was ended. "Agreed," he half moaned, half whistled. "Thsaan Bass will not be killed. You will keep sssilent. Agreement?"

"Yes. Agreement. But you must tell them now, not wait."

"Find. Bring here." Black pinpoint pupils in flat black orbs looked away from her upon some alien vision. Betsy withdrew quickly, to look for Zig and James.

She had overheard their panicky conversation accidentally, working under a heavy lift vehicle when James brought the aircar down nearby. Ziggy was there to meet him. He'd been waiting quite a while, dozing, most likely. His clothes were stained with old sweat and new. The first word out of James's mouth was Bass's name, else Betsy might have made her presence known, and the two men would have delayed their talk. She had kept silent and listened.

It was perverse of her to maintain such an interest in Bass. He obviously hated her, scorned her weakness and depravity; else he wouldn't avoid her so pointedly. He must know she was never in port on Saturday—the one time she'd stayed there with him had been an exception.

Sorayan said he hated both of them, probably some twist of his religious background. Sora complained that Saturday nights with him were as romantic and sensual as trips to the outhouse, but Ziggy made her serve him. Everyone gets the same chances, he said. "That way you're free of the bastard, Bet," Ziggy would say. "If he won't even call you to say he's sorry, I'm not going to push him on you. Sora can handle it."

But somewhere deep inside, Betsy didn't want to be free of Bass Cannon. There had been something good between them, there by the river, and it hadn't been just sex. He had cared for her in spite of her rough treatment of him, and when he had said he would see her again, he had meant it. But he hadn't, ever. Was it pride? Was he ashamed to be emotionally involved with a whore? Was her situation just too complicated for him? Could it be because she was doomed to stay on Phastillan, and he was leaving, going home? There were no answers. None. But still, she hoped . . . until she heard Ziggy tell James to get a gun, that they'd have to kill him.

Her first reaction, when she realized that she was going to try to save him, was selfish: If he's grateful to me, then perhaps . . . Once begun, her resolve gained a momentum of its own. She'd have done the same for anyone, she told herself, but in the shadows within, she knew that was a lie. She wasn't that brave.

From Ziggy's bragging, from his frequent importunements to leave Phastillan with him—when the time was right, he said—she knew about his secret wealth—gold, not just credit. She'd finally given up trying to convince him it wouldn't work, her going with him. Let him believe what he wants, she decided. When he's ready, he'll go with or without me, and once off Phastillan, he'll be happier without—even if he never knows why.

Ziggy, James, and Thesakan; hoarded gold and frozen credits. She had heard snatches, and guessed the details. Her confrontation with Thesakan had been bluff and innuendo, but it had worked. Bass would live. But what now? What about her? Could she go about her work, just waiting, hoping he would learn who arranged his reprieve? She supposed so. She'd done all she could.

James and Ziggy were at the aircar. She told them Thesakan wanted them right away, pretending she knew nothing else. When they'd gone, she breathed a sigh of relief and hustled to finish her repair job so she could soon be far from the port. Her next one was halfway across the continent, on the western coast. But she was still under the lift vehicle when they returned, with Thesakan, and lifted recklessly off into the darkness.

CHAPTER

NINETEEN

VoiceLog 3.24(r), Shipsoft Corporation, Tacoma, S3
Timecode 772.811.4216

> We're down to a third of *RR*'s takeoff fuel weight. Legally, we can't lift off from AgroProd #2 without topping up. I don't suppose legalities mean much here, on a viking-run planet. De Witte denies it, of course, and it looks like an ordinary ag-world, dying for lack of trace elements. Damn our owner. Why couldn't we have loaded the holds with zinc and copper and all those treasures so common Earthward, instead of Jovia 22Cs?
> I ramble. The efficient way port control handed us down from orbit was my first clue. That didn't fit the farmtown facade. When Mark saw all the fresh burns on the landing field, he was sure a fleet had gathered here—and it wasn't Navy.
> He recalibrated the most accessible missiles, ten of them. De Witte plans to take one portside to show his customers. Unless his rat-mind detects something in our eyes, he'll take one of ours. Its warhead will blow a microsecond after power-up. Even a diagnostic check will trigger it. If we can't lift out of here after it blows, we'll trigger the rest of them right in the hold.

> Alta Van Voort, acting captain, *Reef Runner IV*.

Bass pulled damp socks from his reddened feet, wishing futilely that he had enough water to wash them. It wouldn't do to go lame on his third day of walking. The stream he followed was now a gully. It sank into the earth gradually, mile by mile, and he had hardly noticed when the stones under his feet became entirely dry.

Spreading the socks on a still-warm rock, he wiggled his half-numb, tingling toes in the faint breeze, then settled as comfortably as he could on a sparse, newly gathered bed of moss. I must be safe, he told himself. James would have come back by now if he were going to at all.

Darkness arrived immediately after the sun set, red-gold, without cloud or obscuring haze—a harsh sunset unlike the pink diffusion of light that reached the settled psatla lands, and equally unlike the glorious full-palette paintings that washed the western coastal skies.

Sleep was slow in coming. Bass studied the slowly turning stars, the almost-familiar constellations. He traced an imaginary course from where he lay, out along the swath of starless black that was the Reef, past bright stars and dim. That one! Small, bright-white and only slightly flickering in the dry air above him. He pretended the unnamed star was Mirasol, was home. It could really be, he told himself. But he doubted it. The bit of sky his eyes could encompass was immense, filled with stars in spite of the Reef's dominance, and the vista he saw would be repeated many times, in many such patterns, from other vantages on his planet of exile.

Lights! His night-adjusted eyes spotted the glow far to the north just as he was about to drift off to sleep. The landing site—the impoundment! James is back, looking for me! He's had time to think things over. Will he have a gun this time? Bass focused on the faint line of the aircar's ground beam, which varied in intensity as the vehicle moved about. It cut off abruptly.

What now? Had he given up? The red flash of running lights answered him. James was coming straight down the streambed, just as Bass had. He must have spent a day or so quartering the dam area for me, Bass realized. If he were an outdoorsman, he would have done what he's doing now a lot sooner.

Bass cursed his shortsightedness. Had he taken any course other than the easiest one, such a craft couldn't have found him in days, or at all. But here he was, in the streambed, the only place James had left to search! The red and green blinking lights were over him. The intense glare of the beam pinned him to the pebbly ground like an insect specimen.

"Bass! I have some people who wan' to talk wizh you! Don' ron, zhere ees nowhere to go." James's amplified voice, the whine of repulsors, fragmented the night. Bass stood, brushing dry crumbs of vegetation from his shirt and trousers. The craft sank to the ground only meters away. Blinding light was the single focus of his existence, the source from which, any second, the bullet or laser beam would come.

People who wanted to talk with him? Perhaps he had time, yet. Minutes? An hour? Who? Could he get on board, force a takeoff, a crash, anything to get away? How many were there?

Three shadow outlines blurred the beam, breaking it momentarily. He recognized James, then saw the glitter of a gun in his hand. A second shadow was Ziggy. Of course! No wonder James had insisted on handling the terminal restarts himself! One was Ziggy's, at the port.

The third shape was psatla. Was it just the glaring, contrasty light, or was the being darker than any psatla he'd ever seen? As they came close, he confirmed that the psatla was indeed a stranger. Thesakan. It had to be. What's his part in this? What will a psatla do with a million credits? What *gadesh* does he seek?

"We're not going to kill you, Bass. Not if you cooperate." That was Ziggy. "You screwed up with your meddling, but you've still got a friend who wants you alive." Ziggy was no longer the jovial tavernkeeper. In the concentrated white light, Bass noted the haggard droop of his plump features, the stained pouches under his eyes. Another bartender! No resemblance to Henry Myers, Bass thought, but if what he says is true—if I live through this—I'll do my drinking in my room from now on.

James, too, showed signs of strain: a tick at the corner of his mouth, eyes blinking more frequently than stirred-up dust and dry moss warranted, and knuckles white on the handgrip of a projectile gun.

Thesakan was unreadable, impassive, alien, a blot, highlights from the search beam shifting like tiny stars across glistening body plates that unfolded ever so slightly for hundreds of tiny *ksta* mouths to breathe, to smell his desperation. Then they closed tightly again, rasping.

"We're going to move you to a different place," Ziggy said. "You'll be out of the way for a few days. Don't do anything to make us hurt you."

"Why should I believe you?" Bass asked bitterly.

"Because you're still alive right now. Thesakan says you're only a temporary threat, until arrangements are made. Just do as you're told, huh?"

Bass nodded sullenly. At Ziggy's gesture he took the forward seat next to the pilot's. Ziggy climbed in behind, then Thesakan. A glimpse of James's empty hands told him the gun had been passed to Ziggy, an invisible pressure at the back of his head.

The 'car's generators whined up past audibility. James took them up into thick, silent darkness. In spite of his helplessness and anxiety—or perhaps because of them—Bass fell asleep until the aircar's motion changed. They were over rough terrain; the vehicle pitched and trembled in irregular currents, rose and fell erratically. Airflow through the ventilator was distinctly chilly. Mountains? James flew as if he was over familiar ground.

Dawn broke over low rocky hills. James lowered the aircar into the shadow of a steep-walled valley, a depression of pitted limestone and thin moss. He let the 'car drift laterally to the base of a worn cliff, directly in front of a patch of still-deep darkness: a cave.

"Your new home—for a while," Ziggy said unnecessarily. "You can get out. There's food and water—and equipment, but don't mess with that. You can't use it, and you'll only make me angry."

Bass looked intently at James, who avoided his gaze. Kicking open the door panel, Bass climbed down to the shelving rock. When the repulsor whine rose behind him, he walked straight into the cave, not looking back.

Inside were answers to several of his questions. The first thing he saw in the wan light was the in-system radio that James had claimed couldn't be made, but obviously had been. There was a half-parsec subspace set, also. That one wasn't a cobble job. Though scarred, it was a high-quality instrument.

The trader that crashed! It was theirs, for sneaking in to pick up the contents of the impoundment. That's how this one-tavern planet rated its own pirate vessel. Someone was careless. Perhaps the trader was followed in-system after selling a previous cargo; it must have been tempting prey. What will Ziggy and friends do now? Are there other ships involved, or are they finished?

He wondered who his "friend" was. Swadeth, most likely. But if so, why hadn't he been freed already? Was he being held hostage against James's and Ziggy's safe passage offworld? He'd know

sooner or later. Meanwhile, Ziggy had said there was food here
. . . he hadn't eaten since the trip out from the port.

Fortified with tinned soup heated on a tiny pellet-fueled stove,
Bass explored further. The cave had to be part of a larger system
underlying the valley and surrounding hills. The conspirators had
only made use of the dry area near the entrance. By lantern light
he examined the radios: neither was independently powered. A
coil of insulated wire, with jacks, was used to tap into an aircar's
generator.

There was little Bass could do. He was a thousand miles from
the nearest settled area, on the far side of Phastillan's most for-
bidding mountains. Walking out seemed pointless—as Ziggy had
said, if they'd been planning to kill him, they would have done
so. He would wait.

From then on, he ate whenever boredom overcame him and
slept fitfully on a pile of tarpaulins. He explored the near side of
his valley prison, but found little that interested him. It was a
bleak place, inhabited by small creatures that uttered raucous cries
when he approached, and by toothy, birdlike beasts that preyed
upon them. He tossed stones at the small creatures, which resem-
bled long-legged turtles. He broke one open, intending to roast
it, but the stench was so foul that he gagged and tossed it away.
After that, he threw stones at both kinds of beast, but only to pass
the time, not to kill.

Uncounted days passed before the aircar returned. James flew
it. The other occupants were psatla, and strangers. James had no
gun this time, but the psatla could easily hide weapons under their
chitin plates, among white, writhing snake muscles.

"Has my ransom been paid?" Bass's voice was husky with
disuse.

"Ransom? Who would pay money to free you?" James had
taken the question literally.

"Then why are you here?"

James didn't reply. Bass watched the three psatla disembark.
"What's going on?"

"Old gray-scales zhere ees Phaniik Reis," James replied sotto
voce. The psatla was more gold than gray, except around the
edges of his chitin. "Zhe ozzers are *Pralasek-thes* Phthaas an'
Pralasek-thes Sfel. Zhey go to see for zhemselves zhe evidence,
to confairm zhat you are truly one of zhe peerotes—pie-rats—who
almos' destroyed Phastillan."

The lie had been told, and believed. Bass's rising hopes fell.
He slumped in his seat and turned his head to hide tears of sick

rage and frustration. His face twisted like a grief-stricken child's. His hands shook. Whatever counterclaims he made would never prevail. "You filthy bastard! Why, James? Couldn't you think of a better way to clear yourselves? You didn't even try to buy my silence! And all I want is to get off this stinking planet!"

"E'ees *gadesh,* don' you see? You had too motch! Besides, you don' need money—you are Bass Cannon, zhe heir of a whole worl'. How could we buy you?" Scorn—and the bitterness of brooding on Bass's accident of birth—oozed from James's words. "We needed zhe money to get off Phastillan. Bot you? What do you need zhat we could pay you off?"

"You stupid, stupid fools!" Bass murmured, and James had to lean close to hear him. "All you needed to buy me, heart and soul, was a ticket home."

James shook his head. "Zhere ees steel zhe matter uff *gadesh,* no? Zhe *pralasekt,* even Swadeth, zhey all gain *gadesh* wizh your fall." Bass was dumbfounded. Swadeth? What would he gain from my misfortune? Has Swadeth betrayed me, too?

"What's going to happen now?" he asked plaintively.

"We go back to zhe port. After zhat—zhe *sfalek-thes,* 'e weel decide." The three psatla returned, having seen what they needed to see, having made their impenetrable decisions. Bass couldn't bring himself to address them, nor to continue speaking with James. The trip back to the port was made in unbroken silence.

CHAPTER
TWENTY

"Why, Swadeth?" Bass tried to keep from whining, but his voice echoed shrilly from the concrete walls of the storeroom, his cell. "Why didn't you stand up for me? You know I'm not guilty of anything."

"What is 'guilt,' Bass? What is 'betray'?" Swadeth paused, but he wasn't really awaiting an answer. "Human words," he continued. "But all is *gadesh*. I advised you to learn *gadesh*. Your learning was at fault—no one else is accountable."

"What did I do?"

"You served the *psalaat*-Reis well. You created *psalaat-ni*, a small path all your own."

"How did I do that? Create my own path, I mean. I only did what I was contracted to do."

"You were *psaalek*, a small, weak branch. But you worked to save all Phastillan, the action of a *sfalek*, even a *sfalek-thes*. Your strength was perhaps equal to that, but your understanding was insufficient for such *gadesh*."

"I contracted to do my best, that's all." Bass's hands trembled with inexpressible rage, and tears forced themselves from the corners of his eyes. "You still haven't answered my question. What *psalaat* did I create?"

"The liaison with offworld pirates was one such small path, at odds with the vision of Phaniik Reis."

"You can't believe I was involved in that. You got my message about the pond—even though it was too late. You knew I was going to investigate. Why would I do that if I was already involved? It makes no sense."

"What I believe is of no matter. You were involved. Consider. Those who consorted with the offworld buyers risked much. Had their chosen *psalaat-ni* ultimately strengthened Phaniik Reis's own *psalaat*, their gains in *gadesh* would have threatened others. Had their path proven the wider, with few impediments along it, and had none raised substantial objections to it, then it is no trifling possibility that a new branching would have occurred; two *psalaat-thes* would have existed. Was that the nature of your *psalaat*? To supplant Phaniik Reis himself?

"No, I need no answer from you. It is enough that Phaniik Reis might believe it so, for otherwise, why would you have gone so far beyond a contract that required only that you set up the system and demonstrate that it functioned? Your actions can be interpreted as *psalaat* or insanity, and the *sfalek-thes* believes you sane."

"That's it, then? You're throwing me to the wolves?"

"Wolves?"

"Predators. *Flades'lel teres klestu sut.*"

"You still say funny things, Bass. I serve *psalaat*, no more. I soothe and make even."

Bass sighed, a bitter rush of tired air, letting go his last hopes. Swadeth explained his upcoming fate: exile. Not the honored exile of a path follower such as the departed Ghisk. No such luck. He would be sent to a circumpolar station, which psatla only reluctantly visited. The harsh climate of high latitudes was inimical to their temperate-adapted bodies. *Tsfeneke* worked there in shifts, one month on and one off. *Psalekt* came and went, never staying long. Only exiles called the stations home.

Swadeth informed Bass that his contract was considered fulfilled from the moment his last student had graduated. No one had told Bass. There had been no reason for him to have been more than a transient, waiting for a ship out.

"Psatla do not bind time in little bundles for trading," Swadeth had once told him. Had Bass understood that earlier, it would have served him well. Now the situation was reversed, for his exile was also unbound by time, indefinite.

"What of the isolation syndrome? I'll go crazy again. Will I see other humans at all?"

"It is not for me to say. It is not likely. But that served you well when first you were *thsaan* in my house. Perhaps again you will make use of it." Yeah, Bass thought bitterly. And who will benefit most from my slavery? But still, he gave his ex-employer the benefit of certain doubts. He understood a bit more about psatla now: nuances of meaning that humans attached to sexuality weren't included in Swadeth's fund of human knowledge, Bass realized. To him, sexual congress was still a small death, the fragmentation of identity into a thousand subbeings, *ksta*. The jetting release of living seed was a diminution, a tragedy. No wonder Swadeth never mentioned the syndrome during my first months, Bass thought. He must believe he's saved me from a tragic human compulsion—that he helped me, during those driven, undistracted months, to be a "normal" psatla.

The thought of years in that same state depressed Bass as much as not being able to go home. He hadn't suffered from the lack of sexuality those first months, but neither had he been truly aware of the loss. Now he would know. He would be aware that he was a half man, a pseudopsatla unable to confront members of his own species without subjecting himself to the humiliation of mindless rut.

Saturday night went by unnoticed. He stopped counting days. He asked for nothing, not even news of outside. Perhaps he went a bit mad. At any rate, when two strange psatla came for him, he followed them obediently. He climbed in the aircar silently, blinking in the wash of unaccustomed sunlight, and kept his eyes closed during the ten-hour journey north.

* * *

"You place great value on that human," a psatla said as the aircar whined overhead. "Will he be productive?" There was no sound, only breeze-wafted essences that carried meanings directly to the myriad brains of his fellow being. What was actually said was this: FEAR (odor) + SENSE OF LOSS (pheromone-stimulated emotion) > UNCERTAINTY (concurrent fight-and-flight pheromones) + HUMAN (generalized scent) > EGG-HATCHING (odor redolent of sulfurous mud, of warm moss) + HUMAN + *GADESH* (strong essence of a dominance pheromone, like charisma).

The reply: HUMAN + *GADESH*/CHARISMA + WARM MUD/COOL MUD (a scent cycle, seasons passing, repeated several times) > STALKING BEAST (pheromone eliciting tension of hunting, waiting) + (name scent of first psatla) + FEAR > RAW POWER (*gadesh*, amplified, carrying sharp, spiky whiffs of ozone) + MACHINE OIL (scent) + SHUTTLECRAFT EXHAUST (a relatively new convention connoting anything off-world) + PSATLA (generalized odor) + HUMAN > PSATLA/HUMAN/PSATLA/HUMAN PSAT . . . (rapid odor-cycling, gradually diminishing in intensity and fading). It might have been represented in sound speech as, "Be prepared to witness power that will change psatla and humans beyond recognition, from Phastillan to the farthest worlds."

"Alone, he will accomplish that? In exile? Did you thus arrange events now-past?"

"I arranged little," Swadeth exhaled. "I sowed seeds once, many seasons past. Surely you remember that—and the maple tree now growing before your *asaph*? Events created themselves, while I observed.

"*Esepthen ketheset sfataah,*" he continued, aloud now. "Have you not read the patterns he bears? Exile will shape him, not hold him."

"Fear, and the odor of my own *gadesh*, conceal much from me of late. Perhaps I will be soon *ksta* alone, and this assemblage called Phaniik Reis will be but memory."

Swadeth's own *ksta* could not help but writhe and twist in purely physiological sympathy.

CHAPTER
TWENTY-ONE

VoiceLog 3.24(r), Shipsoft Corporation, Tacoma, S3
Timecode 772.883.6564

> We're under power again, in space. The Vikings took one of
our modified missiles for testing in a buried arms bunker near
the field. They wouldn't allow any of us off the ship, so de
Witte is still with us, and still armed.
> I hope the Jovia took out all their munitions when it blew. It
looked horrible. The ground literally bulged, then collapsed
into a crater. I threw *RR*'s stabilizers on right away, and we still
almost toppled. It only took de Witte a second to realize he'd
lost his customers' goodwill, not to mention the customers
themselves, and he ordered us up and away. We took a few
burns from portside defense lasers, but the Jovia's seismics had
nixed their calibration.
> The owner didn't connect *us* with the explosion.

> Alta Van Voort, acting captain, *Reef Runner IV*.

Brown, rolling hills huddled against a cold, leaden sky. Clouds
blanketed all, conserving meager heat for the few tough plants
rooted in scant, half-frozen soil. Lichens grew between the bare
rocks of the Kenesthet region, some giants as high as a man's belt
buckle. Propagated by wind, nourished on weathered rock, they
had no scent, color, or sexuality. The landscape was pallid, drab.
Scent and odor existed only in the warm pockets of the station,
which had no name. Its stone hovels housed five hundred psatla, but
none called it home.
    One of five such settlements, its inhabitants monitored weather,
currents, magnetic variables that affected planetforming, *psalaat-*

thes. To psatla who dealt with the information it sent, the station was terminal 151. Bass couldn't remember when he had issued that terminal, or to whom. Its codes were different, limiting him to sensor-repair information and schematics, weather charts, area maps, and simple utilities. His exile was total.

Thsaan Bass felt an affinity with the lichens. He, too, was bleak and brown, sexless and dry. The *tsfeneke* who shared his exile were no better, dull creatures with lusterless chitin and failing minds. Bass did not rage at his fate. The old wounds received at Stef Myers's hands regulated him, and perhaps psatla hormones negated feelings not sexual. He knew the signs of rising emotion, the incipient stabbing below his ear, the thoughts not then and there, and he suppressed them and proceeded with his undemanding duties.

Bass took long walks across dismal hills and let his mind roam, examining the upwelling memories his passive state allowed. Memories? He thought of them as *ksta, ksta* of a particularly human kind, concealed in the writhing coils of DNA—recordings of events long past, ancestral memories. Were they true, or was he psychotic? He had endured much, and lost much. Psychosis was not unlikely. Perhaps they were only the recollections of dreams. In 2476, his first year in exile, a particularly vivid dream started it all:

He was on Earth itself. The whole planet was the private preserve of the Megacorporate families. He had seen, in overflying it, the vast parklands, the nostalgic ivied ruins of ancient cities, maintained solely to stimulate the poetic impulses of the privileged few. On other Earthward worlds, on other trade missions, he had seen equally vast plantations worked by serfs whose scant upkeep cost less than fuel for machinery. He had seen cities that were great blocks of identical buildings, where millions lived in tiny identical rooms and worked long hours on thankless tasks. Thus his view of the Earthside merchants he faced was jaundiced, at best. They were the foppish, overdressed scions of Megacorporate houses, and they stank of perfume and drugged smoke. He carefully played the buffoon's part they cast for him. "Uh . . . your offer, it's really kind, sirs," he stumbled. "Yes, generous, but the cargo's owner set the price at seven-twenty a square. If I sell it for less, he'll take my ship."

"How is that?" The merchants were not voluble. Every time they speak, Bass thought, they're forced to inhale. What provincial stink do I carry?

"He has a note against my ship. He'll call it due."

The merchant brightened, tapping overlong, lacquered finger-nails on his satin-clad knee. "If we pay your note and six-seventy . . . whether you go home again . . ."

"Uh, I owe . . . seventy thousand on the ship. And there's berthing fees here . . ." Scorn showed outright in the merchant's eyes. These corrupt pustules consider *me* no better than a pirate, Bass thought. So be it. My pride means nothing, as long as I get what I want from them.

"Done!" The second merchant slapped the thick mahogany tabletop. "Six-seventy plus seventy thousand to you, the fees waived . . . now get out of here before I puke."

Bass rose, bowed, and shut off his pocket recorder. It had been an unnecessary precaution—they were, by their lights, stealing him blind, and they knew it. But, a stitch in time, as his father used to say . . .

My father? Jack Cannon? No, my father never said that. Dream-fabric had fluttered in the breeze of reality and shredded before eyes opening not on the huge moon of Earth, on ancient city streets, but on a lone incandescent globe lighting sod walls. The station. Phastillan.

Bass knew how that dream ended: there had been profit enough to return to Cannon's Orb with three leased ships, men, women, tools . . .

The dreams didn't fade with daylight. Days, months later, he recalled them like actual experiences. Details unrecognized during the dreaming emerged clearly in retrospect.

He negotiated a truce between fur-clad tribes. Firelit glints of polished bronze and iron were burnt into memory, and faces: bearded, weathered skin contrasting with red and golden hair. Their language was smoothly elided, often guttural, always powerful, the raw stuff of heroic hexameter. Bass sometimes rolled forth its sounds as he trod the lichen-spotted plain, rhythms he believed would evolve, centuries after the dream-time, into the Greek of Homer's age.

Was Earth's moon so large, a looming disk overhead, a silver shield, a great stone suspended by a whisker? He could check that against records, if he could access them. He "remembered" measuring it against his thumbnail, at arm's length. He wore fine maroon cloth that time, under a rough fur cape. A wide gold bracelet encircled his wrist, ornate geometric designs gleaming silvery by moonlight.

All the dreams had things in common. They were all in the past, their clear, vivid details were consistent, and they were young

men's dreams. Bass's position wasn't always central; in one dream
he was an errand boy bringing messages to wool-suited, necktied
deliberators in a high-ceilinged chamber.

Bass was less skeptical than another might have been. He recalled a Cottertown gypsy who read auras and spoke confidently
of other incarnations, past lives. Even Crowe Academy military
historians admitted, without affirming, the claims of Subotai, Pat-
ton, and Mejanian to expertise born of more than one lifetime in
command. And his father's faith implicitly accepted reincarna-
tion, the migration of ancient souls. Was there some actual, rational basis for that belief which had accompanied man from the
very dawn of time?

Bass didn't believe in anything at all, but he asked himself: Are
the dreams *ksta*? Are they ancestral memories bursting the dam
of consciousness? They were consistent with Swadeth's intron
hypothesis: the recollections of the old could not be genetically
transmitted to their children long since born. If he had access to
histories, to a library photo collection of ancient artifacts, recorded "reality," he would know. What did "Indians" look like?
What was a rune? A hood ornament? A necktie?

CHAPTER
TWENTY-TWO

> >LOGFUNCTN:420.124.8878 COMMENT:

It is time. Our fuel is nearly gone. New Detroit colony was
reduced to cannibalism. They suffered no food shortages, only
a dearth of those trace elements rare throughout transReef, for
which the only source left is . . . each other. Needless to say,
they had no fuels.

The only inhabited world within *Matteo*'s reach is a nonhuman one. For me, that's just as well, though my crew will
surely suffer for it. Perhaps the aliens will be free of the blind,

grasping, and all-too-human behavior that is destroying us.
Tonight I will announce our final destination . . . Phastillan.

Jacomo Pirel, captain, *Matteo d'Ajoba*

A torpid, dust-covered laborer grew agitated as Bass passed. Chitin clattered harshly and the slight breeze reeked of machine oil
and musk. Bass held his breath. Sometimes such exudations stimulated anomalous emotion, disorienting, often downright unpleasant. Everyone had moments of déjà vu evoked by odors. The
human olfactory nerve alone was unprotected by a myelin sheath;
chemical stimuli could bypass the brain's censors and draw forth
responses as intense as "reality."

TransReef humans disliked things that denied the patent dual-
ism of their culture: body and mind were *not* one. Man and environment, man and animal, were distinct, apart. There was no
relieving yin within yang. It was a circle divided across its di-
ameter, geometric, inflexible. But Bass was stripped of his culture, his emotions, his association with his own kind. He was
lichen, wind-beaten, passive, and aloof . . . but he was curious.
What did the psatla's reaction mean?

He stopped. Agitated activity slowed, then ceased. He peered
at the three putty-ball eyes raised to him. "What did your *ksta*
know of me, just then?"

"You are he-without-*ksta*," the *tsfeneke* replied ambiguously.
"Your true-speech is without sense." Tight-held chitin plates,
overlapping edges flat against *ksta*: tension.

Was it afraid of him, or of his question? Fine discrimination of
scent could be cultivated, he knew. Master chefs and king's
poison-sniffers staked their reputations and lives on well-trained
noses. Bass, always open, always credulous, accepted his ability
to comprehend bits of psatla speech, while concluding that human
senses could only grasp vague meaning in them. But he had never
turned the situation around: What did his odors communicate to
them? "What did I say that caused you discomfort?"

Again, the psatla rattled, scraping a ratchety cricket tune. "I
may not say, human-beast. Go now. My *ksta* cringe from you."

"When I am satisfied, not before." *May* not say . . . not *cannot* say. "Who commands your silence?"

The *tsfeneke* pondered, closed tight, vibrating. "*Sfalek-ni*
Swadeth requires it, unless your speech is sane. It is not so. I
think it cannot be so." Putty eyes turned away.

Swadeth. Dronelike, Bass focused always on affairs at hand—

his work, his dreams, a meal—swathed in a veil of apathy which the name "Swadeth" slashed through like a deadly blade. Spinning on his heel, he half walked, half ran out of the compound. His steps took him, unthinking, out to a lichen-covered outcrop of bedrock. Steep-angled sunlight warmed the rock, so he settled gratefully in its lee.

Swadeth. He hasn't forgotten me! he told himself. He's set conditions on me. Sane? What does that mean? Something to do with scent, communication. With *ksta*.

His mind swirled. Memories ran like speeded-up holotapes, an instance here, an observation there. Warm rock lulled him even as his thoughts raced. First impressions: Phastillan's overwhelming perfumes. Event and odor, word and scent, action accompanied with a reek, a tingle, an evanescent whiff. He remembered all, and sorted them. The air grew chill. The sun sank while he lay motionless. The rock beneath him cooled even while synapses heated like long-unused, corroded wires now glowing with current.

Only the bitter chill of subarctic summer night forced him to get up. Stumbling over rocks and lichen, like a *beteph* to its stall he trudged to his room. He slept. Deep within, racing currents persevered, sorting and shuffling every psatla word he'd heard, and the fragrances that had accompanied it.

Through the short days of winter, when biting winds kept psatla inside, he "listened," absorbing through untrained membranes the sense and scents of psatla conversation. Much eluded him. The range and complexity of "sane" speech exceeded his chemosensory capacity, though Psatla sound-speech took on nuances he'd never suspected. But, of course, he could never respond in kind.

Or could he? Humans, too, spoke silently. His father had used more than sound and gesture to enthrall his congregation. Bass remembered him pumping up for his performance, building his charisma, his "inspiration." Inspiration: breathing in. Breathing what? Who? Dominance and submission: chest-beating. *He exudes confidence,* people said. *The sweet smell of success. He's in bad odor at court. I smell a rat.*

"You have to set your attitude first, Bass. You can't walk into a man's office and give him your bid unless you're confident. He'll know. He'll smell your fear and use it against you. You won't have a chance." Confidence: dominance, ancient prehuman speech— a pheromone. Was that the answer? Humans deny their animal selves. Jack would never have credited his lofty position to a feral, primate stink. But Bass . . . Bass had no pride. He was *thsaan* to *tsfeneke*, lichen, nothing. Man, and animal. He practiced. He learned.

On his warm rock in summer, later in the lonely cold of isolated sensor-line shacks, throughout the winter when sun was only a memory, he played out the roles of his father, his dreams. Without hope or ambition, he learned to create them, to shape his own weakened emotions. In such rudimentary fashion, might he control his exudations, make them comprehensible to psatla? Make them sane?

The exiles gathered only at mealtime—forty of them ate when Bass did—so at mealtimes he conducted his experiment. Squatting over a warm pot with four psatla, dipping small morsels with his handmade ladle, he remembered Saturday night: Sorayan. Deliberately dwelling on mindless passion, he remembered sensation, emotion.

The room was silent. Silent? He emerged from his reverie aware that he had indeed spoken clearly to psatla. "Do my thoughts trouble you?" His voice was harsh in the humid crowding. Had he said what he meant to? "Thoughts of the small death, of *ksta* breaking from *ksta*, are not welcome among exiles, doomed to the great death like Edephaa last year, and others before him." Psatla bodies turned toward him, eyes swiveled, flattening to focus on his face. "For my impropriety, I beg forgiveness. I plead necessity. My speech is rude, my *ksta* untrained." He singled out the laborer who had given him his first clue. "Pfaskiit," he said quietly, "though I spoke of things painful to psatla far from warm soil and female *ksta*, was my speaking understood?"

"It was, *fsa*-psatla. Your words and my *ksta*'s suffering are one. What of it?"

"My speech, then, was sane?"

"Your speaking was unwelcome. All suffered for it."

"I am aware of that. But my words and the *ksta*-voice are consonant?" Bass's gaze swept the two score gathered there. "You all understand word and scent alike?"

"We understood both," Pfaskiit agreed, though reluctantly.

"As my speaking was sane, then I am sane as well. The *sfalek-ni* Swadeth's condition is met. Is it so?"

"It is so." Psatla do not sigh. but the impression conveyed by their low rush of sound, gesture, and aroma had the same effect. A release of long-held tension—relief. From that moment on,

Bass was less alone in his exile. There were "other" psatla, others of his kind sharing the loneliness, the cold.

Limited to the conveyance of raw emotion, human speech was inexact. Human anger expressed panicky self-destructiveness, which was not "sane." Sadness, despair, and melancholia induced in psatla only calm acceptance, mild resignation. When Bass radiated calm assurance, psatla reacted with respect. Strong commitment to an idea, a methodology, generated enthusiastic obedience to his every whim.

Many weeks passed before the uneven correspondence of input to output made sense. *Psalaat*: mind's struggle to order environment. Not a plan, but active participation in the flux of event and circumstance. *Psalaat* was not static. It was incessant, thoughtful effort. And speech did not convey meaning, but impetus. Bass's nascent self-confidence did not make psatla confident in him, it made them obey.

With Swadeth's condition met, he questioned particular scents, even requested they be repeated for him. "What is security?" Warm compost, a forest-floor aroma of mushrooms and mildew.

Fine discrimination eluded him. Old Earth's finest chefs might have done better, but some limits are absolute. Pheromones are odorless. They act along membrane-blood-brain paths, bypassing the senses. From a state of absolute calm, Bass could register the rise and fall of emotions that didn't originate within himself, but that was all.

He came to understand *gadesh*. The seeds of understanding had been there all along. Much as the conviction had come to him unbidden that Phastillan was a crux world, a dispersal point for a new humanity, so his understanding of psatla came, subliminally, disguised as bits and pieces of unremarkable information, raw data that fit no preconceived scheme.

His new comprehension couldn't be articulated in English or Psatla, but his mind no longer sought certainty amid variation. *Psalaat* was flux. There were no rules. But beneath the shifting balances of power and influence lay an immutable iron core: *gadesh*.

Psatla manipulated environment to a degree humans scarcely dreamed of. The genomes, the very heredity of species, were environment, and psatla changed such bioforms at will. Ideally, psatla planets recapitulated their homeworld. Actually, they were compromises, homeworld biota and native forms commingled and changed. *Gadesh* was a brake upon change. It conserved.

For psatla were capable of changing themselves, too. Psatla they remained only because of the overriding dictum of *fsa-psataleth-fsat*, "never to become not-psatla." Changing themselves, mutating their own genes, would have been easier than changing worlds, but at what point would the changers have ceased to be psatla at all?

The complex institution of *gadesh* controlled psatla mutability, and *psalaat* was a blueprint for controlled change. Challenges and proposals forced *sfalekt*, even *sfalekt-thes*, to defend and update their visions. Conservative visions were most correct until defeated, and to defeat them experimental paths must be undeniably superior.

Gadesh is recognition of pure vision and containment, and Bass understood both. The chaos he had sensed in *Sally*'s datastreams, in the log dumps and newscubes, was *fsa-gadeh*, uncontrolled, and insane. It was human. "The pressure of events," men said; historic imperatives, manifest destiny, progress: these were *fsa-gadeh psalaa-fse kten*, the juggernaut, an uncontrollable force. Madness. Now Bass knew what had to be done. He knew the proper levers to pull, and was no longer afraid to pull them. His hope to return to the Orb no longer had urgency. There were more important tasks. The crisis of transReef humanity would not abate, it could not. Mad expansion, uncontrolled breeding, minds wide open to the words of charismatic fools, all those and more were the human heritage. Pirates—parasites and vampires—were a human curse, the useless remnants of ancient dominant-maleness. Once such raiders left fresh genes in their wake, babes of rape, new blood and strong that invigorated isolated populations. Such radical exogamy was a boon to future generations. Now, only fear and devastation followed them.

Human culture was a massive synthesis of religions, ethics, mores, and technology, the only bulwark against chaos, and it had scattered and differentiated among the transReef worlds. Culture would not prevent dissolution. Chaos would grow inexorably into the bleak universe of Bass's shipboard vision unless radical steps were taken—unless humanity was brought under the aegis of *gadesh*, bound to a greater vision than ever before. *Psalaat*. The *psalaat-thes* of Bass Cannon.

Ego was not involved. Bass knew he must gain power over his species, and others, power no individual had ever possessed. He took no pleasure in it. I am nothing. There is only *psalaat*. He would plunge into the stream of it, not attempt to balance, as he had done, on the peak of a standing wave.

Gadesh . . . stability . . . control. *Psalaat*: inhuman, inconceivable change; a war against entropy. It must occur. There was no other way. But he knew that without some luck, some opening, he would grow old and die in his exile, for no other's vision would be served by aiding him.

That chance came near the end of his second year in the north.

CHAPTER
TWENTY-THREE

KEYBOARD FILECODE XXXXX [SIMULATED]
>>[CLOSE] [ERASE] [TRANSLATE]
>TRANSLATE
>>[TARGET LANGUAGE?]
>ENGLISH VAR 3 LITERAL
ENT 1.5>>>Seventy slave women sold on Carbuncle. Ten we have kept for our use. Twenty we slew, when their tears and hatred bored us. The ten, too, will die when we tire of their dull Hebrew eyes, their swelling bellies. The star-trails are no place for gravid sluts and mongrel bastards.

The ship must be impeccable when next we land. There must be no blood, no single Hebrew hair, no dusty trace of drugs long sold. Even our weapons must be jettisoned, for the next planetfall is our last. Our raids have been in vain. There is no fuel to be taken. We have enough to reach but one lone non-human settlement, a world called Phastillan. [DATECODE MISSING]

Bass was several miles from the station when the aircar streaked overhead. It had to be new exiles arriving; supplies and regular visitors arrived in crude cargo floaters.

Spinning his battered vehicle on two wheels, he raced back the way he had come. Two psatla had disembarked and were standing by the aircar, looking lost and disoriented. Psatla were shocked by their first exposure to clear, unscented northern air—it was like becoming abruptly deaf or blind, he speculated.

Bass had no specific plan, only a conviction that change, variation, was a basis for opportunity. He pulled alongside the two to pick them up. The aircar pilot was human. Bass's pounding heart, his sudden sweat, icy in the steady wind from the island's center, his trembling reaction to human chemistry assured him of it. Was James hiding in there, ashamed of his part in Bass's ill fortune, afraid of a violent confrontation?

Bass motioned the psatla aboard his four-wheeler, then pulled quickly away. No one was outside the station, where he pulled to a stop and turned to inspect his passengers. He recognized one. The psatla was smaller than average, and quite green—the green of new growth, seldom seen in Bass's barren exile.

"I see the *pralasek-ni* Kstala, once my student," he said formally. It wouldn't hurt to remind him, though no *gadesh* was created unless the psatla came to consider him useful once again.

"You see Kstala, now *tsfeneke*," the psatla replied. Damn! Bass thought. Kstala broken to *tsfeneke*! What use will he be now?

The other psatla was the color of basalt. His rough chitin hung loosely, the edges dull and curling; he was old, or ill. He seemed familiar. "I see one whose name I do not know," Bass ventured.

"You see the *tsfeneke* Thesakan."

Bass couldn't conceal a start, hearing that name. Stilling unproductive rage, he turned to opportunity. Both psatla were casualties of some intrigue, even a delayed result of the one that had landed him there. Battle. *Gadesh. Psalaat* against *psalaat*, shaking the foundations of existence. Were Kstala and Thesakan permanently exiled, as he was? It would be a bitter disappointment were it so, but he had to know. All avenues had to be explored.

"Tell me of events in the warm lands. Perhaps advantage will accrue." Advantage: *gadesenth-ni*, a potential for active intervention in the flow of *gadesh*; leverage, or the hope of it. An alliance of rejects? Better than no alliance. He had long since pieced together a sketch of events since his exile. Swadeth had successfully ridden the storm. When Bass had fallen, he had fallen alone. The heavy-metal embezzlement had never become general knowledge. Swadeth ignored it. Phaniik Reis never knew the details. James and Ziggy survived untouched, still avoiding the slightest *gadesh*.

Small, duckweed green Kstala was voluble. His fall, and Thesakan's, had originated with a desperate maneuver by Zig and James. The two humans had amassed resources useless on Phastillan. They had tried to escape with all the hoarded gold, not theirs alone. In the data net, Kstala discovered forged shipping lists and blew the whistle. Ziggy and James survived intact, shorn of their gold and still stuck on Phastillan. In the shifting *gadesh* that ensued, Kstala was sacrificed and Thesakan broken. *Pralasekt* Sfel and Phthaas, whom Kstala had implicated, abandoned *psalaat-ni* for the greater path of Phaniik Reis. Their settling-ponds and biorefineries were abandoned.

Concerning the greater polity of transReef, all was less calm. Incoming shipping was totally unpredictable. The immediate cause was piracy. The root causes were politico-economic: key mining worlds had rebelled and had turned to raiding. The Panaikos Council, never strong, had disbanded, and many council members had no homeworlds to return to. Larkspur Colony was gone, its population enslaved, sold as miners and serfs. Perfection, Sardonyx, Tbilisi . . . abandoned. Without radioactive ores, there was no power to sustain Camden's atmosphere plants, and terraforming had ceased. Refugees strained the capacities of more fortunate worlds, hastening their own declines.

Chaos, Bass thought. The destroyer of plans and the plow that turns fresh soil for seed of my *psalaat*. Root and stem of my salvation. The years and their hardships had shaped Vassily James Cannon in strange ways. The boy who had left Cannon's Orb would not have recognized the thoughts of the man. "*Gadesenth-ni* awaits," he told his companions. "I would show you the path, but my way is barred. I cannot access the computer."

Kstala's rattling and the sharp, minty odor of excitement told Bass what he wanted to know: no one had thought to deactivate Kstala's access code.

Bass's next acts puzzled the psatla. They watched him cut his hair short. Then, with an eager, feral smile, he reached into his faded shirt, pulled forth a cloth-wrapped packet, and unrolled it with gentle, reverent hands. He spread hair-fine wires and stretched them over stiffened fingers, placing the delicate net upon his cropped head. A cabled strand, made of thousands of microscopic conductors, terminated in an interface plate. Still smiling fixedly, he tucked the surplus cable in his pocket. Only then did he lead his observers to the terminal room.

Kstala logged on and moved aside. Bass drew the interface from his pocket and set the clear crystalline block against terminal 151's socket. Toy sparks kindled, dancing in crystalline depths.

His fingers remembered the strings of code. He had prepared for the moment, practicing on the formerly useless terminal, terrified that he might forget a vital number. He murmured a fervent prayer to no particular god and tapped a final key.

From terminal to satellite to mainframe the burst of code carried its powerful message. For two long milliseconds the entire Phastillan network shut down as it assimilated the override command. No human or psatla noticed, but from that moment on, the whole system belonged to Bass alone. His lone terminal controlled the network. He could never be locked out of it again.

For an hour, Bass sat entranced, his fingers limp on the obsolete keyboard, his thoughts a thousand miles from the small, dank room. No expression crossed his face, but his eyes shone with drugged intensity. Outwardly he was silent, still and passive; within, his intensity was greater than ever in his life . . .

A black blot, flat, unreflecting, formed in the haze before his unfocused eyes. He imaged it as contracting, compressing. First wavering, stretching, becoming diffuse, it eventually followed his mental command, and became first a disk, then a shrinking dot, and finally a point.

It split. *Two*, he subvocalized. *Two* dots, *two* chickens, *two* psatla, *two* grabbits. *Two*. Haze coalesced into a line connecting the points. *Line. Geometry. Two points define a line.* Bass reviewed the first three theorems he could remember. *Three* theorems. *Three points, three trees, three coffee cups, three ksta . . . four . . . five. Five dots . . . six.* His mind rocked with the impact of quasiphysical forces shaking his synapses, triggering bursts of unconnected thought, irrelevant, forgotten memories, erotica, numbers, concepts . . .

At last it stopped. Unfocused haze coalesced again: [MOD2OPSYS 3.32]. Bass sighed. I'm through. I'm past the threshold that drives men insane. Every hat user had to get past this point, to surrender the autonomy of the mind for the time the hat's brain-mapping took. He would not have to go through it again unless he used a different hat. What he saw was the hat software's logon prompt.

ME. He pictured the letters as a tag a space right of the prompt. RUN.

Again, field forces took over his brain. Stimulus, image, stimulus. Number. Seven. Three thousand. Stimulus: a harsh discordancy. Stimulus: B-flat. Notes. Tonic, subdominant, a triad. Tonality: whistle-hoot, whine-plunk. Banjo, piano. [MUSIC. CHECK?] GO. Victoriously, Bass heard the exultant opening fanfare of Tchaikovsky's Fourth. The interface is building, he thought. I'm getting there. Banks of figures scrolled. A data base. Tabulated values. unlabeled. Mine production figures, ten years old. Not Phastillan numbers, but part of the hat program's sample data set.

INSTRUCT:GRAPHICS, he commanded. A swirl of black numbers broke apart. A flat graph, then 3-D mountaintops. STIBNITE PRODUCTION BY MONTH: MINE FIVE > CORRELATE AGAINST DAY OF WEEK AND WORKER ABSENTEEISM. Again, a three-dimensional graph rewarded him. AUDITORY AND VISUAL: MINE FIVE. A mine cart crossed his field of view, rumbling. Dead-faced, sweating miners wearing dust masks and goggles swore muffled oaths and trudged wearily by.

Images, figures, and sounds erupted inside his head or sprang holographically before his eyes. Aside from an occasional pause for his input, he was no more in control of the process than he would have been under a heavy hallucinogen dose. He understood what was happening, though, and didn't fear it. Men's fear was what drove them mad.

Starting with the first amorphous image, the blob, the hat had continuously monitored and recorded his relevant cerebral activity, guided by its own generalized brain-map. As he responded to each experimental stimulus with thought or image, it responded with new stimuli until it, and Bass, arrived at a consensus: the concept "two." As the program swept through his memories, it sought, at first, "two." New stimuli, new variables defined, new images, sensations, sounds were catalogued.

From numbers to concepts to visual images to sounds and music, the correlation process deepened. Bass, in turn, worked to define the command structure that suited him, the conceptual operating system where I/O required safe, conventional block letters on a gray, misty screen. When that was established, he took control of the process.

SAMPLE FREQUENCY FEED 0–20,000 HERTZ: COMPARE WITH MEMORY > "KYRAITO S'IL LIXEN" (SPELLCHECK); COMPARE > "JINGLE BELLS"; COMPARE > "SAM HALL." RATIONALIZE. The growing program responded, fine-tuning Bass's limited musical memory against its data bank. From then on, it would be able to "play" any musical work in its stores, and Bass would "hear" it as perfectly as his own imperfect ability allowed. And so with all things.

The process took a long time, and Bass wasn't easily satisfied. He wanted flawless performance and exactitude. If he called up an image of the Best-of-Century Laura Endicott rose, he had to be sure that the pale blue-violet petals were the exact shade rose fanciers and judges had seen, under display lights chromatically adjusted to Earth sunlight, latitude 41°30'N, longitude 93°30', day 170. If he asked for a holoview of ships lost, when and where, he wanted them displayed in the exact shade of scarlet he most associated with danger.

Finally, stiff from sitting motionless, his eyes hardly able to refocus on the reality of terminal 151, he was finished. The psatla had used the time to settle into their own bare quarters. At least Kstala did so. Thesakan grew more quiet, more withdrawn. His illness was aggravated by bleak surroundings, by cold, by his lack of conviction that Bass would return him to the fertile, green lands he craved. He hunched in the warmest corner of his sleeping area, apathetic, drab, and forlorn.

Within his own still-intact file area, mentally flitting like a fire-fly spark among reeds, Bass activated programs even as his mind skimmed over them. Moments later, the printer hummed softly, extruding twelve sheets of text.

Unplugging again, he motioned the psatla to follow him outside. They sat in the wind shadow of the terminal hut while Bass revealed their fates. "*Tsfeneke* Kstala will be absolved of complicity in false-*psalaat* when I transfer these to *Pralasek* Lesthef's files." He turned to the other psatla. "For the *tsfeneke* Thesakan, I have no such good news. Your involvement in the radioactives scheme was total. I could not expunge your part in it."

"Isss underssstood," Thesakan said, a mere croak overlaid with breathy hissing. He betrayed no emotion, no twitch or twisting of corded muscle beneath his dulled, chitinous exterior. "Now? Disssposssition?"

"I can aid your impending dissolution . . . if you wish it of me."

"Explain."

"*Pralasek-thes* Sfel's involvement in failed *psalaat* is masked by your own. You will consequently remain here, to die."

The psatla finally showed signs of agitation. "Die," Thesakan grated. "To ssstrew my *ksta* on unliving sssoil." Chitinous extremities whirred softly like winged beetles in a sticky web. Arm segments writhed, his body swayed. Bass waited, hoping he would recover. Slowly Thesakan, once master of thousands, mastered himself.

Bass continued. "This information shows Sfel's *psalaat* truly, and defines yours as well. The *sfalek-thes* will reexamine your plight. You will be called to account for yourself—but unless you take action, I will see you here again. I offer only a brief respite."

''Action. What?'' The psatla knew what the answer was, but had little desire to hear it.

''Your *ksta* can burrow in good earth. When you are called to Asaph Phaniikan, you must act.''

Dark gray chitin drew tight around Thesakan's resolve. He became as he had been so long ago: tight and hard, an expressionless insect-being. ''Give me paperss. It iss enough.''

''Almost enough,'' Bass said. ''There is a thing you must do for me.''

''What thing?''

''You will see *Sfalek-ni* Swadeth at Asaph Phaniikan, and you will remind him that I await his time of need, and Phaniik Reis's. Will you do that?''

''Do that. I. Yesss.'' Thesakan recognized the aroma of *psalaat*. He knew it well.

Bass extracted a similar promise from Kstala, explaining that the need he foresaw would become evident within two years—that the Sfalekt would be consumed with fear for the futures of *psalaat-thes* and Phastillan itself. ''The roots under Phaniik Reis will tremble as if sunk in unsound soil. He will ask of Swadeth and Khestaat: 'Why?' They will not answer, but will repeat the question. *Gadesh* will hang suspended, ripe fruit within reach of tsfeneke on the smallest limbs of Reis. From Lesthef to Bephest to Kstala will the question rise: 'Why?' Then will you remind Bephest that I am here, awaiting the call of Phaniik Reis. You will tell him what I have done this day, for you and for Thesakan. You will tell him that I told you of events not yet transpired, that I foretold even his asking.''

Kstala knew few humans beside Bass; he had only seen them going about their tinkering business with machines. But in spite of his lack of familiarity and his brief acquaintance, he perceived the changes time had wrought. The man was dried out, thin, stiffer and more brittle-seeming than before, though all humans seemed so anyway. He consumed himself with an inner fire so carefully banked that only Kstala might taste it, and know it burned at all.

And who was Kstala? A psatla trained to use machine-minds, true, but still what he had always been, what his *ksta*-borne capabilities dictated: *enef-seh-kstes-selut*, one-whose-*ksta*-taste-deeply, a specialist in reading chemical essences as others read scrolls or books. What he read in Bass Cannon was not frustration, anger, or the madness of long exile—it was *psalaat*, all-encompassing *psalaat* unlimited by planetary or solar system boundaries. It was *psalaat-thes-kfaseh*, the path-crossing-all-paths: overview and ultimate synthesis.

He could not read Bass's mind. He only sensed the exudations of confidence, of racing thoughts revising themselves with each new datum, of powerful plans held patiently in check, awaiting their moment. He was afraid to ask Bass for details, afraid of what he might hear. But ask he did.

"My *psalaat*?" Bass replied. "It is this: There will be no more psatla. Nor humans. The distinctions of species will become as the growth rings and color of your carapace, that distinguish you from Thesakan, or the difference between my light hair and another's dark; they will become inconsequential, irrelevant." He would say no more.

Bass's words and essences combined to make disbelief impossible. Kstala's mind recoiled from the man's confidence, his absolute assurance that he was right, that his terrifying path would become real. Bass's were *sfalek-thes* thoughts.

CHAPTER

TWENTY-FOUR

VoiceLog 3.24(r), Shipsoft Corporation, Tacoma, S3
Timecode 772.902.9968

> Our last three stops were wasted fuel. We're down to standby reserves, and no one is selling. No one has any to sell, with the mine worlds all in viking hands, and a viking noose around the Reef passages. Not even pirates can get enough.
> Our last decel, at Hammond's Egg, turned into a flyby—they're firing at anything coming in-system.
> There's only one registered port in range, with the Egg off limits. It's Class C, emergency services only, no fuel dump. It's not even a *human* world. Once we set down, we're grounded

for the duration, maybe forever. I hope those pissants don't *really* smell so bad.

> Alta Van Voort, acting captain, *Reef Runner IV*.

Kstala and Thesakan were recalled, but Bass wasn't there to witness their departure. He had resumed his interrupted trip to the fallen monitoring tower. It didn't matter, he told himself on returning. Psatla don't wave good-bye.

From that time on, terminal 151 recorded increased activity. Phastillan's data base had continued to expand during Bass's exile, and not just via the planet's keyboards—someone had continued dumping ships' logs into the system. One dump contained the entire library of a luxury liner. Seeing that, Bass thought of his dreams.

No method of viewing computer holograms surpassed Bass's hat. There was none of the distortion that accompanied projections with the hat; ancient armbands and swords, museum pieces, were so real he wanted to touch them. Only old newspaper photographs became no clearer than their originals unless he enhanced them.

There were no "hood ornaments." There were photos of automobiles—not the ones Bass "remembered," but then, the automobile era had lasted a hundred years. There had been many manufacturers, many styles. He had no better luck with jewelry or neckties. The geometric bracelet in the Hellenic dream had been much copied over two millennia. Some buildings he "remembered" were hauntingly echoed in old, flat photographs, but others bore disappointingly little resemblance to his dream images: the capital of the United States of America, ca. 1990 C.E., more closely approximated an ancient temple than the lean glass-and-stone edifice his dream self had worked in.

If the dreams represented reality, perhaps he would someday confirm it. The likelihood seemed slight. Stubbornly, though—perhaps because it was so important to psatla that lives not evaporate in death—he clung to his personal conviction that those lives he'd shared were real, not products of his altered brain. Despite this belief, he reluctantly confined himself to more productive efforts.

When all was prepared for that critical future moment Bass awaited, he again abandoned terminal 151 to routine queries of machine-part stores and schematics, and for two long years he returned to his lichen existence. Occasionally, in the depths of winter, when savage winds kept him from venturing out, he checked the terminal for news from the southlands, for developments offworld.

Across transReef, chaos bloomed. Piracy and revolution sapped the lifeblood of the spacelanes. Even Phastillan, poor refuge that it was, became temporary home to several ships. Bass studied every detail. He kept a list in his room:

Matteo d'Ajoba, trader. Net tonnage 7500. Cargo of record: semiautomatic production machinery, control units, repair & replacement components. Crew: 18 + 3 officers.

Reef Runner IV, yacht. N.T. 14. Cargo of record: none. (Note: cargo bay held 84 space-to-space seeker missiles, unregistered.) Crew: 3 + 2 officers.

High Line *Prince*, transReef liner. Passengers: 962 refugees from Consolidated Industries #14. Cargo of record: none. Crew: 39 + 7 officers (surviving).

Enzo Vinella, trader. N.T. 10,000. Cargo of record: n/a (record blocks sealed, loc: Phastillan Port Authority vault). Crew: 20 + 4 officers.

Behind the dry listings of cargo and tonnages lay other facts. The *Reef Runner* had attempted to deliver her illegal missiles to an equally illegal buyer, but had departed with her cargo unsold and her hull laser-scarred when negotiations broke down. The *Vinella* was battle-scarred, too, but no records told of her battles.

The *Matteo d'Ajoba*'s log read like a traveler's diary of transReef. A veteran trader, undaunted by unsettled conditions, she was forced to remain on Phastillan only for lack of fuel. Bass imagined her master, Jacomo Pirel, to be a synthesis of the *Carrington*'s Captain Sotheny and Alois Battersea of the *Sally B*. He wanted to meet Captain Pirel.

The High Line *Prince* had the most tales to tell. They weren't pretty stories. A pirate fleet had taken over on C. I. #14, a mining world, after a violent siege. Many died in fire and famine, more died during conquest. Survivors were methodically culled: those with indispensable skills were branded and chained, then sent to their jobs; the rest were stripped and lined up. Pirate officers took their pick of the young and lovely—women, men, even children. The rest were herded, before the eyes of their loved ones, to the edges of open mine shafts, then ordered to jump. It was a measure of the horror the pirates instilled that few refused to leap. The dead were lucky. The living were less than slaves.

For two years the conquerors enjoyed the fruits of victory. The mines continued to produce. Ships from planets dying for lack of metals, desperate for fuel, came and went, and the pirate rulers of C.I. #14 became rich. Elsewhere their growing wealth and power were joylessly noted.

A consortium of thugs calling themselves vikings were rapidly becoming transReef's major power. They controlled the Earthward passages through the Reef and several mining worlds, and they tolerated no competition. Consolidated Industries #14 was marked for destruction. Class One warships—the last of Earth's transReef fleet to surrender when their fuel ran out—seeded Consolidated Industries #14 with corebreaker bombs. There was no conquest, only doom. The pirates abandoned slaves and wealth and fled to their ships. The ruined planet turned dark as ash and dust and smoke hid the sun. Broken men, lost, degraded women, little boys and girls with minds no longer young activated distress beacons; then they waited.

Captain Ade Folgrin was cautious. His great liner threaded the spacelanes with sensors at maximum range. Thus his first officer noticed the weak signals from afar, on the *Prince*'s starboard-inferior scope. The captain was awakened and the beacons' messages replayed. The twelve hundred survivors plucked from the planet's surface were a miserable lot. Medical officers with excellent equipment cured physical ills, but there were no cures for the sicknesses within. Only time would heal those—some of them.

There was only one port the *Prince* could reach. For Phastillan's human population, her arrival meant only extra work—the port was ill equipped to handle such a great ship. To psatla, it represented a further drain on limited resources. For Bass Cannon, the refugee passengers were the answer to a prayer. The *psalaat* he contemplated in exile required changes in human mores and social behavior, changes that would distress the most adaptable members of his species. What better material could he have than pitiful refugees for whom the worst he could offer was an improvement?

Bass wasn't walking to remember, but to forget. A psatla had died—it wasn't just dissolution, but the true death, forever. The *tsfeneke* had been visibly old. Beneath unkempt chitin, wormlike *ksta* writhed like snakes confined in too small a basket. Incapable of rudimentary communication, its component organisms drew back into themselves, and nerve linkages attenuated and broke. Bass appreciated the effort of will he put forth to remain whole for an hour, a minute longer. Perhaps the psatla hoped he would survive to expiate his crime, to be transported south where his ksta could burrow, to be reborn as young psatla with hope for the future, wiser for the fragmentary experiences he bequeathed them.

His efforts were in vain. It was a rare sun-drenched afternoon. Stimulated by warmth, he moved haltingly beyond the clustered huts on dirty beige *ksta* barely able to act concertedly, and discovered a patch of thickened soil. Gravelly, devoid of humus, the soft dampness still provided more stimulus than the *tsfeneke* could counter with will alone. Soft chitin flaked off like wet rags, exposing ghostlike whiteness. Bass watched helplessly, horrified. The psatla trembled and inexorably slumped to the dirt, separating into several hundred individual, thrashing white *ksta*, already dying. There was no depth of soil to burrow in, no shelter from the sun or the dry air.

Bass wiped his face on his sleeve, ignoring the stink of vomit, and started walking, away from his coexiles, all faced with such dissolution. He walked further than usual, to a range of hills that formed the station's inland horizon. The image of the dying *tsfeneke* merged with his memory of Thesakan. Thank God he had sent him south! Whether or not Thesakan's *ksta* kept the memory of him alive, he had believed it so, and he had gone back to richer soil than here. When Bass returned past the spot where the nameless psatla had died, he was grateful for moonless darkness, but in the light of his imagination he still saw writhing worm fragments—bits of sentience dying, drying on the hard, harsh ground.

On the way back to the station, an aircar passed low overhead, to the east of him, the second 'car in as many years. This time, though, he was in no rush to meet it—he knew it would land at the station, and that it had come for only one reason. His exile was at an end.

CHAPTER

TWENTY-FIVE

Seven years before, Phastillan had been home to only fifty-two humans, and now there were over a thousand. Bass hadn't really expected a familiar face. The pilot peered blindly into the darkness. "Who's there?" he said in guttural psatla, crudely shaping the slippery words.

"I am *Thsaan* Bass Cannon. Have you come for me?"

"You sound like a pissant. Move over in the light where I can see you." Suspicion created by fear—groundless fear, for psatla treachery was never an attack from the shadows. It was a violence of the soul. If Bass had truly been psatla the pilot would have had less cause for fear, not more. But he was new on Phastillan. Bass shrugged and obeyed him.

"Can you see me now?" Bass kept his distance, barely within the ring of light from the craft. Even now his nostrils absorbed human molecules not his own, which coursed through his psatla-saturated blood and made their way to his brain, his glands and organs. "I've been out here for four years," he explained. "If you know about Phastillan at all, you know what that means. Are the on-board breathing units still sealed?"

The pilot nodded.

"Toss one out to me. Please don't handle it any more than you have to." After a moment's fumbling, a plastic-wrapped packet slapped down onto the gravel. An air canister followed it. Gingerly, Bass picked them up and retreated several feet.

"I'm going to put this on," he said in a loud voice, "and then I'll come on board. Perhaps it will isolate me sufficiently. If not, you're going to have a miserable passenger." He opened the pack and threw the plastic wrapper down. Psatla would find it in the morning, and make use of it. Fitting the cylinder, he cracked the valve to purge it, then stretched the helmetlike mask over his face.

The telltale remained silent. Pressure inside was higher than outside, so he was secure.

"All set," he said as he climbed into the craft and took the seat farthest from the pilot. A bulbous console separated them. "Where are you taking me? The port?"

"Nobody told you? I'm supposed to take you to the head pissant himself, Phaniik Reis."

"Ah!" Bass smiled inside his concealing mask. "My *thsaan* opens low among roots, in the shadow of greatness. That's better than I hoped."

"Huh?" The pilot glanced nervously at Bass, surely wondering if his passenger was sane.

"I said 'Great!' Are you new on Phastillan? At one time, I knew everyone here."

"I've been here a couple years. I was third officer on the *Matteo* till she sat down for good."

"Ah, yes. The merchantman. I hope to meet your Captain Pirel sometime."

The pilot looked at him curiously. Bass, in worn, shabby clothing, hardly seemed the type to hobnob with shipcaptains. "Yeah. 'Scuse me, now—I've got a schedule to keep." Bass shrugged and retreated into his thoughts. He would meet with Phaniik Reis. After that meeting, he would either emerge as the single most powerful individual on Phastillan, and ultimately in all transReef space, or he would be banished once more, forever. He had made his plans for success. For failure, he needed none. For failure, lichen thoughts would again suffice.

Most urgent, assuming the meeting went well, was to readapt himself for contact with his fellow humans. He wasn't looking forward to it—not yet. But in spite of the mask's isolation, the pores of his skin still breathed. He couldn't escape it forever, and he feared that once some unknown threshold had been reached, he wouldn't want to. When that happened, he wanted to be in a position to take the "cure" properly. The car was airborne, the pilot less busy. "What's the port like nowadays?" Bass asked. "Is Phastillan still a one-tavern planet?"

"Uh. Yup. I guess it's bigger now—the port, I mean. It was a real mess for a while. Hardly any food except pissant stuff, and all those people staying on the *Prince* even after the shit tanks were full. Now they've got gardens and chickens. But I hear it's still pretty bad there."

"Are there still girls there? At the bar?"

"There's whores, if that's what you want. I don't hold with that kinda stuff. I got a woman, off my own ship.'' He sounded smug, condescending. Too bad—Bass wanted to know about Betsy. The intensity of his disappointment, still not knowing, surprised him. Emotion, he thought. It's already happening. He fell silent after that. Speech increased his metabolic rate, limiting the time he could spend, masked or not, among humans. Thinking was a less active pursuit. He thought about the isolation syndrome.

One of the *Prince*'s officers was, as required on liners, a physician. He had observed Phastillan's effect on humans, and studied it. He had noted, as had others, that reactions intensified with the length of isolation. But no one else had recognized that after three months a saturation point was reached. Bass's reaction, when it ensued, should be no worse than that first time. He wouldn't die of it.

With psatla cooperation, the doctor might have learned more, but they had been reticent, and his final report had been only a technical version of ''I give up.'' That suited Bass. His *psalaat* required human ignorance of such things.

The aircar's whine wavered. Below sprawled a broad patch of interposed squares and rectangles, brown and gray against matted green rain forest. Asaph Phaniikan, its wood and withe no different, from above, than that of any *asaph*. Bass hoped to study its style before meeting its master. The house would say much about he who had ordained its creation.

He collected air cylinders from all six masks. The 'car set down with a slight jar. ''See you, fella. Should I wish yuh luck with the head pissant? I don't envy yuh one bit.''

''I can use all the good wishes I can get,'' Bass replied fervently.

''Wull, good luck then. Mebbe I'll see yuh again some time.'' As the aircar lifted, Bass kicked off his worn boots and luxuriated in the feel and smell of warm, damp moss against his soles. It was the first time in four years he'd felt it.

CHAPTER
TWENTY-SIX

Phaniik Reis's great hall was packed with high-ranking psatla. Had the crowd been human, the air in the low-ceilinged room would have been unbreathably humid, but there were no men there at all.

Bass recognized Swadeth, Sfel, and several others, but acknowledged none of them, striding directly toward the "head pissant" himself. He carried his air cylinder in one hand, its mask thrown over a shoulder. He was glad he didn't need it. Psatla's airborne words were barely readable with his limited human olfactory sense, and he would need every advantage he could muster. Carefully monitoring his own thoughts, concentrating on plans, possibilities, and potentials, he was confident that his own exudations were the same ones Kstala had sensed—*psalaat*, and thus strength: *gadesh*.

Phaniik Reis shone. His luster was gold, not greenish brass. Had he once been duller and graying around his joints, none would have known it. Swadeth was only slightly less brilliant. The *sfalek-thes*'s three eyes were shifting, moving points of darkness, tiny windows opening on the depths of space.

"I see *Thsaan* Vassily James Cannon," Phaniik Reis declared. His voice was reedy and vague, at odds with his appearance. How old was he? How near to dissolution? That's all I'd need, Bass moaned silently, to get my chance and lose it in another shuffle of *gadesh*. Quickly, he suppressed all negative thought. Possibility . . . potential.

"I see the *sfalek-thes* Phaniik Reis," he replied equally formally.

"Echoes of the strange *gadesh* of the *thsaan* dance among my branches." Phaniik Reis got right to the point. "Are they dis-

161

torted reverberations, I ask, or has such strength grown up unknown to me?''

He equates my *gadesh* with strength, Bass thought. That means he knows what's coming. My seed must have been well planted by Kstala and Thesakan. How will he react if I push a little? "For how long does the deep-planted seed remain hidden? How long does it lie dormant among great roots awaiting the winds that shake earth and loosen soil?''

Phaniik Reis's reaction was immediate and decisive. His segmented carapaces clamped shut, rasping, then opened only enough for sibilant words to issue forth. ''All must depart at once, save he who addresses me.'' *Psaalekt* and *pralasekt* alike turned away at once toward the room's many doorways. Only Swadeth hesitated almost imperceptibly.

Bass read Swadeth's agitation from the corner of his eye: twitching limbs and a jerkiness in his usually smooth-flowing motion. Bass grinned. Let him get a taste of *gadesh*, human-style. He swept his budding satisfaction away, rationalizing it as rightness, conviction.

The timber-framed room seemed suddenly large when it was empty. ''How does a human come to speak of *psalaat-thes*, the great path, without fear of his own uprooting? Have you wisdom denied the Reis?'' Bass read suspicion, even threat in the old one's quiet words, but the *sfalek-thes* held himself loosely, and Bass caught glimpses of protruding *ksta* moving, twisting . . .

''The *sfalek-thes* Phaniik Reis was once *ksek-psalaat*,'' Bass replied. ''A trailblazer, an iconoclast—a pathbreaker. Is he too stiff with old bark and heavy-laden with limbs now?'' Question met with question: challenge.

''Before what wind must Reis bow?'' An answer in kind.

''Winds from beyond Phastillan brought new seed to Reis soil. They put forth roots and stem. A follower of old ways might root out *fsa-esefek* weeds. I hope that Phaniik Reis is less bound.''

''How does this weed grow?''

''As mold and fungus unite,'' Bass said, using the names *fsent-si nef* and *esthess*, two psatla-homeworld genera which were symbiotes in a lichenlike manner. ''As grass and legume entwine roots with advantage, so must Reis and humans.''

The *sfalek-thes* shifted to household speech, less flowery and more direct, shallow, but less subject to giving offense. ''Humans speak with equals while bent-in-the-middle. Sitting? Is it your wish?''

''I will sit.'' I've done it! Bass exulted. He's scared, and he's got no answers. He's accepting me as equal. Now I can show him why he needs me, needs every human on Phastillan. Bass sat.

Phaniik Reis, embodiment of his race and his planet, creaked with the unaccustomed flexing of chitin and hunkered down on Bass's level, eye to eye.

"Will the *sfalek-thes* make a spoor for me with his own perceptions?" Bass still spoke in formal mode. Clarity. Confidence.

"I elucidate," sighed Phaniik Reis. "No more human ships come to trade. In long-past this would not have mattered, for psatla settled only where our own skills were enough to change worlds. Phastillan and the Reis *psalaat* are different. Without *fsa-psatla* machines, all will destabilize. This I know."

"You assumed human expansion patterns to be like your own," Bass commented. "But human branches break from their stems and root themselves anew. The human path is neither straight nor consistent. Our evolving took many paths, and did not wholly abandon old ones that no longer served."

"How can that be?" whispered Phaniik Reis.

"First was the scent path, where two-legged apes spoke as did ancestral psatla," Bass explained. "Later, harsh living on treeless grasslands demanded strict measures, and humans came to live always on the edge of the small death, to have desires not only in season, but all the time. We came also to accept the wishes of those who had *gadeh-presh*."

"*Gadeh-presh?* I do not know this. It is *gadesh* through . . . *gadesh*? Through . . . ability?"

"It is a human pheromone that my tongue shapes as 'charisma.' "

"Ah. And that is the second human path?"

"So I believe. The third took sound and made spoken tongues, where things-that-are-not could exist. I call it *gadeh-fesaal*, *gadesh*-like-wind, which fools the eye and ear, as dead leaves flutter like birds and voices howl without mouths."

"Lies? You dignify such as *psalaat*?"

"Lies, yes, but also speculation, the creation of not-events that might be. Therein rests my own *gadesh*: to see what might be, and to prevent it from being."

"There is, too, the machine-path and the counting-of-nothings," the *sfalek-thes* murmured, citing mechanics and mathematics.

"Rather the evolution of minds to conceive them," Bass corrected him, then continued. "The final human path we call culture, or society. It defines 'rules,' paths-followed-without-thinking. Humans depend from many limbs on the tree of culture, each hand grasping twigs and branchlets according to individual reach and circumstance, no two people in like manner. The limbs of culture are religion, law, custom, ethics, economics . . . they are many.''

''And humans follow all those paths, at once?''

''Culture is human *psalaat-thes*,'' Bass confirmed, ''but it is not strong. The older paths arise again and again, and override *psalaat-thes*. Leaders arise whose *gadeh-presh*, whose charisma, creates destruction and death. There have been many such. Hitler, Timur the Lame, Temujin, Baku Khan . . . men with no *psalaat* save conquest. Whole civilizations fell before them.''

''Why was it so? Was *psalaat-thes* so weak?''

''The power of such men, though they may be wise, foolish, or insane, is learned-in-*ksta*. Culture is learned-in-one-life.'' Bass hesitated, not sure the *sfalek-thes* understood. His eyes never left Phaniik Reis as he sought some sign, however ambiguous, of the impact of his words.

''*Gadeh-presh* is . . . genetic,'' said Phaniik Reis, finally. ''Culture is only-now, and thus weak.''

''Exactly so,'' Bass agreed. ''And my *psalaat* must destroy both.''

''Then humans must return to the root of their being,'' Phaniik Reis decreed. ''And *psalaat-thes* will make them . . . psatla. There will be no more humans, if your path is chosen.''

The words brought a chill, and Bass's skin tightened. But though coldly spoken in sibilant psatla tones, they were no more than the truth, no more than necessity as Bass saw it. Humans would not, in his *psalaat*, be truly human, ever again.

''Chaos,'' Phaniik Reis said, returning to their earlier talk, ''is the destruction of culture-*psalaat* by older paths emerging. I taste the sourness of them in all humans except you. Your *psalaat* will change those oldest paths, but that is for later. Chaos is now. What does the *gadeh-fesaal* of the computer say?''

''Conflicting interests have been generated,'' Bass went on, relaxing slightly. ''Whole paths are abandoned, and Phastillan lies on an abandoned human path. Machinery will wear out, stockpiles will diminish, and the parts of Phastillan you have made proper for psatla are not yet stable. Your control requires machines to manipulate current and storm, or Phastillan will revert and psatla will die.''

Bass's words were hard. Through gaps in his chitin caused by the psatla's unnatural posture, Bass saw the tug and pull of snakelike *ksta*: a visible analogy of the "internal struggle" a human might experience when faced with only undesirable options.

The *sfalek-thes* studied his visitor. Did he seek a flaw, a failing—however minor—that would cast doubt, allowing the *thsaan* and its frightening *psalaat* to be dismissed out of hand? Bass tasted deep soil on the air, teeming with life. *Psalaat. Psalaat-thes*, he thought. Then he noticed the trembling among the *sfalek-thes*'s least tightly bound *ksta*, and knew his error. Deep soil is refuge for such *ksta*. Phaniik Reis holds on by will alone. Time is short.

"Without human tinkerers, *psalaat-thes* is incomplete," Bass pressed, "and Phastillan will die. Your strategy extends *fsa-psatla* utility beyond transportation and simple tools. But you assumed a natural stability that was in truth only a human artifact. My *psalaat* is a path beyond." He attempted to "speak" in true psatla fashion, controlling his thoughts rigorously, dwelling calmly and optimistically upon his future, his path, and the *sfalek-thes*'s place in it. Would his own molecular exudations reach Phaniik Reis? Would he sense them, translate them? "Set your fears for the Reis *psalaat* aside for now," Bass said firmly, confidently. "A solution exists which will permit its continuance, and Reis growth; but you must first understand chaos." Was he going too far? Did he dare talk down to this ruler of a world?

Phaniik Reis revealed nothing. His prevailing scent was mild and sweetly acid like fresh-squeezed sodafruit, bringing a rush of nostalgic memories to Bass's mind. Is is intentional? Is he toying with me? Why? Then he remembered an earlier context for the scent: teaching Kstala to use the computer. Excitement, he'd thought then. Perhaps. Perhaps something else, too.

Unsure of his impact on the *sfalek-thes*, he pressed on. "It is not true chaos, only complexity. You are used to that in organic things, in *psalaat*. Now you must understand what humans call sociodynamics. With information from the data banks I have made analyses and predictions, to reassure you that Phastillan need not die."

The psatla remained still, passive. Finally, he spoke. Ozone and sodafruit wafted on his words. "Teach me," he said.

Over the next several hours, Bass taught. It was a history lesson—human history.

"The seeds of chaos are threefold," Bass told Phaniik Reis. "First, the dense Reef itself; second, the rapidity of human expansion beyond it, into transReef; and last, the very nature of the worlds here.'' There was more, of course, but Phaniik Reis had shown that he understood the human terms, the biological terms of the equation. Those were the critical ones. Those Bass would not speak of again to psatla or human, for his *psalaat-thes* was a new and tender shoot, and it craved obscurity and deep shade while it put its roots down deep. Psatla alone would speak of it, in ways no human could interpret—and psatla would soon be very busy indeed.

The Reef had barred human expansion toward the galactic core, Bass explained. Earthward, humans once claimed only a paltry group of suns, and other sentient races bordered them on all sides. Before the first ship threaded the Reef, human space had been a seedpod ready to explode, and interstellar war threatened. It wasn't relief from population pressure that drew the war god's teeth, but the knowledge that there was indeed a frontier.

''The early colony ships picked rich, fertile worlds. Later arrivals took what they could get, and few prospered. All transReef lacks elements heavier than iron, and the further from the Reef, the worse it gets.'' Phaniik Reis was rigid, intense. ''The less hospitable the worlds, the more dependent they are on trade.'' Bass took a deep breath.

''The scattered traces of radioactives are barely enough to fuel interstellar trade, and the few worlds that have them are living hells, mined by prisoners—exiles. Rebellions have destroyed machinery, even mines. The Earthside corporations that own them cut their losses and left the rebels to starve or make do.'' That, Bass explained, had been the situation a mere decade past. At that time several disparate factors had united to create the chaos Phaniik Reis perceived.

''Most marginal settlements failed, but some refused to die entirely; they've captured ships, and they send them out as pirates. Vikings, they call themselves. They've allied with survivors on the mine worlds to control every fuel source.

''The Panaikos Council once regulated trade and colonization, and Earth's military vessels backed it, but with the Reef passages blockaded, the fleet surrendered when it ran out of fuel, and the council broke up four years ago.

''The mine worlds don't produce much, now that no Earthward manufactured parts get through, and what the rebels inherited is junk. Commerce has stopped, and ships have put into port to stay. No fuel is being traded as far out as Phastillan, so the *Matteo* and the others are stuck.

''And now,'' Bass said, having brought the *sfalek-thes* to the present moment, "there is the future—Phastillan's future, and my *psalaat*."

"Such were Kstala's and Thesakan's promises," Phaniik Reis's whispery voice replied. "That you 'see' through the machines that which is not-yet, but will-be. You claim that sight?"

"Let me show you, *Sfalek-thes*. I will need a terminal. Is there one here?" Bass knew there was: a superb, full-surround holo-vision unit from the *Prince*'s first-class theater, a computer, image processor, and simulator, Captain Folgrin's gift. With his hat, Bass could make Phaniik Reis feel like he was on the bridge of a warship, or show him a strategic view of all transReef space . . . now, or years in the future. He planned to do all that, and more.

At a motion from Phaniik Reis, Bass rose. Outside, the *sfalek-thes* ordered the unit to be brought to his own quarters. Bass studied his host's house as they walked. Where Swadeth's compound and the other *asapht* were mostly wood, blending closely with the surrounding soil, Phaniik Reis's dwelling proclaimed a different attitude: wood vied with uncut stone. Soft moss formed only narrow pathways bordered with gravels and shade-grass. Openings to the outside were veiled by curved passageways and screens of loose-woven vines. The *asaph* stated Phaniik Reis's understanding: it encompassed all of Phastillan.

Bass noted patches of sharp-edged breccia, painful to psatla "feet." Walkers would suffer cuts and stone bruises unless they went around them. Bass made a point of walking directly across, though his feet were bare and his calluses thin. Phaniik Reis couldn't miss his unspoken statement.

The terminal had arrived ahead of them. Bass turned it on and called up graphs, maps, and columns of figures to illustrate the history lesson he'd given. Phaniik Reis—judging by his incisive questions and hisses of surprise as he traced this line or that—understood what he was seeing. Bass's respect for him jumped several notches. Old he might be, but not yet doddering.

Carefully unrolling the hat, Bass settled it on his head. Tiny sparks like miniature stars glittered as he snapped the interface into place. "Now," he said, "knowing the past, we peer into the future."

In the hours that followed, Phaniik Reis, ruler of a world, sat entranced like a child as the bright colors of Bass's *psalaat* danced in the very air about him, sparkling off his golden self. He watched the growth of the bloodred blot of viking conquest, the breaking of the Reef-passage blockade by Earth's forces, and a war of attrition that followed. He saw corebreaker bombs create new belts of asteroids out of viking homeworlds, and saw the beginnings of a revival as the first timid traders ventured outward, still far from the green pinpoint that was Phastillan.

"When will the ships reach us?" Phaniik Reis's tone was flat and breathy.

"At this point," Bass said as the holo-glow faded, "transReef is free of organized threat—but still unpoliced and ungoverned. Beyond 2493, fourteen years from now, the decisions of individual humans and specific worlds will be paramount, and those I can't predict at all."

"Fourteen years is not long. For fourteen years, Phastillan can endure."

"Just so," Bass agreed, "but I suspect that trade with Phastillan won't resume in forty, if at all."

"Then the Reis *psalaat* will not exist. Only humans will survive here. The rain forests will be poor dry sticks and dust." Wafted odors of methane vied with the caustic bite of wood lye, of water and ashes, filling the chamber.

"It need not be so, *Sfalek-thes*. Observe further." Years reeled back. Phastillan glowed emerald green, alone among red viking star clouds, light-centuries from Earthside amber. "It is 2483, four years from now," Bass said. "My *psalaat* grows beyond Phastillan." With a thought, he caused a distant, unnamed star to become a verdant point. "Eden . . . Hope . . . Crowe . . . Novay," he droned as star after star turned the green of Phastillan. "Albriten's World, Potsdam, and Helikon," he continued. "Journey's End. All future homes of the Reis." He stopped for breath, though the shifting greenness continued to expand. "That is my *psalaat*!" He froze the display.

Phaniik Reis writhed, shifting in the grip of great emotion. Chitin plates rubbed and grated like insect song, ringing. "The year is 2489," Bass told him. "Observe further. *Psalaat* grows." Phaniik Reis saw the green of Phastillan sweep over the viking worlds, snuffing them like water over embers. He saw it splash against amber Earthside sands and sweep on by, even trickling down the Reef tunnels until Earth, and the suns around it, were as green as the leaves brushing the *asaph*'s roof. "It is 2590," Bass said. "My *psalaat* is complete."

"I see, but I fail to understand," whispered Phaniik Reis, basking in a brilliant green glow that cascaded off the gold of his carapaces. "I see the green of Reis in every star."

"It can be so." Bass allowed the psatla time to absorb what he saw, to speculate.

"I will assume," Phaniik Reis eventually said, somewhat recovered, "that your *psalaat* can be explained and your claims substantiated, but tomorrow is soon enough for it. Tonight I will stand long in evening rain, and then I will sleep."

"I, too, will sleep well tonight. Is there a place here for me? I dare not return among my own kind."

"Of course. The strange human exchange of *fsa-ksta* would overcome you. Ask in the refectory we passed coming here. You will be guided. But I have one last question." He paused, awaiting Bass's nod. "When you named the worlds where Reis might someday dwell, you did not identify the first of those worlds. Does that one have a name, too?"

"A lovely name, *Sfalek-thes*. That world is called 'Cannon's Orb.' "

CHAPTER
TWENTY-SEVEN

Bass spent the next day closeted with Phaniik Reis. His *psalaat* was exposed for the first time to a critical, acute mind, a mind whose separate *ksta* encompassed a world. This is it! Bass tensed whenever the *sfalek-thes* pored overlong over a datum or chart fearing he had found a fallacy, a fatal error. But each time, Phaniik Reis motioned him to continue.

After a particularly long exposition, Phaniik Reis spoke. "Languages are indeed strange," he said in what Bass interpreted as a pensive manner. "Psatla speak in essences that partake of the substance of reality they represent, and you humans reflect reality with vibrations in air . . . and here, you show me realities-perhaps, written as tiny sparks that glow on a glass screen. This is all quite well, Bass Cannon, but speak to me now in different words. Tell me of pain."

"Of pain, *Sfalek-thes*?"

"Show me the fear, the anger, and the death agonies of those who will be shaped by this new *psalaat-thes*."

Bass was taken aback. *Psalaat-thes*. The "big picture." The numbers were clear and correct. The saving path was narrow. Whatever suffering *psalaat* created was lessened, in the long run, for the greatest number of beings, on Phastillan and beyond. What did Phaniik Reis want?

"Show me you understand the cost of *psalaat-thes*, human. Show me Psatla, and humans, and others yet unmet who will *not* enjoy the new future you foresee." The sibilant voice was harsh with sharp consonants, and the tang of hot iron, blood, and crushed caterpillars was thick in Bass's nostrils.

Show him? But how? The screens showed graphic abstractions, not people or psatla. Given time, Bass could have created pictures of them with the hat, but *psalaat-thes* itself was a sweeping generalization, a statistically significant prediction, not individuals. With a sickness in the pit of his stomach, Bass realized that this was to be Phaniik Reis's true test of his vision. And in that moment, he knew what he had to do.

As if he were at that moment wearing his hat, Bass let his mind expand into the reality that the terminal screen sketched in phosphor symbols. Like a great ship of space, he moved among worlds, seeking. Finding an unnamed world that felt right, he plunged to its surface.

He was no longer Bass Cannon. He was a young girl . . .

Alone, gaunt and spindly from starvation, with only a numb hollow where her stomach had once been, she clung with stick fingers to the chain-link fence that surrounded the abandoned spaceport and gazed with rheumy eyes across its emptiness. It wasn't her first trip to the port. On the days she discovered a nest of fat insects, a cluster of bag-worms, even a steaming heap of animal feces rich in undigested seeds, she used the scant energy she gained from them to crawl from her burrow, to totter through the empty town to that same place by the fence. Someday, someday, she assured herself, her parents would come back for her . . .

He was psatla. His universe was tangible chemistries where light and sound impinged but lightly on perception. His *ksta* sensed the ozone tang of the hand-laser even before they felt its fiery touch. *Ksta* scented burning *ksta*, tasted the agony of crackling flesh, and felt the sudden dissolving of their bonds. He was briefly aware of his mind's fragmentation as chitin fluttered and *ksta* wriggled to the ashy, dead ground. Then, without unified mind, there was no being to regret the passing of the sapience that had been Kafekl, *tsfeneke* of the Ptakekl sept, on the world called Sfontassan.

He was L/Halas Oberst, night-shift foreman in shaft twenty sub A, and he was alone in the dark. Even in the cold depth of sunless, airless rock that was Centaurus Combine Planetoid III, he had enjoyed light-globes and sour, oily pumped-in-air. Even though he was a debt-convict who would never again see Sol's smog-masked glory over the domes of New Mecklenburg, or feel the reassuringly heavy gravity of Mars, at least he had been able to console himself with bright barracks lights, coin-op holoshows, and occasional half-hour trysts with company whores.

Now the conveyor-belt elevators no longer rattled upward, the air grew cold and thin as it leaked out through the cracks in the shattered planetoid, and the darkness was absolute. His bloody hands covered his face, unseen, and for a moment they muffled his sobs. From within the rock, he imagined he could feel the vibration of the last ship leaving, pushing away, and he knew he was going to die. Sobs turned to screams, and muffling fingers turned to claws that raked the skin from his grimy, contorted face.

In a brief return to sanity, minutes or hours later, he only feared he would not die soon enough.

L/Halas Oberst, Kafekl tei Ptakekl, a starved girl whose starved brain remembered no name . . . and others, so many others. Bass's mind swooped like a great hawk over world after world, seeking similar prey. He suffered slow starvation and quicker deaths by gang rape and gun, he felt the despair of those who could not die soon enough . . . and yet, as he alit one final time in the withe and wood chamber of Phaniik Reis, as his reeking sweat cooled upon him, he knew with absolute certainty that he would continue his *psalaat-thes*, for he had seen not only what suffering his path would cause, but the greater agony, too, that would happen on any other path.

"There will be great risk to Phastillan, too," he said when his mind cleared, when the vapors of Oberst's agony and Kafekl's burning *ksta* evaporated from his clothes through porous walls and roof and into the damp coolness beyond. "Phastillan will become well known as a rich gem in this crown of poor, dying stars. Many will covet the prosperity my *psalaat* will bring, but few will have anything to trade for a share in it. I forsee us attacked by desperate forces, and I cannot promise that we will prevail.''

"I would know the worsst and the best of your forssseeing for thiss world," Phaniik Reis hissed.

"At best," Bass replied after much thought, "many strangers will come to Phastillan for refuge or for wealth, and all will not accept *psalaat*, or psatla, or my own human-folk here. Humans will die, and many psatla will take the path through the soil. That will create new awarenesses in place of old, and Phastillan will change greatly.

"At worst, those who come to conquer will shatter Phastillan like a nutshell crushed between stones."

Phaniik Reis whistled—sadly, Bass thought. "At worst, then," the psatla said, "we will die more quickly than without your *psalaat*. That may be opportune. At best, much will change, and this world and many others will flourish."

"It is as you say, *Sfalek-thes*."

They stopped for food. A wooden dipper was brought for Bass, and he shared a common pot with the ruler of the world. They paused again when afternoon rain spattered the boulders outside. Bass threw off his clothing and joined his host, relishing cool drops on his body, a sensual assurance that Phastillan, at least, still lived.

At the end of the longest day of Bass's life, he made his decision, his final commitment. He scrawled a code on a scrap of paper and handed it to the *sfalek-thes*. "This is an override code. With this, nothing in the system can be hidden from you." Bass now had no secrets, no hiding places should things go wrong. It won't matter anyway, he reassured himself. Either he buys my whole package, or I go back to the arctic. I won't see any more psatla dying there than will die here, in a few years. "How long will it be before you decide?"

"How long is a river? How long is a thought, a hope? Is there urgency I have not perceived?"

"To the contrary—my readjustment to my own kind may take several days. Should I continue to postpone it?"

"By no means postpone it. You will not be greatly changed?"

"It won't affect my *psalaat*."

"Go, then. Return in four days."

There were several 'phones in the *asaph*, and a satellite uplink. Bass could call anywhere on the planet. He took a 'phone to the room where he had slept. After much hesitation, several nervously miskeyed numbers, and as many impulsively broken connections, he reached the port office.

"Portmaster. Hang on a minute." Bass waited. He'd never forgotten that voice. In the background was a mélange of tinny music, overloud voices, and the clinking of ice and glasses. "Sorry. Busy night here. Who's this?"

"Ziggy. This's Bass Cannon." Was that his own voice, that flat, psatla hiss? On the other end, there was a long silence.

"Who? Is this a joke? I mean, is it really? I . . . I thought you were . . . up north somewhere . . ."

"Stow it, Ziggy. No games. You know what happened, and so do I. But that's over, now. I don't want revenge, I want answers." Bass's toneless vocalization reflected his ambivalence. Should he hate? He didn't. Should he despise the other man? He felt nothing. But his lack of emotion affected Zig.

"Well, sure . . . I suppose . . . say, are you nearby? We ought to talk about this."

"This? What's 'this'? Forget it, Zig. Your paranoia is pointless. I have no interest in you and your affairs, past or present, and I am not vulnerable to your plots or threats. Just answer my questions without evasion. First, where is Betsy?"

"Last I knew, she was here," Zig answered. "This morning." He sniggered. "Been a long time for you, I suppose." His jocularity fell flat.

"Don't suppose," Bass commanded, still without discernible emotion. "Find her. The *sfalek-thes*'s aircar will be on the main apron at oh-seven-hundred tomorrow. Make sure she's there."

"Ah . . . sure, Bass. Seven Ay Em." Bass knew he would obey.

"One more thing—are the officers of the four ships readily available? Are any of them in the bar?"

"A couple. Off the *Prince*, I think."

"Tell them to notify all the captains there'll be a meeting in the *Prince*'s main dining room in five days, maybe sooner. Phaniik Reis will preside."

"Phaniik Reis himself?" The name-dropping made Ziggy even more obsequious. "Of course, Bass. But what will I tell them? I mean, what's it about? They'll want to know."

"Tell them nothing. Ask nothing. Phaniik Reis will address them. The *Prince*'s main salon is preferred, but any large room will do. Pass the message."

"Uh-huh. I will. I don't understand any of this, though. Like, where you fit in."

"You'll know soon—when everybody does. Get it done." Bass switched off abruptly, before the barkeeper could provoke him. He had not called Ziggy to rehash old grievances. He just didn't know anyone else he could have talked to.

His arrangements anticipated Phaniik Reis's decision, of course, but even if the *sfalek-thes* rejected his plan nothing would be lost. Nor would Ziggy try anything tricky. The man was an opportunist, but he would do nothing unless he knew what he was up against. He hadn't even demanded proof of Bass's authority; the ordering alone had intimidated him. That, and Phaniik Reis's name.

Betsy! Had he been foolish? A woman he hadn't seen in years? One who had pointedly avoided him? Why her—should he have asked for some new girl to "cure" him? Ziggy would be eager to help him regardless, to have a new hold on him. His hands were shaking, he noticed. Betsy.

CHAPTER
TWENTY-EIGHT

She had awaited this moment for years on end, without hope. Hope starves on humdrum fare. She'd clung to a remote, comfortable fantasy. Bass would return: they would meet, wordlessly, and take a long, silent walk; somewhere they'd stop to make love, a long blending of flesh, leading nowhere. Like their last time, but better.

The *asaph* of Phaniik Reis was below. "Andy?" Her voice grated against her own quiet thoughts. The pilot turned his head. "Will you circle awhile—over the ocean? I need time to think."

"Say when, Bet. I'm in no hurry." Wordlessly, his hands moved on the controls. Phastillan's surface tilted, and the *asaph* receded in trackless greenery. Ahead, flat metallic ocean reflected high, gray clouds. She nodded, already lost in thought. Dreams were a product of one mind, not two. Anything goes. They ignored ugly details, impossibilities. They should be left alone: little bright pebbles in a still pool. When you plucked them into the air, they dried to dull stones. Already, her dream was faded: he should have come to her, not sent for her like some busy official calling out for sandwiches.

She was afraid it would be no good, that no trace of her dream would remain. She wanted him. She wanted more than Phastillan would let her have: love, security, long days and years . . . his children. Afraid, convinced that it could never be, she constructed a whore's defense: he just needs a lay to get straightened out, and I'm the only one he knows, the only bottle in the first-aid kit with a familiar brand name.

He probably doesn't know he owes me, she thought. Thesakan was exiled for a while, but he probably didn't see Bass. They wouldn't have talked, anyway. Even if he knows I saved his life, he'll just pay me off in my own favorite coin. A good three-day rut. And, love or not, I'll take his payment. After all, he's been out there almost forever . . . Her thoughts betrayed her. Electricity sparked in her groin, coursed up her belly. Treacherous nipples hardened and her shirt's fabric scraped them like sandpaper. She hated the unbidden wetness between her thighs, the saltier moisture that blurred her vision. Fingernails cut into her palms. Pain staved off desire. He was still miles away. Her present enemy was only Pavlovian reflex, Phastillan's price.

Does he still hate me for that first time? Will he laugh when he's had me, then throw me away? Ugly fantasies! Fear feeds on non-knowledge. It only gets worse while I stall . . . "Andy? Let's go. I'll never be readier than I am." Andy's sweet, she thought. He knows when to be quiet. The 'car swung about, tilting the ocean as it banked. Ahead, green forest spread beyond brown, rocky coast.

Bass awakened before dawn and waited. When the aircar sank out of mauve and old-rose clouds, he was masked, standing on the apron. He'd bathed thoroughly. Biochemical stimulation would be put off for a while; he needed time. He needed to talk with Betsy before talk became impossible. But would she come? Would the 'car be empty? Skids rasped on rough concrete. Glassine canopies slid up and outward, and maroon doors opened down, forming a ladder.

Betsy climbed down gracefully. Bass followed her round back-

side with avid eyes. When she turned to face him, her own eyes
were guarded, fearful, only partly because she could read nothing
in the glazed windows of his mask.

"Hi, Bet. The years have been good to you." How inane! I
plan everything else. I should have planned something, anything,
to say. He kept hands at his sides. Even in a ship-type jumpsuit,
he could tell she'd changed little, even improved. Her face is still
unlined, he noted. She's only a little plump. Voluptuous. Bass
noted her narrow waist beneath the tightly cinched canvas belt,
her fine-boned ankles and wrists, her sleek healthiness. His bitter
false memories evaporated.

"Hi, Bass." Her voice was tremulous. "I can't see you behind
that mask."

"Yeah. Sorry. I'm a six-monther again—but I have to talk to
you! Can you put up with the mask? Do you mind?"

He's as nervous as I am, she was shocked to discover. Even
muffled by the ungainly mask, she had heard his voice break. "I
don't know," she said. "Ask me later. Where shall we go?"

"Over there. That rise with the tree." Bass had picked the spot
with care. Forest and *asaph* lay on one side. Mossy excrudes-
cences of bedrock on the other channeled the breeze like a funnel.
Side by side on the branch that stretched like a park bench, the
wind would carry betraying pheromones away.

Once they were seated, a prudent three feet between them,
Bass spoke first. "Something happened between you and me,
Bet, something alien chemistry can't explain. We both knew
it, and I guess it scared you off, so you hid from me. Tell me
what happened?"

Her face twisted, an expression he couldn't read. "Hide from
you? I didn't hide. I asked about you. I wanted to see you again,
but Ziggy told me you wanted Sorayan. He tricked me." It's true,
she told herself. But not the whole truth. "I suppose I let him do
it. I was bitter. I had a glimpse of something I wanted, and couldn't
have. I still can't." She shrugged. "Phastillan is no place for
lovers, just one-night stands. Besides, you were going home, remember? Do you think I could have gone with you? To Cannon's
Orb? Can you see me sitting in your church every Sunday? Chat-
ting with all the good little housewives?"

"You didn't give me a chance, did you? Couldn't we have
talked? We'd have found out what Zig was doing. And we're not
stupid. We could have worked something out. Damn it, we had
something! Don't tell me you didn't feel it."

"I won't lie to you. I did. I suppose I fell in love with you.

That's what they call it, anyway—I wouldn't know. But it couldn't have worked.''

"How do you know? If you don't care anymore, why did you come, today?''

"Bass, you're sweet,'' she said sadly, shaking her head. "You're older now, but you're still innocent. I'm sorry if this hurts you, but I'm here because Ziggy ordered me to—he thinks you're going to have him shipped off to the pole. I'm a bribe. Are you that powerful all of a sudden? Never mind! It doesn't matter.''

Bass said nothing. It hurt. He hadn't thought she would have come unless she wanted to. He hadn't understood Zig's part in it. A pimp. Her owner, not just the bookkeeper. A slimy pimp. She was right. He was still innocent, and a fool.

Still, he wanted to hear everything she had to say. Why? He wanted to know how to convince her to stay. On the other hand, maybe she could convince him his fantasies were the daydreams of a man too long alone. She was helping him right along with that. And she hadn't finished.

"You already know the other reason I'm here,'' she said tonelessly. "I'm an addict. All Zig had to do was tell me how long you'd been out . . . and here I am.'' She shook her head abruptly, bodily denying her words, motion turned graceful by the floating wave of her silky, fresh-washed hair. "You'd think with a thousand new people on Phastillan I'd be the happiest tart in the galaxy, wouldn't you?'' She spat the question defiantly, a glove at his feet. "Five hundred fresh males to solve li'l Bet's problem? But they all huddle on the *Prince*. Most never even see pissants. It's a real system. Shall I tell you about it?''

"If you wish.'' Why is she telling me all this? To turn me away? Or is she testing me, seeing if I can look beyond all these sordid details? "I want to hear whatever you want to say.''

She nodded. Her hair fell around her face, obscuring it. "When a man leaves the *Prince* they won't let him back in until he's been screwed. If he's married, they send his wife out, otherwise they send one of us. They avoid going out. Why shouldn't they? The pissants send them food, and the ship can run forever, just lights and ventilation. The competition's fierce. I was lucky you asked for me, you know? It wasn't my turn,'' she spat, glaring defiantly. "So if you've got a place, let's go. Otherwise I'll yank that mask off right here.''

"Just a few minutes, okay? I've still got something to say. Something I've had years to think about. You can wait ten minutes.''

She nodded, apathetic now. Bass wondered if her mercurial temperament, her jolting mood shifts, were hers alone or part of Phastillan's effects.

Drawing a deep breath to marshal his thoughts wasn't easy in the restricting mask. He wanted to speak convincingly, ignoring what she'd said to push him away. "Don't decide I'm crazy until I finish, all right? Hear me out?" Again she nodded, hiding her expression behind a haze of sunlit hair. "I'm in love with you. No—don't say anything. You promised. It's not just sex. I've gone for years without that, without even thinking about it. But I still thought of you all the time. Maybe there's nothing left between us, but I think there is. I think you do, too.

"You've wasted a lot of time whipping yourself for being who you are, but it doesn't have to be that way. You've made hard choices, like staying here on Phastillan, and did the best you could with what you were dealt. That's more than most people do. But there's one thing you haven't really tried." After several seconds' motionless silence, he realized that she wasn't going to respond. "Me. That's what I want you to try. Living with me, eating and sleeping with me. Loving me. For however long it takes to know if it's going to work."

He could see by the set of her shoulders that she was ready to tell him it wouldn't work. But she kept her promise to let him have his say. Brushing her hair back from her face, she silently raised her eyes to his.

"I don't mean just shacking up in Port," he said. "I want you to be my woman in every way, my partner and confidante—my wife. So take your time thinking about it . . . and don't say no just because you're afraid it won't work, not if you want it to." Watching low, distant clouds build up for evening rain, he gathered his thoughts, mastering the tension that threatened to overcome his resolve. Should he tell her how his vision would change Phastillan, how much different everything would be? He wanted to reassure her, but he wasn't selling *psalaat*, just himself. She still watched him expectantly, knowing he wasn't finished. A little hint wouldn't hurt, he decided. "Phastillan is going to change. It's going to be easier for oddballs and outcasts like us. Humans are going to spread all over the planet, working with psatla—even the refugees holed up on the *Prince*. It won't be so hard on you. You won't be humiliated, ever."

Seeing her eyes flash with angry denial, he spoke quickly. "Don't tell me you don't feel that—not under the 'system' you just told me about. Maybe it wasn't that way before." The fire he'd kindled died, and she listened passively. "I . . . I don't want your promise to be faithful. I won't promise either. Sex on Phastillan is always going to be potluck. We can be together when . . . when it's right . . . but it won't always happen that way." He was finished. Betsy didn't say no. She didn't say anything, just looked at him, unblinking. Her eyes glistened with tears, but none fell.

When she did speak, her voice was emotionless. "I don't know what you have planned for Phastillan. I know you're suddenly a powerful man, even among psatla, so I'll just accept that you know what you're talking about—only about the changes, I mean." For the first time, he saw her smile. It was a child's prankish grin, but her eyes still glittered like polished metal. "I haven't thought of marriage since . . . I suppose my ex is dead of old age by now. I suppose you have it all figured out how things will work for us?"

Bass didn't let her constantly shifting attitudes throw him off. "I'll be working among psatla. I want to build a place—I want us to build it. Somewhere away from everyone, where we can meet. Between times, we'll be on our own. We'll have to, otherwise . . . there won't be any 'magic.' "

"I can't believe this!" She laughed harshly. "You know it's crazy, don't you?" She sat with her legs apart, elbows on thighs and hands swinging randomly, rhythmlessly. Again, her hair hid her eyes. "How could it work? You're obviously on your way up. How will it look—me, I mean. Your wife? They'd laugh. You'd get nowhere with any of the humans. My God, I've slept with most of them!"

"That will change," he said confidently. "They'll do exactly as I wish. I'll tame them."

"Humans can't be regulated like that, Bass. We're not wild animals."

"That's my point. We're domesticated. Sentients domesticate themselves. All our laws and morals regulate our drives. We'll adapt to Phastillan the same way we always have, by adjusting them to fit the new conditions. We're stuck here, so we have to. Besides," he said in a faraway tone, so softly she could hardly make out the words, "the psatla will help, if . . . But that's premature. I'll be able to tell you more later."

"Can't we just go on the way we are? The refugees keeping 'normal,' while the rest of us work for the psatla?"

"It won't work. By the time things settle down out there," he gestured skyward, "the Reis will be dead and the humans who still survive will be living on seaweed. We need the psatla to keep up the planet, and they need us to fix what breaks. Since the ship people won't come out on their own, I'll force them—as soon as I'm 'cured.' "

"And that's where I fit in, huh?" She shook her head, grimacing. She'd been weak for a few minutes, letting herself believe she could be happy, ordinary, and normal. Bass painted a pretty picture—just what she wanted to see. But this is Phastillan, she reminded herself, and I'm a whore. "Look, let's just get down to business. You're here, I'm here, so we'll take that mask off, and when you're normal again, you can change the world and forget about me until next time. Okay?"

"No! Not okay. Oh, I'll take off the mask. We'll both go nuts for a while. And then we'll separate, but I won't let you hide from me again. There won't be any Saturday nights—with Sorayan or anyone else. And I'm going to keep the pressure on until you stop being afraid of caring about anything."

"No matter what I want?" She spoke angrily. "Even if I hate you for it?"

"Will you hate me?"

"I don't know. I'm afraid of you. Afraid of being hurt. If I let myself care about you . . . love you . . ." She stumbled over the words, but her eyes met his steadily. ". . . if it doesn't work out, I don't think I'll want to live at all."

"I'm afraid, too," he admitted quietly. "For both of us. But if we don't try, we're already dead inside, aren't we?" He took her hand in his gloved one. "Let's go inside. I'm running out of air for this thing."

CHAPTER
TWENTY-NINE

Betsy sent him on ahead. "I have to get some things from the 'car," she said. "No—you go on in, and I'll find you. Psatla will guide me. Go."

Odors assaulted his nostrils: psatla cooking smells, overtones of spices he couldn't identify. Cuisine varied from one *asaph* to another. A faint perfume wafted past his door, evoking memories of a long-ago night at Phastillan port. Betsy? Had she come? Then where was she? He was hypernaturally aware of his sensation. His heart beat slowly; his breathing was smooth; the faint roar of his blood ebbed and flowed regularly, leaving no tingling tide-rush in his hands and feet. His body knew Betsy was nowhere about.

Outside, all was tranquil beneath an indistinct glow of cloud-hazed stars. He sat on the edge of his mossy bed to wait, refusing to go out, to hunt her down. It hurt, that she had said nothing about leaving. He was convinced that she was gone. Not that he didn't understand. He did. She was afraid of another failure, another hurt. Afraid of admitting what she really wanted, because if she did and then it didn't work, she wouldn't be able to go back to lying to herself anymore, to say, "I didn't want it anyway." She would have to live with it. I could have her found, Bass thought, have her brought back here—even dragged back. Phaniik Reis would see to it, if I asked. But what good would it be, then? I'd be as alone in her unwilling presence as I am now. Alone! God, I'm tired of being alone.

Eventually he settled down more comfortably. If she came back, it had to be her own decision, her risk. He slept. Later, he got up to undress, tossing his clothing in a heap beside the bed.

He'd been dreaming that Betsy had come. Then, when he opened his eyes, he still saw her silhouette obscuring the starlight. The sky beyond was clear. The faint rasp of cloth against skin had awakened him to a dream become real.

He steadied himself for the assault on his senses that their interacting presences would engender. She stood only a step from him, turned slightly away as she undressed. When her heavy belt clunked on the floor, she stiffened, listening for changes in his breathing, then unbuttoned her shirt and let it fall. Bass watched from half-closed eyes.

Her skin was as smooth as he remembered it, unpebbled by chill in the warm coastal night. He realized that he should be insane with desire. He wasn't. He watched her, appreciated her, but still his heart beat slowly, his breath came and went in silence.

As he watched her free her breasts from the bra's confinement, as she slid her thumbs inside the waistband of flimsy panties and slid them down over her full buttocks and legs, he felt a vague warmth in his groin. A strange, almost forgotten sensation: he was becoming aroused. Would it begin now?

Motionless, he watched with the intensity of a man who knew he would soon be blind, absorbing details and hoarding them against the long night ahead: the dimples over her buttocks were deep and symmetrical; a slight crease marked the meeting of roundnesses at the backs of her thighs; as she straightened up, the backs of her knees were smooth-corded, white. Her belly smoothed as she stood upright, without flattening completely away. He yearned to reach for her, to run his hands along her sides and press himself against her, but he was loath to break the quiet spell that enfolded him.

Undressed, she ran her hands over her breasts and belly—as he wanted to do—then stroked her hips, smoothing invisible wrinkles left by her fallen clothing. She quietly pulled back the coverlet and slipped in beside him. Her skin was cool and she smelled of fresh violets and springwater. His hands sought her, and they came together at last, with no room between them for doubt or fears.

Sunlight spread green-gold brilliance across their shared pillow and Betsy's hair sparkled like the stars of the galaxy's core. Her head was cradled on his shoulder. "Where did you go?" he murmured. "I thought you'd run away."

"I did. I went to the landing apron, but Andy—the pilot—had already left. The aircar was gone."

"But you were gone almost all night . . ."

"I took a walk, and I got turned around in the dark. I guess I hadn't noticed where I was going, and psatla don't make trails. I really was lost." He felt, rather than saw, her shrug. "I suppose I could have yelled for help, or climbed a tree or something, but I still needed to think about what you'd said."

"Did you sleep? Out there?"

She giggled. "Of course I did. I sleep out on the job, anyway. There're always dry spots, even when it rains."

"And you did think about us, about what I said?"

The question deserved no answer. She snuggled closer. His eyes meditatively swept the ceiling, as if he beheld some magnificent scene drawn in leaf-dappled, rough-split wood. "I can hardly believe we're on Phastillan," she murmured. "It was all us, wasn't it? Not pheromones."

"It was a gift," he said. "We're lucky. It probably won't happen again." He didn't elaborate, and he was glad she didn't ask what he meant. It had only just become clear to him. *Psalaat.* Psatla control of human lives, going far beyond what anyone believed possible . . . A gift, and a terrifying threat, if what he'd begun to suspect was true—if psatla were capable of modifying human genetic codes, then whether or not they actually did wouldn't matter. Risk and potential alike would increase manyfold. If Betsy figured it out, too, and talked with others, there would be riots among the refugees, psatla would be slaughtered wholesale by enraged humans, and afterward . . . a vision enveloped him, a vista of bleak worlds, of humans herded into alien ghettos, of Phastillan barren and dead . . . she mustn't know. It was *psalaat.*

Minutes later, seeing she was still awake and watching him, he said, "That first time, when I was new here—something happened for you too, didn't it? It was special, not just business as usual."

"Very special," she replied in a childlike voice. "And I don't want to talk about it. Too special. When you never came back, I thought I'd die. I wanted to. I vowed I'd never be hurt like that again."

"Damn Ziggy, anyway! Even exile would have been tolerable if I'd known you were waiting for me."

"You really think so?" Her eyes glittered mischievously.

"Hmmh. I don't know. Probably harder, actually."

"Still, you wouldn't have been exiled at all, but for him."

"I thought that, too, for a while. But I would have. It was *gadesh*—Swadeth and Phaniik Reis would have found another way to isolate me. They had plans within plans . . ."

"Do you hate them?"

"I feel sorry for them. They took a big risk, even though Swadeth knew more about me, from the start, than I knew about myself. My exile was his gamble: that I could become enough of a psatla to put *psalaat* ahead of my human desires. For his own scheme to succeed, I had to put it ahead of my desire for you, my family, the Orb, everything, or they'd have lost their last chance for Phastillan to live."

He saw her puzzled look. "It took exile to bring out abilities only Swadeth knew I had. I might have gone through life not knowing my own potential, and even if I had, it would have taken too long to learn what I am, with a kinder teacher."

Betsy didn't ask what he meant, what special aptitudes he had. There would be opportunity to ask questions later. Years of opportunity, she hoped, though fear still nagged her. "Go on," she prodded him.

"Swadeth had less choice than I did. He knew he needed some-one to bridge the psatla-human gap, but he also knew that if I succeeded, if I succeed from now on, then everyone—psatla and human—will be subject to my *psalaat*. I'm a juggernaut. They started me rolling, now all they can do is watch, and stay out of my way."

CHAPTER
THIRTY

Phaniik Reis gave Bass carte blanche, accepting his *psalaat*: humans became psatla, by definition, when Bass proved he could "speak." His odd dreams of times past? *Ksta*, Phaniik Reis decided, a biochemical mechanism to bridge the gap of generations. So humans were to be cherished, manipulated and used only for the greater good of both species. It was a qualitative jump in psatla perception of their universe. They were no longer alone.

Sfalek Bass, hardly less than coequal with Phaniik Reis himself, would be the chief advocate for his race's colony and, by extension, for all humankind. At this point his *gadesh* was assumed. Psatla would accept him because Phaniik Reis did, though uneasily. Human acceptance would be Bass's problem.

Psatla tradition demanded that the incumbent *sfalek*, Khestaat, be ousted or "kicked upstairs," but in this case he would continue his duties, while Bass administered human affairs.

Until now, no human had been other than *thsaan*, an adjunct without a real place in the Reis system. Now, suddenly, all humans were part of that system, on their own unique branch. Integration of the working humans who had been on Phastillan for years would have been strain enough; integrating what seemed to psatla a vast number of refugees was almost inconceivable. Until now, they had been parasites, temporary residents who hoped they would soon depart. Whether the new system worked would depend on the ability of unorganized, despondent, and ineffectual humans to form a functioning assembly psatla could identify with.

That was what Bass told the four captains and their officers in the *Prince*'s elegant salon, now tatty with wear and planetside grime. Despite his earlier promise, Phaniik Reis was not present, nor was he needed. Bass's acceptance by psatla, and his aura of *gadesh*, sensed by all, was enough. His introductory remarks stressed the down-to-earth requirements of survival, of adaptation. He built up their importance to the planet, to their fellow humans, and to him. It surprised him that he succeeded so well. They listened. They accepted him, his authority, and the skeletal *psalaat* he presented.

"You men, along with Madame Captain Van Voort and your crews, are the only people on this planet with military training," he said in summation. "You are the only ones with concrete personnel-handling skills, as valuable now as your ship-handling ones will be later on. You have all seen my projections—worst case and best. Now, are you with me?

Fat Jacomo Pirel, *Matteo d'Ajoba*'s first officer, bobbed his head immediately. *Enzo Vinella*'s Ma'mut al-Jebel's eyes darted around the room, assessing the others. Alta Van Voort remained expressionless. Only Ade Folgrin of the High Line *Prince* spoke, looking neither right nor left.

"I am in a different situation than are the rest of you," Folgrin stated. "Captain Pirel, you own your vessel and answer to no one. Ma'mut, you hold shares in *Vinella* and your men will support you. You, Madame Captain, have an owner with whom to confer. I represent an Earthside corporation, and though my masters have surely written off me and the *Prince*, they still command my loyalty. Unless the *Prince* is confiscated by whatever passes for a government here on Phastillan, I can offer nothing but verbal support. I'm sorry."

"Assuming such confiscation," Bass asked, "how would you react to it?"

Folgrin shrugged his bony shoulders. "I would remain with my ship unless it's used in a way I can't condone—piracy, for example."

"As an alternative," Bass inquired, "are you empowered to contract the use of the *Prince*?"

"The *Prince* is a luxury passenger vessel. I can justify wear and tear by her present occupants on humane grounds, but your

plan calls for no liners. I couldn't agree to her modification for
other purposes. Not, that is, as a corporate representative."

Bass nodded. "Very well, Captain. I confiscate the High Line
Prince in the name of the Reis sept and the *sfalek-thes* Phaniik
Reis. We'll draw up suitable papers shortly."

Folgrin smiled ruefully. He had expected no less, but had been
unprepared for Bass's speedy decision.

"I was raised on a contract world," Bass continued, "and I
place great value on formal agreement between people. Will you—
will all of you—contract yourselves, and your ships, under Panaikos Council standard contracts?"

Al-Jebel spoke up. "The council is defunct. What good is a
contract without enforcement?"

"As good as any contract has ever been," Bass said, resolving
to watch him carefully. "My word and yours. How many disputes
ever reached the council, anyway? Out mutual intent is enough."

"Then draw one up," Jacomo Pirel said, grinning, "and I'll
sign. Bear in mind my desire to someday become a wealthy re-
tiree."

"As prime contractors with me," Bass said with a matching
smile, "you'll each have a substantial claim on my own wealth,
with Reis backing. It will be a respectable sum if—when—we
succeed. Madame Captain? You look doubtful."

"I shouldn't be here at all," she said with a dejected shake of
her head. "My husband and I only pilot the *Reef Runner*.
Dingenes de Witte should speak for himself."

Bass shook his head. "Owner de Witte is an overaged, pam-
pered schoolboy. For carrying contraband missiles to sell to vikings, I should have him hanged. For botching the sale, his family
should disown him. I won't contract with him. Buy the ship from
him."

"We haven't the money." Her plain, cleanly chiseled face
twisted. "It was my father's ship until de Witte's family drove
him into bankruptcy. All we could hold were our pilots' berths."

Bass met her objection. "The only currency of value is heavy
metal," he replied, "and the Reis sept will soon control that
market. Push him to sell. Offer him thirty thousand troy ounces
of gold, in ten annual payments. Phastillan will back you."

"Is there that much gold in all transReef?" She was amazed.
Thirty thousand troy ounces. Was that twelve or sixteen to the
pound? Even using the smaller figure, she calculated quickly, it
would be a ton and a quarter. How big was a ton of gold?

"He can have three thousand ounces when he signs. Reregister the ship in your name, contracted to me."

"Is it legal? The gold?"

"It's Reis gold. There is no ownership among psatla, only *gadesh*, which gives control. Control I currently enjoy."

"I'll see what can be arranged," she said. Was that a gleam in her eye, or a tear?

The shifty-eyed Ma'mut agreed that a contract was possible provided Bass supplied fuel metals to get *Vinella* under way. Bass resolved to dole fuel sparingly to Ma'mut's ship, else the *Vinella* would never be seen again. Such crew-shared ships were on the edge between commerce and piracy in the best of times and, though her papers seemed in order, Bass had found no past references to the *Vinella* anywhere. He resolved also to keep Ma'mut from becoming familiar with his plans for defending Phastillan.

Nevertheless, he would soon have his cadre. Folgrin was quiet, competent, capable of handling responsibility, and almost painfully honest, though inflexible.

Jacomo Pirel, fat and slow-moving, was bright, not averse to swift decisions, and had held legitimate rank in the Earthside space forces only twenty years in his subjective past.

Alta Van Voort seemed willing enough, with the promise of owning her ship, but she was a yacht pilot who took, not gave, orders. Never mind. He had not yet met Van Voort's husband, Mark.

He dismissed al-Jebel and Van Voort to make their arrangements, and held the other two on the pretext of finalizing contracts with them. "We have more important business than paperwork," he told them. "Captain Folgrin, you are appointed 'mayor' of Phastillan's human population. You have a head start, as ninety percent of them shipped on the *Prince*. Among them are engineers whose skills are unused. Outside are psatla who have methods of refining low-grade ores using gene-tailored bacteria. I want you to get the two groups together." His words came forth with staccato intensity. They were old words, thought out months, even years, in advance.

"You'll have to work with *Pralasek-thes* Phthaas. Are you familiar with psatla hierarchies? Good. You two will need rank. You, Ade, are *sfalek-ni*. You'll be able to command all but three psatla—Khestaat, Phaniik Reis himself, and my former boss, Swadeth. I suggest you work closely with Swadeth. He's your counterpart among psatla. But tread lightly. *Sfalek-ni* is an exalted title, one you'll have to work hard to justify."

"If you doubt me, perhaps a lesser one would suffice," Folgrin said without heat.

"I have no doubts. I merely caution that psatla will be observant. And you must be titled—that's part of our adaptation to our sharers-of-life." Folgrin only nodded at the psatla term, accepting his commission with immovable calm.

"Jacomo," Bass said, turning abruptly, "you are *pralasekthes*. You will nominally answer to Ade, but your responsibility is military. When rumor spreads that we're producing radioactives, we'll become a prime target, so I've outlined defenses including satellites and ships armed with *Reef Runner*'s missiles."

Before Pirel could comment, Bass raised a hand to forestall him. "It's strictly a concept—modify it, even junk it if you've a better one. And a militia of some kind . . . see what you can come up with."

Both men were eager to start. Life in space was monotonous, but it was familiar and purposeful. On Phastillan, they had suffered boredom of a different kind. Folgrin escorted Bass through his enormous ship to the lock where an aircar waited. Bass noted a pungency even in the immaculately maintained service corridors: food, both cooking and spoiled; feces and sweat; and there were other, subtler essences, too—fear and despair. The continuing occupancy of the refugees couldn't continue much longer.

Bass's long weekend with Betsy had sated him emotionally and physically. They had enjoyed heightened sexuality without the rutting compulsion of the syndrome. He treasured the memory of those five days, knowing they were truly a gift that wouldn't soon be repeated. The rules had been set aside one time, at great risk to *psalaat*. Should the humans, even Betsy—especially Betsy— discover that they were not invariant, there would be hell to pay.

They had lingered two days after Bass became "normal." Even then, their lovemaking had been fulfilling, and they had talked. The years had been kind to Betsy in some ways. The hurt, the feeling of being dealt a bad hand in life, had receded, leaving only wistful sadness. Even ecstasy wasn't as important to her as it had been.

"How did you get the captains to agree with you?" she asked. "Especially the swarthy one—Ma'mut? I'd have thought he'd hold out for more than a promise of fuel."

"They must have liked the way I smelled, or something,"

Bass told her with a grin. "I have these special pheromones, you see . . ." She took his answer for flippancy. Perhaps it was.

After the meeting with the captains, Bass continued in exceptionally high spirits. *It's going to work*, he told himself. *I'm sure of it now*.

Weeks passed. Bass coopted a room and a terminal in Asaph Phaniikaan. Betsy went about her own business—machinery needed tending and continued to break down.

Folgrin's progress with the refugees only seemed slow. Bass religiously scanned the reports he sent in. One Assan Hasturian emerged as a guiding force—a refugee who only needed a job and an objective to pull him out of withdrawal and chronic depression on the *Prince*. Others followed his lead, and with the return of hope and ambition came conflict. In an altercation between the engineers and *Pralasek-thes* Sfel over the allocation of machinery, the humans called Bass to settle the dispute. He declared Hasturian *pralasek-thes*. Sfel, smelling Hasturian's men's confidence in him, didn't dispute his right to the title—had the matter been referred to Swadeth and Folgrin, Sfel would have lost *gadesh*, and Hasturian would have had to explain himself to nonengineers. The dispute evaporated and a compromise was reached.

Bass seldom interfered in disputes, seldom even voiced an opinion. Both his captains noticed, though, that his silent presence eased strain and diminished contention. "Pheromones," he joked. "Just psatla magic." Of course that was a joke.

There were no social scientists on Phastillan. Humans and psatla had to integrate their efforts on a scale never tried before, with only seat-of-the-pants guidance from Bass. Perhaps it was better that way. Conventional thinking—and conventional ethics—might only slow the plunge into social chaos that awaited the humans. It hadn't happened yet. Ade coddled the engineers, allowing them to return to the *Prince* between jobs and to "take their medicine" as the price of readmittance. Something would have to be done about that . . .

Asaph Swadethan had not changed occupants as Bass had once expected. Swadeth had never relinquished it. Bass postponed visiting several times, wanting to be in control when he met Swadeth again, to know that his hostility toward the *sfalek-ni* had died. He had been manipulated, but as his own *psalaat* grew, so did his sympathy for his manipulator. He now understood the coldness of *psalaat*.

The day he chose was stormy and uncommonly cold. The recent closing of a causeway between northern islands now diverted cold currents away from a headland that the psatla coveted, and the clammy days were a temporary result of shifting equilibrium. He flew Phaniik Reis's Stollivant himself, welcoming the turbulence that diverted his thoughts from his impending confrontation.

He entered by the same portal as that first time, six years earlier. His former mentor seemed happy to see him. "You have learned well, *Sfalek* Bass. I am well credited by your strength and your *psalaat*. In psatla, one cannot say 'I am proud of you,' but the concept is apt for expressing my pleasure in your vast *gadesh*. For all your protestations, you have learned it well."

"English expresses my feelings best, too, Swadeth. I'm grateful for your harsh teaching—though once I felt betrayed. Perhaps someday our mutual understanding will be shared by our races.

"In fact," Bass said portentously, "that is why I am here."

Swadeth's posture, his loose carapace, betokened his receptivity. His *ksta*, surfaces exposed, "listened" to what Bass "said." He could almost feel their tiny, vestigial eyes upon him. Earthy fragrances rose from Swadeth.

"I want to start a school," Bass told him. "Humans and psatla must learn together, and I can't wait for it to happen on its own. My people must learn *gadesh*—unselfish service and the effort which rewards itself." Bass purposefully divided the *gadesh*-concept, though it would sound odd to Swadeth. "At the same time, if the Reis are to venture among men, on human worlds, they must learn pride and conscience, loyalty and reciprocity—and above all, tact."

"Those words are without meaning among humans," Swadeth observed. "What is the point?"

"You're a cynic, Swadeth. Humans know what such words mean." He grinned. "Perhaps you'll be able to teach them to mean them. But lessons need not begin with such things. If they can learn the Reis hierarchy and their places in it, and the rudiments of *psalaat*, I'd consider it a good beginning. For psatla . . . what must they understand to work alongside men? I'll let you decide that."

Bass smelled pepper so pure and strong that he felt like sneezing. He had a rudimentary understanding of the psatla scent vocabulary, but the distinct fresh-ground-pepper aroma was entirely new.

"You don't want to start a school, Bass," Swadeth said, with an odd body tremor. The flat statement brought Bass up short.

"What?" he blurted, then more quietly: "Explain, please."

As yet another fit of trembling rattled Swadeth's chitin, he said, "You want me to start one. It is your revenge, is it not? For those harsh lessons?"

Psatla did not laugh, but Bass laughed for both of them. When they parted, an hour or so later, he was still laughing inside. Every time he smelled pepper, he would laugh again. Of all the elusive elements that were uniquely human, surely the most alien to psatla was humor. And Swadeth had made a joke.

He reviewed the conclusions he and Swadeth had reached. The school was to be more than a social experiment. Questions raised by Bass's dreams must be explored. *Ksta*, or soul, was too important to be left to human theologians. Psatla must taste human cells, strip them bare and dissect them atom by atom until there was no doubt at all.

Psatla tasters like Kstala would not stop there, Bass knew. Humans, now a branch of psatla, were *psalaat*, environment, and had to be totally understood. *Gadesh* demanded that no secrets remain.

Bass's mind was black as he set the aircar down. He had just sold the entire human race. Knowledge is power. In psatla, a tautology: *gadesh* is *gadesh*. Psatla would care for their human kin just as Bass cared for his fingernails, his hair. He only hoped that, as men learned to be psatla, psatla would learn . . . kindness.

CHAPTER

THIRTY-ONE

Three months after Bass's return from exile, much progress had been made. Bass and Betsy's gentle passion had truly been a gift, a fleeting affair never repeated. That didn't matter. Though Saturday nights with Sorayan had been distasteful medicine endured to mute Phastillan's influence, to preserve a remnant of his humanity, with Betsy he didn't care; it was *their* ardor, *their* need.

Abandoned biorefining ponds were reopened, and the hills above reseeded with voracious bacteria. Precipitates as thick as mud made bright crusts on pond banks. *Bephest*-powered wagons and crude floaters hauled the precious, deadly ores away.

When a pond was cleared, psatla returned to *asapht*, humans to the *Prince* and their rituals of return. Ade Folgrin threw up his hands in despair at his failure to motivate them to vacate the ship. He asked Bass to help.

"Public speaking, Ade? After years in exile, among psatla? I wish my father were here instead."

"Your father was a preacher. Did you hear him speak often?"

"Often enough." Is he still alive? Could he be? "He was impressive. But I've never addressed a crowd. What if I can't?"

"Pretend you're him. You sold your *psalaat* to us, didn't you? They need to be pushed into moving. They're afraid of Phastillan, so maybe a bigger fear will make them move. But you're the *sfalek*," he said with a grin. "I only work here."

As soon as Ade departed, Bass left for Asaph Swadethan, the new school. He had to talk with Swadeth.

The *sfalek-ni* met him outside, in a grove of the oldest trees on Phastillan. The mossy soil was springy and damp; the chatter of *zethalt* leaping from branch to branch overhead was piercing.

"I will come, of course," Swadeth agreed, carapaces spread

192

wide, *ksta* breathing clean forest air, "but you can sway them without help, you know."

"I don't think you have any idea how stubborn they can be. I offer only risk and disruption."

"I know this much, Bass: You must convince yourself. Your words won't move them."

Then he understood. "You expect me to sway a thousand human beings with scent talk? A psatla trick?"

"You influenced Assan Hasturian as well as Sfel—and the ships' captains, too. Look within, Bass."

"But only a few at a time, in closed rooms. Not an open-air meeting with a thousand people who hardly know they have noses!"

"Did your species evolve in closed rooms?"

"My species? Are you saying that scent speech is a human trait? I know I implied that to convert Phaniik Reis, but . . ."

"I did not give it to you. As for the thousand . . . charisma is a spark. Once it is ignited in those close to you, others will carry your flame, your *psalaat*." Then Swadeth closed, contracted. He withdrew without moving away, his chitin plates closing, overlapping like beetles' wings. The hard, bronzed shape before Bass could have been cast in metal. Bass was dismissed. He turned his back on Swadeth. Overhead, the *zethalt* were as noisy as ever.

From a rude podium built close to the *Prince*, Bass surveyed an ocean of bobbing heads, brown and pink faces, some raised to gawk at him, most showing no interest at all. An amateur band, with players and instruments from several homeworlds, kept up a loud, insistent tune until Bass motioned them to stop. The assorted horns tootled to a stop one after the other, in midmeasure. Bass drew a deep breath, and leaned toward the ampliphone.

"You have heard of *psalaat*," he began conversationally. "A plan. Psatla set great store by plans. If an idea is good, they back it. As they support mine." He shook his head, almost sadly. "You weren't consulted. You have no rights here. You are refugees. Not citizens. Not psatla. I hope to change that." Hook their self-interest. Follow my notes until I get used to this. Words aren't the message, only a palatable disguise.

"But how? What is this *psalaat*? Be patient. We—you—are victims of history. In your past are the seeds of your future. TransReef is a frontier. Humans love frontiers, because as long as our horizons are limitless, we can look ever outward and ignore the beasts within ourselves. Once, when there were no new frontiers, we sought solutions to overpopulation, to famine and war, and cures for crime and prejudice. Had we remained trapped Earthside, with the Reef at our backs, we might have exorcised the demons of murder, rape, and conquest . . . the very demons that destroyed your planet, your lives.''

Bass surprised himself. The echoes of his words were full and resonant. His eyes swept over the upturned faces; no eyes were roaming, no attention elsewhere. The spark. Had it caught yet? Were ancient human pheromones being triggered out there? Too soon. Wait and see.

''Humans respond to pressure by moving on. When there is no frontier, we slaughter ourselves instead. Backed against the Reef, we prepared for interspecies war.

''It almost happened. We could never have beaten the coalition of nonhuman races we faced. Our survivors would have been animals in alien zoos. We knew that. Our leaders knew it. But they still led us toward war, and we still followed! Were our ancestors insane? Are we?'' Bass paused. He wasn't out of breath; he hadn't forgotten what came next. It just felt right. The very silence was part of his message. No coughing marred that silence. No one murmured to his neighbor. All eyes met his.

''Were we insane, or victims of our evolution a million years before? Even as we teetered on the brink of extinction, scientists inquired why some men are leaders, no matter where they lead, and why we were trapped in a cycle of production, consumption, and more production that had stripped our homeworld bare in one generation and our offworld colonies in the next.

''Humanity was trapped between self-ignorance and interstellar war. But the discovery of a million empty worlds beyond the Reef changed that. We again followed our ancient, genetic directive: we migrated. We called it a new opportunity, but as a species, we'd lost our chance . . . to evolve.

''We fled the depleted soils of Earth. But these new transReef soils we've rooted in are not the dirt of home. Vital traces are lacking. Our growth is stunted. Colonies flourish as seedlings, then wither and die.'' The echoes of Bass's voice haunted him, old and familiar. He laughed under his breath, turning it into a dry cough. May I present the Reverend John ''Jack'' Cannon, courtesy of his son? Why not? I can do it. All I have to do is to let go, let him take over. All those Sunday mornings . . . Again he addressed the throng, his notes abandoned.

''You know about those missing elements, don't you? That's why you're here. Many of you once mined those fuels, those heavy metals. But there is more to our malaise than deficiencies in our industrial diet. On our outward journey to the stars, we carried all our unexamined pathologies. Those, you know first-hand. Rape. Murder. Torture.'' Between each word he paused, hearing his father's sonorous tones in his own voice.

"We have gone too far, we are spread too thinly. No longer can we gather the brilliant minds and resources for a crash program of cures for our social ills. Between us and success lie centuries of willful ignorance. Pirates. Vikings.

"From pirates and vikings, from starvation on a dying world, there is no rescue. Perhaps it is too late for humanity altogether. The evidence points to that conclusion. My conclusion.'' Bass sipped water grown tepid in his glass. He had brought them to the present, to this moment when all their fears were exposed. Quietly, almost sadly, he continued.

"*Psalaat*. It is a plan, and the planner. Hope and destiny. A psatla word for psatla concepts. There will be more such psatla words, if we survive. Without them, without the words and the psatla themselves, we will die. We'll die on Phastillan, and everywhere transReef. We are new shoots on the human tree, too far from Earth's roots to be fed, too tender to survive the winter of interstellar chaos. Blight is spreading, blight we carry in our very genes, which has waited patiently for this moment when our resistance is down.

"If we die, so will the psatla of Phastillan, for their fate is in our clever hands, tied to our machines. But while our psatla hosts have accepted their dependence on us, we haven't reciprocated. We haven't even acknowledged that our continuing survival rests with them.

"Without the active aid of psatla here and on a thousand other transReef worlds, human civilization will cease to exist. We'll starve, we'll fight, we'll die. How can psatla help us? You'll have to wait for an answer to that. For now, trust me. It is so. Ask yourself instead how we can enlist their aid. What must we do?''

Bass paused to survey his audience, to sense their mood. They were intent, he could tell by their silence. They were afraid. Afraid of more hard times like those they had endured all too recently. Phastillan wasn't much, but it was better than Consolidated #14. He wanted more than their fear. He wanted anger, a surge of raw adrenaline to open them up to him, make them suggestible, make them believe.

" 'What are you?' psatla ask. 'Do you know?' '' He shook his head. "You must first become aware of what you are not.'' His voice rose gradually, phrase by phrase. "Are you masters of a world? No longer! Are you rich? Influential? No! Then what are you?" His voice rang out over their heads. "You're refugees. Rejects! Discarded trash saved from extinction because the *Prince*'s captain thought you might, someday, somehow, be worth something again!" Some cringed, hung their heads in mute admission. Others, he sensed, were hot sparks in the gray, ashen crowd. Sparks, but not yet flame.

Again, he softened his voice. "You must learn what you are not. Not masters of a world, not useful or productive. Can you claim otherwise? You depend on psatla for food, on the *Prince* for shelter, on Phastillan for your very lives. You are beggars and parasites. Look at yourselves."

Bass stepped back from the podium. Muttering blended with weeping. Scattered cries of misery and anger were indistinguishable. Frighten them, then whet their expectations, then cast them down. Bass stood impassively, a silent focus for building rage. They wanted answers, not insults and vague philogophy. Voices rose in confusion and indignation, and transmuted to anger. Who was he, to drag them out to listen to history lessons, to platitudes and insults?

Bass waited. The air reeked. He watched intently, judging their temper, preparing to give them the answers they craved. He raised hands over his shoulders, palms outward. His father's gesture. At first no one noticed, but by one, angry eyes raked over him and the crowd fell silent. With nudges and gestures, like ripples from pebbles thrown into still water, silence spread outward. He lowered his hands. How long had he held them so? His arms felt numb.

"Is that all?" he asked. "After all my sound and fury, all my high-sounding words? That you are helpless in a universe of helplessness? A 'plan' to integrate you with . . . wormbags? Oh, yes, I've heard the term. It's accurate enough, but that's not the point, is it? It's a special kind of word, that isolates the speaker, a word like 'ship-scum,' like 'dreg' or 'reffie.' You know those words. That's what 'native' humans call you."

He raised his hands for silence. It was a long time coming; their anger, so long buried, was not easily stifled again. "What did I tell you only minutes ago?" He was Jack Cannon, gently scolding schoolchildren for inattention: *Who was Joseph? What kind of coat did his father give him? And what did Gautama's sire give? Did you listen? Did you read your lesson?* Aloud, he said, "Without psatla help, we will die. Don't you want to live? To see your children grow up? Your grandchildren?'' The blurred pink-and-tan mass of faces was motionless, rapt. Charisma. I've caught them. Is it only a psatla pheromone, Swadeth's, or my own? No matter. Could Julius Caesar take credit for his glands' exudations? Or Moses? As long as they'll follow me . . .

''Phastillan is a hinge-point of history. I saw that before I set foot here. It is why I am here. Psatla aren't just 'wormbags.' They have a crucial part to play. And you? You aren't just refugees, you know. You are forerunners of a new humanity—pioneers of an age without murder, rape, or genocidal war; a new humanity whose interests will be so totally merged with those of psatla that distinctions between the two species will vanish, will not matter anywhere but in your beds.'' He waited, smiling, until a scattered chuckle rewarded him. ''Of course, change is rarely easy. But we'll survive it.

''You have listened to me. I haven't told you much, not nearly enough, but I'm not accustomed to speaking. Will you listen, with open minds, to someone who can tell you what the future holds?'' He saw their eyes seeking below the podium to see whom he meant. ''Will you listen to my mentor, my trusted friend?'' He sensed curiosity, their uncritical receptiveness. Anger had evaporated. They were his, soft clay in his hands, changing mood as he changed his tone of voice, hanging on his every smile and frown, reflecting him. If he told them it was raining, they would cover their heads.

Commitment, murmured a voice inside. Make them commit themselves. Bring them down to the altar, son. ''Will you listen?'' he asked again, louder than before. Their nods and yeses were tinged with impatience. ''Will you listen?'' he cried. ''Will you trust my teacher as you trust me?'' Louder now, he could hear individual voices. ''Tell me, then! Tell me you'll hear and remember his words!''

The upwelling sound of their commitment pushed at him. Its power frightened him. ''Yes,'' they shouted with a thousand voices. Power. So much power he could make them do anything. ''Yes!'' they roared. What did he want? Husbands would proffer their wives, fathers their daughters. Food? Drink? Their last mouthfuls would be his. I am the alpha male, he thought, the archetypical primate, the warlord. They scent my strength, my conviction, and they follow. No sheep are more easily led.

Bass stepped back from the stand and held out his hand as Swadeth ascended the short ramp. He shifted aside. The psatla grasped the ampliphone in thin, white *ksta*. The silence was dense and viscous.

Psatla seldom wore more than a belt with pouches, or swaddlinglike protection against winter cold, but Swadeth was draped in a toga, an academician's robe. From a distance he was a scholar who had swapped his mortarboard for a bronzed helmet. Swadeth was clever, minimizing visible differences between himself and his audience. "Greetings, future friends. From me, from the *sfalek-thes* Phaniik Reis, and from all psatla." He nodded as he spoke, pinpointing individuals in the crowd, acknowledging them. As a result, everyone near where he looked felt as if he were speaking to them specifically.

"My friend Bass spoke of dependence. I prefer to call it mutuality. You scratch my back, and I will scratch yours—figuratively speaking, of course. We psatla don't itch, thank the stars!" He paused while mild laughter subsided.

"The *sfalek* Bass called you beggars and parasites. Those were harsh words. Too harsh for me. I call you survivors, for you have passed the truest test: you are here, alive.

"You have passed one test, but psatla and humans must, together, pass another. Can we learn to live together? Our survival depends upon it.

"What form will our mutuality take? Who will do what? You humans will get most of the dirty work, I'm afraid—making machinery and running it, building factories and running them. Ships and starships, too—yes, the starlanes will open again. We psatla will help by supplying biorefined ores, by growing your food, for we work best with living things. Is that a reasonable division of labors?"

Bass watched them respond just as they might to a human. Heads nodded, turning to each other, shrugging, murmuring assent. It wasn't loud, but it was clearly positive. Swadeth raised sinuous arms much as Bass had done. "If you wish, papers can be drawn up, a treaty between our races. Psatla won't vote on it—that's not how we resolve things—but we will decide. I can't tell you what that decision will be, because it's as hard for us as for you. We'll have to give up our own cherished independence, and many psatla are afraid to put themselves in human hands. I'm sure you have similar fears.

"Until now, you humans have been the aliens on Phastillan, my planet. Soon, I hope you will be psatla." Uneasy laughter interrupted him. "That sounds funny to you, doesn't it? Try turning it around, then: How easy will it be for you to consider someone like me as a human, and treat me as one?

"This man"—Swadeth gestured toward Bass—"has convinced Phaniik Reis, our leader, that psatla and human can integrate. But we are different, and it won't be easy. Consider this: We psatla manage our world from the lowest bacterium to the highest species, ourselves. Will you permit us to manage you also? To control your exploitive and destructive ways? Can you adapt? Can we trust you to try? Think carefully when you vote. Are you willing to surrender to us just as you surrendered to Captain Folgrin and his crew? Just as we psatla, needing you to build and run the machines that make Phastillan live, surrender to you?"

"Even now, I read your reactions to my words: control, management, surrender. You are afraid. You hate. Yes, hate—ready to spring forth and destroy all of us. If you fear us as aliens who will enslave you then the *psalaat* of Sfalek Bass will fail. If we psatla give reign to our fears that you'll dominate us with your machines and technology, that *psalaat* will fail." Swadeth paused to let his words sink in. "To succeed, we must strive for symbiosis. Psatla must trust, without benefit of understanding. You humans must trust, equally without understanding, that we will cherish you as psatla yourselves.

"Think carefully before you vote. If you can't commit your children and your grandchildren to this mutual course, you will be allowed to leave Phastillan without bitterness or prejudice. A ship will be provided, fueled and stocked, to work out your human destinies as you will. There must be no shadow of coercion or desperation—those of you who stay, who join with us as a new entity in the universe, I welcome you." Swadeth stepped back, finished. At first the small sounds of the crowd were like mud bubbles popping here and there, but they grew denser and louder as Swadeth moved to stand next to Bass, until the sound of clapping hands and shouting became an encompassing, indistinguishable waterfall of sound.

Bass smiled and waved as the band struck up the same marching tune as before. He smiled, even though he alone knew there was more to it than Swadeth even hinted at. Once humans agreed in principle, sweeping changes would begin. The big surprises would come later, when carefully fostered circumstances broke down the patterns and preconceptions they now lived by. The promised future would differ only in degree from what they would vote on, just as a wooden boat differs only in degree from a starship, but the final result of those changes would be unthinkably alien to psatla and humans alike. They would begin soon, awaiting only commitment to his *psalaat*.

CHAPTER
THIRTY-TWO

The voting took place that evening. A few humans who missed the meeting voted no. Later, they changed their minds. No ship was readied for departure. No humans left Phastillan.

With a larger population the experiment might have bogged down in self-interest. With a happier, better-adapted one, it would have been still more difficult. But Phastillan's refugees weren't even from a single homeworld—C.I. #14 had been an industry, not a home. They were remnants of broken tribes, with nowhere else to go. It was Phastillan or nothing.

With a base culture less structured than the Reis model, the test might have come to nothing, but given a crisp mold to fit, the humans flowed into it as rapidly as their old mores were broken by Phastillan and its strange, pervasive perfumes.

Offered functional work outside, residents abandoned the *Prince*. As the numbers of those remaining diminished, the corridors became lonely thoroughfares, until even the most fearful took assignments away from the ship. Mothers and small children cleared garden plots outside new, sunny quarters near the port—but out of sight of the *Prince*.

In remote places the new settlers built small refineries and ground-based defense installations. Under concealing trees they cleared roadways which skirted *ksta*-rich humus. Factories crowded in limestone caves, invisible from space. Only the settling ponds with their slurries and clever bacteria were exposed. Raiders would see nothing of value. There were no targets except ships.

The work itself forced decentralization: ore-crushers had to be near the mines that supplied them, refineries near settling ponds.

Available techniques and tools were designed for colony worlds starting out, not factory planets.

The *Matteo*'s cargo of machinery need not have been scattered to remote *asapht*, nor did goods and equipment have to go overland on animal-powered carts. Humans didn't really have to live in the *asapht* where they worked, sleep on mossy, psatla beds, or dip homemade ladles into psatla soup pots. But scattered between port and refining complexes, between polar weather stations and equatorial islands, newcomers were forced to ride the same sexual roller coaster as Phastillan's original humans. As Bass had foreseen—as he had hoped—sexual mores and standards were shaken and shattered by exposure to psatla and Phastillan. The real reason for the scattering was, for Bass, the gravel patches his bare feet had painfully trod in Asaph Phaniikan. *Psalaat* required discomfort, awareness, and adaptation.

"You've seen psatla sort seeds," he said to Betsy one idyllic afternoon. "Winnowing. They toss seeds and husks into the air and let the wind blow the husks away. I don't have time to pick through my human seeds one grain at a time. Most of them will adapt once their cultural chaff is blown away."

"Biologists call it adaptive radiation," he told Ade Folgrin. "When reptiles evolved hard-shelled eggs, they spread over the dry lands with no life-forms to oppose them, and they evolved into thousands of species. Only a few were really efficient, like the dinosaurs." He looked questioningly at Ade, wondering if he'd lost him.

"Ornithischians and saurischians. I went to school," Ade teased. "Go on."

"Yeah. Right. When some of them evolved homeothermy and hairy scales to keep heat in, they 'radiated' into newer, colder environments. Tree dwellers probably grew feathers to keep warm or cool, and only later used them to glide between branches. The air was a new environment, a new 'radiation' again."

"Let me say it, Bass," Ade interrupted impatiently. Our 'eggs' are spaceships—portable environments. We've 'radiated' to thousands of worlds, though our adaptations have been technical and social, not biological. Is that where you're leading?"

"Uh-huh. But we radiated too far—transReef can't support us, as we are. Eventually, we'll be back to animal power, and other races with fuels and metals will move in. We'll be slaves. Serfs. Other psatla planets, 'finished' ones, will go on as always, but Phastillan will be dead. So we have to adapt to the psatla. I don't know how we'll do it, not exactly."

"You don't know? I thought *psalaat* accounted for such things." Ade's crinkled half smile revealed that he was baiting Bass.

"Getting them all off the *Prince* was *psalaat*. How they adapt is up to them. They'll have to find their own ways to handle psatla pheromones . . . and themselves. In social evolution failures don't have to die—not if they watch the successes, and do likewise."

Among the former refugees, contract-worlders fit in rapidly. *Gadesh* was rigid adherence to their unwritten contracts. Those shaped by dictatorial company worlds looked 'up'—or down, by psatla convention—to their sources of power and well-being. Their *gadesh* was obedience and accomplishment, pleasing those from whose stronger branches they depended. Individualists found *gadesh* when success rewarded them with freedom to choose their own paths.

Humans who didn't learn psatla sound speech adopted its vocabulary. *Gadesh* signified success, reward and recognition; it was noblesse oblige, pride, and smug satisfaction, force applied and influence exercised. Determination, confident purpose, intuitive rightness, high hopes and dreams, fate, destiny, moira, and fatima—all were lumped together as *psalaat*, and meaning was gained, not lost, in the translation.

There were suicides. Some women couldn't cope with their own wanton behavior. One homosexual man adapted to his new craving for the opposite sex; his lifelong partner died alone.

There were quarrels, and jealous fights which required mediation.

There were murders. Husbands killed wives and wives' lovers; wives killed husbands. Two psatla were slashed and stabbed by a Universal Sacrament priest who considered them incarnations of Satan. Their *ksta* returned to soil. They would be back.

There were no murders for gain. There was no profit to be made on Phastillan. There was only work, obsessive work punctuated with ecstasy and frenzied release. No one was punished. Who could judge them? Who had not felt the same madness?

When another ship landed, descending on its last fuel pellets, seventy-two new faces climbed down and were whisked away to *asaph* and mine and refinery. They, too, would adapt or die.

In a year there were no more violent deaths or suicides, only sheepish faces, and halfway through the second year of Bass's *psalaat* even those were gone. No single pattern of sexual behavior emerged, but no one missed it. And over three hundred women were pregnant. Hormonal birth-control medications were ineffective on Phastillan—only surgical sterilization worked. Bass was pleased by the swelling bellies. Humans born on Phastillan would grow up amid the swirl of psatla essences, of shifting moralities and family structures, and they would find their own ways.

Bass and Betsy weren't immune to the turmoil. Bass lived in Asaph Phaniikan, a terminal his steady companion. Betsy flitted about Phastillan at a mad pace. The engineers could design and build machinery, but they were engineers, she complained, not mechanics. And the psatla? Human influences were not contagious. Simple adjustment and lubrication were still beyond their grasp. Things broke down unrelentingly.

She trained mechanically inclined settlers to assist her. Computer-taught knowledge wasn't enough. She demanded ingenuity and open minds, because Phastillan's human-made tools were all old and had been repaired with scavenged parts from hand pumps and starships. Betsy demanded artistry. Perhaps by coincidence, most of her "artists" were women.

What pleased Bass most was simply that Phastillan was *working*. The emerging society he saw, stripped of the baggage of abandoned cultures, inhibitions, and individual pasts, was functioning, and its adherents seemed to look forward with hope again, without fear of the new psatla-human symbiosis.

They called themselves "Phastillans" now, after much clumsy experimentation with "Phastillians," "Phastillanians," and "Phastillites." Besides, the way they said it, with just a touch of pride, it could be written with or without the apostrophe: *We are Phastillans. We are Phastillan's. We belong.*

Few humans let their thoughts range far beyond Phastillan, though. Too many remembered only pain and degradation and loss. But for Bass and those close to him the universe beyond was real and immediate. Newcomers who trickled in, ship by dying ship, had to be interviewed by him, by Ade Folgrin, the Van Voorts or Jake Pirel, and their tales recorded. It was a depressing task at times.

Hokkaido. TransReef's industrial hub had ground to a halt. There was no power to run the factories, no raw material to form. Never an agricultural heavyweight, Hokkaido lost a third of its population to starvation and rioting before stabilizing at a low energy level. Dietary trace elements weren't a problem, yet—most were also industrial raw materials, and could be refined from the waste heaps and stock-bin sweepings of idled industrial sites. Hokkaido figured prominently into Bass's future plans.

Lonesome. Of the entire colony, only two survivors had lived to tell of the dry, hot dying. Without power, the desalinization plants stopped, and thirst drove men mad. By the time scavenging raiders gave coup de grace to the last few, the dome-cities were home to only mummified remains. Of the two men who had escaped in a cargo hull and reached Phastillan, one died soon thereafter. It was unlikely that the colony, marginal at its inception, would ever be rebuilt even in good times.

Annalisa. An ironic, bitter tale. An ancient asteroid buried in Annalisan bedrock was a prime source of zinc. Shafts sunk through miles of overburden once flowed with the life-giving metallic ore, necessary to Earth-origin plants and animals alike. But Annalisa's mines were closed when ships from Elysiou raided them. Defenders hid in the caverns and blew shut the main shafts. When the raiders departed, frustrated, only a hand-carried trickle of zinc ores flowed upward through personnel tunnels and air shafts. There was no power to run excavation machinery to re-open the mines.

Elysiou. "Why didn't you trade with Annalisa instead of raid it?" Bass asked one refugee from Elysiou. "You had agricultural wealth, and needed only small quantities of zinc and selenium in exchange. You doomed your own planet to death from deficiencies."

"Nobody thought of that," the refugee replied. Bass sent him away in disgust. "Such a one," he said, "has only his genes to give to Phastillan."

Bass commissioned psatla housegrowers and a human carpenter to build him an *asaph* like no other. Set on a brush-covered hill north of the forest zone, it overlooked a rock-wrapped arm of the sea. Walls of rounded stones were set with tight-growing lichen; floors were slaty flags and moss. Sunlight pierced bubbly handmade glass and dappled the floor.

Woven partitions rolled up for open or private space. Psatla bacteria kept a composter fresh, and went dormant when only black humus remained. The "kitchen" was a slate shelf and a firepit. Mossy stones cupped a sand-bottomed pool stocked with tiny iridescent crabs for steaming and eating with the crisp, white tubers that grew in the sand below them.

No one lived there. It wasn't a house, just a quiet niche where Bass and Betsy met when time and circumstance allowed. They found the time and created the circumstances, a roughly monthly cycle. They worked apart for three weeks and spent the fourth together, beginning with passionate madness, ending with long, sated hours catching up on incidents and experiences of their time apart.

It was an odd relationship; they had little in common except enthusiasm, competence, and their love of long rambling walks. But there was trust, and a tacit assumption that come what may, they would spend one-fourth of their lives together.

Fidelity wasn't part of their bond, though Bass had few chance encounters. He was in psatla company most of the time. But Betsy's work took her to remote outposts where she couldn't avoid isolated human males. Perhaps she planned it that way—Bass never asked. Their own accommodation worked one week out of four, and nothing else mattered.

They even talked about children. Betsy's infertility was surgical, reversible, but she said she wasn't ready. Until her aides could handle the most demanding tasks, she would hold off. There was more to her refusal, though: fear, and doubt of her own worth. Bass hoped that her scars would heal on this new Phastillan, but he sensed that it was still too soon. They did agree that her children would be Bass's. They both wanted the blood-tie between them.

CHAPTER

THIRTY-THREE

By the third year of Bass's *psalaat*, Phastillan seemed secure. Defensive satellites were in orbit, powered by Phastillan-refined fuel. They were simple, their weaponry crude. Triggered by ground-based lasers, their missiles were programmed to seek out anything that moved. Their warheads, doctored for maximum EMP, could devastate lightly shielded shipboard cybernetics even if they missed. Real warships would barely notice them, but no one expected to defend against anything more formidable than converted merchantmen.

The *Matteo* was ready to lift. The stubby merchant sat proudly on her concrete apron, loaded with refined uranium and other metals in short supply throughout transReef. She had been modified for the voyage. Four tubes were mounted conspicuously at her waist, holding missiles from *Reef Runner*'s illicit cargo. Those were not homemade toys—a direct hit could take out a fleet scout, even a light cruiser. The first venture of the Phastillan Trading Company was about to begin. A small beginning, only one elderly vessel, but it was backed with the hopes of a world.

Departure Day promised to become Phastillan's first holiday. The *Matteo* was draped with bright streamers. Grandstands had been built, and a speakers' platform with an awning. All but essential work was suspended, and by noon the port swarmed with humans and psatla.

Though mass celebration was alien to the Reis, psatla got into the spirit of things, even drinking home-brewed beer. If it affected them, no one could tell. Music filled the sunny afternoon, sometimes lilting, often strident—Phastillan's own band. It was amateur entertainment, to be sure, but it celebrated everyone's victory: fuel for the *Matteo* and fuel to sell. The work of their hands.

Phastillan's humans were from a score of planets, so the band played traditional airs from all of them, and colonists demonstrated homeworld dances to an approving crowd. A fine haze of dust hung in the air, stirred by quickly moving feet. Families brought food, and spread blankets only meters from the landing apron. Drinks were passed around. Children played in the shadows of grounded starships.

Several ball games were in progress. Conflicting rules from diverse worlds were modified on the spot. Whatever the rules, humans from the farthest colonies would recognize the game; five hundred years from Earth, baseball had hardly changed at all.

The day wore on. Children tired and parents bedded them down on blankets. One by one the ball games ended, their final innings played, and as the band handed their instruments down from the platform, the rulers of Phastillan ascended. Crowds moved to the wooden grandstands, humans and psatla, chitin against cloth.

Ade Folgrin spoke first, warmly praising everyone's fortitude and perseverance. "The first tangible success of our united effort stands before you," he told them. "That ship, fueled and loaded with the substance of your lives, your work. Our prayers and hopes will rise with it, that it may bring life to still another world."

He leaned forward, his quiet tone never changing, imparting intimate confidence. "Its destination, secret until now, is the planet Hokkaido. If Hokkaido has survived, that fuel will sustain it and revitalize its factories, and trade with Hokkaido will rejuvenate us. And the *Matteo*'s voyage is only the first of many ventures of humans and psatla together.''

Jacomo Pirel, still nominal master of the ship, thanked everyone for their efforts to get his beloved ship spaceworthy again, though he himself would not be making the trip with his crew.

Swadeth was a runaway hit with the human celebrants. He announced that his school was ready to enroll psatla and human students, and though it was small now, he assured them it would someday be a center of learning for all transReef.

''It is acceptable, I think, to give my small school a grandiose name, one it will grow into. To commemorate its naming, I had an emblem made to symbolize its purpose.'' He turned to the awning poles and unfastened a cord. Bass, like everyone else, had thought the rolled cloth was an awning. It fell open and hung in the still air, a great, green flag emblazoned with the name and insignia of Swadeth's school.

At first the massed audience was mute as necks craned to see it. Then, among those near enough, there was a spattering of chuckles, then laughs, and finally a roar of hilarity that spread as fast as minds registered what their eyes saw. A name, Phastillan University, was sewn in yellow letters along the banner's lower hem. At the sides, a man and a psatla reached out to each other, joining hands over the initials PU. The free hands of both beings were held in front of their faces, though only the human had a nose to pinch.

Swadeth let the laughter die to weak, teary-eyed gurgles, pleased with the success of his joke. ''Psatla never invented humor,'' he told them. ''It is your gift to us. Humor respects nothing, and has no proper boundaries. On Phastillan, anxiety abounds but there are too few jokes. I hope that will change. I will not ask you, my human audience, not to fear psatla, but don't spare us in your jokes. Laugh at us, as you do at yourselves. We will be honored, not offended.''

To quell the babble, he raised his arms. ''P.U. is seeking students,'' he said. ''The qualifications are curiosity, irreverence, and suspicion of ideas and solutions, new and old. Courses will be open-ended and will lead to no degree, but if students feel that paper credentials are essential, perhaps we can draw up a 'certificate of endurance' for them. We, psatla and humans, will study each other. If it appeals to you, apply.'' Describing the goals of P.U., Swadeth told anecdotes about psatla-human difficulties he'd witnessed, some dating back almost to the founding of Phastillan's colony.

Just how old is Swadeth, Bass wondered. *If he were human, I'd think he was in his fifties, by the way he acts and speaks. Was he really here two centuries ago? He or his* ksta?

Even lacking a human face, Swadeth made them laugh. He was a deadpan comedian, and a mime. Swadeth's understanding of humans ran deep, Bass realized. *Had it always been so?* His humor was right on the mark. Nothing was too sacred for his wit, least of all the confused and confusing human attempts to adjust their sexuality and their lives to psatla influences.

Swadeth had seen what the human leaders had missed, and in a masterful coup of *gadesh* had remedied a social illness. He had reintroduced the tension-release of humor, giving humans permission to laugh at psatla—and at themselves. His mild jokes were only a beginning. From then on, Bass knew, jokes would arise to recognize new stressful situations. *Did you hear about the horny housewife and the psatla . . . ? What did the psatla say to the guy with the hard-on? Nothing. He gave him some dirt.* Would they be truly funny? Who could say? Cultures changed, and few jokes seemed funny a decade later. None survived transferral to another culture. Phastillan's jokes would be funny enough when they were needed. And later, who would remember them, or care?

A rotating green beacon in the *Matteo*'s nose announced her readiness. The last celebrants moved out from her shade and the squat ship stood alone. As the band struck up an ancient farewell, she rose slowly, scarcely disturbing the warm evening air. In two minutes, she was a speck in the sky. In three, she was gone.

CHAPTER
THIRTY-FOUR

Voicelog 3.24(r), Shipsoft Corporation, Tacoma, S3
Timecode 773.281.4005

>Outward bound. This is my final entry in this sublog. From now on, the official log will be the real one again. Freedom! Owner de Witte is no longer aboard, and no longer owner. I understand he has worked his way up to night-shift foreman on a mushroom farm or some such. Don't they grow mushrooms in the dark and feed them . . . [COMMAND MODE] [TO IDENTIFY UNRECOGNIZED POSSIBLE PHONEMES STATE USERNAME NOW] Alta Van Voort. [SOUND-PATTERN FOLLOWS] . . . [IDENTIFY WORD OR CANCEL] Correction. Relevant sound. Not a word. File as 'Giggle.'

>Alta Van Voort, acting captain, *Reef Runner IV*.

The *Matteo* was gone for a year. Much had been left unsaid on Departure Day. *Psalaat-thes* was more than the rejuvenation of trade and the acquisition of industrial goods for Phastillan. When other ships went out, when refueled Hokkaidan ships sought trade on their own, Phastillan's reputation would go with them, and increasingly jealous eyes would turn her way. *Psalaat* demanded that, too.

When *Matteo* returned, two other ships followed only minutes behind: the *Nippon Maru*, a ten-thousand-ton freighter, and the *Samurai*, an armed trader of two thousand tons' burden, both from Hokkaido. Of primary interest was their cargo. All three had full holds—the price Hokkaido had paid for seventy-five hundred tons of vital pure elements heavier than iron, along with preserved foods and supplements rich in zinc and selenium, all

rare among the transReef stars. Once Hokkaido's dormant factories were powered up and workers recalled, the Hokkaidans had
manufactured tons of replacement parts for obsolescent Phastillan
machinery, utilitarian aircars, and computer hardware, things
Phastillan couldn't produce on its own.

August 4, 2482 was declared Phastillan's third official holiday.
Matteo's crew and the Hokkaidans were feted, speeches were
made, and a new round of jokes circulated, invariably concerning
sexually deprived Hokkaidan crewmen and their lack of success
with Phastillan's women. Shore leave was a big disappointment
to them. They'd heard rumors that Phastillan's very air was aph-
rodisiac, its women more responsive than their most exaggerated
fantasies. What they encountered was a busy, hardworking place,
with sexuality in the air, all right, but not for them. They were
fended off politely but with vast disinterest.

When the new jokes reached Bass's ears, he reacted immediately, arranging for Hokkaidans to deliver and install their cargos
in remote psatla communities. By subterfuge, their returns were
delayed for weeks while they breathed, ate, and worked amid the
subtle vapors of *ksta*-rich forest soils. The aircar crews that picked
them up were volunteers and female. New jokes made the rounds.

Betsy was one of the pilots. Bass hadn't wanted her to go—his
pre-Phastillan conditioning wouldn't quite die. He couldn't rationalize it as an accident. His wife had intentionally left him to
make love to other men, and he waited, outwardly complacent,
trusting her to return to him. A lifetime on Phastillan wouldn't
make that easy.

"You understand, don't you?" she asked Bass plaintively. "It's
one last fling before I get unfixed." Bass understood conditioned
fear. Pregnancy nullified psatla pheromones; for Betsy, that would
be like the bad old days before Phastillan. Bass was more optimistic. Still, he suspected she would always need that kind of
reassurance. He remembered old Orb settlers who spoke of long,
shivering winters in the High Ranges, of the chairs and bedframes
they had burned to stay warm. He remembered homesteads piled
high with firewood decades after solar-heat units had been installed. Old habits, old fears . . .

"Of course I understand. I know you'll come back, that's what
matters. This is still Phastillan, but you're still you." At this Betsy
wrinkled her brow. "And I wouldn't change a thing," he added.
She departed reassured. Funny, he thought. She's going off after
horny Hokkaidans, and I have to reassure her it's okay. He prom-

ised himself she'd be four or five months pregnant when the next ships came in.

Bass had a brief, unplanned affair. The girl, just eighteen and almost a decade his junior, was awed by the *sfalek*'s attentions, as if he were more than a man. Neither his physical attributes nor his skill met her expectations, but they parted friends. She was forever cured of hero worship.

Betsy returned haggard and uncommunicative. Bass took her to their mountain retreat. Physically sated, they huddled in the chill of evening to watch a splendid sunset. "We're all cripples, aren't we?" she mused apologetically. "All beaten in one way or another, twisted a little or a lot, depending. Just making do."

"Like anyone, anywhere, I think. It's nothing to torment ourselves about. Besides, everywhere else, things are falling apart. All those proud, lovely worlds . . . and we're building something new."

Children! Bass made sidelong references to Betsy's arrested fertility every time they were together. Never outright suggestions, his remarks were couched in safe, negative terms: "With almost every woman on the planet pregnant or nursing, you're almost the only one who can still choose when you want a baby " *When*. Not *if*.

Betsy wasn't self-analytical. She was happy and strong, or unhappy and weak—more often the latter, she believed. She didn't articulate her feelings, though exposure to Bass was changing that. She absorbed his values without always agreeing with them.

For Bass, individuals were foci of circumstances. Strengths, weaknesses, intelligence, even dreams and aspirations were only the visible flowering of twining causal vines. What made Bass unique among all the men of her experience was his emotional integration. He didn't hate anyone. He didn't get angry.

She'd known men who never showed an angry face to the world—but no man could hide from his whore. She had been a vehicle for fantasies, an outlet for emotions and urges hidden from the rest of the world. Some things she had done with them were odd, at worst humiliating. Others—tried once and never again— were painful, even damaging. Some things a seasoned street-walker would have refused. She shied from such memories, but not from thoughts of the men who had wanted them done—the strong, rational men. Always them. They hadn't lacked anger or hatred, the need to dominate and degrade; they had just packaged it and saved it for her. Bass wasn't like that. If he hated anyone at all, she would know.

Bass didn't even hate Zig. The pimp still had his job at the port, didn't he? And his bar? She marveled at Bass's calm acceptance of him. When she visited the port on business, Zig treated her coolly, respectfully, without trading on their past relationship and without servility. Ziggy had come to accept Bass's matter-of-fact treatment; his *psalaat-ni* had failed, and he was in no position to do anything except his job. Bass knew that, and Zig knew it. That was Bass's particular magic, she reflected. If he believed something of you . . . if he did, how could you help but believe him?

Seeing herself through his eyes . . . yes, she liked who she was, who she was becoming. At first she'd asked herself, "Does he love me?" Later, the question had been, "Why does he love me?" Then, "What is it about me that he loves? What's so great about me?" Now she knew. She saw herself with clear eyes, without self-hatred.

Sometimes she imagined herself as one of her machines—a tractor, for instance, not all that well made, ill-suited to the tasks demanded of it. A machine with rude vents sawed in a cowling, the radiator hung on hand-welded brackets, and hand-turned bushings. Crude adaptations that kept it working. All-purpose machinery: bolt on a pulley to run a sawmill; drop a pin through its shaft extension for a drill rig or a pile driver; connect jumper leads here, or an air hose there . . . it could do anything.

So could she. She was competent. After a millennium of emancipation, most women still weren't. If anyone had kept Phastillan running all these years, it was her. And as a woman . . . she kept her man happy, didn't she? And how many others had she delighted, and been pleased by? The others were just sex, just Phastillan—but whatever she did, she did it well. She adapted. She survived. Her relationship with Bass worked. Nothing else mattered.

So. Children. They would adapt—whatever they became would be "normal." Could she adapt to them? Could she handle the responsibility? Mechanic. Crew chief. A good whore. Woman and wife. The machinery is all there, too—just a simple reconnection required. Why not a . . . mother?

CHAPTER
THIRTY-FIVE

Vinella departed with less fanfare than *Matteo*. For Phastillan's second ship, the occasion was less momentous, and the mission was limited: pharmaceuticals, machinery, and bacteria cultures destined for Yellow Dog, an inhospitable world whose nonhuman indigenes mined ore pockets for a small human minority in return for tools and trinkets. Neither Bass nor Jake Pirel trusted her captain with a cargo of heavy metals. She had fuel for one round-trip to Yellow Dog—and there were no other inhabited systems within her range.

Bass and Betsy missed *Vinella*'s return. They were busy welcoming little Adam Cannon to Phastillan. Phaniik Reis and Swadeth were present at the birthing, the greatest gift of understanding Betsy and Bass could give. The psatla were honored witnesses, and both were less shaken by it than an uninitiated human might have been.

The boy was named Adam Esaphaan Cannon. Esaphaan had been a *sfalek-thes*, of whose *ksta* and memory Phaniik Reis partook.

Betsy and Bass seldom strayed far from Asaph Phaniikan. Adam was a magnet that drew them home. Betsy nursed him for nine months, then several young psatla coopted him. They guided him, kept him out of mischief, even taught him to walk. He was always returned clean and well-fed. He spoke as many psatla words as human ones.

As the child of Bass's blood grew, so did the offspring of his mind, his *psalaat*. Phastillan exported energy and economic life to nearby stars. Word went out that Phastillan was trading in fuel metals, and foreign ships arrived from distant worlds. But some ships weren't what they seemed. Psatla interviewed all officers and crews, not just refugees and immigrants. Sometimes, smelling lies and evasions, they exposed hostile spies and scouts. Their vessels were commandeered, and none left Phastillan with what they learned. They were small fry. When officers of one suspiciously well fueled merchant vessel were questioned, though, psatla drugs induced the ship's second officer to reveal that they were the spearhead of a major viking fleet. Phastillan had indeed been getting attention. The same viking consortium that had captured the fuelless Earthward naval vessels, the same group that even now held the Reef passages in a stranglehold, was eyeing Phastillan askance as a monopoly-breaker. They wanted no other suppliers of fuels.

Without explaining his reasons, Bass had a hard time convincing Pirel and Folgrin to go along with his plan for that ship. It was to go free. The second officer could not be returned to his companions, so a story was concocted that he had stepped on something poisonous, had died, and his body had become too infested to be returned to his shipmates. The crew and officers were suspicious. They were presented with a suitably unrecognizable corpse, well rotted and aswarm with harmless maggots. The ship had to be allowed to depart, with all its ill-gained knowledge of Phastillan's prosperity, with its surreptitiously scanned data on the planetary defenses. Pirel remained bitterly frustrated with Bass's unexplained insistence, but like the good officer he was, he adhered to his commander's words.

Bass wanted a prison camp for the other foreign agents, but Swadeth suggested exile. Psatla took the captives in custody, and there was no trouble from them.

Later, Bass heard rumors that psatla were using them as guinea pigs for behavior-modification experiments. That frightened him, but only months after he decided to visit the camp where his old fellow prisoner Kstala kept them did he drum up the courage to go. *Psalaat*, he reminded himself. This is it, what I fear most, to view the result of my race's betrayal.

"Some things best experienced," Kstala said. He led the way to a clearing, where wan dawn illuminated a fence of upturned trees, roots pointing inward. When sunlight warmed the corral's packed dirt, its inhabitants stirred. Huddled lumps rose from trampled moss, stretched, and yawned like well-fed dogs. Human dogs. Bass counted eight of them, seven males, naked and dusty with dirt and dried moss.

The eighth rose up beneath Bass's hiding place. She sniffed, turned her head from side to side, and looked directly at him.

Carla Stratton. A fifth columnist who had knifed a refinery worker she'd been cultivating when he had second thoughts. She was blond, with eyes colored like Betsy's. She smiled—but what does a smile mean when the pretty blue eyes above it are dull?

She mewled like a cat in heat, a hideous sound from a human throat, and approached the spiky barrier. She was too close to see now, against the stump fence, but Bass heard her. He heard mewing, cooing. In his mind he saw her dirt-streaked body and her vacuous smile as she urinated copiously, darkening the moss beneath her heels. Scent-marking. *May I have this dance, sailor? Here's my phone number. Call me anytime.*

Kstala gestured and they moved to a new vantage point. No longer downwind, the female—Bass couldn't think of her as a woman—lost interest and wandered among her male companions, sniffing and cooing. One hooted wordlessly and made hostile, darting motions. Another was on his hands and knees, rooting in the soft soil for his breakfast. She approached him, squatted by his skyward-pointing rump, and stretched out a hand. Gently, aimlessly, she fondled him. He hooted softly, a placid sound without surprise. She dropped to her elbows and knees, presenting like a cat, and, aroused by the sight of her—or by some subtler communication—he mounted her from behind. He thrust once, twice, a third time, then quivered weakly. And that was all. He backed away, slick and detumescent, and by the time she regained her feet he was rooting as if nothing had happened. Like dogs, Bass thought. No love, no little gestures, just a quick, efficient exchange, then business as usual.

The female approached the seventh male, who repulsed her, hooting threateningly. She dropped to her knees again and dug with grimy hands for whatever the others were eating. Wiggling, white, they looked like larvae.

"Grubs," Kstala confirmed. "Nutritious."

"It's permanent, isn't it?" Bass restrained his urge to gag. "They'll never be human again."

"Still human, *Sfalek* Bass. But very small life-forms stop thinking. Only scent-talk thoughts. *Ktek-elas kai tfelesteh psith.*"

Bass understood. The psatla's experimental bacteria absorbed neurotransmitters and inhibited synapses in critical brain areas. "But why do they still react sexually?" he asked Kstala.

"Very-old ideas in body—old ways before human speaking-thinking. Nothing cover them up."

Old mammalian patterns human cerebral evolution had suppressed? Ancient pheromones filling the vacuum Kstala's "bugs" created? Is our humanity that thin a veneer? Bass wondered. Beneath our thoughts and posturing, are we still apes—or less than apes? Those were human beings, once. Vikings, yes, but human. And Kstala doesn't see anything wrong with what he's done!

"They not love like humans," Kstala volunteered. "Leave babies in dirt. I give babies to other human-womans. Babies okay babies. Smart."

The sex cells weren't affected, Bass realized. The transformation was permanent, but the children of these beasts would be normal—or at least whatever Kstala thought of as normal. "Couldn't you have sterilized them, Kstala?" he asked as they walked back to the aircar. "Wouldn't it have been better than breeding orphans?"

"Orphans? No!" Kstala's *ksta*-voices wavered, unsynchronized, indignant. Triple eyes rolled separately, further sign of his upset. "Babies good. Woman-humans like babies. Keep. Love them." Kstala was adamant. "Not-enough different ideas in humans here, Bass. Keep good ideas, save bad ones, too, maybe change some. Important."

Ideas: human genes. A few thousand sets are too small a pool. Bass praised Kstala's work despite his revulsion. Psatla knew the value of a large "file" of spare genes. You never knew what you might need. What should he do now? These creatures were thieves and murderers, pirates who had planned raids on his home, his planet. Let Kstala have his two-legged laboratory mice.

Bass didn't see much of Ade Folgrin. The mayor adjudicated, soothed, and organized. If Phastillan had a government, it was Ade. He was necessary and well loved, but he wasn't happy. It wasn't until Ade found out about Kstala's experimental laboratory that he came to Bass.

"My God, Bass! Your little green friend is turning men and women into animals up there. You can't allow it to continue. They're not human anymore!"

"But I must allow it," Bass asserted. "They were spies and murderers. Now they provide answers that our future on Phastillan, and as a race, depend on. Besides, we humans do worse by our enemies than Kstala has done. Ask yourself what our lives would be like if the vikings had succeeded."

"It's wrong, Bass. Human beings are God's work. It's not our place or the psatla's to meddle. And that's only the worst example of what's happening here. What have psatla pheromones done to our morals, our religions? There's not a single church on Phastillan! Lust—that's all that's left. We should find ways to nullify their filthy hormones, but you've done worse than nothing! You've institutionalized their stink, their corruption. You've encouraged people to adapt to Phastillan, not to fight it.''

"I wish you didn't feel that way—but I can't say I'm surprised. I was afraid that the changes would be too much for you to accept.''

"Am I that predictable?'' Ade snarled.

"You've shaped yourself to fit a difficult mold, Ade. You demand more of yourself than a mortal can give. Look at you, man! You look like hell. Your hands shake. Your clothes hang on you like sacks—how much weight have you lost? What's happened to your hair? Haven't you punished yourself enough?''

"I don't know what you're talking about!''

"Forgiveness, Ade! I'm talking about forgiving yourself for not being able to resist Phastillan. You have a wife a thousand light-years away, and you torture yourself to remain faithful to her, starving yourself, wearing cheap perfume to drive women away, to shield yourself from your most natural urges.''

"Natural?'' Folgrin spat. "How is it 'natural'? Apes and dogs are 'natural.' Humans should be more! But psatla are making us 'natural,' and that's making me sick.''

"Ade, humans have always been driven. Do you think psatla have created the urges that torment you?'' Bass's eyes were ice-blue magnets, demanding, hypnotizing. "They've not made you inhuman, Ade. The pheromones have only intensified what you already are—they've made you more human.''

"Is that what you think? That we've never been more than zoo monkeys fornicating in public cages? Damn you, Bass! Damn you and your psatla and your *psalaat*!'' Folgrin's face was pale and deadly gray. "I pity you, Bass. You disgust me, and I pity you . . . what do think of yourself?''

"I'll live with myself. I'll cope because I believe in survival. I believe in humanity, too.'' He shrugged eloquently, though his eyes were tired and sad. "When the crisis is past, we'll be able to afford second thoughts. But for now our loss of dignity is the price of living at all.'' Bass stretched out a hand. "Ade, I need you. We all do. Won't you stop destroying yourself? Forgive yourself for being only a man, won't you?''

"Are you manipulating me, Bass?'' Folgrin grated. "Are you playing with my mind and my emotions?''

Bass was startled. He tried to divert him. "Of course I am, Ade. I'm trying to convince you to live.''

"You know what I mean," Folgrin insisted, refusing to be steered. "You control people. I've seen sworn enemies arm in arm after you spoke with them. I've seen the effect you have on crowds, too—and you're not that good a speaker. Are you doing it now?"

Bass wasn't trying, but the rigid control he'd once exercised over his emotions had given way to a more gentle "steering." He didn't plan the release of chemical messengers as did psatla. It just happened. When he was confident, people trusted him. When he was frustrated, they appeased him. But he wasn't influencing Folgrin, who was too sure of his rightness, too full of inner strength. Bass told him that.

"I still trust you not to lie to me, Bass. I'm not sure why, but I do. You've almost convinced me, you know—that I could adapt, and still live with myself. But it won't work."

Bass put his hand on the other man's shoulder. Thin, he realized. He's grown old, like my father. Tears rose unbidden in his eyes and ebbed like rainwater from soft moss. "I know, Ade," he murmured. "You're not the kind of man to bend. I'm the one who's killing you, you know. Me, my *psalaat*."

Folgrin cut him off. "It's not your fault, Bass. Remember the dinosaurs? I'm an evolutionary casualty, that's all." He smiled, a skeletal grimace. "I'll go back to work now," he said softly, "and when my time comes, I'll take my rigid genes to my grave. One good thing—I haven't passed them on."

"If you think that, you don't understand at all, Ade. You're a good man and a leader. We need you and your genes."

"No, you don't. You're probably right, that it's human to adapt. Then I'm not human enough." Folgrin leaned on the twisted-root doorframe, his body as bent as the psatla wood. "Grant me the freedom to die, Bass. Don't interfere with me."

"I won't interfere, Ade. I only wish . . . no, I'm sorry—no more words. You have my respect, always. And my love. Take that with you."

"I will, Bass."

Tears came easily. And tears were welcomed. They washed away grief, diluted rage at the cruelty of *psalaat*, and left him empty. It was the emptiness of exile, the vast, cold vacuum of *gadesh*.

CHAPTER
THIRTY-SIX

Ade didn't die, not then or for a long time thereafter. He was needed then, and more than ever in the days that followed, and Captain Folgrin had never been one to shirk responsibility, even responsibilities only he could perceive.

The first sign of trouble was, for Bass, when an agitated psatla youngling awakened him with trembling *ksta*-fingers and clacking carapace. Bass scented his message before he was awake enough to speak: FEAR (subjective, in Bass himself; a pheromone) > BURNT MACHINE OIL + HUMAN + COLD DRY GRANITE + IRON + SHUTTLE EXHAUST > SOUR SOIL/ANAEROBIC DECOMPOSITION/STAGNANT WATER (a mélange: danger/death of *ksta*, a convention). Fear: danger to Phastillan/ecosystem/psatla from non-Phastillan humans, from space (place-of-iron-stones, i.e. asteroids).

He pulled on trousers, threw a blanket around his shoulders, and raced to his terminal. < < COM OVERRIDE:BCI + PORT: FOLGRIN > >, he keyed.

A reply scrolled up his screen: < < SAT IV (S ORBIT) REPORTED H-DRIVE SHUTDOWN EMISSION, 320D STELLAR EQUATOR, + IOD ECLIPTIC. SAT III + SAT IV INOP. SAT VIII (P ORB) REPORTS CHEM DRIVE TRACES POS: 322D SE, +IOD ECLIPTIC. ASSUME HOSTILES. GROUND ALERT. SAT/SHIP DEFENSE DEPLOYED. > > < < BASS: THIS IS IT. VIKINGS. THANK GOD JAKE PIREL'S HERE, NOT SPACING. CALL PORT. ADE 0407:23 > >

Four-oh-seven—only ten minutes before. His heart was pounding, partly from the youngling's pheromones. "Calm yourself," he told it gently, "and care for Adam while I'm gone." Where'd Betsy go? he wondered. Up north somewhere? Damn, I want her with me.

Bass had to get his emotions under control. His present condition could cause panic. He concentrated on warm sun on salt-washed stones; seaweed and slow-lapping waves; flash and glitter of calm water where the white clouds were reflected on ultramarine deeps.

The com room stank of interspecies fears. Bass turned to a young engineer with Hokkaidan features. "Samisen, report, please."

"At ten-oh-nine last night," she replied, machinelike, in a clear, high voice, "a drive wake, magnitude point-oh-four-two, was recorded by distant-warning satellite B-3A, and shortly later by B-7C." Bass translated mentally: the B series were automated sensor units built on the old asteroid-mining platforms abandoned after Phastillan's initial planetforming. Their crude electronics, manufactured by the nonhumans who had deposited psatla on the hostile planet untold ages before, were only marginally compatible with human-made equipment and were incapable of fine discrimination. They were set to respond to any anomalous readings at all. "Signal processing by central facility revealed three synchronous drive patterns which emerged and shut down simultaneously," Samisen droned. "Satellite B-3A ceased transmission at 2445 and B-7C at 2454 yesterday."

This is it! Bass realized. Jacomo Pirel's first-case prediction of enemy strategy was that a force of large size would be preceded by stealthed scouts with indetectible drive wakes. That they *were* detected might be because the intruders' skill and equipment were marginal.

"Have the intruders done a whole-system scan of us yet?" he asked. Samisen's machine-precise facade broke for a moment. She raised an eyebrow at Bass, surprised that he should know about that. Pirel's briefings had been detailed, though, and his time-stretched lifetime spanned the period prior to transReef's colonization, when war among the Earthward worlds had been imminent. Pirel's own naval training had thus included all the standard scenarios for invading an occupied system. A major viking fleet, necessarily including some of the surrendered Earthward fleet, would likely employ the strategies Pirel knew, not suspecting that anyone on Phastillan would be familiar with centuries-old but still state-of-the-art plans. Pirel had suspected that the invasion, when it came, would proceed in stiffly choreographed fashion, and that viking officers would be even less flexible in its execution than Earthward officers would have been.

"An all-freq burst of point-two-five seconds' duration was recorded at oh-one-three-one." Samisen droned.

Bass reviewed. Under three hours to shut down drives, stabilize orbit, triangulate in-system emissions, and send a chem-drive pinnace to disable the satellites. Five hours to complete the passive scans, and then a short active scan burst. Yes, those were Earthfleet-equipped scouts for sure. When the scan burst was analyzed, the enemy would have a good picture of Phastillan's defenses.

"Samisen? Is there more? In the last three hours?" Scout-sized comps might take several hours to analyze returning signals. "And what's the signal delay between the scouts' location and Phastillan?"

"No emissions recorded. Transit time from the near-Oort location to Phastillan's current position is almost exactly ninety-six hours."

Four days! The invasion had actually begun four days earlier! "Get me Jake Pirel, Samisen." By the book, he said to himself. 640 AU out, and they came in sub-C so there'd be no instantaneous FTL wake to alert us. Exactly by the book. The viking officers don't have enough intuitive understanding to deviate one whit from the program. That may save Phastillan.

"Bass? Jake here. Are you current?" Pirel's voice wavered and crackled.

"Here, Jake. I have the latest reports. What are you doing about them?"

"I've prepared our passive defenses and I've sent our fleet of thirty unarmed hulks out, in offensive formation as planned. If the invaders maneuver according to expectation, our ships will be on an interception course. That may slow them down, because the scouts' burst won't show that they're unarmed freighters."

"And?"

"And nothing. If the scouts represent a major incoming fleet, it won't hesitate after the first unarmed hulk blows. Even a small contingent, evenly matched in number with ours, wouldn't hesitate to use probing fire to reveal our sham."

"So now we wait. Any idea how long?"

"Standard OP calls for a single scout to relay scan findings to the fleet, staying sub-C to maintain the ninety-six-hour time lag. Rendezvous should be just beyond our detectors' suspected range, so eight hours should see the fleet under way. Five hours later, they can be in-system. That depends on what the scout reports, and the fleet's capabilities."

"Explain, please." Bass's request was for the benefit of the others present—com crew and the *asaph* residents hovering nearby, awaiting news of their fate.

"A small fleet will have choices—to enter detec range at flank speed and smash through our defenses, or to come in at low V, with greater range of maneuver. A large fleet, assessing its risk as minimal, will follow the course I've outlined—an efficient one, at midspeed, that will allow for decel into Phastillan orbit."

"You expect the latter, then—the hulks will slow them up."

"The hulks might entirely deter a small fleet. That's their primary function. We'll have to wait and see."

"Again, when?"

"With a signal lag of ninety-six hours, a fast approaching fleet will Doppler-up on its own wake-echoes. We won't have time to react. Look, Bass . . . there isn't really anything we can do." Pirel's face twisted in sad frustration.

Bass silenced him with a raised hand. "We'll give battle in our *own* way, Jake. Just do what you can." He rubbed sleep from his eyes. "I think I'll rest for an hour or so. Samisen, when you go off watch, advise your relief to page me if anything develops." With an air of immense calm that had nothing to do with nonchalance, Bass left the com room.

The fleet didn't emerge for eighteen hours, so its makeup remained problematical. There was nothing for Bass to do in the meantime. Atmospheric disturbances over the poles meant he couldn't get through to Betsy. Unless she showed up soon, she'd be trapped at some weather station for the duration. Jake was ready to put all air traffic under central control.

Com was quiet when he was summoned there. Too quiet. Bass suspected why, and Jake confirmed. "One hundred and eight ships, Bass, and not just any ships. They're flinging the entire Earthward fleet against us."

"Is it too early to tell what they plan?"

"They're using main engines, not reaction-drive, so there's no surprise intended. Those drive wakes are realtime, not lagged." Bass understood. From the looks he received, few others present did. "On reaction-drive engines, the ships could have built up velocity outside our detection range and coasted in-system at just below C. We'd have had no warning of their approach until they used the mains for rapid decel."

"What their approach means to us is that they probably won't use corebreakers," Jake interjected. "No sense using a fleet that size merely to deliver a few hell-bombs we couldn't intercept anyway."

Bass felt rather than heard the collective sigh of relief that filled the com room. "What about our hulk fleet?" he asked Pirel.

"They're on course . . . wait, Bass! A new development. Let me put this on holo for you." Bass nodded to the com supervisor, and a cool glow lit the center of the room just above eye level. Bright sparks within glowed red, green, and white. From every vantage point, background was obscured, and the holoimage became the "real" reality. "Green is us, our fleet," Jake explained. "Red is them. This is Phastillan." A smallish white glow flickered. A larger white point, almost a minuscule sphere, was Phastillan's sun. Other sparks were outer planets, and haze represented the two sparse asteroid belts. "Notice the red fleet has split," Pirel commented. "The main fleet will go into stellar orbit at Oort distance, and the rest, thirty-odd ships, are coming in. I'm ordering our hulks to evade, Bass."

"Wait, Jake! Why?"

"They're no use, only a delaying measure. The most the invaders would do is shift vector slightly and lob a few nasties their way in passing."

"Hold that order a moment, Jake. When will the red fleet arrive in Phastillan orbit?"

"Four hours, at their present V."

"I need more time, Jake, now that I know what we face. If they shift to avoid our hulks, how much time will I gain?"

"Twenty hours, maybe twenty-four. Even a small vector change will cost them that. But, Bass—they won't just avoid our ships. They can get most of their course change by throwing mass. Missiles. Some of our ships will be hit. Men will die. Is a few extra hours worth that?"

"Jake, I need the time. There are things that must be done. Vital things that couldn't be foreseen until I knew what we faced. If it would cost every one of our ships, and all their crews, I'd still need that time. Don't give us up too soon, Jake. They won't die in vain, if I succeed."

Reluctantly, Pirel agreed to withhold the evasion order. The unarmed ships would continue to simulate a defense force; they would be targeted, and missiles would explode among them. The parting look Pirel gave Bass was cold, but he was a military man. He took orders. Other faces, in the com room, registered other emotions, all veiled. Not one pair of eyes met Bass's as he stood up. How many men had he condemned? A hundred? More? Like monkeys averting their eyes from death or fire, they denied with those downcast stares that Bass was one of them. He had become an elemental, a force less human than even the psatla they lived among.

"Gordon," Bass snapped, "see that my aircar is ready. Phephiis, bring a basket of food and coffee to it." He dashed outside, where the old Stollivant waited, already powered up.

Harsh, heavy breathing fogged the 'car's screens as his hands danced over its controls. The rising scream of repulsors drowned out all other sound as he edged the craft out from overhanging branches into the clear night. Betsy kept his 'car perfectly tuned, and at three hundred feet he found a following wind. He made good time. Several times en route his hand reached, as if by its own accord, to activate the 'car's com, to call off the hulk fleet. Each time, Bass withdrew it reluctantly. *Psalaat*. The *Matteo*'s first voyage had been a die cast into the heavens, and this was the gamble, now, even if men must die. There were worse fates than death in battle. Bass could visualize a hundred worlds where death was slow, where it was preceded by degradation as on Consolidated #14, a thousand others where it had been or would be almost that bad . . .

Kstala was waiting when he touched down. Having heard the news, he found Bass's arrival no surprise. The basket held sweet, mealy cakes that reminded Bass of corn bread with honey, along with freshly brewed Phastillan coffee. He shot questions at Kstala between mouthfuls and sips of hot coffee, and felt optimistic, apprehensive, and guilty as Kstala spoke.

He made his arrangements, burying his mental agony at what must ensue, at what he commanded of Kstala, behind his concern for the time: the deadline less than ten hours away when the viking fleet assumed orbit around Phastillan.

Before he left Kstala, Bass visited the compound where the former spies were held. He saw only two—white wraiths combing berries from ground-hugging foliage. One was female. Bass couldn't see her face, but her belly hung conspicuously low. Pregnant? His mind cowered from the thought. What horrors had he helped create? What fate would befit a viking child on Phastillan?

In the aircar again, he was crowded by psatla-made packages, green pods sealed shut with sap, containing . . . what he had come for. Psatla, too, rode with him, chitin tight-held with tension. Aircar travel was not usual for them, but they were Kstala's protegees, each with a certain expertise Bass cringed from thinking about.

Hours passed as the 'car droned through darkened skies. At one *asaph*, Bass released one psatla and a share of the pods. At another, and another, at mining camps and fish hatcheries, he released others. The 'car became less crowded, the supply of pods less cumbersome. Bass never lost track of the time. Finally, when he dared hold off no longer, he called Jake.

"They're here, Bass. Four ships are moving into P-orbit and the rest are trailing the planet."

"What are the four?" Bass's voice was thick with fatigue. It had been twenty hours.

"Fleet warships. Three Viper-class platforms and a heavy cruiser or a mother ship. The drive wake could be either."

"Can we be absolutely sure they're not Earthside or friendly?" Pirel was silent. "Jake?" Bass prompted.

"Does it really matter, Bass? Either way, our course of action's the same: we do nothing. There's nothing we can do."

"How long can we hold them? Hours? Days?"

"Minutes, perhaps. Those are warships. If the big one is a cruiser, with corebreakers, we're helpless. If it's a mother ship, with a flock of light attack fighters, we can hold out indefinitely. It'll cost us every industry and habitation on the surface—the bioponds, the refineries, the *asapht*. What do you think?"

"I don't know yet, Jake. Hold the fort. I'll be back in radio contact at oh-nine-hundred tomorrow. I still have things to arrange and I won't dare use com. Don't give up yet, Jake. Stall them, hold them in orbit—tell them our 'government' is assembling to surrender, anything you can think of. Just give me one more day."

Jacomo assented. His carrier wave abruptly stopped. The crackle and hiss of static from some far-distant thunderstorm was all Boss could hear.

Bass climbed into the aircar. It was nine o'clock, and his time was up. He had flown steadily for almost forty hours at high speed, had made a score of stops, and had spoken personally with eight ranking psatla on three continents. He hadn't dared have a human pilot along to relieve him. Humans talk. They speculate. He was exhausted, but it was all over now. He toggled the 'car's com.

"Bass? Damn it, man, where have you been? Have you been keeping up?" Bass told Jacomo he'd heard nothing since his last call and asked for an update.

"They're vikings, all right. Their high command's evidently had spies on Hokkaido for years. It took them this long to free up ships from the Reef blockade. They've wiped our satellites and issued an ultimatum: unconditional surrender—us and the psatla.''

"The fourth ship—what is it?''

"A mother ship. No corebreakers, or they'd have blown us already. They don't have the hardware to destroy us, and they know it. We've got a chance.''

"How, Jake?''

"They couldn't have refuelled on the way here, so they're barely operational. The whole fleet has to be on short rations. They didn't *say* that, but all the questions about our food stocks gave them away. And I think their takeover of the mine worlds hasn't helped them much, either. They must have destroyed too much in the fighting. We can hold them. In months, or a year, they'll have to power down; then we'll dictate terms.''

"Jake, we don't have years. We don't have a month.''

"What? I don't understand.''

"Ships come in every week. The vikings'll take them and their fuel. We'll lose them all, and their crews. The *Matteo* is due to return soon—or had you forgotten?''

"Bass, I'm a fool. A damned fool! I should resign command.''

"Don't be a real fool, Jake. You can't resign. You've got to handle the surrender.''

"Surrender? We can warn off the *Matteo* and the others, buy more time. They won't have reinforcements coming. We can still take them, eventually.''

"Jake, I'm asking you to trust me. Really trust me. We've got to surrender. It is *psalaat. Geth estekes tif psalatak-thif kes.* We can't talk of it now.'' Bass had spoken in psatla in case vikings were monitoring. He'd said, "The path they make here will be soon overgrown.'' It was the best he could do. "Will you do it?''

Jake Pirel demonstrated his confidence in Bass, a confidence perhaps born of prehuman genetic dicta, but nurtured by years of working together, of trust. He agreed to surrender his command to the vikings. Secretly, though, despite Bass's assurance, he resolved to surrender also his life. Failure wasn't easy for him.

"Honor, Jake!'' Bass guessed his thoughts. "You owe it to all of us, to your oath, to see it through to the end. I need you now, and for years to come. There's no easy way out.''

"Very well, Bass.'' Jacomo Pirel sighed. "I'll do as you say.''

CHAPTER
THIRTY-SEVEN

Before the surrender was formalized, Viper-class gunships abristle with weaponry grounded at the port, at Asaph Phaniikan, and at Asaph Swadethan, the school. They chose bare, stony landing-places for their own stability, not out of consideration for the psatla's precious soils. The mother ship remained in orbit.

Fighter craft made threatening passes over *asapht*, settling-ponds, and other clusters of occupation and industry, but only on the first day. Not enough fuel for such extravagances, Jake thought, congratulating himself on at least one astute guess. And they haven't bombed anything. That means they'll use Phastillan, not destroy it.

While the ships were assuming orbit, Bass flew to Asaph Swadethan and hid his aircar in deep forest. It would take time for his plans to reach fruition—if they did. He entered the school on foot and became just another student. Elsewhere—though Bass only heard about it later—Ade Folgrin, was made prisoner. Jake Pirel, according to plan, retired to a hidden listening-post deep within a hillside cave, where roots and vines and arching trees concealed an elaborate collection of com antennae. He would be in touch with every electromagnetic phenomenon on and around Phastillan, and as long as the vikings did not destroy Phastillan's remaining satellites or the massive computer at Asaph Swadethan he would see, in his holoset, every ship movement within sensor range.

He would see everything, hear everything—but he was forbidden to act. Being a prisoner, he often thought in the long, lonely days that followed, would have been less soul-destroying for a man of action like himself.

Bass hoped Betsy had followed their contingency plan and had gone to ground at some out-of-the-way station. Psatla would find her, and bring Adam. There must be no trails leading to Bass, and no family for an enemy to use against him.

Had he heard the viking admiral's rage, he would have congratulated himself on his foresight—the admiral wanted the "traitor" who had sold out his species to the "goddamn alien wormbags." Bass didn't blame him. It wasn't far from the truth.

At Asaph Swadethan, he listened to announcements relayed from the admiral's ship: Phastillan's humans and psatla were commanded to carry on with subsistence tasks and otherwise remain within *asaph*, village, and house.

A day passed, then a week without further word from outside. The conquerors banned travel and telecommunication. Bass fidgeted. He paced his room. He attended classes, then walked out abruptly halfway through them. Where was Betsy? Was Adam well? Kstala? Swadeth? The *asaph* was an island in a green sea, isolated, alone.

Bass was almost relieved to hear news of a budding resistance movement, carried by a quivering *tsfeneke* from Jake's lair. Workers at a collecting-pond and refinery complex northwest of Asaph Swadethan, the young psatla told him with odors of gunpowder, scorched flesh and fabric, and meat rotting in pungent soil, had murdered viking pickets and buried their bodies in secret. They had cached captured viking weapons in a rockfall cave. Bass left with a psatla guide that same night. Thankfully, the vikings at Asaph Swadethan had not instituted close control measures over their captives, so he would not be missed. Others would cover for him.

It was a three-day walk to the ponds. Once Bass had arrived, another day passed as he waited in a gully near the facility for word to be passed inward, and for a meeting to be arranged. When a small group of refinery workers met with Bass, their leader, *Pralasek* Helm Stegler, wasn't happy to see him. "You want us to endure this? I was a slave once, and I tell you I'm not going to be one again."

"They'll start killing you, once they know for sure that Phastillan doesn't have any large predators, as you told them. They'll know who to blame for the deaths."

"You think I *care*? You think any of us care? We were on C-Fourteen, man. These pigs haven't even *started* on Phastillan yet."

Bass pondered Stegler's flushed face. "Walk with me, Helm," he said. "Alone." With an apologetic glance toward his men, Stegler accompanied Bass farther down the dry wash. They were gone an hour, and when they returned, the *pralasek-ni* had agreed to follow Bass's instructions. There would be no rebellion.

As Bass left with his psatla guide, he was satisfied to hear Stegler explaining the situation to his associates. "The vikings are in for a surprise. No, I can't tell you what, exactly, but our part in it is *important*. We have to keep those pigs quiet. If we can keep 'em *happy*, so much the better. Yeah, Sack, I know what that'll mean. I been here as long as you. So what? You tellin' me you never did it with nobody? Sure, and your mother's a psatla, too.

"Anyway," Bass heard, "if we screw up here, and production drops, then what? Then these bastards start thinking, if they can't use us, if we aren't making fuel metals, then why not just get rid of us all? You think they can't? You ever been on a planet with a corebreaker in its gut? Well listen, asshole, I was on C-Fourteen, see, and . . ."

Totally satisfied that his wishes would be honored, Bass faded into the darkness. It was a long hike back to Asaph Swadethan.

Eight days after the surrender, viking crewmen stamped through the *asaph*, heedless of moss torn beneath booted feet, and herded everyone outside. Viking troops itched to use their rifle butts on their captives. There had been few incidents, and no opportunity to exercise the prerogatives of conquerors. For that, Bass was grateful for the size of the invasion force. A smaller force might have been slacker, less disciplined, and more likely to perpetuate atrocities like those on Melchior or C-14, but this was a fleet of over a hundred ships, thousands of men, and by necessity it had to be almost as disciplined as had been the Earthward naval vessels they now commanded. Otherwise their force would have broken up at the first differences of opinion among captains. Nonetheless, Bass read animal violence in several vikings' eyes. He remained calm. *Psalaat,* he told himself. This is necessary. It is inevitable. Be calm. No one must die.

His companions took their cues from him. They gathered quietly and without protest at the base of the ship, where a huge com screen stood at eye level, aswirl with abstract images. Vague figures swirled on the screen until all were assembled, then solidified: a fat viking, an admiral by his braid, and beside him another. His voice burbled between loose, fatty jowls, hardly understandable. Did some obscure backworld accent shape his words, or was his flawed speech the result of the old head injury that depressed his left temple and made his asymmetrical face seem as soft as wet clay? He confined his brief oration to gloating over the bloodless viking victory, advised his audience to be punctiliously obedient, and then turned the pickup over to his lieutenant who, the listeners were told, would instruct them in their duties and responsibilities to the Provisional Government of Phastillan.

The lieutenant wore his hat brim low over his eyes and sported a small, foppish mustache. His voice was a petulant whine, a vocal sneer. Bass hated voices like that. The scratchy, narrow-range audio system drove speakers built into the landing struts of the ship. They were meant for the use of loading supervisors when cargo came aboard, and they worsened the lieutenant's already unpleasant delivery.

"First, your rights," he said with a sharp, humorless grin while some on-board engineer focused in on his narrow, mousy face. "You have none. Human treatment is for humans—are you human? You gave up your race when you made unnatural union with wormbags." He said it as if "unnatural union" meant sex with psatla. And "wormbags"—Bass hadn't heard that pejorative in years. He suspected that psatla would bear the brunt of sick viking hostility.

"Do you want to be human again? You don't, do you? But you'll learn. And the first thing you'll learn are rules—our rules.

"One: No more schools. When we want you to learn something, we'll teach it.

"Two: Stay inside unless you're called for work details. Fencing in your pens will be your first job.

"Three: Learn who you can fuck, and when." His stiff grin turned malicious. "You can't fuck anybody. Women and men will be separated until you prove you're human again. No fraternizing. No more sick, wormbag sex."

"Four: Orders. You resist, and we may decide you aren't worth saving." He peered outward as if nearsighted. "If anything happens to my men, you will be executed. If an officer stubs his toe on a root . . . it's your planet and your root. You should have removed it. Is that clear? I warn you, I'm looking for an example."

Bass was proud of his fellows. They listened. They did nothing. No one so much as coughed. None showed anger, only a cold disinterest, almost disgust. It wasn't easy for them. They stank of anger, but they followed instructions: Remain neutral no matter what they say or do. Obey them. Stay alive.

When the lieutenant finished his harangue the com screen swirled into meaningless patterns again. The prisoners made no move, still staring much as they had while the vikings addressed them. They were in mental shock, Bass knew. He knew, too, that it was a dangerous moment. One wrong word, one casual insult or brandished rifle butt, and they might explode into riot.

It didn't happen. A viking sergeant picked a tall man in the crowd. "Get your people back in their pen," he commanded, conferring on him temporary leadership. The prisoners were herded back to the *asaph* by one of their own.

In minutes, they knew something was very wrong—the psatla were gone. The vikings had made a second sweep. But where had the psatla been taken? No vehicles had come or gone. Few believed they would be back. The lieutenant's acid words didn't bode well for "wormbags." It wasn't exactly an unforseen development, but only Bass had worried about it, before, and for unsentimental reasons. Psatla were necessary to the ore-concentration process, and that process was important to the vikings. Self-interest dictated that they preserve psatla. Had Bass miscalculated? Would the conquerors, in a fit of xenophobic violence, destroy the fount of their anticipated prosperity?

Bass didn't fear psatla annihilation. The planetside garrisons didn't have enough troops, and Phastillan's humans wouldn't help them. Before psatla could be "processed" in death camps or herded under the guns of the grounded ships, they would disintegrate, and their *ksta* would burrow. His concern was for a future only he could see. Psatla culture, the Reis *psalaat*, was a construct maintained by embodied psatla, by unique concatenations of past and present experience that humans identified as individuals. If too many psatla chose the path-through-the-soil too soon, an insufficient number of embodied psatla would remain to shape the experience of emerging *tsfeneke*. The new combinations of experience-past that each young psatla represented would uninhibitedly create *psalaat*, several *psalaat't*, with unpredictable, even chaotic results. Only the *ksta* of those who had directly known and understood Bass's schemes in their entirety would influence the new ones, and their influence would be dilute. *Psalaat-thes* could yet fail.

Asaph Swadethan's humans scurried through room after room looking for psatla. Wisely, their guards stood aside. Their leaders wanted an incident, but in the confined spaces of the *asaph* such could have been disastrous to viking and prisoner alike. There were few signs of struggle, only torn chitin, disturbed moss, and a shallow rut where something had been dragged. Chitin plates in a neat, psatla-shaped pile, unbroken, told a story easy to read: a young psatla—the chitin was pale green and thin—had struggled with hard-shod vikings, had closed itself tightly and been dragged outside. Not understanding hostile scents, alien voices, it escaped in the only way it knew: into the soil from which it had emerged. *Ksta* broke from *ksta* and burrowed in black humus, leaving only still-new chitin behind. It had probably happened before the vikings had time to react—not that they could have done a thing about it. Not death, Bass told himself. Only fragmentation and postponement . . . a reshuffling, an interlude of darkness between bright, conscious lives. No *ksta* were found dead or dying, no other chitin heaps lay emptily about. The exodus had been orderly. It was small comfort.

Guards sorted men into half the *asaph* and women into the other, quietly, without meeting resistance. No tearful couples had to be pulled apart, but men looked at each other with shamed, sickened eyes. Primeval imperatives demanded that they fight to defend their women, their honor, but they didn't fight. Like sheep, they allowed themselves to be herded back into the fold. Bass took his original quarters. He spotted movement in the woods outside—guards. He'd seen no light-amplifying gear, but that didn't mean the vikings had none. There could be sonic alarms, or tripwires.

Had he miscalculated? Would psatla be decimated before his preparations could take effect? What was happening elsewhere on Phastillan? There was no way to find out without psatla to carry Jake's messages. Bass was again in exile. He missed the psatla more than he'd yearned for his own kind that other time.

Another assembly! Bass pulled his aching body out of bed. He'd been on the fencing crew for two days and was blistered and sore. A viking crewman rattled his heavy rifle impatiently but kept his distance. Bass greeted him civilly—there had been no incident yet, no pretext for violence, though Bass sensed it was coming. Docility only intensified viking suspicion that a plot was brewing. But days had passed quietly and they were still alive, all of them.

The scene for the assembly was the same. Only the women were missing. The huge com screen first swirled in meaningless patterns, then resolved into the hawk face of a viking admiral, a new face beamed down from orbit or beyond. The admiral mouthed platitudes, urged them to cooperate passively with their captors, and informed them that the psatla were not dead, but were everywhere hostage for the humans' good behavior. Production must proceed, they were told, and the fleet's reserves must be replenished. He told them how lucky they were to be alive, how patient his men had been. But the meeting's main topic was Bass himself. For that, the screen resolved into the face of the unpleasant-voiced lieutenant. "One man is responsible for your perversions," the lieutenant told them. "One man who masterminded your sick surrender to the wormbags. You know who he is—most of you know him personally. Vassily James Cannon."

There was no reaction except curious glances. Hardly anyone on Phastillan knew his full name. Most didn't even know his surname; he was *Sfalek* Bass, or just Bass. Swadeth could have told them, or Betsy, if they'd found her. Bass forced himself to doubt that. She was hidden, safe with Adam . . . she had to be. James Aubasson had known his name, Bass thought, but that was years ago. He had left Phastillan. Was he back now, with the vikings? Ziggy Anson? No, not him. Any part he might have played was long past. There were no photos or holos of Bass, and any verbal description of him would apply to a dozen men at Asaph Swadethan alone.

There was another hitch in Bass's plan. His control over his people was indirect, and too often stemmed from personal contact with individuals. There had been too little time to train trusted men and women to use his own kind of *gadesh*—if that was indeed possible. There could yet be rebellion. Without communication, unable to travel for fear of being identified merely by his presence, Bass could not stop them. Phastillan could yet erupt in a bloodbath. "You are hiding him," the lieutenant said. "You don't owe him anything. If he hadn't perverted you, we wouldn't even be here, would we? We want him. To show you how badly we do, I'm going to read a list of hostages who will die, one a day, until one of you turns him in."

It was a long list. He stumbled over names like Lesthef and Gisseth, Swadeth and Kstala, less over the human ones: Folgrin, Pirel, Van Voort. There were forty names. Some spy or informer had done his work well; all the names were there, everyone without whom Phastillan couldn't work. Bass suspected he exaggerated. Jacomo Pirel, for one, was surely still safe in his cave. Alta and Mark Van Voort were offworld—*Reef Runner* wasn't due back for months.

"The psatla will die first," the lieutenant said, "because we don't want to waste humans. Make it easy on yourselves—just point Cannon out, or tell one of your guards. No one else has to know, and when we have him, the hostages go free—the humans, at least.'' His eyes traversed the assemblage as if he were really there, not aboard a ship at the port. Bass's fellows froze, afraid their slightest random movements might provide a clue to his presence.

When they returned to the *asaph*, speculation was guarded. The lieutenant's offer of freedom for human hostages only seemed to confirm the vikings' determination to exterminate psatla. As for Bass, the vikings believed they had to have him or risk Phastillan's humans rising against them. Just the opposite was true, of course, but they had no way of knowing it. If worse came to worst, if executions were imminent, he could surrender to them to buy time. Even with Bass dead, *psalaat* would limp ahead, at least for a while; too many plans had been laid and implemented for it to stop completely, short of planetary devastation.

But he was important to Phastillan, too. Even if its captors departed tomorrow, the planet's survival was not assured. Without Bass, many feared that the alliance of psatla and humans would falter. He was a symbol to Phastillan's humans. Though few knew his face or remembered him from the one time he had addressed them as a group, the *concept* of their human *sfalek* was a unifying factor. Some believed he had a plan to drive the invaders off, or to disappear into the deep forests and evade them until help came. Others suspected that psatla would perform a hat trick and somehow save them all. Bass wouldn't confirm their speculations or deny them. Their hopes kept them alive, for now.

CHAPTER
THIRTY-EIGHT

The raiders showed no sign of leaving; they dug in. The entire population of the *asaph*, men and women in shifts, excavated an earthwork around the ship, then erected a log palisade. Digging and clearing was hot, dirty work. The psatla's beloved humus dried to a fine, pervasive dust that clogged pores and irritated noses. Viking guards were most severely affected. Many retired to the ship to cool fiery, itching skin in cold-water baths. Headaches, red eyes, and rashes were endemic.

A nervous middle-aged prisoner sidled up to Bass as he entered his room. He was a recent immigrant, on Phastillan less than six months. In a whisper, he told Bass of a conversation between two guards. The troops were to be allowed to have their way with Phastillan's women. Bass's anxious visitor had overheard their avid intent, their graphic fantasies. They would teach the pissants' whores about real men. A bit of rape would soften them up. The women might even reveal who Bass was. The guards would be promoted, and would have their pick of more women.

Bass's informant apologized profusely for putting Bass in danger by contacting him, but he had a wife on the other side of the *asaph*. Bass assured him there was little danger. No surveillance devices had been found. "If you'd stop acting so frightened, there'd be nothing to notice," Bass chided him, then sat down on the bed. He leaned back, crossing one leg over the other, and motioned the other man to sit. "You've been on Phastillan about six months. Is that right?"

"Almost six, now."

"Then you've experienced the 'effect' several times?"

"Ah . . . three? Yes, three times." He blushed hotly. "Always with my wife, though," he said defensively.

"I suppose I can't blame you for your fears," Bass mused. "Perhaps I can reassure you that rape should be the least of your— or your wife's—worries.

"Human pheromones," he explained, "evolved before our species could speak. There are pheromones that affect sex and others that control dominance, cooperative action, you name it." He saw that his visitor was looking strangely at him. "Bear with me awhile—Nils, isn't it?"

"Yes. Nils Abrams."

"Bear with me, Nils. I'll get to the point soon."

"I . . . sure." Bass didn't get to the point right away, but Nils listened.

Before there was speech, Bass told him, there were pheromones, and now, a million, two million years later, they still controlled things. Like menses, repeating every four weeks. The Earth's giant moon may have inspired it, but pheromones regulated it. When women lived together, as in ship's dorms, they synchronized their cycles, and women living closely with men had more regular ones.

''You can even see our pheromone heritage: haven't you ever wondered why humans have hair in such odd places? Because hair, especially curly hair, has more surface area to distribute pheromones. Axillary glands—armpits—regulate menses, pubic ones control sexuality. And beards—almost all Phastillan men have them, without even knowing why.''

''I guess I grew mine, just seeing all the others,'' Nils reflected. ''Why do we have them, anyway?''

''Our ancestors had to have a boss, Nils. One of them had to command. Survival depended on quick, united action, and there wasn't ever time to explain things or argue. Since males were bigger and stronger, they did most of the fighting, and the male with the most 'stuff,' certain pheromones, ran the show. His beard pheromones made the others suggestible, submissive, even angry.''

''It wasn't very fair, was it? For the women, especially.''

''It was fair enough—males made the decisions, but the females chose which males.''

''How? How did they choose?''

''They chose by paying attention to a particular male and hanging around him. A male, surrounded by admiring females, would experience a rise in hormones that made him quicker, smarter and more sexually potent than other males. And around him, the hormone levels of the other males would drop. You see? A biologic chain of command.''

''That makes sense. I suppose we still have that, in a way. Politicians, people like that. But where does rape come in?''

''There's more than one kind of rape. Invaders fall into one category, and criminal rapists into another. Can you see that there's a difference?''

''Well, invaders—conquerors—would be dominant males, wouldn't they? Just by winning?''

''Just so. To the victor, the spoils. It isn't nice, but it's survival. Exogamy. Conquerors come and go, leaving their seed, and the species is strengthened by it. They don't kill women, not like criminal rapists do.''

''What's so different about rapists? Aren't they just primitive dominant-types that haven't been civilized enough?''

''Actually, just the opposite. They're not dominant at all. They're psychotics—zero-dominance males. Rape stimulates hormones that make them feel dominant. It's a powerful drug—they feel powerful for a while, but it doesn't last because it's not real. Women don't admire them and men don't respect them. It's not genuine power. That's why they have to do it again and again. They're hormone addicts.''

Nils pondered. ''It might've had value, once. I mean, how could a new guy become boss? Maybe he had to have a kick in the glands.''

''I hadn't thought of that.'' Bass sounded surprised. ''Perhaps you're right. At any rate,'' he went on, ''biochemical evolution stopped at the prelanguage level until Phastillan.''

''The 'psatla effect'? It is more than just sex, then.''

''Uh-huh. Psatla pheromones lock out some of ours, and stimulate others, so we don't react the same anymore.''

''They change our glands, you mean? The way we work? Then I suppose our children will inherit the changes, and . . .''

''No!'' Bass said vehemently. ''Nils, I don't want you to speculate like that around anyone else, okay? If people thought psatla could manipulate or change their genes, they'd panic.''

''If you say so.'' Nils sounded unconvinced. ''You're the *sfalek*, not me. All that doesn't bother me, much. I'm more worried about my wife, and those guards out there.''

''Nils—I don't think the vikings will be a problem much longer. What's important now is to keep things quiet.''

''I hope you're right. I guess we've been pretty lucky so far. Stories I heard about what they do, sometimes, on other worlds . . .'' He shook his head jerkily.

''That won't happen here, Nils. Can I tell you a secret? One that can never go beyond this room?''

Nils nodded uncertainly, proud to be confidant to the *sfalek*, unsure why he was chosen. But Bass knew, as he had known about Alois Battersea, Ade, and Jake Pirel. And he couldn't keep it bottled up inside anymore. As deceptively simple as Nils Abrams seemed, he was a good man, and right then, above all, Bass needed a friend.

''Yeah, okay,'' Nils said.

Settling comfortably, leaning against the woven wall, Bass used body talk to speak to Nils. And tension ebbed from the other's frame, leaving focused interest. ''Psatla are experimenting with us, Nils,'' Bass said, and paused to assess the other's reaction. Attentive curiosity. No outrage, no sign of fear. This man is unusual, he realized. He seems naive, stupid at first, but he's not. If we survive this crisis, I'll watch him, see what he becomes . . .

''Their idea, and mine, is to breed some of those ancient survival pheromones out of the human race.''

"Like the boss males," Nils interjected. "Politicians and police."

"Perhaps those. Letting someone run things when his only qualification is his hormone count doesn't make sense. We're not hunters and grubbers anymore, or hunted by animals that're bigger and hungrier than us. Our only real enemy now is us."

"Too bad those pheromones can't just leave love alone, and work on stuff like leaders who get us into wars."

"I wish it were that easy! But everything is tied together. Dominance, sex, and love. It'll take years to sort it out. There're no guarantees we'll still be . . . human."

Nils surprised him again. "Is that so bad? Humans aren't that special, I sometimes think." Bass recognized the bitterness of a small man without power or influence of his own, a man who had endured a lifetime under the thumbs of more powerful men. But he saw more—an indefinable acceptance of possibilities that had its own strength, its *gadesh*.

"We aren't special, really," Bass agreed. "We're organically evolved beings, made by our biological past. But most people can't see it. They worship mankind as it is now—even God is a human image, not subject to change. Men have been hanged for insisting otherwise."

"Religion!" Nils spat it like an expletive. "I never had any, you know? I don't like politicians or priests. We'd be well rid of them all. There wouldn't be any wars then."

"I don't know. There are other species out there, too—who can say what they'll do? No more human wars, I hope. No more suicidal ones. But I was going to explain about rape—"

"Yeah. No need. I can figure it out, now. If those guards tried to rape somebody, I'll bet they'd be, they'd be . . . you know, when you can't do it?"

"Impotent. Uh-huh. Pheromones again—female hormones that interfere with serotonin in the brain. Unless Phastillan women want sex, no man will get any. The vikings will be having it soon, but it won't be rape. Our women have some surprises for these 'conquerors,' Nils."

Nils eyed him askance. "You mean our women . . . they'll let those . . ."

"It has to be, Nils. It's *psalaat*."

Psalaat. The magic word. Nils had been on Phastillan long enough to absorb its mystique. "I wish . . . no, can't have everything, I suppose." His brow wrinkled with obvious pain. "Our own men, that's one thing. Sex, I mean. If May—if my wife does it with a Phastillan man, I mean . . . that's no different'n anybody else here, you know? It's those vikings. I don't know what I'd do if she got . . . if she had a baby.''

"Do you think there's something genetically wrong with them? Nils, ask yourself what May would do with a baby—any baby at all.''

"Yeah, I know. She loves babies. Always holding other people's, then giving me those looks . . . we haven't had time, that's all.''

"There'll be time now, Nils. Soon. This whole nightmare will be over.''

"I hope so," Nils replied doubtfully. "I guess we're done now, aren't we? You got to get some sleep." Having made the decision in almost motherly fashion, the small man rose to his feet. "Don't get up,"he said, holding his palm outward. Bass waited until Nils had shut the door, then stepped outside to contemplate, and to water his ferns. He slept soundly that night, less troubled than on any night since the vikings landed.

CHAPTER
THIRTY-NINE

News of a second attempt at resistance was delivered to Bass by another *tsfeneke* working with Jake. Psatla were seldom seen at Asaph Swadethan now, but everyone knew they were out there, elusive as tree snakes in the forests and swamps. Those kept penned by vikings were there only as a sop to the conquerors' egos, a pacifier, helping them believe they were in total control. This one carried a note from Pirel. Port workers, forced to labor directly under viking overseers and more resentful than most of Phastillan's inhabitants, planned to sabotage a landing strut on the warship stationed there. When the ship sprawled horizontal, they would overcome the stunned and injured vikings on board with sheer numbers and capture their weapons. Then they would flee to the swamps, and planned to snipe and sabotage where and when they could.

It was a futile plan, and it served no purpose but self-gratification. Jake's written protests to the plot's leaders had had no effect. They were operating on anger, not rationality, and they weren't heeding outside commands. Bass decided he had to go there himself.

He had to walk. No aircar could avoid being spotted by shipboard or orbital scanners. The normally short trip took him two days, and when he and the pstala who had accompanied him arrived at the forest verge, in sight of the towering warship, his feet were too swollen to fit in his moccasins. Rather than braving the hard-packed portside soil and the risk of being recognized as an intruder, he waited until dusk, then hailed a worker returning to the port complex. A message was carried, and only a short time later a slight human approached his place of concealment. Coming closer, she was revealed as a slender Hokkaidan woman, Sunam Ree—scarcely more than a girl—whom he had met once, months before the invasion.

She wore quasimilitary gear: a pistol belt and bandolier over a costume of shorts, canvas boots, and an open vest that barely concealed her small breasts. A Hokkaidan Merchant Service patch served as a unit designation. Bass wasn't impressed. It was petty showmanship, and she surely hadn't donned the weaponry until she was safely away from the port buildings.

Bass began quietly enough, listening to her plan—it was hers, he discovered, and she was the ringleader of the movement. "Nothing good can come of this," he said finally. "Many will die, and for what? For a few of you to feel a little less helpless, for a short time?" He refrained from voicing the simile he perceived, that the potential rebels were like hapless apes beating their chests in noisy threat against hunters with rifles, poor primitive beasts for whom any action, however futile, was better than none.

"At least we can make them respect us!" she said angrily. "That's worth something, for morale, at least. Others will hear what we've done, and they'll kill a few vik bastards, too. It's better than kissing butt, like you're doing. Why haven't you taken to the hills yourself, 'Sfalek' Bass? You're supposed to be our leader, for gossake, with Folgrin locked up and Pirel, our frigging 'general,' saving his own ass, sending us notes like that." Bass quietly refrained from pointing out that what Pirel was doing, what she so strongly disapproved of, was exactly what she was condemning

Bass for *not* doing. He understood that he couldn't expect a sensible response.

"Don't anger them, Pirel says? That's bullshit. I'm angry. I'm more than angry. My brother was on the *Sammy J.*, did you know that? The only family I had left, and they killed him. I'm going to see there's a fair trade, ship for ship." The green *tsfeneke* with Bass trembled and rattled, and buttoned itself up tight as a chestnut. To a psatla, Ree's exudations were psychotic.

Bass kept trying to reach her, to get past the anger and grief, the helpless need to *do* something, anything, to ease her psychic pain. He was confident. He exuded confidence in his *psalaat*. He visualized himself as a dominant-male primate and willed her to acquiescence. His efforts were in vain. Sunam Ree was too grief-stricken, too filled with hate; Bass's subtle machinations didn't faze her. Sadly, without looking at her again, he turned to his lime-green companion. "Phessift," he said, and the psatla responded by lifting one chitin flake, revealing a single *ksta*, which it raised and rotated about like a periscope, tasting the air. The single *ksta* mouth released a tiny hiss, like a leaking tire. "Phessift," Bass repeated, "it is time. You know what to do."

Given a specific task, the *tsfeneke* was no longer unsure. With incredible speed it whirled, and the single exposed *ksta* separated from it and flew like a crossbow bolt across the short distance to Sunam Ree. It struck her high on the rise of her left breast, between vest and bandolier. She screamed and grasped the wriggling white snake that burrowed into her, but she couldn't tear it loose. Blood oozed from where the *ksta* clung.

"Don't!" Bass grunted, pulling her arm away, prying her clenched fingers loose. "You'll only tear your skin more." Ree's face was a death mask. Hatred and pain contorted her grimace into a grinning skull. Slowly, almost imperceptibly at first, Bass felt her grip loosen. "You're relieved of duty, Ensign Sunam," he murmured, and let go of her arm. She stood alone, swaying. Her face relaxed into flaccid stupidity. Only her eyes glared hatefully at Bass and the treacherous psatla.

"I'm sorry about your brother, Ree. I sent him to his death. Hate me. But trust me in this one thing: You *will* have your revenge. You will have it, and it will sicken you in ways you can't even imagine now. But I can't trust you to believe me, and to remain silent. Your grief is too strong. I must be sure you won't act on it. The psatla drug in your veins will keep you silent for now, and psatla will keep you safe, and out of sight, until matters resolve themselves. But think of this: Your rage has no outlet. It can consume only you, and *it will destroy you*, unless you can let it go.''

He saw no comprehension in her eyes, and suspected she would allow her rage to destroy her. Locked in psatla-induced passivity, she would not surrender, but would become insane. If so, then psatla would have no choice but to further dose her, and add her to the herd, the hidden cattle—Kstala's ''pets.'' It was not an easy thing to do, Bass reflected as Phessift led her away unresisting. He was saddened, but he felt no guilt at all. He had asked nothing of her that he himself would not have done—that he had not done. His memory ranged back to the dark, early days on the *Sally B. Halpern*, to his pain and rage, and his coming to terms with it. Then further back, to the other ship, the *Carrington*, to his drawn-out lashings, endured in silence. But unbeknownst even to him, he was terribly unfair to her: she was not Bass Cannon.

He slept among ferns until the predawn dew chilled him. Then he stretched and waited quietly for Phessift to bring Sunam Ree's subordinates to meet him. In Ree's absence, he had little trouble persuading them to abandon their campaign. He was *sfalek*, of course. He offered them no explanation for Sunam Ree's disappearance, which probably helped convince them, too.

One day the Viper-class ship that dominated Asaph Swadethan lifted skyward, leaving five depressions from her landing legs, a circular earthwork, and a garrison. Her captain rubbed dust-reddened eyes and silently rejoiced. His most fervent prayer had been answered: he had been ordered home. Other ships were leaving, too. As Bass had hoped, and as he had expected, keeping a fleet that represented a major portion of viking resources on and around Phastillan just wasn't practical now that the vikings felt secure in their conquest. Garrison troops and a few courier ships would suffice, aground at key *asapht* and the port, with a relay craft or two in orbit.

For the residents of the *asaph* the ship's rising was cause for no rational joy, but everyone felt a burden lift, as if the ship's departure was a sign that soon they would be entirely free. But the other ships still kept to their posts, two on-planet and the third in orbit, and the garrison left by the departing ship soon made its presence known. That very night the men planned a minor invasion of their own—on the women's quarters in the *asaph*. It wouldn't be rape; the intention might be there, but the vikings were in for a different experience. They had been on Phastillan long enough. Now Phastillan would conquer them. The *asaph*'s women would be no more victims than assailants, and they knew what to expect. Remembering that first time with Betsy, Bass shivered hotly, and the hairs on his neck stood up.

Even as it began, as viking men by ones and twos at first, then in raucous, laughing clusters, pushed through wicker doors, slid aside panels, and sought out their prey in the maze that was the women's quarter of Asaph Swadethan, Bass acted. He didn't do what many had expected of him, or had hoped. He didn't exhort them to take up kitchen knives and pitchforks, to move in and slay vikings while the slavemasters were helpless, coupled with the settlers' wives, mothers and daughters in a delirium of passion only Phastillan could create. Instead he and Nils, who took on the responsibilities of aide-de-camp, moved among the men, soothing and reassuring, cooling anger and restraining. Nothing is wrong; do nothing; let it happen—it's only Phastillan. They must adapt, as must we. This must happen. No one will suffer. Let it be. Phastillan's old-timers took it in stride—it was only sex, after all—but for relative newcomers the viking incursion among their wives and daughters raised ancient specters of degradation and defeat. Many lives were changed that night. The vikings got what they came for, and more, but no women were raped. No one was killed.

Power was exercised, and dominance, but it was not viking power or viking dominance. The triumph belonged to Phastillan: to the still-missing psatla and the rich soil teeming with *ksta*, to rich human-female bodies and rich human-female blood teeming with descendants of the bacteria and viruses Kstala had bred and Bass had delivered to every *asaph*, every settlement on Phastillan. In those moments and hours, ten million years of human evolutionary demand culminated. Half a million generations of genetic tradition commanded impregnation, demanded it with the power and conviction of ancient mammalian adaptation, honed to perfection, was freed of cultural, moral, and intellectual restraint.

High, delicately bossed female crania, eyes seemingly overlarge in light-boned female faces, jutting breasts and swelling, fecund hips all demanded fulfillment. Unshaven female axillae and dark pubic clumps ripe with unscented volatiles were freed all in that moment by ancient prehuman demand and psatla art.

Culture, nurture, and a paltry few millennia of clever artificial restriction became evanescent fantasy, and were inundated in wave after wave of ancient primate lust. Every woman, viking and Phastillan alike, threw off the carefully nurtured "flaws" that had bound her. No obesity made her unlovely, no scars repelled her lovers, no breasts were too large, too pendulous, too small. No male-defined ugliness confined her, for she was Astarte and Aphrodite incarnate, fount and prototype of Olympian lust, and no man was immune to her.

Don Juan and Zeus, satyr and Dionysos, viking males were transformed into priapic machines of infinite stamina, and their deep wells of precious semen gushed forth a multimillion-year heritage, humanity itself written on scrolling, coiling molecules, the story told and retold with every thrust.

It was bacchanal, that night—the all-consuming madness of maenad and Baal, the reign of goat and bull—and it was not Phastillan alone that created it, but the tides and seasons and moon-phases of distant Earth, unremembered, but not forgotten.

Phage: an "eater," a tiny particle of deoxyribonucleic acid surrounded by a protein sheath. Its ancestors rearranged their victims' DNA into replicas of themselves. Now, a new element was introduced: purpose. Not phage-purpose, of course, but psatla-purpose, and Bass Cannon's *psalaat*.

The hot vapors of coitus might seem, to phages, like the collision of star clusters and galaxies, each human cell a world where tiny phage-starships sought their programmed destinations.

Unsheathed olfactory nerves were the only pathways from the world outside to the human brain. Phages, like ships penetrating the Reef, passed through. Braving the synapse gaps, tricking them into accepting phages as proper neurotransmitter enzymes, they migrated brainward along the nerve filaments and locked themselves in nerve-cell and brain-cell genes. Phages no longer, they became strings of codons—genes—and like genes, they awaited the proper stimulus to act. Phage had become prophage.

Bass felt his men's pain, their jaw-clenching helplessness and loss of self-esteem. Now in the throes of a madness all Phastillan's humans knew so well, the vikings were as helpless as coupling dogs. Honor, pride, and the whole rich panoply of human expectations demanded that the settlers slay the marauders, the enemy, that they preserve the fertile ground within the *asaph* for their own seed. Bass Cannon and Nils Abrams at Asaph Swadethan, Ade Folgrin, released from his cell at the port, and selected others at every *asaph*, village, and facility where women lived, all told them, "No, wait. Let Phastillan itself vanquish them." They waited, and Bass, no less agonized than they, waited with them. But *psalaat* ruled him more than ever; Phastillan needed the vikings' genes, and needed them to take the women's secret plague. Without your knowledge or consent, our women steal your worth, he thought. Emptied of semen, you are empty shells to be tossed away, rubbish on our middens.

Psatla, too, felt the power of the primal human genes, the wild, wordless life-song, and many heard a death-song as well. The human pheromones on the wind, similar enough to those of the psatla to create the effect, stimulated psatla to their own sexual frenzy, and one after another young *tsfeneke* with little self-control and old psatla with little physical cohesion succumbed to the small death and spread their *ksta* in Phastillan's soil.

Less suddenly than it had begun, the effect muted. The sun rose and fell one time, and the sounds of evening were less lusty than before. Moans and thrashing now alternated with giggles and harsh laughter in the women's quarters across Phastillan. The second sunrise brought quietude, and as the second day grew ripe, pale faces peered from *asapht* windows, Phastillan faces and viking ones awakening to the cool reality of their separation, men from women.

That day and the next viking guards returned to their neglected duties, their expressions thoughtful, sheepish, or smug according to their natures. One look all held in common, and that was fear. Had they indeed conquered Phastillan? Guards assigned to the men's quarters found themselves being less abusive toward their prisoners, who in turn looked upon the guards with cool understanding of their unwanted common bond. Day followed day. Quiet, subdued days and intervening nights. No more sounds of nocturnal activity in the women's quarters reached the other side.

A courier ship, the one that had towered over Asaph Swadethan, had gone. Kstala and two of his aides had arranged to be among the hostages taken aboard. Jake Pirel reported that across Phastillan ships had landed and lifted, ships carrying psatla. Intercepted communications revealed that psatla were to be taken to other viking worlds as slaves, to produce metal ores upon demand. Jake confirmed that the effect had speeded up a plan already developed. Vikings had been carefully led to believe that the effect was Phastillan's, not psatla's, and that it would not repeat itself on other worlds. Bass visualized the movement of ships that Pirel described, red sparks separating from Phastillan, joining others in orbit. He pictured frightened psatla being herded from hold to hold, *ksta* clinging to each other by will alone. He imagined the red-plotted courses bound outward toward the Oortcloud fleet, and the frightened psatla being retransferred, and the departure thereafter of dozens of large vessels, each on different courses, each headed away from Phastillan until they were beyond recall in the abyss between stars.

It was time. Day followed day, each one the same. Bass awaited word from outside—he didn't know how it would be delivered, only that it had to be soon; the lieutenant called assemblies every day now. The subject of his ravings was always the same: Where is Vassily James Cannon? He threatened, cajoled, and bribed, to no avail. Only tenuous threads of discipline held him in check. If his threats were made good, there would be no choice—Bass would have to surrender. Only *psalaat* made him wait. Kstala's tiny pets must be well distributed even on the farthest ships. No vessel must remain untouched. Pinnaces flitted between viking ships, and Pirel reported their movements ninety-six hours later. When he judged that every vessel had been touched by men from another, when the chain of psatla infestation looped back on itself, he scrawled three words on a scrap of paper. The note was delivered by psatla who slipped through woods and swamp and prairie-burn like green and brown ghosts. IT IS TIME, Pirel's note said.

Mitosis: somatic cells divided, and divided again. Each time, a prophage divided, too—it was part and parcel of the cell now. Prophages, along with millions of other genes, awaited their proper moment of expression. They lay dormant in neurons and adrenal cortices and hypothalami and sweat-gland cells, awaiting a stimulus, a signal to proceed.

Outside—a universe away, for a tiny prophage gene—psatla in forest concentration camps of hastily strung wire spoke among themselves, speaking even to their fellows across hundreds of miles, their words carried on invisible, silent currents of air: sophisticated molecules, DNA-like codes translated as light, volatile proteins.

"Is it time?" psatla wondered. "Are you ready?" they asked.

Time. When every guard outside makeshift psatla prisons has returned from village or *asaph* reeking of the small death of human sexual congress, then it would be time. When every viking man on guard and every viking woman on the ships was infected with Kstala's pets, it would be time.

It was deep night when the waiting ended. Viking boots thudded on the shredded moss of the *asaph*'s floors, and weapon fittings jingled. Somewhere outside a deep male voice howled without words. Bass knew that eerie sound; it was time. Shots were fired, muted quickly in damp forest air. A viking kicked Bass's door in, then harshly ordered him out. Time. The man's eyes shone wide with uncomprehending terror and Bass knew what he feared. He heard more howls and a familiar, clear, high hooting. Gripping his captor by the wrist, ignoring the pistol in the man's other hand, Bass caught his eyes. "Don't be afraid. Remember your training. Fear kills. Panic kills."

"They've gone mad! They've all gone mad. The sergeant . . ."

"Yes. They are mad, right now. But don't be afraid. It's like the other time, like with the women. It will pass. It will end." For us, it will end, he appended silently. For Phastillan, there will be an end to vikings. But for you, this night will go on forever. It is your only night, your last.

His words seemed to have some effect. "Outside," the viking commanded. "Assemble at the screen." Perhaps this one would do no violence before he succumbed like the others. He was still coherent, and Bass didn't dare try to take the pistol from him.

It is time. His heart pounding, Bass moved, stumbling in darkness. Outside, starlight and a clear sky made the going easier. Others joined him, prisoners all. In the black night he couldn't tell for sure, but it seemed that there were too few guards.

Stimulus: psatla sang. A scent-symphony composed in notes of floating enzymes blew on Phastillan's well-planned winds. It was a symphony "heard" by psatla everywhere, even carried skyward on clothing and skin and hair to ships in orbit, where psatla hostages began to sing. Across Phastillan the song carried, and beyond. Psatla on even the farthest vessels smelled their captors' fear when the reports of strange behavior came in, and they guessed that it was time.

Psatla words, psatla songs penetrated human nasal membranes and blood-vessel walls. They rushed and tumbled in bloodstreams, notes seeking their places, musical eighth-notes on the score sheets of human DNA.

The fortification was unlit. Shapes could be seen within, moving, shifting. Below, men of the *asaph* stood huddled against a psychic chill. To one side was another group, vague silhouettes. Bass's nostrils told him they were women—a dozen, twenty at most. No guards stood atop the walled berm. It was time. Bass breathed deeply, readying himself.

From the woods came sounds of thrashing and running. Voices

called out harshly, muffled by humidity, out of breath. An eerie, hollow hoot answered them. Shots were fired, and nearby howls stopped, but other voices began farther away, shrill and malevolent, deep in the trees.

Bass darted for the darkness of the forest. No guards called out, no shots reverberated. He ran, no longer stumbling, his feet knowing his destination: a place where he and Betsy had met and trysted many times. The aircar was there, and the port was only minutes away. There was someone he had to see before it was too late.

The lieutenant's voice snarled from the aircar's com, too. "This is your last chance," he howled. "I want Cannon now! You hear me, Bass Cannon? Come out or the hostages die!" His breath came in short gasps, panicky, hollow rales. "You out there! You want your infected bitches to die? Your fine, leading citizens, too? To die like my men are dying? It's a plague, you fools, and Cannon can stop it! You'll be next! Your precious wormbags have infected us all!" It was the first Bass had heard of deaths among the vikings. He knew that no plague had killed them—they had died with frightened comrades' bullets in them, died when they'd howled and hooted in animal panic and strove to tear off the clothing that clung like terrifying leeches to their bodies as their human minds faded, forever.

Prophages, long dormant, awakened. They twisted, forcing apart the double-helical strands. Carefully, precisely, gene strands were cut and patched into new codes, their messages altered.

In an endocrine cell prophages coded for a hormone that suppresses "fight" chemicals. Aggression ceased, and anger. All that was left, when adrenaline surged, was to flee.

In some other unnamed cell, prophages and RNA polymerase created a template that would through the interaction of ribosomes and fragmentary transfer RNA, string together a protein, an enzyme, that neutralized male sexual desire. It would swim in human bloodstreams until it, too, was neutralized by yet another "song," a human-female one tied to the endless circling of Phastillan about its sun.

In brain cells, prophages were genes expressing a neurotransmitter in one cell, a neurosuppressor in another. Prophage-patterned proteins opened broad neural pathways here and there, while other paths were broken. Like detour signs at synaptic crossroads, prophage-proteins directed traveling nerve impulses in new directions. Only sex cells remained unchanged. Sperm and ova still carried their original messages. Offspring of the changed ones would still be . . . human.

Bass keyed the aircar's com and quickly found the lieutenant's channel. Boosting his transmitter to override a mishmash of anxious queries and commands, he said, "This is Cannon, Lieutenant. I'm coming in. No one must die—not your people or mine. Hold your men back."

"Cannon! This is your doing! Make it stop, or they're *going* to die."

"This is Phastillan, Lieutenant," Bass said regretfully. "Nothing can stop it. But no one needs to die. Your job is to keep order until this is over."

"My job? My job is to have you under arms," the wild, harsh voice returned.

"And you will, shortly. But no killing. I'm coming in, but if my people die . . ." He left it unsaid. There was really nothing he could do. Repulsors screamed, and the 'car jounced and shot skyward. The trees were a sea of midnight green below, sparked here and there with fires, lights, and an occasional muzzle flare or laser burst.

"Cannon can stop it," the lieutenant's electronic voice repeated inanely. Bass shook his head sadly. Nothing could stop it now. When vikings had mated with Phastillan's women the exchange had been a simple one: viking genes for Kstala's tiny pets. Psatla had made their human symbiotes immune. What else had psatla done? Bass pushed curiosity aside. There would be time later, if he survived this night, this counterinvasion. No, nothing could stop it now. Plague and *psalaat* spread together.

The port was below him. Fighters from the mother ship squalled by overhead. Below, men scrambled among buildings and flames. Bass dropped the 'car near a floodlit Viper.

Five men guarded Folgrin and several women, herding them into the light with urgent, ungentle rifle barrels. In a hatch above, a madman shrieked, his foppish mustache leaping like a mad, bristly worm. He saw Bass drop from the 'car and suspicion lit his insane eyes. Did he somehow recognize him, or was it only a lucky guess? "Cannon!" he shrieked. "Up here with me, or they die!" Four riflemen stepped back and took aim at dark, huddled shapes.

Bass stepped forward. He passed among the condemned. Hands reached out to stop him, clutching his arms, but he shook them off and walked steadily toward the ship. Two rifles came to bear upon him. Only two—a third rifleman dropped his weapon and stood idly by, his head swiveling, seeking, confused. Another was missing, having dropped to all fours and crept into the darkness.

"I'm coming up there to talk with you, Lieutenant," Bass said, loudly, calmly. Soon the viking would be beyond rational conversation. Bass hoped to stall him for only a vital minute or two, to keep him from giving the command to fire. Ordering his thoughts as he walked, he created a fantasy in his mind:

Hot sun beats down on my tawny, brindled fur and warms rough breccia under my hands and feet. My nose feels females nearby and males lurking and cringing. Only one other is above in the rocks, barking and chattering his defiance of me. He is puffed up with rage and fear.

I climb up. He grins and yawns empty threats. I face him. He smells my power and my juices on the wind. His fur is musky and he is aroused, but anger fuels his arousal, not fawning females. His fear stinks, and females scorn him.

I am unafraid and my blood surges with strength and quickness; females edge toward me. I am male and large and smart, and the females are mine. The high place is mine.

No one stopped Bass's ascent to the hatch. A wan, predawn glow cast itself halfway across the sky. Several vikings huddled tightly against the far wall beyond the airlock, making themselves small, surrendering to him.

The lieutenant stood alone in the lock, abandoned. Fear and anger prickled the air between the two men, and a wild, angry light shone in the viking officer's eyes. Anger—and fear. Expression after expression raced across his face. He hated Bass. He feared him. He was confused, confounded, lost. Something was happening to him, something odd and terrifying that he didn't understand at all. Who was he afraid of? Who did he hate?

"Hoo!" he howled. "Hoo! Hoo, hwaow! Hoooo!" He danced back from Bass and crouched among his fellows, stepping on his fallen cap.

"Hoo, haaaah, hwaoh, hah!" said the others in unruly chorus. "Heh heh heh hooo!"

Bass squatted in front of him. So young! he thought. He's still a boy, almost. Star-years. He's traveled fast, on old ships, but he's paid for those years out of time. Now he'll pay forever, and he'll never grow up a man. The viking's eyes were wild and raw, no longer remembering, reacting only to the scents and pheromones of Bass's dominance. The sharp tang of urine rose from a darkening patch on his trousers, from a growing puddle beneath him.

"Hwaoh, hoo!" he said as the light faded, this time forever. Bass rose and turned his back on the once-men who crouched with heads turned away, whose averted eyes looked everywhere but at him. One slipped back into the ship, scrabbling over crates and boxes, clawing desperately and moaning.

Below the ship, women sought out mates and friends. The guards' rifles were meaningless sticks, dropped on hard pavement. Ade approached the platform with two others. "Try to get the clothes off them," Bass commanded, "or they'll become infected from their wastes. Get them away from the port somewhere, anywhere, and turn them loose—we'll round them up later and psatla can care for them."

"Bass—what is this? What's wrong with them?" Ade's voice cracked with fear. Will we get it, too, whatever it is? was his unspoken question.

"Wrong?" Bass shook his head slowly. "Nothing's wrong, Ade. These are Kstala's creation. They've adapted. They're Phastillan's now. Our planet's own *Bos primigenis*—wild cattle. It was a trade. Their genes for . . ." He realized he was rambling. Stress by-products made his limbs feel like soft mud, and his thoughts were fuzzy and ill-defined. Shaking his head hard to clear it, he told them he had to rest in his aircar. "An hour or so. I don't think it's necessary, but put out an all-channel call, code word 'cattle drive.' The cadres will know what to do. We have to save as many as we can. And send some crews out to find the psatla—those still alive. They know what's happened, but I want to see them, all of them."

These simple, straight pathways through viking brains were not new. They were the dusty savanna-ways, the slow ponderings of remote australopithecine ancestors, and even more ancient paths through sun-dappled branches—vine-to-vine and tree-to-tree passages of dimly remembered predecessors.

Vikings—eaters of worlds. Starship-fliers, corsairs on sun-paths. They were gone. No longer driven, their purpose fulfilled—though they, like the viruses that conquered them, neither knew their purpose nor cared—they were bound into the gene-stuff of Phastillan: dormant strings of codons, waiting. Waiting.

Night passed. Dawn broke clear and rosy, a new day like no other. Bass stood by the com console in port control. Overhead, a lone fighter streaked the midmorning sky. Whistles and crackles spat from the console's speaker as the radio tech changed from one setting to the next. He turned to Bass. "I'm on his frequency."

Bass took the pickup from the tech. "Phastillan control to unidentified fighter. Your forces have surrendered. You are ordered to land and turn yourself over to planetary authority. Acknowledge, please."

The carrier registered nothing. Then, softly, progressively louder as the craft made another rackety circling pass over the *asaph*, the pilot spoke: "Hooo!" he said. "Hah, hoo, hwahh. Heh heh hooo!"

Bass shook his head. He spun on his heel and left the room. Outside, the day was hot and humid. He caught the fighter's glitter low over the trees, miles off. Perhaps the pilot's hands and eyes still remembered skills his mind forgot. Bass squinted, waiting. The sun hurt his unshaded eyes. Then he saw it. Above the trees rose a column of wet, white smoke laced with greasy black. Burnt plastic and nearby trees were quickly consumed in a raging blaze, a blaze soon quenched in Phastillan's moist, dew-laden air. The cloud that rose like twisting, living *ksta* was for a while steam-white, and then it was gone.

Bass imagined the pilot's last moments in his cramped, unfamiliar cage. Had he been afraid? Had he clawed at his harness and lashed out with bleeding fists at bright baubles strewn on panels before him? Had he stared bemused at the rushing vistas of treetops and hills? Bass heard silent echoes of the sounds preceding his final impact: "Hoo! Heh heh hwaoh. Hoa. Hoo! Hoo!"

CHAPTER

FORTY

Bass listened anxiously to reports of death and damage, but after forty-eight hours there was little more to be heard. Phastillan had gotten off lightly. Only a few humans had died. Psatla casualties were higher, but no planned pogrom had been carried out. Confined like cattle in wire pens, some had chosen the small death as the price of freedom. Fences were no barrier to burrowing *ksta*. Many younglings would emerge in the years to come, Bass knew, who would remind him of others he'd known, now gone. It was the psatla way, and Phastillan's: in chaos and disruption are the future's solutions forged. In disbanded *ksta* are a new generation, with shuffled memories and genes, new answers to all the old questions. But enough psatla had survived intact for *psalaat* to continue.

Living psatla, returning singly or in groups, were welcomed by men and women with laughter, tears, and hugs that rattled their chitinous armor. They endured the embraces stoically, all the while reveling in the joyous perfumes that suffused the air.

Phastillan's recovery began at once. The cadres, those in place in the beginning and others Bass had converted from rebellion, organized citizens not involved in pressing tasks to care for the erstwhile vikings. Much had to be done. Simple things were deadly to them, even belts, boots, and trousers. They had to be led to places with adequate forage, of kinds they could digest, before they starved. Immune to most of Phastillan's microorganisms, they still suffered human-borne infections, and many had open sores or infected injuries incurred in their headlong flight from all things . . . human.

The hostages, even those on the orbiting mother ship, were free. Swadeth's return occasioned an enthusiastic celebration at the *asaph* that bore his name. He told how they took the mother

ship with a new strain of virus that only pacified—excised mad
ambition without the devastating effects they'd all witnessed on
Phastillan. Developed while the vikings held Phastillan, there had
been no way to distribute it. Ships rose from Phastillan and pointed
outward toward the Oort cloud. On board were Phastillan prisoners, human and psatla alike, and viking crewmen, too. Would
psatla meddling have left those vikings more human than their
comrades on Phastillan who had suffered the original form of the
plague? Bass was reluctant to ask. One way or another, they had
to be brought back. Their genes were needed. *Psalaat*.

Bass wondered how it had all been done. What, exactly, had
kept Phastillan's folk from succumbing? He knew timing had been
important, that Kstala's viruses had inserted themselves in the
interval between the vikings' exposure to Phastillan and their adaptation to it. The implications were disquieting: psatla had med-
dled with human genes before. They had done it all along.
Immunity to a plague that made mindless apes of "normal" humans was one such change—what else had psatla done? The
changes weren't superficial. Some were genetic modifications,
not bacterial tinkering; the essence of all things human was not
sacred to psatla. Of course, with humans now officially considered psatla, the ancient dictum "never-to-become-not-psatla" applied, but what did that really mean? Could *fsa-psatla* be equated
with inhuman? Not human? Antihuman? What would psatla make
of it? More to the point, what would they make of men and
women—and how far would they go? Was he, Bass Cannon, really
a traitor to his own kind, a quisling, a Hitlerian manipulator? Had
there been any choice? One damnation or another. Chaos or *psalaat*. Either way his unique vision qualified him to make the
choices he had made, because no one else had: not the world
leaders of transReef, nor the defunct Panaikos Council, nor the
ordinary people who had chosen their own shortsighted paths and
had died or become vikings. Compared with the alternatives, his
psalaat was gentle, gradual, and kind. He shrugged off his guilt.
There had been no alternatives, and there was no going back. His
psalaat was only one path. Psatla had others, and they might
confide in him, or not. The one who could have told him everything he wanted to know was gone: Kstala.

Phastillan's counterstroke against the viking homeworlds
wouldn't happen right away. Kstala would wait until it was too
late to contain the "pets" his *ksta* carried. It was the new plague,
Swadeth assured Bass, so it would spread quietly as waves of
disinterest and a yearning for quiet peace. Perhaps another viking

expedition would still be mounted, but it would be much delayed. Another admiral would be cautious, not knowing the fate of his predecessor, and in time, he, too, would succumb.

The hordes of former vikings, hooting and scratching in mindless confusion, were a weight on Bass's shoulders. He had caused their degradation. He had given his race into the white, boneless hands of psatla manipulators. Before, *psalaat* had been reason enough for his surrender, but seeing the vacuous faces, he couldn't help wonder how Betsy would look, or Adam. The power had been given psatla to do what they deemed best, but he couldn't help doubting.

Betsy arrived at Asaph Swadethan with little Adam in tow. She swept in unannounced and deposited Adam in a willing psatla's arms, instructing him to deliver the child, and the note pinned on his tiny jumpsuit, to Swadeth.

The *sfalek-ni* Swadeth, with a well-fed Adam comfortably sleeping in his arms, opened the folded paper with slender, dexterous *ksta*. His three eyes, their covering skin now almost entirely gold, darted unconcertedly over Betsy's note, each one reading a separate portion of it. As he read, his arm chitin and body segments trembled, droning like grasshoppers in a dry meadow. There was no mockery in his psatla laughter, nor condescension toward the determined human female who asked him to baby-sit her tiny offspring and send her husband to meet her "in our favorite spot—he'll know where I mean." Swadeth approved of her planning and forethought. She had food and blankets, she wrote, and even a tarpaulin tent to shelter herself and her mate while the estrous frenzy was upon them.

Bass and Betsy weren't disturbed in their woodland glade. Even uncaptured vikings who still wandered noisily nearby seemed to sense their need and skirted their campsite. Little Adam's sister, Elizabeth, was born two hundred and sixty-one days later, a month before the final, vital detail of Bass's *psalaat* fell into place.

There's nothing now but to wait, Bass told himself repeatedly over the months before *psalaat* matured. The ships must go out, and return. They must seed all the worlds with hope that Phastillan can give them what they need to survive, that Phastillan is the key, perhaps not to the ending of chaos, but to the rejuvenation of transReef, this isolated litter of human-dominated stars. The ships must come, from Lonesome, from Stand Pat and Coeur, and from . . .

Bass didn't linger among such thoughts, nor did he recapitulate the lichen thought of his exile. Though *psalaat* must wait upon circumstance, there was still much call for his time. Urgent messages in his incoming data file were as common as days. He selected one from the queue with that particular blend of excitement and annoyance that characterized that whole period of his life. The message was from Helm Stegler, at the refinery north of Asaph Swadethan. Stube Ryman, one of Helm's men, had killed an ex-viking. Helm didn't say "murdered" him, just "killed"— and that was the problem. Bass ordered his aircar readied, and carried his coffee mug out with him. It was going to be a long day.

Ryman wasn't locked up. There were no detention facilities, so he just waited in his room, with a tough-looking companion at the door. Bass was shocked. Stube had been a good-looking man when Bass last saw him. His broken, twisted nose wasn't good-looking now. His asymmetrical face reminded Bass of the viking admiral's, a malleable-seeming mass, expressionless. His one good eye wasn't expressionless, though; Bass read hatred there, and defiance. "Stube?" he began.

" 'Stube,' you say? Like you don't recognize me, eh? Well, that's no surprise to me. I didn't recognize me either, when the bandages came off."

"Did you have to kill him, Stube? The man who did that to you is long gone. You killed an animal."

"Yeah? Well, I'm glad to hear *you* say that, Cannon. I really am. So fine me for hunting wild pig out of season."

"It's not that simple. You killed his genes, too. You killed his father, his forefathers . . . all the generations that led up to him."

"Look, that sounds like mystical guff to me. I never touched his four fathers, or his mothers, either. How about let's settle this, so I can get back to work?"

Bass sighed. He hadn't expected this one to be easy. That was why he had come. "I'll discuss it with Helm, and others. They'll let you know what's decided." He departed.

Assan Hasturian arrived just as Bass came outside. "Stube was with me on C-Fourteen, Bass. I have a right to speak for him."

"I don't deny it, 'San. But who will speak *against* him? Who will speak for . . . for the one who was once Horge Samlson?"

"Horgey whatsisname was just like the ones who killed everything Stube loved, on C-Fourteen. And you saw Stube's face. Doesn't that count for something?"

"I regret that. Stube lost much, here and on C-Fourteen. But that doesn't excuse him. He's set an awkward precedent. Can any sentient human be allowed to have his way with our unintelligent charges? Is rape permissible? The abuse of their children? Where will it end, 'San? I want it to end right here.''

"How? What can you do that's fair to Stube, too?''

"I am going to charge him with murder. He will be tried.''

"Bass, that's nuts. No one on this planet will convict him.''

"I wonder. What are we, 'San? What are we Phastillans, anyway?''

"I don't follow.''

"You voted on Treaty Day, didn't you? How did you vote?''

Assan Hasturian turned pale. "Bass, that's not fair. You can't do that.''

"I can. I will. You voted to become psatla, 'San, and so did Stube. And psatla will try him.''

The trial date was set. Hasturian would defend the accused. Swadeth would prosecute. A jury of six psatla and six humans would render judgment. Ade Folgrin would preside. It would take time to arrange, and Pirel wanted Bass to tour Phastillan's new defenses. Bass thought the time was opportune. Out there, beyond Phastillan, no one would corner him in out-of-court defense of Stube Ryman.

Bass was impressed with Pirel's arrangements from the moment they achieved orbit. Close-orbiting ex-viking ships were thick as flies. Nothing could get through them. A total of fifty ships had remained in-system when the plague hit, and every one was now under Phastillan command. There were several major dreadnoughts patrolling in overlapping half shells as far out as the Oort cloud. The 680-AU sensor range of the old defense setup was expanded by forty percent. Now not even an FTL spaceframe with a corebreaker payload could get past.

"What's the duty tour on those patrols, Jake?'' Bass asked, thinking of his satellite repair job so long ago. "What do they do about the 'effect' when they come home?''

Jake merely smiled. "I think you'll want to see for yourself, Bass. Can you take three days for a short FTL hop? I have a cruiser waiting. The crew would be honored to have you aboard.'' Bass smiled and agreed to go. Three whole days. By then, he hoped, Stube Ryman's trial would be under way.

The Earthward navy might have tolerated what the vikings had done to the *Grand Sirius*, the pride of their fleet; there was nothing that paint and scrubbing couldn't cure. But the ship Bass toured would have given a navy man ulcers. There was dirt on the decks.

Not trash; dirt. And moss, and things growing in it. Phastillan things. There wasn't room for trees, but some of the potted bushes were a fair substitute. The psatla loved them. Psatla? "Jake, how many psatla are aboard?"

"Just over a hundred."

"Incredible. And human crew?"

"Seventy-five. All told, she's overstaffed by fifty—that's with the psatla, of course."

"How did you do it? And why, for gossake?"

"Nobody wanted to be odd man out when they went home, so they asked for the psatla. And psatla? Well, they've been traveling on ships since humans were furry little things, to hear Swadeth tell it. They can adapt, too. And if you really mean to start psatla colonies on Hokkaido and—"

"Keep that under your hat, Jake. I'm not ready for that to get out yet. But this—it's incredible. Doesn't all this green stuff muck up the air system?"

"Muck it up? Nobody's wearing boots. Except when the mosses sporulate, the filters stay cleaner than ever."

Bass shook his head. Maybe things weren't as difficult as they seemed each time he checked his incoming file. Some people were solving their own problems without his help—and helping him, too. *Psalaat,* he thought. The juggernaut gains momentum.

He got back to Phastillan in time for the trial. As predicted, the jury was hung fifty-fifty. Using his right as judge, under a precedent he claimed was usual among psatla, Swadeth made his own decision. Exile. Lifetime exile, under conditions much like those Bass had endured. Nobody was really happy with the outcome of the trial, but at least it established that the ex-vikings had a place on Phastillan, too, and that their all-too-human pasts weren't to return to haunt them—or kill them.

Bass got back almost in time for Elizabeth Cannon to be born, too; he had to hurry to be at Betsy's side to see little Liz nurse for the first time. True to form, Betsy had continued to work up to the last moment, so the happy event took place on a rocky island in the subtemperate southern sea. The hospital was a stone hut, the equipment Betsy's aircar first-aid kit, and the doctor an old psatla from Asaph Lesthefan who was in charge of climate modification for the southern hemisphere. Employing wafted odors of blood, distinctly female sweat, and—how did he ever know?—baby powder, the *pralasek* Anethk reassured Bass that all had gone quite well.

"Well?" Betsy challenged him when he arrived at her bedside, out of breath. "Do you approve?" He did, deeply. The small, still-wet baby was almost as pretty, to him, as his wife—who was almost as wet, and not nearly as fresh-smelling. Betsy didn't care. She knew how profoundly she had changed, and though the children were not a cause of her newfound self-worth, they were surely a symbol of it. Perhaps, she pondered, eyeing her husband as he eyed the new infant, I'll always be a bit of a whore, and not comfortable with my exalted status, but at least I'm not as uncomfortable as Bass looks right now.

Bass was indeed discomfited. Baby Elizabeth had just left a creamy-tan deposit on her mother's flaccid belly, and the *pralasek* Anethk's busy *ksta* were ingesting it.

"It's just baby poop, Bass," his wife said, grinning.

"Yeah, that's what it is, all right," he replied. "But I don't think I'll share a pot of stew with Anethk tonight." Betsy didn't bat an eye. Bass was pleased, once he had time to think about it all. It was nice to realize that in some ways, others were much better adapted to Phastillan, and to psatla ways, than he was.

CHAPTER
FORTY-ONE

The awaited day finally arrived. As with so many important events, the long wait had dulled the edge of urgency Bass had attempted to instill in others. There were screwups, and he wasn't notified of the arrival of the first ship from Cannon's Orb. He didn't know it was in-system until it roared by over his very head, on a typical glide-path entry that minimized pollutants at the expense of minor atmospheric disturbances. He was en route to one of the southern *asapht*, and he immediately turned the 'car ninety-five degrees and headed for the spaceport. He had recognized the ship: his father's old lumber trader, now rejuvenated, the blue-and-gold maple leaf and antique bucksaw bright on her hull.

He raged all the way to the port. The ship's passage left a trail of static that gimmicked his 'com and he couldn't even growl at Ade for the oversight, but he made up for it when he arrived. The post staff had never seen Bass angry before. Not that his anger was any worse, objectively, than that of any other medium-height, sandy-bearded Phastillan's—but he was the *sfalek*, and they were genuinely afraid. Ade, ever kind, stood between his staff and his boss, and sheltered them. He hadn't known about the ship either, but Bass wasn't about to find that out, not from him. Anger washed over the larger man like pounding surf over salt-rotted crags, with much roaring and splashing, and no more short-term effect than water on long-enduring rock. Ade endured, and eventually Bass became calm enough to issue an order.

"I want that ship quarantined, Ade. I don't want a word to pass to or from that vessel unless I'm right there to okay it!" The ex-captain had never seen Bass so tense. "This ship is special," he explained. "I need to know everything about it. Everything. I want the log dumps, the personnel records . . . but make it all sound S.O.P., okay?"

"That's easy enough. Bass. May I ask why?"

"*Gadesh*, Ade. Cannon's Orb is going to have a lesson in *gadesh*." He spun on his heel and left through the still-open door.

M. V. BARRED SPIRAL. Permanent Registry: Cannon's Orb (NT 4700). Trader Class Tf-7, 75m tons cap. Cargo of Record: None.

Bass tapped the printout against his leg and smiled an odd, contented smile. Betsy called it his "murky, mean look," and claimed he only showed it when he was about to do something shocking or make someone very uncomfortable. He flipped past the flimsy cover to the second page, a list of the ship's crew and passengers. The latter interested him most:

Dovstran, Alexei
          Bio: 39 std. Abs: 39 std. POR Cannon's Orb, NT4702
Nickerson, Oliver
          Bio: 39 std. Abs: 39 std. POR Cannon's Orb, NT4702
Santiago, Roberto
          Bio: 38 std. Abs: 38 std. POR Cannon's Orb, NT4702
T'song, Wayne
          Bio: 40 std. Abs: 40 std. POR Cannon's Orb, NT4702
Van Elderen, Jacobus
          Bio: 61 std. Abs: 61 std. POR Cannon's Orb, NT4702

Alex, Ollie, Rob, and Wayne. Only Stef isn't here. Interesting, Bass thought. Their ship has the newer drives, so their ages still match. Not with mine, though. Even Rob is eight years older than me. I wonder how it will feel to see them again? God! How many times did this happen to Dad? He must be a hundred fifty, absolute. The difference is, Jack *used* the time-stretch. It only *happened* to me, and I begrudged every day, every year of it. But, like him, I've used my time well. Have they? They must have, or they wouldn't be here, representing the Orb. What luck! Them . . . *Psalaat*, Bass knew, was unaffected by the identities of the Orbers. Any Orb ship, any responsible men, would have done as well—but he exulted that he would be able to face these very four again, and on his own turf, his terms. Joseph's brothers have come to Egypt at last, Father. They come begging grain. Even now, Pharaoh prepares for an audience with them . . .

Inwardly aswirl with mixed emotions, Bass seemed cool, and his calculating mien gave Ade severe misgivings. "From your expression, I'd guess you found what you wanted," Ade commented. "I think my arrangements will meet your approval, too. The five representatives of the Orb will be brought to Asaph Phaniikan at noon tomorrow. The meeting hall, the empty room next to it . . . It's all arranged."

"There's been no contact with them? They haven't had questions?"

"I imagine they're on their best behavior. They're suppliants, not trading partners—not yet, at any rate." He eyed Bass dubiously. "I'm taking your word that you're not engaged in a vendetta."

"I wish I could reassure you, Ade. It is truly *gadesh*, not revenge. Phaniik Reis and Swadeth both have agreed to it." There was no other man to whom Bass would have spoken that way, like a boy pleading with an adamant father. "The Orb will be a test case. If they accept my *psalaat*—in modified form—they'll be the first of many worlds like Phastillan, psatla and human. We can't continue to supply our neighbors unless other worlds take some of the burden, or the mining worlds will have to be reopened—with Earthside capital—and the cycle of chaos will start all over, repeating until we've destroyed ourselves."

"And you want them to let psatla colonize their world?"

"They're here because they're desperate. I could probably order them to take psatla with them, but our symbiotes aren't just components in biorefineries, which is how they'd use them. I can't advance humanity's cause at psatla expense. The Orb is going to have to beg for a psatla colony.''

"And you'll trick them into doing it? Is that it?"

"I'll manipulate them into opening their minds, I hope, because neither force nor trickery will work, in the long run.''

"What *will* work?" Ade sounded less dubious than he had moments earlier.

"I want to train a human *sfalek-ni* from the Orb, then send him home again.''

Despite Ade's raised eyebrows, Bass was satisfied that his wishes would be met. He slipped out of port as quietly as he could and returned to Asaph Phaniikan to prepare a reception for his childhood friends, his betrayers.

The architecture of a typical *asaph* lent itself admirably to eavesdropping, and Asaph Phaniikan's wood and wicker walls were no barrier to sound. Bass felt no differently than he had as a child, creeping to his father's study door at night to listen to the adult conversations held within. His schoolmates' voices had deepened with age, so he couldn't tell, at first, who spoke.

First voice: "God, what a weird place. And that bed—if that's what it is—it looks like it grew here. Are we supposed to sleep on that?''

Second voice: "Try it, Ollie—it's comfortable enough, and it smells good. Some kind of moss, and straw.''

First voice—Ollie: "It's probably got bugs. I wish I'd brought an air mattress.''

Third voice: "Shut up, Ollie. This place doesn't have any poisonous ones. I want to get things figured out. Let me get it straight: The portmaster—Folgrin?—said we'd meet with their head whatever-it-is . . .''

Second voice: *"Sfalek-ni."*

Third voice: "Yeah, Sefalik-whatever. Said we'd meet him tomorrow to talk about trade. So we've got a real problem, fellows.''

Ollie: "Nothing to trade, you mean? We don't know what they want, yet. Once we find out, we'll go back to the Orb for it.''

Third voice: "Maybe. If we can show them things they want, and if they'll advance us the fuel. Old Man Cannon wasn't exactly generous with it. We're a suicide mission—either we talk them out of some, or we'll be smelling all this shit the rest of our lives.''

Second voice: "It's not exactly suicide, Alex. None of us is going to die.''

Third voice—Alex: "You know what I mean. You call this

living? A bark hut full of pissants? We should have held out for enough fuel to return. At least we could have bargained with the bugs.''

Second voice, impatiently: ''You volunteered, remember? If we'd taken more, what about the Orb's defenses? You can't run particle beams with steam engines.''

Ollie: ''Rob's right, Alex. We knew what we were doing and why we all volunteered.''

Fourth voice, an older man who had to be Jake Van Elderen: ''I haven't brought this up before—the time never seemed right—but I don't really know why you volunteered, Ollie—or any of you, for that matter. Jack could have sent other expendables, like me.''

Ollie: ''We thought we owed it to him, Jake. It's an old story.''

Jake: ''Why? You don't owe him more than anyone else on the Orb, yet you, Jack's prime contractors, all volunteered for a last-ditch, possibly one-way, trip.''

Second voice: ''Guilt, that's why! Guilt and expiation. You could almost say this trip is a pilgrimage, a penance . . . or a taste of hell.''

Fifth voice, a smooth, high tenor that Bass immediately recognized as Wayne T'song: ''Shut up, Rob! You don't speak for the rest of us.''

Second voice—Rob: ''Does it really matter? We were fools to have come. Besides, all that was twenty-two years ago.''

Ollie: ''Both of you shut up! What about this meeting? We've got to tell this *sfalek* something.''

Jake: ''How about the truth? Whatever we promise him, the Cannons will deliver. Ben gave me a free rein—anything that won't harm Orb security.''

Alex: ''What about his old man? What did Jack Cannon say?''

Jake: ''Nothing. Ben did all the talking. The power has passed from father to son, Alex—you might as well get used to it.''

Alex: ''The kid! If Bass was still alive it'd be different, but . . .''

Jake: ''Ben Cannon is twenty-two. He's no child.''

Bass's hands trembled. His vision blurred. He'd expected changes—he'd known from the ship's papers and from his own travels on the *Sally B.* that much time had slipped away from him. He'd known his father would be old, very old, even dead, and that Bass Cannon would be only a memory, and not even a fresh one.

A rough calculation showed him Jack Cannon hadn't waited long to replace him. Interchangeable sons. Components in Cannon's machine—if one malfunctioned, just plug in another. No wonder Dad's still alive, Bass thought bitterly. He had to hang around to see how my replacement worked out before he would pass his little empire on.

Bass shook his head and rejected his unworthy thoughts. It was Raquel's doing. Mom. She would have planned it, and Jack wouldn't even have known, until it was too late to say no. Dad would've resented . . . Ben . . . at first, I think. But he'd have pretended, for Mom's sake, and before long those pretensions would have become real.

I wonder what he's like? he wondered. Not like me. They wouldn't make the same mistakes twice, and besides, his . . . Ben's Orb isn't the same one I grew up on. It must be a harder place, with no room for luxuries like . . . Lorraine. Funny, how I haven't thought of her in so many years. And I was so sure, back then, that I'd never forget. Crowe Academy was another luxury. Ben will never have had the opportunity to wear a fancy uniform. He'll have been more grown-up than I was, at the same age, and more responsible.

I wonder if there's been anyone to take him fishing, or grabbit-hunting? Not Dad. Not at his age, now. Bass felt a brief jolt of pity. Ben Cannon could never have had the companionship with his father that he, Bass, had had. I wish I'd been there to . . . tears sprang to Bass's eyes. What might it have been like if I'd had a kid brother to take fishing, to help over the humps of growing up? Would that have changed me, too? But no, he realized, it wouldn't have happened. One son, one heir. Dad and Mom wouldn't have thought of producing a second son, a disinherited one, and Jack would never have conceived of dividing his empire. Only my absence created the conditions for Ben to exist.

I wonder what he's really like? I can't even imagine. The old man, Jake Van Elderen, approves of him. He's not a rebel, then, not an unruly troublemaker. At twenty-two, he's taken over from Dad already. Serious, then, and responsible. Not like me at all. I suppose Dad and Mom learned from me how not to raise him. Maybe that's for the best—one son to practice on, to dote on and spoil, and then throw away. No mistakes with number two. No coddling, no feeling sorry for how life bats him about. Just one big lesson, psatla-style.

Bass knew he wasn't being fair to anyone. He'd made his own errors. He could have chosen otherwise. He felt left out, of course, cheated of not having had a brother to grow up with, but that was fate. His feelings didn't have to make perfect sense.

Excitement grew in him then. Fate. No, not fate, but *psalaat*. What does Ben Cannon mean—not to me, but to *psalaat-thes*?

Bass had expected a ship from Cannon's Orb. Ever since the *Matteo*'s first celebrated departure, every ship to leave orbit had not one but two unstated missions: to tempt the coalescing groups of viking conquerors into making their first united, large-scale attack on the planet, and to bring this one Orber ship to Phastillan.

He couldn't have predicted who would be on board. If he had known no one, he would have had to choose one of them, or sent them home again to choose the best, the most beautiful . . . the Athenian children from whose midst he would pluck his Theseus. When he had seen the crew list, with Rob on it, his speculations had changed. Rob. Not knowing Rob's role in his banishment, he was still sure that his best friend had opposed it—or perhaps proposed it, to save him from a worse fate? But Bass still doubted Rob. Not his complicity in Bass's exile, but his capability. Was Rob hard enough to deal in *psalaat*? Could he make correct decisions for a world? But now there was another choice, another option. A better one?

Ben . . . Benjamin? . . . Cannon. My brother. Raised in my father's house, nursed by my mother, shaped by the forces that shaped me. He's already older than I was when I left the Orb. Is he the one? The *Barred Spiral* is a fast ship. It's worth eight months' delay to find out.

CHAPTER
FORTY-TWO

The chamber where Bass had first faced Phaniik Reis was crowded to capacity. Humans and psatla intermingled. He would be close enough to hear what was said, but it was Swadeth's show. Swadeth, whose ever-subtler understanding of humans complemented his instinctive comprehension of the *gadesh* Bass had conceived.

Only heavy silence announced the Orb delegation. There were

no heralds or fanfares, just booted feet falling heavily on green, tender moss. Bass tried not to stare at the changes twenty-two years had wrought. Ollie was obese, his face oily with sweat, though the hall was still morning-cool. Wayne's thin beard accented his Asian features: a mandarin in a jumpsuit. Was that Alex—the tall one with the bald pate? How odd, Bass thought. All the times we drew beards and mustaches on our own computerized images, none of us ever pictured ourselves bald. Alex still walked with a halting gait, each step a conscious decision.

Rob! Bass's vision blurred. He squeezed his eyelids to hold betraying tears, but they trickled into his beard. Rob's brisk little mustache only accented his perpetual boyishness. He'll go to his grave with that same innocent wonder, Bass realized. He's still my friend. God, let him still be my friend!

The other man might have been a vague face in chapel: Jacobus "Jake" Van Elderen. He led the pitiful delegation, which drew up in a rank before the *sfalek-ni* Swadeth.

Swadeth stepped forward. Bass tried to remember what the *sfalek-ni* had looked like to him the first time they'd met, and what he'd thought of psatla then. What must these men think? He looked closely at his psatla friend, at the alien shape now grown familiar to his eye. Yes, Bass could call him "friend," for Swadeth, alone of all psatla, surely understood the word. The Orbers see an impenetrable mystery, a being so foreign that they sense no common ground. They are desperate for signs of similarity, for something they can interpret, however wrongly, as a counterpart to something in themselves. And Swadeth, with his carefully cultivated mannerisms, will give them that, in just the way he wants them to have it. It is the Turing Test. If the alien black box returns intelligent responses, responses indistinguishable from human ones, then it *is* human, in a sense. If Swadeth *acts* like my friend, and does not act as my enemy, then he is my friend. Process doesn't matter. The means of cerebration, whether *ksta* or synapse, is irrelevant. Only output can be read. It's no different between humans. I can't see inside these men's heads. I can only listen and interpret, and decide, and Swadeth will provide the stimuli for their words. Bass looked at Swadeth again, and saw him as he must seem to the Orb men.

Swadeth was a dark bronze and he shone with metallic intensity, his colors swirling like sunlight on oily water. He carried himself in almost human fashion, and nodded, consciously bending only where humans bend. The newcomers didn't know that, but they read his curt imperiousness before he spoke. His psatla eyes, like round clay balls set deep in their hooded crests, were impenetrable.

Van Elderen stepped forth. "I am Jacobus Van Elderen, *Sfalekni*, representing the people of Cannon's Orb. I and my associates have come to discuss trade between our worlds."

Swadeth took his cue from Jake's stiff mode of address, though he could be jovially informal when he wanted to be. "You wish not to waste words, sir, so let me ask you: Your holds are empty, so what will you trade for our metals?"

"Whatever you ask, within our ability to deliver it. You know our situation is desperate. Either you help us, or Cannon's Orb will collapse, pirates or vikings will inundate us, and the opportunity for trade will be gone. I've given your people a catalogue of the Orb's products and production figures. Pick what you wish."

"Indeed, you sound like a desperate man, Jacobus Van Elderen. Anything? And in what quantity?" Swadeth played with him, supple *ksta* extending like folded hands with steepled forefingers, pensive and vaguely impatient.

"I understand that Phastillan has an interest in keeping worlds like ours from reversion to savagery. If that's true, then 'shop' cautiously, and allow us enough to survive."

"Sir, the situation is not so simple. Excepting a few cuttings and rooted plants, a colony or two of insects, Cannon's Orb has nothing we want—machinery is what we need, but you produce none. And have you seen our forests? We need no wood. We acquired what we needed from your world a generation ago, from a trader." He gestured stiffly, humanly, at the opening to the outside. "Our maple trees, like the one right out there, are flourishing. See? Even now, their winged seeds scatter, rustling and whirring on the slightest breezes." He moved his upper *ksta* and chitin from side to side, like a man shaking his head slowly, regretfully. "No, trade is out of the question. Our arrangements must be more flexible."

"What do you have in mind?" Faced with Swadeth's smooth urbanity, his air of regal impatience, Van Elderen became abrupt, a country bumpkin. Bass stifled a chuckle. A good-sized bar in Cottertown, together with its parking lot, was larger than any settlement on Phastillan. So much for Swadeth's urbanity.

"Truly, Phastillan—that is to say, the Reis sept and its human adjuncts—wishes to save worlds like yours from . . . inutility. But there are difficulties. Allow me to describe them, and perhaps you will have constructive thoughts to offer.

"One, we have no desire to gut Phastillan for others' benefit. We are not a mining world. Our distribution of elements is the same as that of most transReef worlds. Source minerals are no more common, or more concentrated, than on Cannon's Orb.

"Two, we want no neighbors to be so oversupplied with metallic wealth that they become targets or willing suppliers for predators.

"Three, interstellar transport of such goods is dangerous. Ships coming and going are vulnerable to piracy, and their capture would only resupply our foes, perpetuating the problem."

Bass marveled anew at Swadeth's mimicry. He had again extruded five slender *ksta*, and again manipulated them like human hands, this time raising a "finger" on each count, touching it delicately with the "index finger" of his other "hand." No longer an imperious Pharaoh, he was now a slightly effete professor lecturing to note-taking underclassmen. Where does he find his material? Bass wondered. Old holotapes?

"Four," Swadeth continued, "our production methods are unique, a cooperative effort of humans and psatla. The process, by itself, is not exportable. Those are our qualifications, Jacobus Van Elderen. Can they be circumvented?"

Van Elderen's wolfish, flint-hard grin broke his face into planes delineated by deep-run wrinkles. "Imperial dreams, *Sfalek-ni*? Is psatla domination the price of your fuel?"

"Your grin tells me you don't believe that, Jake. May I call you that?"

"Of course you may—Swadeth," the human countered quickly. The intercourse took on a different tone. An understanding had been reached; accommodation would follow. "No, I don't believe you dream of empire. But you want a psatla colony on the Orb."

"At times I regret not having a human face behind this . . . mask . . . if only so I could grin as ferally as you."

Bass saw that only Rob understood the exchange. Innuendo had always been lost on Wayne and Alex. Ollie reddened, aware that an arrangement had been made, unable to fathom it, and prepared to bluster. Jake raised a hand to restrain his fellows and addressed Swadeth again. "What will it entail? What place will psatla have among us?"

"Initially, their impact will be minimal. In return for a few hundred thousand acres of swamplands infested with—grabbits? Isn't that what you call your pests? In return, psatla will develop and maintain mineral-extraction facilities sufficient for your needs. As a side benefit, they'll control the grabbits."

Initially, Swadeth had said. That word wasn't lost on Van Elderen, who waited patiently as if Swadeth had paused only for breath. "Eventually," Swadeth continued, leaning forward to impart greater intensity to his words, "eventually, the price will be the utter destruction of your social order, your morality and religion, and the reshaping of your entire culture to accommodate the presence of psatla in every aspect of your lives. Your cities will wither, and you will reside in villages like this—'*asapht*,' they are called. Psatla words, spoken and unspoken, will enter your vocabulary and shape your behavior, for concepts exist only as constructs of language, and yours is too spare a tongue. Don't misunderstand—psatla, too, will be changed by you, by your world, and by your own concepts. But that is not your concern. It will be your children's, and your grandchildren's. That surrender to sweeping change is the ultimate price of our aid. Will you pay it?" Swadeth raised four curled "fingers" to his chin. His posture said *Take your time, think about it.*

Jake nodded ponderously. Turning from Swadeth, he surveyed the crowded chamber, the psatla and humans side by side, the flesh, fabric, and myriad chitinous hues pressed together without disharmony. Again, he nodded, then spoke to Swadeth. "Whatever the cost, I see no distress here. Can I believe this same harmony will prevail?"

"If not," Swadeth replied in heavy tones, "then we are doomed here on Phastillan and throughout transReef, for on the very adaptation you observe here hangs our mutual survival."

"There's no choice, is there? How shall we seal our bargain?"

"A token of your good faith, and of *Sfalek-thes* Jack Cannon's," Swadeth said, too smoothly. "That is all."

"What token?"

"An intelligent, adaptable Orb citizen to learn our ways and eventually to escort psatla colonists to their new home. Cannon's son, Ben."

"Ben? A hostage?" Van Elderen was visibly shaken. Bargaining with every life on the Orb he could take in stride, but in the matter of one specific young man . . .

"Hostage, guest, or student. Call it what you wish. *Psalaat* . . ." Swadeth made no apology for using the psatla word, nor did he define it for his audience. ". . . *psalaat* requires him. He will learn, and will eventually return, a *sfalek-thes* in his own right. For that, only Cannon blood will do, wouldn't you say?"

"You may be right," Jake agreed, "but you've asked for the

one thing I can't promise, *Sfalek-ni*. Jack Cannon lost one son, and has no others.''

''Nevertheless, that is the price of survival,'' Swadeth murmured, unmoved. ''Return to Cannon's Orb with my proposal. Fuel will be furnished, both for your ship and enough to maintain your planetary defenses for eighteen months. You can be home in four months, and here again in four more. I am sure that Jack Cannon will agree to my terms before your new supplies dwindle dangerously.''

''I'm less certain than you, *Sfalek-ni*, but at least the additional fuel will extend the Orb's survival awhile. For that, I thank you. Are you finished here? I have much to think about.''

''We are finished, for now.'' Swadeth took a single, sliding step backward. It was as if a door had closed, a curtain dropped. Jake stepped back among his compatriots and, after a brief murmured discussion, led them from the hall.

Bass was smugly gratified at the apprehension in their eyes as they passed unreadable chitin countenances in shades of gold, gray, green, and brown, blank, pinhole eyes that bored into them but gave nothing back, and human faces just as impenetrable as psatla ones. Bass couldn't remember what it was like to look upon alien faces without understanding. Psatla were just people to him now, as expressive in the flaring of body plates, the twitch and tremor of *ksta*, as were mobile human faces. If he had ever thought differently, those thoughts were buried beneath the immense burden of his responsibility for both species, his frightening *gadesh*.

The hall emptied silently. Bass took the ancient Stollivant of Phaniik Reis northward, to his tiny *asaph*. He regretted that he could not talk with the Orbers—with Rob, at least. There is so much I want to know, he mused. And Rob—I ache for the long years behind us, ten more for him than for me. What of our friendship? Could it be rekindled? Would it be only a disappointment, a taste of too-sweet childhood candy no longer palatable to an adult tongue?

Little Adam had never seen a starship rise. He asked countless questions in a piping voice, indiscriminately mixing English and Psatla words. Bass believed his son would eventually sort out the two languages. His thought patterns would remain dual, neither psatla nor human, but Phastillan.

He had playmates of both species at Asaph Phaniikan. The human ones were children, and though newly joined psatla were only confused and unsure, and not the blank slates humans considered babes to be, there were still enough similarities between the two for a bond to form.

Adam spoke casually of his *"ksta"* and their memories, and sometimes surprised his parents with references to times and places he should never have heard of, let alone experienced. Were there truly veins of racial memory in the human mind—memories transmitted from one generation to the next on the strands of microscopic, chromosomal *ksta*? At Phastillan University, humans and psatla sought answers to such questions. They spoke of secondary codes, homeobox-interpreted and located on intron areas of chromosomes. They studied reverse-coded gene sequences and postulated that the human genome was, in its entirety, a collection of ancestral memories. Much that they said flowed over Bass without seeping in. He still had dreams, once in a while.

The *Barred Spiral* was ungainly, a trader modified by weapon platforms. Her hold was full, and her strained overtones protested the weight of her cargo as she rose into a pale violet and gray overcast sky.

"The other ones were never shiny, Papa," Adam said. "What are the funny bumps on it?"

"What other ones, son?"

"I don't member. I wasn't me yet."

"Who were you?"

"Him. A grown-up man."

"Oh."

"What are they, Papa?"

"What? Oh, the bumps. Laser pods. They shine bright lights on bad ships, to make them go away."

"I don't like them. They hurt."

"They do?"

"Uh-huh. They make fires."

The ship's main engines began their takeoff whine, and the *Barred Spiral* rose on a column of dissonance and troubled air, a glittering gem catching sunlight from a patch of clear sky low on the horizon. It was a spark, and then only a bright afterimage against the roiling clouds.

Bass waited. Eight months was no long time; he'd waited much longer in exile. Four months for the *Barred Spiral* to reach the Orb, and four months back. But Phastillan allowed him no time to brood, to speculate on what would transpire on his homeworld, or thereafter. Even when no crises called for his skills or authority there was much to be seen to, and seen. There had been no time for sightseeing before. During his obsessed early days on Phastillan, working on the computer at Asaph Swadethan, he had not been interested; later, with James Aubasson piloting him to the remote terminal sites, he'd spent most of his airtime sleeping or working, and saw mostly vast vistas of thick coastal forest, gray rock and heath, and wide expanses of glittering open water. In exile, there had been only dreary landscapes where gray, lichenous rock and gravels merged imperceptibly with gray, textureless clouds.

Now things had changed. People all over wanted to see him, to partake of the mana of the leader who had, they believed, saved them from death or worse. There was a magic in the laying of curses, the laying on of hands. He didn't begrudge Phastillans their superstitions, which were if anything less awesome than the truth, and he wanted to see more of the planet whose destiny he shaped.

He flew first to Asaph Athkletan, until recently a grassy, otherwise barren isle, sun-drenched and bathed in a warm equatorial current. Hans Holke, whose gardening efforts the *pralasek-ni* Athklet had once aided, was experimenting with multicropping, adapting Earth-origin domestic plants to psatla-style agriculture. Fat-grained wheat grew in the light shade of leggy citrus seedlings. Edible gourds twined on branches, trained with psatla artifice to shade tender bark and to avoid obstructing sunlight from the glossy orange, lemon, and lime leaves. Beneficent insects crawled among gourd stems, over and under leaves, and across the ground below. Birds and birdlike creatures—mammals, reptiles, and others less classifiable—pecked at insects, keeping populations under control.

"Ain't so busy I can't enjoy a hobby," Holke explained when Bass remarked on white-columned stonework rising from a rocky, sea-girt pinnacle. "My dad was a mason, an' I carried his tools to four worlds, before here. 'Sides, all this new Hokkaidan stuff—weather monitors an' such—don't need much fixing, so I got time." Time. So many Phastillans had time, now. Time for work, and enough left over for another full-time task, whether building secure little havens for themselves, exploring, experimenting . . . or loving, when the time was upon them.

What Bass liked to call "neighborhood taverns" were springing up near every significant worksite, whether *asaph*, refinery, or cropland. Though they were often no more than a corner room or two in a rambling psatla structure, a few duplicated the feel, if not the actuality, of some homeworld's ambience. One thing all had in common was good liquor. Psatla could duplicate malt, hops, grapes or grain, sometimes by trial and error, sometimes by verbal description alone, and Phastillans enjoyed a quality and variety of beers, wines, and distillations few worlds could have duplicated.

Absalom Ismail, a brewer by trade, had survived the destruction of Jerusalem Colony by hiding in a mash cooker when raiders hit it. He ran the Insomnia Lodge on the island, so named because Ismail worked days in the fields with Holke and only drew beer after dark. His best was a red-brown beer he claimed came from Colorado, on Earth. Bass was well into his second glass when he noticed the odd looks the brewer was giving him. Ismail looked as if he had something to say. Bass didn't think he was afraid of him, *sfalek* or no, but the man was clearly vacillating. When the only other customer left, Bass spoke. "What is it, Ab? What's on your mind?"

"Uh, Bass—ah, *Sfalek* Bass—it's about a man I saw in port last week, when I was picking up my new inox kettle. I . . . I think I know him."

"Oh?" Bass's hair prickled on his neck. Jerusalem had been wiped out. Every male the raiders could find, Jew or gentile, had been slain, and the women abducted. Few had shown up in the aftermath of the viking defeat, and none Absalom Ismail had known. "Who is it? Who did you see?"

"Ma'mut, his name is. I heard someone call him that."

"Ma'mut al-Jebel? The captain of the *Enzo Vinella*?"

"He was at port, and I saw him go out to a ship. That's all I know."

"The *Vinella* is in port—it could be him. What about this man, Ab? Did you know him on Jerusalem? Don't be afraid to say what's on your mind."

Ismail's face contorted suddenly, and tears sprang to his eyes. His fists clenched and he forced the words out. "He was the one. He killed them. Him and his crew."

"He was a raider? You're sure? You couldn't be mistaken?"

"That—man—killed—my father—and—" Ismail groaned and turned his head away, sobs shaking his thin shoulders. Bass jumped up, spilling his beer, and put his arms around him. It was all he could do right then. Other men, other times, he could influence with his own thoughts and emotions, but not now. There were no prehuman pheromones that create comfort, that mute grief or assuage psychic wounds. There were only dominance and its kin, and sexuality. He could only hold the man, and share in his agony. Bass Cannon was as helpless as he felt.

He held Ab Ismail until the sobbing ceased, then led him to a chair. He poured beer into two glasses and gave one to Ab. "It's entirely likely that Ma'mut al-Jebel was one of the raiders who destroyed Jerusalem, Ab. We don't have the facilities on Phastillan to deal with tampered ship's logs, so I can't prove it. And without other witnesses . . . what do you want me to do, Ab?''

"I . . . I don't know what to do. If I see him again . . . I'm not a violent man, but . . .''

"You know what official policy is, don't you?''

"Uh . . . yeah. Nothing counts from before. But . . .''

"It has to be that way. But if you can prove he is a mass murderer, he'll be banished. His ship is Phastillan's now. His original crew all sold out their shares. He'll be sent off, empty-handed, if he's convicted.''

"You're the *sfalek*. Can't you . . .''

"Without proof? Ab, I can't do that. And you can't kill him. You'd destroy yourself. I know that. You said it—you're not a violent man.'' He sighed. "What I'm going to ask you isn't fair to you, Ab. But I'm asking anyway. Will you stay out of port while *Vinella*'s in? Stay home here, and go on with your life? There are things I can do, ways I can keep Ma'mut from ever hurting anyone again. Will that be enough? Will you trust me to do that?''

"I . . . I don't know.''

"No, I suppose not. Will you keep away from him, for now? Until you can be sure I mean what I say? Will you give me six months?''

"And then? And then what?''

"By then I hope there won't be anything you need to do.''

Absalom Ismail agreed to tend his tavern and his patch of hops, to serve his customers, and to not visit the port, for now. Bass left him sitting in his tiny barroom, staring at the sunlight that turned the fine brew crimson as it passed through his glass.

Bass visited Asaph Lesthefan next, though he hadn't planned to. One of Kstala's protégés was breeding a species of Hokkaidan fireweed that would survive on the open grassy lands, springing up after brushfires and providing cover for tender sapling trees. Later, in leaf-shadow, *Psaalek* Sfithis hoped they would bear fruit and provide forage for the tall, pale beasts that roamed the adjacent forests.

A week later, a single psatla sought out Ma'mut al-Jebel as the captain walked back to his ship after dark. Ma'mut never saw the stiffened *ksta* that latched onto his neck, though he felt its penetrating bite and had time to grunt and reach a hand toward it before he collapsed. His glazed eyes never registered Sfithis's presence when the psatla collected its *ksta*, and, after "tasting" the captain's blood, administered a second, subtler dosage.

"It is done, *Sfalek* Bass," the psatla said later. "He is like those others, now." Indeed, Bass realized when he contrived to meet the captain, the old Ma'mut was gone. The shifty, predatory brightness was gone from his eyes. His answers to Bass's penetrating questions about cargoes, navigation hazards, and *Vinella*'s reworked drives were answered clearly and coherently. Bass had a nagging feeling that Ma'mut had lost something besides his aggression, true, but he seemed no less able for it. But then, they had all lost something. Absalom . . . But that's over, now, Bass thought. Phastillan is a new start for us all. It would be a pity to destroy that with old vendettas, for the sake of the dead, not the living.

There were many other visits, in the months while the *Barred Spiral* thrummed and plowed toward Cannon's Orb, but no problems so painful arose again, for which Bass was very glad. A *sfalek* couldn't afford a conscience, he had long since decided.

CHAPTER
FORTY-THREE

FILE > JOURNAL:JVE
ENTR > 0502

I approach C.O. with heavy heart and paranoid fear. I was with Jack in the dark days following Bass's death and I watched him with his second son when Ben was a babe, a boy, and a young man. Ben is a fine man. No father could ask for better. And the Sfalek-ni Swadeth could not have asked a higher price. Will this be the final burden for Jack? I pray nightly for God's strength in him.

My shipmates' behavior troubles me too. Guilt and expiation. Rob said. I have come to suspect that they are in some way responsible for Bass Cannon's death, and that someone on

Phastillan knows of it. Did they murder him? Could the other boy, Stef, be behind these machinations? Didn't he disappear, go offworld, soon after Bass's death? Time will tell. I do know now that I have no choice but to be aboard the second flight to Phastillan—if indeed Jack authorizes it. I must see these events, and my growing suspicions, through to the end.

The *Barred Spiral* dodged sunward toward Mirasol under variable thrust, on a course the clutter of ships in planetary orbit couldn't have matched even with unlimited fuel. Two ships had been circling like vultures months before the *Barred Spiral* had departed—desperate vessels short on fuel and hoping for an easy catch. The rest were hulks abandoned since *Spiral* had left.

The *Spiral* lived up to her name. She plummeted planetward, then applied fuel-wasting thrust to decelerate just before she dropped into air. One of the orbiting vessels reacted by accelerating, and for a moment fear crossed the tense faces peering at the *Spiral*'s com display.

Their anxiety was short-lived. When the *Spiral* flipped over for a tail-down landing as if she had fuel to spare—which she did— the other realized its mistake, and cut thrust. There was no way it could catch them.

Jack Cannon was among the first notified of the *Barred Spiral*'s return, and he arrived at the Cottertown port before the ship's hatches opened. His son Ben flew in moments later, breaking regs by overflying the heated vessel and putting down on the landing apron beside her. While curious, anxious crowds gathered by the port fences, Jack and Ben Cannon remained inside the ship for almost two hours. When they finally descended the main ramp, Jack looked pale and drawn, but the vid cameras centered on Ben, not on him. Ben's right hand was raised thumb up in the old sign. Arm in arm, they pushed through the crowd to a waiting aircar.

"No! Absolutely, finally, no!" Jack Cannon looked his years. His white hair, usually a dignified crown for the Orb's longtime monarch, was sweat-greasy and rumpled.

"Dad, it's not your choice. I have to go."

"A hostage! No! What about the Hokkaidans and Faraways? No hostages were taken from them! Why are we being singled out?" Jack shook his tangled mane. "It doesn't make sense, son. No sense at all."

"This Swadeth only *spoke* like a man, Jack," Van Elderen pointed out. "He isn't one. How can we know his motivations?

He claims Ben would learn, become a *sfalek*—whatever that may imply—and be returned to us. I can't tell you why, but . . . I believe him.''

"You forget, Jake—or perhaps you never knew. I've been on Phastillan. I've met psatla, had coffee with them in their strange overgrown grass huts, and traded with them.''

The maple trees, Jake remembered, his eyes widening. Of course. I sometimes forget how old Jack is, realtime. He could have . . . he did bring those maples, those gnarled ancient trees, to Phastillan when they were but sprigs. Is there a relationship between his trading and this strange, twisted, biblical tale I can't push from my mind? He sighed. "I see. And what impressions did you form of psatla, so long ago?''

"They are devious beings,'' Jack stated, his voice harsh and grating. "They don't think as we do. Their thoughts range far ahead, and they plan for futures that no individual among them will witness.''

"Much as a young Jack Cannon did? Planning the future of a world none but he would see grow mature? Is that why you don't like them, Jack? Are they *too much* like you?''

"Excuse me, sirs.'' It was Rob who spoke—Rob, who was always silent in such august presences. Sensing that the chasm between the two old friends grew wider each moment, he spoke in desperation. "What if we sent someone else instead? Someone who . . . could pretend to be Ben? I could . . . I mean, I'm older, but I don't look it.''

Jack's eyes bored into him. "Why, Rob? Why would you do that?'' Jake Van Elderen didn't question Rob's offer. He let his suspicions molder in silence.

"I can't explain, sir. It's just . . . an obligation I feel.''

Jack turned to Van Elderen. "Jake? Would it work? Would they recognize Rob?''

Jake pondered, but not, at first, Jack's question. Is this the expiation Rob spoke of? To sacrifice himself as penance for some unspoken deed? Perhaps to save himself from the responsibility for another Cannon life, either Jack's or Ben's? But that's useless speculation. The question is, would it work? Not if, as I believe, Swadeth, or someone, knows exactly what they want. But I can't say that to Jack. "I think someone would—perhaps not the psatla, but there were humans who saw all of us. We could still claim that he was Ben, though—that he'd made the first trip incognito.''

"Aren't you all forgetting something?'' Ben was flushed, barely suppressed his anger. "Me! Dad . . . are you taking over again?

Is that it?'' He did not allow Jack time to reply. ''Rob, your offer is appreciated, whatever your reasons for it, but to quote my father's new favorite word: 'No!' It won't work. They'll surely see through it, and we'll have dug our own grave. Dad, Jake, I've got to see this through myself. Didn't you say their representative, Swadeth, promised that I'd return as a . . . a . . .''

''*Sfalek-thes,*'' Jake interjected, ''their highest rank. A god-king, I believe. A pharaoh. He said their plan—*psalaat*—demanded it. *Psalaat* is a strong word, like 'destiny,' perhaps.''

''Was a set length of time mentioned?'' Ben asked.

''Not exactly. Years, not months, though. We'd have to accept what they decide.''

''I plan to accept their terms, regardless,'' Ben said flatly. ''No, Dad, don't say it! It's not your decision. I'm breaking no contract with you, implied or otherwise.'' Jack couldn't have failed to recognize the implication in his son's words: unless he gave Ben the same free hand in this matter as he had in others, he would be breaking one. He didn't accept his son's rebellion with good grace, but accept it he did.

Ben's thoughts were less straightforward than they seemed. The Orb he had grown up on wasn't the one his long-dead brother had known. While Bass had fretted at the Orb's provincial outlook and compared it unfavorably to other places he'd been, Ben had seen no others; given the reign of chaos among the transReef stars, he'd held out no hope of ever seeing another world. He was Jack Cannon's son, too, with venturer's blood in his veins, and such blood made its own demands. Ben Cannon was determined he would not miss his one chance to set foot on another world. He *would* feel the light of Phastillan's sun.

''It seems so cruel, Bass,'' Betsy said. ''Couldn't you have been honest with them?''

''With Van Elderen, perhaps. Not with the others—I wanted them to sweat.''

''Do you hate them that much? After twelve—or twenty-two—years?''

''I hated them once. Maybe I still do. I don't know.''

''What about me? And the littles?''

''What do you mean?''

''You'd never have had any of us, if it weren't for what they did.''

''If it weren't for you, and Adam and Liz, none of them would have gone home at all. They'd be spending the next twelve years counting lichens!''

"You wouldn't have!" Betsy turned her face from him then. "I don't think I like that part of you," she said to the dark wall beyond.'"I thought you'd stopped hating, but now I'm not sure—it's just cold hate instead of anger. I don't want Adam to grow up like that—vengeful."

"Am I vengeful? Do you really think so?"

"I don't know. I think you've been needlessly cruel. What about your father? Wasn't one loss enough? He's the one who'll be hurt most."

"Jack Cannon is a cleverly disguised dictator. Without his commitment, nothing could be accomplished. I'd spare him if I could, but it isn't possible. This is an experiment; I have to limit the variables. If he knew that I was alive, and behind all this, he'd trust me and agree—and I'd never know if my *psalaat* was enough . . ."

"Your *psalaat*! Damn you, Bass! Is that what everything boils down to—your damned *psalaat*? What about you? What about the man I fell in love with, in spite of myself? Is there anything left of him? I haven't seen him in a while."

"Bets, I'm here! I'm still in love, and I love Adam and Liz. But I can't stop everything else. What would be left for them if I did that? A dead world? I have to finish what I've started, and that means Cannon's Orb must accept the psatla, without other influences. And it's not just *me*, or my *psalaat*. I suspect I'm as much a tool of *psalaat* as a creator of it. An old *psalaat* that was begun a hundred years ago, or two hundred, when Cannon's Orb was a raw new colony and my father was still young."

"I don't understand."

"Jack Cannon never mentioned this world by name, but I'm sure he was here, on Phastillan. I think those maples, the big ones outside Asaph Phaniikan, were seedlings he traded. I know he came home from one voyage with a cure for a blight that was killing our forests. He took more of Phastillan home than he knew. He took *psalaat*, and part of that *psalaat* was . . . me."

Betsy's brow wrinkled. "But you weren't born yet. You weren't even a gleam . . ." Her own eyes gleamed in sudden comprehension. "Your ability to use scent speech? The way you can think like a psatla? Is that what you mean? But how could psatla control events from afar—when you were shanghaied, for instance. And how could they guarantee you'd come to Phastillan?"

"Do those maple trees *guarantee* that any particular seed will flutter onto fertile soil? I don't flatter myself. Dad wasn't the only trader to stop here. There must have been hundreds, even before him. I'm just the one that did manage to flutter down here. Even then, I think I was 'helped.' Maybe Mike Devoro's father, or grandfather, was here once, too—or James's, or even Ziggy Anson's . . . or yours?''

"Not mine. My family were all stay-at-homes. Nobody ever left home except me."

"Yeah? You mean you were born on Earth?"

"Hardly. But you know what I mean."

"Uh-huh. But my point still stands. Psatla *chose* me. The computer work was just bait."

"But, Bass, none of that explains your game with the others. Couldn't you have had it out with them?"

"I could have—but if their guilt didn't make them pledge silence about me, or if I wasn't convinced they wouldn't renege, I'd have had to keep them all here. And some of them—Alex and Ollie, anyway—have families. It's better this way."

"Do you think your father will let Ben come?"

"Even if Jack tries to keep him, he'll come—if he's the man I need. If not, then I'll have to make do with someone else. Maybe Rob. But that won't be the same."

"Is blood that strong? Do you really believe that just because he's your brother—"

"It's more than that. I'm different from most people, in ways even psatla meddling can't explain. What I do with computers, for instance. Interfacing. And I was conceived in a birth lab—I found that out from Rob, of all people. My father seems to sire only daughters by natural means, so Ben has to be a lab baby, too. If anything was done to me there, to my genes, they'll have done it to Ben, too. Only my mother knows."

"What does it matter?" she asked, not understanding.

"Perhaps it doesn't." He sighed. "But I want Ben. I want to meet my brother."

"He may hate you, when he finds out what you've done. Have you thought of that?"

"If he can understand what I've done, what I plan, he won't hate me—and that's another thing: the Orb will be his. I'm not going back. I can't let there be even a suspicion of rivalry between us. I'll be buried on Phastillan—and I'll never leave you."

Betsy's hair fell over her lowered face. Tears, Bass knew. His arm crept out and encircled her shoulder. They were quiet tears, gone as quickly as they'd come. She still didn't look at him. "I believe you, Bass. I believe that you won't let *psalaat* drive us apart. But it's still easier for me if I just pretend you're an ordinary man—most of the time. No *psalaat*, no *gadesh*, just my man."

"Your man, eh? Umm. Aren't you due for a vacation in a week or so?"

"Only if you are," she said with feigned shyness. "You're still my man, you know."

"Magic or not?"

"I can get that anywhere, you fool! Right now, I want you any way I can have you."

"Any way?"

"Try me."

CHAPTER
FORTY-FOUR

Phastillan! After the *Barred Spiral*'s sharp, canned air, the humid atmosphere was redolent, thick with scents of a thousand flowers and myriad spices. It made Ben Cannon's head swirl. He hesitated at the top of the ramp, awed.

This is another world! A whole, new planet, with a yellow sun I can almost look right at. Suddenly the four-month journey shrank as his perspective shifted, and it seemed like he'd stepped directly from home to here, with the ship itself only a doorway.

Ben had been given more information than most Phastillan immigrants. He had read and memorized more than many learned after a year on-planet, and could even speak halting psatla. Swadeth had included language cubes in his briefing package. But there were omissions Ben knew nothing of—there was no discussion of the psatla effect, for one thing.

A ground car jounced across the intensely green carpet of the landing area, avoiding dark patches where ships had set down. There was no dust tail. Ben didn't have to remind himself that this wasn't the Orb. Perhaps it was spring, or perhaps Phastillan was always humid, always emerald and beryl and jade green.

The driver was a man with an ordinary build and sandy hair. He looked a few years older than Ben, with a short beard and a slightly drooping mustache. The Phastillan men who unloaded the ship had beards, too. Is that the style here? Ben wondered. Should I start letting mine grow?

"C'mon down. Are you Ben Cannon?" An ordinary voice, unaccented. Comforting. I'm not a hostage—not if he's all they sent.

"That's me. Are you the reception committee?"

"All there is. We're not too formal here."

Ben descended the stairs formed into the edge of the ramp and climbed into the waiting vehicle. Even idling, the groundcar shuddered with worn, mechanical ague. His host offered neither his name nor his hand. Perhaps, Ben speculated, neither one was customary here. He self-consciously resisted the conditioned urge to offer his own hand in greeting and didn't ask the other man's name.

"I guess you're not," Ben answered him. "From what my shipmates said, I expected to be met with armed troops, at the least. Why the change from the last time the *Spiral* was here?"

"Precautions. You were expected this time. Are you ready for a short tour?"

A tour? "Is that permitted? I'm sorry—I don't mean to sound like I expected a police state, but won't I be expected somewhere?"

"Only by me, really. Your crew has things to attend to, but you can take all the time you want. Even grab an aircar and see the planet—this part of it, anyway."

"I'd love it!" With difficulty, Ben held back a score of questions. He didn't feel like a hostage. Was he, though? After all, what need was there for an armed guard? He couldn't run away home.

The ground car's fat balloon tires made no marks on the furry stuff beneath them, but the aging vehicle emitted a cacophony of grinds, clacks, and wheezes that made relaxed conversation impossible until they stopped at a row of wooden sheds. A monstrous, equally ancient aircar squatted in front. For all its antiquity, it was impeccably maintained, with finely rubbed paintwork and polished fittings of inox brass. "Incredible!" Ben exclaimed. "A Stollivant! I wonder how many of these are still flying?"

"Funny old bus, isn't it? This is the *sfalek-thes*'s own."

Ben delved among his four months' accumulation of facts. "Phaniik Reis's aircar? What's it doing out here?"

"Your tour, remember?" Why was the other man smiling? It was hard to see what went on beneath his beard and drooping mustache.

Then I'm not really a nonentity here, Ben surmised. It's some kind of elaborate stage setting. Ben's studies only hinted at the depths of psatla behavior, but one thing came to mind at that moment: because of the unique way they transmitted memory fragments from one generation to the next, psatla preferred example over mere spoken teaching. Such whole-body experiences were more easily remembered than fine abstractions learned and pondered. *Am I being taught a lesson, psatla-fashion?* he wondered. He decided not to relax with his innocuous-seeming host.

"I've only seen one aircar like this," he commented, running his hand affectionately over its polished chestnut surface. "That was the one I first learned to fly."

"Hmmph," the other replied. "A Stollivant?"

"Exactly like this one, even the color. It's a touch of home."

"Why don't you fly us, then?"

"You mean it? Great!" Ben seemed suddenly much younger than his twenty-odd years. He vaulted into the 'car's cockpit in one motion and settled himself before the flight panel. His host followed more sedately. "Take her up to max," he ordered, "and head toward those hills. I'll show you the heart of the 'new' Phastillan on the way to my place."

"Yours? Who are . . . you know, I don't even know your name. What shall I call you?"

The older man smiled broadly. "How about 'Reis'?"

"Reis? The psatla sept?"

"It's as good as any. I've been adopted, so to say."

"Reis it is, then," Ben agreed, now absolutely convinced that a lesson was under way.

CHAPTER
FORTY-FIVE

"The stage is set, *Sfalek* Bass? The young scion is safely here?" Swadeth spoke in Psatla for the benefit of two *tsfeneke*, brown and soft-chitined from recent emergence. One was considerably darker than the other. Bass sensed a vague familiarity, a nagging, scent-inspired memory of . . . but never mind, now.

"He's settled in, Swadeth. Has your household been instructed?"

"Every one. They won't fail us. Some will be even less communicative than you might wish—ones such as these." He extended a brassy-gold arm toward the *tsfenek't*, extruding a temporary "thumb" momentarily, while his blank, pinholed eyes rolled upward. Bass suppressed a laugh. "Human children will be the least predictable, of course," Swadeth added.

"Students' children? Are there many?"

"Never enough. They are teachers, too. Psatla learn words from them. 'Pal' is a current favorite. Children teach pleasant things: love without *gadesh*, the comfort of body-closeness, even the satisfaction of protecting such young ones who are small and new.

"But tell me, Bass—does he meet your expectations? Will he serve?"

"Swadeth, he's so much like me it's frightening—except that he's better than I ever was."

"How can that be?"

"He's humble where I was arrogant; where I was condescending, he's tolerant. He's as intelligent as I am, more patient—and more perceptive—than I ever was. Is that enough?"

"You are proud of him. You love him. That is well," Swadeth said. "Will he create *gadesh*?"

"More than I have, or you. But no *psalaat* guides him yet, except that which brought him here."

"He was not forced by others, by their opinions?"

"Quite the contrary. From what I could learn, he overrode his parents' and friends' objections to come here. He cares more about his people, his responsibility to them, than about himself." Bass shook his head, bemused. "I think I'm jealous, Swadeth. He's damn near perfect."

"Jealousy is outside my experience, Bass. I am content to understand humor—and perhaps love. I think jealousy must not be pleasant." Swadeth rotated his uppermost carapace from side to side in human negation. "Have you confronted the others? His shipmates?"

"Not yet. They're with Ade at the port. He'll have prepared them by now. We'll play that charade out tonight, before Ade's conscience gets the better of him."

"He means well," Swadeth said.

Bass laughed then. "That's the most un-psatla thing you've ever said! Good intentions? Have we humans corrupted you that much?"

Swadeth, too, laughed. The *ksta* that made up his arm trembled in tight, synchronous rhythm, causing his smallest chitin plates to clatter like baby-rattles.

"I understand," Rob Santiago said, "that everyone on Phastillan has adopted psatla conventions of rank. Is it necessary to carry things that far?"

Ade Folgrin heard his thinly masked suspicion. "It was expedient. We were a scattering of people from a score of worlds, each different. Aren't you really asking whether Cannon's Orb will be required to do likewise?"

"I'm wondering what designs you have on us," Rob snapped back, "and evasion doesn't reassure me. When will this mysterious 'Reis' see us? And where is Ben?"

"Reis is here now," Ade said, having caught Bass's entrance out of the corner of his eye. "Ask him about Ben Cannon." Turning, he addressed Bass. "*Sfalek* Reis, the delegation from Cannon's Orb."

They stared. Bass's appearance, for him quite ordinary and everyday, was a calculated affront. His stained homemade moccasins were worn without socks, and his faded blue trousers had been rudely hacked off midcalf. His shirt was collarless, eye-shattering yellow, and sweat-darkened under the arms. Even his hair and beard were damp, beaded with fine droplets from the light rain outside.

"Where's Ben?" Rob blurted. "What have you done with him?"

"Do you care?" Bass shot back, his hours of quiet meditation and imaging paying off immediately in quick thought and instantaneous reaction. "Is he more to you than payment for your cargo—and our guarantee that it's not danegeld for pirates or vikings?"

Rob paled. Ben. What have I gotten you into? I never should have let you come. I should have been the one. There was no recognition of Bass in his bright, sick stare.

"*Sfalek* Reis," Van Elderen soothed, stalling for time to assimilate the revelation that almost overwhelmed him: This is the man! This is Joseph, the guiding mind behind Swadeth/Pharaoh. Who is he? His speech is almost accentless . . . "We have no doubts that Ben is well," he faltered. "My assistant is overwrought. But is there no alternative to this hostage business? We have demonstrated our good faith."

"Have you?" Bass countered. "I am less confident. But if you have alternatives, suggest them." Was that the controlled arrogance he wanted? Bass didn't look at Ollie, Wayne, or at Alex behind them. Or Rob. If anyone saw through his masquerade, it would be Rob. For years he'd planned this moment, his betrayers all in one room so he could see truth in their eyes, but all he felt was fear that his imposture would be discovered. *Psalaat* was forgotten. He was Bass Cannon of Cannon's Orb, and his playmates might see him as he was, childish and vindictive.

Alexei Dovstran pushed past the others to stand before the *sfalek* Reis. "Keep us instead," he demanded, his face working and twisting. "The four of us, for Ben."

Bass recovered rapidly. "That's noble of you," he sneered, "but what leverage does that leave me?"

Quiet Wayne answered. "The four of us—not Jake, who has no part in this—are prime contractors to Jack Cannon. We control forty percent of the Orb's wealth. Ben is only his father's son, and Jack is old. If Jack dies, your hold on the Orb is broken, for we will be running it."

It made sense. If control had been his objective, he would have been foolish not to agree. But he wanted something else. "I'm sure you can back up your claims. But this is Phastillan, where other things weigh more than contracts and controlling interests. Phaniik Reis wants your motives as well. With so much to lose, why would you throw away all you've gained for the Cannon heir?"

Wayne was momentarily speechless. They had prepared to argue advantage and leverage . . . but motive? "He's Jack's only son. Ben means everything to him. We only want—"

"Do you love him that much?" Bass interrupted. "That old man? Enough to sell yourselves? You can do better than that. You accuse us of evasion—what of yourselves?"

"I don't know what you mean," Wayne stammered.

"Of course you do. Your strong emotion is evident. It fills the air and stifles me, yet you evade—you foist altruistic trash on me." Bass turned away. "Discuss it among yourselves," he said. "Decide what is the cost of lying to me. Put a price on truth."

"Please wait." Rob looked directly at Bass with no sign of recognition. Have I changed that much, Bass wondered sadly, that my boyhood best friend sees only a stranger? "There are explanations," Rob continued, "but they're personal. Jake?" He turned to Van Elderen. "May the rest of us speak privately with the *sfalek*?"

"Of course. Your reasons and motives are your own. But if there are to be changes in our agreements . . ."

"Not by us. We'll only speak of personal situations."

"Agreed, then. *Sfalek-ni* Folgrin, will you show me out?" Ade nodded, and together, formally arm in arm, the two tall, aging men left the room.

Bass spoke first. "Shall we waste no more time on equivocation?"

Rob looked at the others. It was a time for truth, he knew, but none of them volunteered to speak. He sighed resignedly. "We are guilty men," he said. "That's why we're here, and why we've offered ourselves for Ben." The *sfalek*'s basilisk stare was devoid of encouragement or judgment, but Rob drew a deep breath and plunged on. "We four hurt Jack Cannon deeply once. He never found us out, but we've lived with it for more than twenty years, good years. We've prospered. If Ben goes home, we'll have paid our debt as fully as we can. What else can I tell you?"

"You have to ask that?" Bass almost snarled. "I've heard evasions, circumlocutions, and drivel! Guilt? What for? You 'hurt' Jack Cannon? What did you do? You've said nothing. I'll ask you only this one time, so weigh your words: Of what are you guilty?"

Rob's shoulders sank and his hands dropped limply to his sides. Twice he parted his lips to speak, twice he gulped, swallowing his words. "Jack Cannon had another son. We were his friends. I . . . I loved him. He was my best friend. He was beaten and drugged, and his contract was illegally sold to a spacer. We could have saved him, but . . . we did nothing. We were afraid. We helped . . . we made it look as if he had died in an accident."

"Why?" Bass demanded. "He was your friend? I fail to understand. What could you fear so much?"

"There was another man. A boy . . . we were boys still . . . he beat . . . Bass Cannon . . . almost to death. The other boy's father browbeat us, threatened to involve us, to blame us unless we kept silent. We did."

"Still you simplify! I sense that you, Roberto Santiago, would say more. What restrains you? These men? Loyalty to your brothers-in-guilt? Fear of them?" Bass shrugged. "So be silent. I would hear from them." He whirled and stopped abruptly, face-to-face with Wayne. "I would know your motives. Why did you incur such guilt, of such a magnitude that, even decades later, you are prompted to sacrifice all to expiate it? Speak of that, Orb-human."

Wayne cringed before the almost-alien man who leaned over him. With great effort, he forced himself to look directly at his questioner. "I was afraid for Stef, for the boy who beat Bass Cannon. It was all so unfair—Stef was born with nothing. He had nothing, not looks, personality . . . but he worked so hard. He *tried*. And when Bass came in, in his cadet's uniform, when he cut into Stef, made his efforts seem futile and pathetic, I hated

him. What Stef did was wrong, but Bass *deserved* what he got.''
Wayne drew breath, a deep, wavering intake, almost a sob. In
anger, even old, remembered anger, his eyes held Bass's defiantly.

Bass softened visibly. ''This Cannon boy was an arrogant fool,
then. And he was his father's heir. Did you judge him unfit to rule
your world?''

Wayne responded immediately. ''We didn't . . . I didn't think
of that at all. I just hated him for destroying what the five of us
had put together—our contract, our bonuses, and the future we
hoped for.''

''He had the power to destroy your hopes—your *psalaat*?''

''We thought so. Now, looking back, I'm not sure. We did go
on. We worked hard, and we've all been successful. Maybe we
still would have done it, in spite of Bass. Only Stef lost out.''

Bass nodded and dismissed Wayne with a glance. ''Events take
on clarity. It is well, for if our two worlds are to share a future,
we must surely share understanding. Thus far we have revealed
guilt and loyalty, hatred and retrospective doubt. Is there more?''
His eyes captured Alex's gaze.

''I just went along with things. I was angry with Bass, sure,
but when I saw him all bloody, with that big gash on his head, I
was just scared. I was sure that he would die, and I didn't want
to be . . . involved . . . in anything like that.''

''Self-interest, then? Even though you struck no blow, you felt
you would be condemned along with . . . Stef?''

''I knew it. When I saw Bass lying there, I knew *everything*
was all over. It would all have come out in arbitration, how we
just sat at the bar and let Bass go looking for Stef, *knowing* what
Stef planned, *knowing* what would happen. Stef wasn't going to
give Bass a chance to fight. Bass had all that military training,
hand-to-hand combat stuff. When we sat silently, we condemned
ourselves. Stef . . . well, you had to know him. He wasn't as
responsible as the rest of us . . . should have been. Stef was like
an act of God, like a forest fire. He just acted, always. We could
have stopped him.''

Again, the *sfalek* nodded in seeming sympathy. ''I see. Is it fair
to say that by *not* acting, you served your own ends? That Bass
Cannon's demise would have favored your eventual prosperity?''

Alex tensed and shook his head in violent denial. ''No!
We . . . I never thought of that. It was just . . . easier . . . to let
things happen, not to do anything at all.''

Bass held up a hand for silence. ''But later? You left his father in limbo, thinking the son dead. Was that not self-interest, a calculated omission and one you profited from?''

Tears, whether of grief, frustration, or anger, sprang into Alex's eyes. "You don't understand. What good would have come of confessing after everything was done? Bass was gone on an old time-stretching freighter. Nothing could have brought him back. Jack was an old man already, and no one expected . . . no one except Raquel, his wife, believed he'd live two years, let alone two decades and more. It was Ben who gave him a reason to live.''

"Couldn't you have given him the hope of knowing his son left the Orb alive?''

"Hope? Of what? Bass was gone for good, and Jack *trusted* us. In the years while Ben was growing, we became his primes. We were Ben's godfathers. We never betrayed Jack's trust, either. We did everything we could for him, and for Ben. Call it guilt or cowardice, but we did it. We were loyal, and we came to love that old man, too. What good would our confession have done? We did more by being silent. You think it was easy? It would have been *easy* to have hopped a freighter and left Jack a letter. No matter what our motives were at first, what we did was try to make up for everything. You can judge us, if you want—but don't reveal us to Jack Cannon. He doesn't deserve to be hurt again.''

Bass put a hand on Alex's shoulder. "I believe you. I see there is no evil in you, in Roberto Santiago, or in Wayne T'song.'' He turned, slowly this time. "I have not heard from one of you.'' His gaze fell on Oliver Nickerson. The fat man sweated profusely, and refused to match eyes with him. "I think there are motives yet unrevealed,'' Bass said in a portentous voice. "Tell me of those.''

"What's to tell?'' Ollie muttered, head down. "They said it all.'' *They*. The single word conveyed the fat man's utter betrayal by his three companions.

"You have nothing to add?'' Bass asked with false gentleness. "They have spoken for you, too? You are sure?''

"Of course I am!'' Ollie reddened. "What else is there? Look, I don't have to take this! Do whatever you want, blab it all to Jake Van Elderen, to Jack Cannon himself . . . it won't do anybody any good.''

"Of course it wouldn't. I have no intention of airing ancient dirty linen. I thought I made that clear. It is *your motives*, your own self-interests that concern me. Knowing those, I will be in a position to decide the fate of your world.'' The reminder was less than subtle. He again held up a hand to forestall angry protest. "Don't mistake me. I do *not* judge you. I place no moral or ethical weight upon your acts or your omissions. My decision will be pragmatic. Either I can trust you to follow your own natural leanings . . . Roberto's love of Bass Cannon, now conferred upon his father and brother; Wayne's hatred, turned first into regret, then to the desire to atone; Alexei's sacrifice of his own integrity for the greater good, the lesser pain.

"What I have not heard, Oliver Nickerson, is what motivated you then, and what does so now. And I strongly suspect I will *not* hear those things from your own lips. Am I correct?" Ollie's stubborn, sweating silence was answer enough. Bass sighed theatrically. "Then *I* will tell *you*. Fair enough? I will speak of your jealousy of Bass Cannon, who was everything you could never be . . . and not by effort, but by accident of birth and genes. He was slim, was he not? Slim and active? Didn't his cadet-captain's uniform fit to perfection? Could you have worn such a garment in comfort? And he was scion of a planetary house. Could you have filled his shoes? Did you try, all these years? Try and fail?"

Ollie's face flushed with impotent anger, with shame, perhaps, but without a trace of guilt. "Are you, as am I, a *pragmatist*, Oliver Nickerson? A *practical* man? Did you see that young Cannon's removal would further your own ambitions?" Bass's brow furrowed momentarily as a vague memory came to the fore. Ollie's own words, heard through a haze of semiconsciousness and incredible pain: "Look, Rob. Be *practical* . . . this is our future we're deciding here . . ." He continued, recovering his interrupted thought. "Did you decide on grounds of personal advantage to remain silent?" Again, the theatrical sigh. "Never mind. Your silence speaks even where you refuse. I pity you. You could not be Bass Cannon. Your struggle was hopeless from its inception, for even when Cannon was removed from your equation, you failed. There was Ben, and you could not be Ben Cannon, either. For two decades you watched him grow, you watched him move smoothly into the places of power and responsibility you coveted." Bass affected a mien of wistful regret, of pity. But was it truly an affectation? "These others have paid, each in his own way, for their decisions-past. You, too, have paid, and will alone continue to pay. Events and eventual revelation will show you your error." He turned away.

"I am satisfied with your tales, spoken and silent. There is only Stef, now, and his father. Where are they now? Why aren't *they* here instead of you?" I should be enjoying this, Bass thought, but I feel cheaper than they do. Only his compulsion to know what had really happened during his last hours on the Orb kept him from calling off the charade. That, and *psalaat*.

"The father of the other boy is dead," Rob said, "and he—Stef—disappeared. It was a long time ago."

"If this other boy, this man, still lives, then he is the guilty one. But he isn't paying, is he?"

Rob shook his head and uttered a short, bitter laugh. "If you knew Stef Myers, you'd know that just being him is punishment enough. He never stood a chance. We felt sorry for him, tried to be friends, but he always screwed up. If he's alive, he's still screwing up, still hurting himself."

No, Bass said silently, he's not screwing up anymore. He's free of it all—his past, his guilt . . . free of himself. Stef, alone of all of you, has bought absolution. But the price—the price. The delegation was silent, responding to the hand which Bass raised, palm outward. He looked as if he were pondering Rob's apology for Stef. Actually, he was remembering . . .

Stef was on Phastillan. Bass had seen him. He'd found him near Asaph Lesthefan, in a pen vikings had used for the *asaph*'s psatla residents. Recognition hadn't come easily. The first time, Bass had flown halfway home before he turned back to the *asaph*. Of course it's Stef, he'd realized. Stef always picked sinking ships, losers. Even face-to-face, he saw little of Stef in those vacant, bovine eyes.

"That one," he'd asked a Hokkaidan woman watching over the penned herd. "When will he be freed?"

"I don't know, *Sfalek-thes*. As soon as a compatible group can be assembled—a month or two. As for where . . . we've saturated this continent already. The next 'colonies' will be in the south, near Asaph Phtha'an, but he wouldn't fit in there."

"Is there something wrong?"

"It's his MHC category—major histocompatibility complex, that is. We sort them by breeding populations."

"What significance does MHC have for breeding?"

"I'm sorry, *Sfalek-thes*. I assumed you knew. Like most mammals, even humans, they sense variations. If MHC's are too close, like among relatives, the individuals avoid each other during estrus. It prevents inbreeding. If their MHCs are too far apart, they don't react at all, like they're different species entirely. That one is a rare type." She pointed at Stef, who squatted quietly, aimlessly sifting soft humus through the fingers of one hand. "He's so far from the norm we haven't found any others who react positively with him. He's a loser. He probably didn't have a friend in the world, even when he was human. Unless we can put together a group of at least five compatibles, he'll always be that way. Ah . . . *Sfalek*? *Sfalek* Bass? Is something wrong?''

The woman couldn't miss the glitter of tears that ran down Bass's cheeks, even if she didn't hear his despairing moan.

Damn it to hell, Stef! Even now, even with all the twisted memories gone, you're still odd man out. And now I find it was never even your fault. *Bad blood,* they used to say. Bass blinked his vision clear. ''Aren't there others like him? I don't want him to suffer among ones hostile to him. And will his offspring be normal?''

''I'll try to make up a group of at least marginal compatibles. *Sfalek* Bass, ones who won't attack him or drive him away. And as for children . . . the ordinary victims of the plague will have normal children, but this is a preexisting condition. We don't have a real gene lab on Phastillan, and breeding the trait out would take generations.'' She smiled apologetically and shrugged. ''Why does he matter so much? Was he someone you knew?''

''He was.'' Bass's voice cracked. ''He was someone who . . . should beget children who won't be . . . losers. His genes . . . his *ksta* . . . deserve a chance. Is it possible? Can you give him a destiny?''

If the girl was surprised by his words, his emotion, and his psatla-like presumption of human *ksta*, she didn't show it. ''I can make a special effort to find marginal compatibles. I'll have to alert the other containment areas to look out for them and . . .'' Absorbed in the problem Bass had given her, she stared at Stef. Psatla, she thought. How would psatla deal with this? They must have a better way.

Neither she nor Bass knew it then, but he had just given her a destiny—a course that would shape her life and those of all the erstwhile vikings, too.

Bass interrupted her thoughts. ''Will you be able to identify infants that are his?''

''Oh, yes. That'll be easy.''

''Then I have a favor to ask of you.''

''Of course. *Sfalek*. Whatever I can do.''

''I want you oversee him personally. His offspring . . . I wish to adopt them. Will you save them for me?''

Open-mouthed, the young woman stared speechlessly for several seconds before regaining her composure. Then Dr. Sally Masters agreed, of course, to do as the *sfalek* wished.

* * *

With effort, Bass wrenched himself back to the present, where the Orb delegation anxiously awaited his return. He let his eyes travel from Rob to Alex, to Wayne and then Ollie. "Do you all affirm what this man has said? Do you all share equally in this guilt?" One by one, they nodded silently. "Then I have heard enough. I believe you. You may go." He laid a hand on Rob's shoulder. "You and I must talk further. Walk with me outside."

"What happens now?" Alexei asked, his manner even more subdued than usual. "Will Ben be freed?"

"Ben is already free," Bass said. "He chose to be here, to stay and learn. If I sent him home to his father, he would be less free." Ollie and Wayne had stopped inside the door. "Besides, all this was a charade. I merely wanted to exact a measure of truth from you. Confession of one's sins is a good thing—as your odd religion teaches you."

Rob was struck dumb. The others looked beaten by strange turns of events, by the strange *sfalek*'s madness. "Come," Bass said to Rob, "we must talk." Puzzled by his gentle manner, by the hand still resting on his shoulder, Rob followed him through the portal.

"Why? Why did you degrade us like that?" he demanded. "What good has it done?"

"Wait until we are away from here." They walked across the landing area of the port, past the *Barred Spiral* and another ship, into a low, scrubby wood.

"I don't understand," Rob said, pushing aside damp branches. Bass remained silent. They sloshed through a small creek. Bass's moccasins oozed water and were soon dry, but Rob's boots sloshed and squelched. Ahead, a larger stream glittered among the trees.

"You can take those off," Bass said. "Nothing in the soil will hurt you as much as your boot soles hurt the moss."

"I'm sorry," Rob said sincerely. "I forgot how sensitive psatla are about living things." If there was irony in his remark, his voice didn't reveal it. He sat, pulled off the boots.

"The moss will heal in a day or two. Psatla have made Phastillan a forgiving place."

That irony wasn't lost on Rob. "Forgiving? What's to forgive? Us? The dirty little incidents of our past? Our shame?"

"On Cannon's Orb you're taught to seek answers. Here, our young learn the art of questioning. What good are answers if the questions are irrelevant?"

"What question should I ask, *Sfalek*?"

He waited for a reply that was long in coming. "Who am I, Rob? Ask me who I am."

In that one utterance, Bass had dropped the intonations of one who spoke Psatla oftener than English. The nine small words were spoken not by a *sfalek*, not by the inquisitor Reis, but by Bass Cannon, Rob's childhood friend.

Slowly, Rob's eyes rose from his limp boots and his bare, white feet. As if against a terrible resistance, a crushing weight, they lifted until they met Bass's own. Rob struggled to regain his feet, but he trembled so violently that he got no further than his knees. Tears blurred his vision. "My God! Bass?"

That face, at once so familiar, so alien in its harsh set, was blurred with sunlight and with Rob's tears. Old memories filled in what he couldn't see: the face of a younger Bass Cannon that matched the voice Rob heard—a face too young for a beard, without the lines graved by age and cold, bitter exile.

Firm hands pulled Rob to his feet. He brushed his sleeve across his eyes and looked at Bass. "For twenty-two years," he said tremulously, "I've imagined finding you, seeing you again. I considered every possibility except . . . except that I wouldn't know you." He held out his arms.

How strange it's all come out, Bass thought as they hugged. I thought I was the one who suffered, but I'm comforting him. I was his "big brother"; now he's older than me. Bass saw silver-gray in the darkness of Rob's hair. His friend—still his friend—shuddered with great, racking sobs, not making a sound. Our old roles still stand, Bass realized. That hasn't changed.

Rob slowly regained control of his shaking and his tears. "Bass? Does Ben know? My God, we've got to get word to your father!"

"It's been twelve years . . . no, for you it's been twenty-two. There's plenty of time. Besides, how can my death be explained now—if I'm alive?"

Rob was shocked. "It's been only twelve years for you? No wonder I . . . that beard doesn't age you much, only hides . . ." The implication of Bass's statement struck him. "You don't intend to let Jack know you're alive? But why?"

"He accepted my death once—and he's got Ben. I'd be an intruder. And you—Jack trusts you. If he knew the truth, he'd have four more lives to mourn."

"It's not right, Bass. He should be told."

"Will you do it? Even if I ask you not to?"

"I don't know." Rob shook his head. "I just don't know. But what about Ben? Will you tell him?"

"That depends on him. I'll see him again in a few months, after he's . . . been exposed to Phastillan. If he's learned enough by then . . ."

"He really isn't a hostage, is he?"

"Not in any sense." Bass glowed. "I have great hopes for my little brother. He's been well raised." Bass paused as a new thought struck him. "Rob, do you have children? Did you marry?"

"I never found time for it. After you . . . were gone, I pulled back. I spent years up in the mountains, and when I heard about Ben being born, I—"

Bass laughed and slapped him on the back. "I knew it! Do you know, I felt it in him—your touch. Rob, it was so strange! I kept looking for Dad in him, or myself, and instead, I saw you."

"I looked for you in him, Bass. Only I found what I sought."

While they talked, the sun burned off the last of the morning haze. It was too hot for the heavy Orb clothes Rob wore. "Care for a swim?" Bass asked him. "We've got time." Rob could see the old, familiar Bass now, even through his beard. How had he not recognized him at once?

"Why not?" he said, grinning. "Beat you in!" Rob tore off his shirt on the run toward the shimmering water and tripped over his trousers the last few steps, hitting the river's surface with a great splash. "Hey, Bass! Is there anything dangerous in here?"

Bass jumped in. "There is now!" He laughed and pulled Rob under. They splashed and yelled, wrestling like the two boys who still lived inside them despite the varying, inconstant years. Later, they were two bodies stretched out on the soft riverside moss— one white, the other tanned. "Did you marry, Bass?" Rob's wistful tone, more than anything he said, told Bass the depth of his self-denial, the lonely price he'd paid for his guilt.

"After a fashion," Bass replied offhandedly. "But Phastillan is an odd place, and marriage is different here. You'll see what I mean when you've been here awhile."

"You have children, don't you? That's why you won't come home with us, isn't it?"

"Two. A boy and a girl. But they'd do fine without me for a while. I'm staying because I've made my life here. Maybe someday, when it's all over . . ." He shook his head. *"Esaf steh psalaas, psalatak kha gades stehk gadeh."*

"Which means?"

" 'The road taken is glorious, and one's glory makes the road wide.' But that isn't clearer, is it? Psatla sound-speech is that way. 'Obligation follows choice, as honor follows choosing.' " Rob's blank look confirmed he hadn't understood. "Never mind. If you stay, you'll learn."

"Will I be staying, Bass?"

"Only if you choose. You're free to return with the others."

"The others? You're letting them go? Then I really don't understand what all this has been for."

"I don't want to explain it yet, Rob. When I planned it years ago, I wanted revenge, but that's dead. I wanted to know the truth about how I left the Orb, about who was guilty and who wasn't . . . and I'm not quite done with my farce yet. When we go back, I want you to tell the others who I am. Not Jake, though. It's not his affair."

"I can't play with them like that—they're still my friends."

"I don't want you to tell them anything but the truth."

Bass would say no more. He led the way back through the woods, then walked beside Rob over open moss and across the port. Amid the gritty reality of cinder-blocks, corrugated roofs, and blank, steel doors, the brief return to childhood friendship was a waking dream to Rob. Once again, the taller, younger man walking beside him was an enigmatic, powerful stranger. He hoped their brief communion was a beginning, and not just a sad postscript to what once had been.

EPILOGUE
CE 2537. March 14

Many ships plied the darkness between Phastillan and Cannon's Orb. Small ships, for the most part, because the nature of interstellar travel had changed greatly over the decades since the *Barred Spiral*'s historic flight.

Cargoes were smaller now. Most of them consisted not of hard goods but of information: information carried in psatla-derived monomolecules, semiorganic constructs that functioned in the manner of psatla *ksta* and human DNA. Small herds, packs, and flocks of useful nonsentients were transported in coldsleep to new breeding grounds. Humans, psatla, and other sapients—information packets of a different kind—traveled when they wished to, which was not often, and when they had to, which sometimes was.

Exploration hadn't stopped. There were always men and women, psatla, armoths, and others who were chafed by the arbitrary lines defining known space. Perhaps they would encounter new partners out there in the vastness of our galaxy, or perhaps enemies. Few were unduly concerned, though, for a hostile species would be hard put to conquer the diverse confederation that transReef had become.

On the Earthward worlds, powerful men peered anxiously through the twisting corridors of the Caprian Reef at the quiet renaissance of their former colonies. Others, less powerful, looked toward transReef with hope, not fear. As yet, no *ksta* burrowed in the depleted soils of their crowded worlds, but some suspected that the day was not far off. Few transReef ships were allowed through the checkpoints Earthward of the reef, and even Earth-owned vessels were thoroughly searched upon their return homeward.

The ship that burst into Orb space late in the two hundredth year after the Orb's discovery was unusual, but hardly hostile. The man it carried was, to use an archaic term, a pilgrim. There was to be a family reunion.

He had forgotten how bright Mirasol's light was. Phastillan's star was gentler; it didn't burn so whitely. For the first time in sixty-four years, Bass put sunglasses between himself and the light, and stepped off the ship.

"*Sfalek-thes* Cannon?" The young man might have been fifteen or twenty-five. Bass was distracted by the pale violet of his skin and the deep purple intensity of his unshielded eyes. Ultraviolet reflections, he knew, slowed down in passing through the filtering fluid in the lenses of those eyes. They're all like that now, he reminded himself. For the Orb's latest generation, Mirasol was no longer an enemy.

In that violet-toned skin and those iridescent eyes was one full measure of Bass's youthful hopes, as well as his deepest fears. Men the new Orbers were, but men made over to a psatla standard by questing, tasting, changing *ksta*. He had feared the power of those *ksta* once. He had feared, until he understood fully what psatla—what Swadeth and Phaniik Reis—had done. Just as a young Jack Cannon had brought maple trees to Phastillan, so had he carried home with him the unknown beginning of greater change, changes wrought by *ksta* upon his own seed: Bass . . . and Ben. Just as humans gave psatla control over their genes and their ancient primate-bred pheromones, so had psatla given the two brothers a subtle control over their own kind . . . and over psatla.

Those Cannon genes, Bass understood now, could have wrought other changes. The power they gave could have shifted the balance of worlds in quite different ways in the hands of less diffident men—men driven by those ancient drives, men neither shapers of *psalaat* nor shaped by it. Bass could have destroyed Phastillan, once. That was the trade-off psatla had made. They had sent Jack Cannon's genes off, only hoping—had it been only forlorn hope, or truly *psalaat*?—that the seed would someday spin down to Phastillan's waiting soil and would breed true: a maple tree, perhaps, not a bramble or a poison weed. Was it as tenuous a chance as it seemed, or had there been others, too? Other traders, other worlds, other sons? Bass suspected that he and Ben were not alone. There were myriad other worlds in transReef space and beyond, and once, long ago, other traders had called on Phastillan. Had the seeds they'd unknowingly carried taken root as well? And had they bred true?

Bass's thoughts returned to the moment. He'd come full circle. He was home again. But even the distant houses seemed strange— they were open and sprawling, with wide, unshuttered windows stretching from ground to eave, like Phastillan's houses outside the growing forest belts. He remembered a different architecture, which hid its dwellers from the harsh sun. No, he thought, the Orb is no longer my world—except in the larger sense that all the worlds of transReef are mine, now, products of my vision, my *psalaat*. Now it belongs to these violet-hued strangers, and to the psatla whose *ksta* burrow here. Grabbits? Bass had heard they were extinct, casualties of the changes psatla and humans together had wrought. There were collections of bones, and a few stuffed ones. They'd been too voracious, too well adapted, to be allowed to live. Bass had known for a long time that psatla methods could be callous, even cruel.

"*Sfalek-thes?*" The young one is persistent, Bass thought, realizing he'd been daydreaming. I'm not getting senile. It's not in my genes, I've been told. But I am eighty-one—even ninety-one, here—and I've the right to go slowly.

"Yes. And you? What's your name, son?"

"John Cannon, sir . . . Grandfather."

"John . . . then you're Adam's youngest, aren't you?" Bass smiled and held out his arms. "Don't be stuck-up, Grandson. Give me a hug."

The youngster hugged gently at first. Afraid he'll break my old bones, is he? Bass laughed silently and hugged back, strongly. "I didn't break any ribs, did I?'' he jested. ''Where's your father and my brother Ben?''

''They're waiting for you, sir. Up at High Manse.''

''Does Ben still live there?'' Bass wondered aloud. ''There was talk of turning it into a museum, I heard.''

''He'll be the last. For most of us, it's too dark. But it wouldn't seem right to change it—to make the windows bigger or anything—so when he goes, it will be a memorial to . . . to him and your father and . . .''

Again Bass laughed, aloud this time. ''And to me? To the arrogant young pup who was carried off-planet in a crate? Seriously though, son, I'm glad it won't be changed. Perspective. We need to maintain that.''

The truly ancient aircar that awaited him was a memorial in its own right; the maroon Stollivant was as old as the Manse. A hundred years—could that be right? Its sister, the one that had belonged to Phaniik Reis, had been scrapped years before, soon after the old psatla had given his *ksta* to the soil. Phastillan's people weren't so sentimental about things.

But give us another hundred and sixty years, Bass mused. Will there be a museum there, too? No, we're too much like our psatla, too much like our wood-and-wicker *asapht*. Both fade into the soil.

The event that had lured Bass from Phastillan was the Orb's bicentennial. Two hundred years earlier his father had first set foot on the virgin planet, knelt in prayer, and laid claim to it. Bass wished his father had lived for his return, but Jack would have been impossibly old and he had never been told Bass was alive.

Changes had begun soon after Ben returned, bringing a psatla colony with him. Revenge, if Bass had still desired it, was complete. Brooding and bitter, Ollie Nickerson faced the final conclusion that destroyed him: Jack Cannon had created the Orb, and now Ben ruled over its humans and psatla alike. Bass Cannon, his nemesis, ruled Phastillan as *sfalek-thes*, Pharaoh, a god-king. ''Those Cannons always rise to the top,'' he was heard to say in his final delirium.

The Orb's upheaval was no gentler than Phastillan's, long ago, and Jack Cannon had not understood. As the towns and visible signs of his personal conquest faded and were torn down, as their people dispersed into villages and psatla-style communities, it had seemed to him that all he'd accomplished was dissipating as well. When Raquel died quietly one winter afternoon, Jack followed with the same determination he'd shown in his life. Suicide? It wasn't proper to speculate.

Bass dozed in the filtered sunlight penetrating the aircar's canopy. His own eyes held no lilac gleam. The Stollivant ran smoothly, with only a whisper of off-tone chatter from a repulsor a bit out of phase. Someone should fix that, he mused sleepily. I'll bet there's not an ounce of original gear left on the old bus, Dad. Are you going to get a new one one of these years?

"You were right, Dad," he mumbled in his half-sleep. "She's still like new, and we still aren't making them any better, now."

Opening his eyes, he caught his grandson watching him with an expression that bridged the impossible gap between conde-scension and awe. Had he spoken aloud? What was the boy think-ing—that he could speak with the dead? I'll have to straighten him out about that, Bass realized. And the rest of them, too. Those dreams . . . we never did find those neckties, or automobiles . . .

An old ache rose in his chest. Betsy. I wish she were here now, so I could tell her it's turned out all right. But all the real doubts were mine, not hers.

In a high tower, in a window looking out over walls and roofs and other windows, editor Helena Rossignol stared long and hard at six pages of coarse, handmade paper filled with crabbed, old man's handwriting, at the sole historic document on any Earth-ward world that was written by Vassily James Cannon, *Sfalek-thes*. She pondered its worth.

Published now, right on the heels of the news of Cannon's death, it would bring in millions, and the original could be auctioned later for even more. The very thought sent chills racing across her skin.

Ethically, she supposed, because it had been written in re-sponse to her formal query on Anne Harrison's behalf, the letter belonged to King Publications and it was not her choice to publish or not. But it had been delivered by courier to her home, and handed to her in person, and no one else had seen it yet. There were still choices . . .

Helena Rossignol
Executive Editor
King Publications
4021 Centaurus Court
Old New York City, Earth

June 21, 2537

Dear Helena,
    I have left your letter of May 10, 2536 unanswered these many months not out of disinterest but in order to answer

your questions first for myself. Perhaps surprisingly, I had not previously given much thought to myself, my life, or my place in a history yet unwritten.

Before I answer your questions, though, I must regretfully decline your request. I am sure your Anne Harrison is a fine biographer, and I have no doubts that she would give my tales, such as they are, a fair and even-handed treatment, but I am too private a person to willingly have the ramblings and recollections of my old age put before the public. I have, however, enclosed a "to whom it may concern" letter urging that she be given whatever assistance she may require for her research into my life. Among the acts and acquaintances of fourscore and some years, there should be material enough for her purposes, and the credit for writing it will be entirely hers, not mine.

Behind my refusal are considerations less personal, too. Depending on whom Miss Harrison interviews, and when, and where, I will be described as Ahriman or Satan incarnate, as the Jesus, Judas, Moses, or Mohammed of my age, as my species's savior or as a traitor before whose treachery all other betrayals fade to nothing at all—and that is as it should be, for my human "ksta" surely carry them all, whether as gene code or memory, for those "ksta" were once of Earth. Whatever I might say would be subject to the interpretations of my supporters and detractors alike, and I fear that my words might take on an unnatural weight that would be a burden to those who would carry them down yet unexplored future paths. I would much prefer that they tread lightly, and look ahead, not back.

"Psalaat," as you may know, means "path." *Psalaat* are the forest byways of every sentient being's plans and aspirations. Sometimes they wend their solitary ways, momentary disturbances of brush and fern and grass that are soon gone; at other times, they merge as the minds of many join in common hope and endeavor to become well trodden lanes, roads, even highways.

Such was my path, my *psalaat*, in its time. I didn't walk it alone. You asked me if I feel guilty for leading the transReef element of my species down a strange path, hand in hand with psatla, such unthinkably alien beings: I do not. Those who walked with me and those who followed freely chose their *psalaat-ni*, their personal directions. For some of those, the alternative was death from starvation, mineral deficiency, or war, but to deny that they had an alternative to my *psalaat* is to deny them their humanity, their free will, and their souls. There is always a second choice. My own path, without those of other humans and psatla, would forever have remained *psalaat-ni*, and solitary.

Do I regret that there are few great works, few monuments created in the psatla-human gestalt? Again, I do not. Too often, I sometimes suspect, even the most utilitarian monuments like the great dams that hold back Earth's rivers, the ponderous habitats slow-swinging around Centaurus, Sirius, and Sol, the ocean-spanning bridges and continent-girdling cities of your worlds represent no less monumental egos than do the chateaux of France, the pyramids of Giza, and the sculpted face of Liang-Ho Wright that you see when you lift your eyes to your Moon.

Our monuments are subtler ones: they are the flash of violet in the eyes of an Orber who dares, for a brief moment, to glance upward at Mirasol's unshielded glare; they are the green carpet of forest that has, in the last fifty years, crept even to the edges of the northern island of my exile, a monument to Swadeth's "squirrels," his zephalt, and to his *ksta* that now burrow in that same once-dead soil.

Am I satisfied with my own life, with the circuitous path that led me "home" to Cannon's Orb only once, when all was accomplished, when my parents were dead, their bodies long since consumed by hungry *ksta*? I have had many homes: my small "room with a view" in Asaph Swadethan, the labyrinthine passages of Asaph Phaniikan where my children played, and the tiny *asaph* on a mountain ridge where I spend these, my last days, remembering.

Yes, I am satisfied. I am honored that so many psatla, humans, armoths, and others chose to join their *psalaat't* with mine. I am content that my years have been long and full and that, having outlived my wife Elizabeth, my friends Adrian Folgrin and Jacomo Pirel, outlived Phaniik Reis who could never have understood the concept of friendship and Swadeth who understood it so well . . . I am content to have known them and to remember them now, before my own *ksta* merge with theirs in the soil we have all cherished.

And now, your last question: where will *psalaat* lead? It will go where it has always gone, in the direction that hopeful eyes look as they peer into futures yet undecided. Will it someday reach your crowded Earthward worlds, and Earth itself? Will *ksta* someday burrow in the crumbling granite and marble of

New York, in the rust of skyscrapers and the dust of your "monumental" man-made deserts?

That is not *my* psalaat, not my choice, and I will not live to see it. It may be yours, for I surmise that you are still young. There are many in your dormitory-cities, and surely some even on your parkland Earth, who would welcome it. Will you?

Now, in looking back over this epistle that began as a brief note, I discover that I have done just what I claimed I wouldn't do—I've written my old man's ramblings down. Of course, this is just a personal letter, not an autobiography or a memoir, but even so, you may be tempted to publish it. If you do, then my *psalaat* will go on after me, to annoy and inspire and mislead others, useless baggage in all their knapsacks. Nevertheless I will send it, you will read it . . . and then? And then, it is your choice, your *psalaat*, not mine. But consider this: the fate of worlds sometimes hinges on smaller things.

Sincerely,
V. J. Cannon
Asaph Phaniikan, Phastillan

About the Author

L. Warren ''Doug'' Douglas was at one time an archaeologist in the American midwest. He has worked as an illustrator, graphic designer, cartographer, sign painter, and stevedore. He is an accomplished wood-carver and archaeological field illustrator, and he dabbles in oils. His previous publications are scholarly papers in obscure journals, and poems in even more obscure ones.

Doug currently lives in West Michigan with Sue, Neutron, Crystal, and Aunt Louise. Sue is human. He works as a carpenter (weather permitting) and as a writer at the drop of a snowflake. *A Plague of Change* is his first published novel.

DEL REY DISCOVERY

**Experience the wonder of discovery
with Del Rey's newest authors!**

**. . . Because something new is
always worth the risk!**

**TURN THE PAGE FOR AN EXCERPT
FROM THE
NEXT *DEL REY DISCOVERY*:**

Children of the Earth
by Catherine Wells

Coconino heard the scuffing of a moccasined foot behind him, and his already tense body grew more rigid still. Turn around, he willed the approaching figure. Turn around and go back up the trail to the village. Or go on down to the stream, whose quiet gurgle mocks me with its peacefulness. But do not come to my wickiup, you with the weighty step. Do not invade this sanctuary I have created on the canyon floor. Do not intrude on my thoughts, my recollection of the dream of my enemy, and the banded lizard, and the unprotected rock shelf . . .

But the footsteps came inexorably on. Coconino closed his eyes and took a deep breath.

He sat outside his wickiup, enjoying the warm fall afternoon and carefully smoothing the shaft of a new arrow. It was barberry, an excellent strong wood for arrows. Beside him lay four similar shafts ready to be hardened in the hot ashes of the cook fire. The mindless work was what he needed after his restless night, and he had been content in it and his brooding until he heard the step behind him. Now he wished that he had gone hunting instead.

Some twenty yards downstream from him Hummingbird knelt and scooped moist clay from a deposit in the silty ground. She had drawn her long black hair to one side, and it dangled down into the mud, but that didn't seem to bother her. He sometimes wondered which she liked better, fashioning her pots or digging in the mud for the clay from which she made them.

Just a breath of wind pressed her loose leather tunic against her, outlining the slight swelling of her abdomen. Coconino smiled in spite of himself and wondered briefly if having a baby would slow her pace at all. He doubted it. He hoped not; she was a pleasant distraction.

Unlike the shadow that loomed up over him now. Coconino

did not stir from his task, but continued running the shaft through the stone smoothing tool. Perhaps if he ignored the man . . .

"Pardon, Coconino."

Sighing wearily, Coconino put down his work and looked up. His father-in-law, Pine Pitch, was a stocky, heavy-limbed person who walked ponderously. Large protruding lips and slightly angled eyes gave his face an officious expression, but his tone to his son-in-law was always polite.

"Yes, Pine Pitch?" Coconino responded, wondering what new scheme the man had dreamed up to capitalize on his elevated status.

"The Council is concerned," the older man began with great dignity, "that the harvest is so small this year. It has been very dry, you know, and—"

"Yes, I know," Coconino interrupted impatiently. "I have been living here, too."

"Pardon, Coconino," Pine Pitch said. "It is just that newlyweds often have—other things on their minds beside the weather and the crops, and I thought—"

"Please go on, Pine Pitch," Coconino prompted, trying to hurry the man to his point so he would go away again.

"As I was saying," Pine Pitch backtracked maddeningly, "the Council is concerned that the corn and vegetables may not last until spring, so I told them I would speak to you."

Speak to him. Coconino picked up his arrow and studied it thoughtfully. A bird chattered in a nearby tree; the water gurgled in the stream; a hawk soared in the air above them; and still the sense of Pine Pitch's statement escaped him.

"And here you are speaking," he said. "What is it you have to say?"

The man seemed surprised. "Why, I am asking for your help," Pine Pitch said, as though that were perfectly obvious.

Coconino's jaw tightened painfully; he forced himself to relax it. "And what is it you want me to do?" he persisted irritably. "See, I am preparing new arrows for hunting; perhaps I will be able to bring you many deer and some of the Great Antelope. Is that what you meant?"

"That is very good," Pine Pitch said, "but if you could do something about the harvest . . ."

At that Coconino's irritation turned to anger, and he leapt to his feet. "Am I the Mother Earth, to change the way plants grow? Can I give or withhold rains and floods? Can I make the sun shine in Father Sky? I am only a man, Pine Pitch!"

Pine Pitch looked startled. "A man, yes; but you are Coconino."

That was what he said, but what he meant was, You are the great god Coconino.

Coconino paced furiously in front of his wickiup. "Yes, I am Coconino!" he snapped. "Yes, I come from the Time That Was. Yes, I tore the Sky Ship from its place. But I am not a god! You would ascribe to me power that rightfully belongs to the Mother Earth; will you call down Her anger on us all?"

He came to a halt in front of his father-in-law. "I cannot make the corn grow, Pine Pitch. I cannot make the squash swell. I cannot make the trees bear more nuts. The People must do as the People have always done; they must pray to the Mother Earth to feed them from Her bounty. They must go forth upon Her bosom and search for the fruits which She supplies."

Reaching down, he snatched up the half-made arrows. "As for me, Pine Pitch, I will hunt and share my kills, giving thanks to the Mother Earth for all that She supplies. And I will pray with you that She will be merciful"—though why, he thought, she should be merciful to a thick-headed, faithless person like you is beyond me!—"and grant us a mild winter with no sickness. But I can only do what any other man of the People can do!"

Then he added, as salve to his own pride, "What any other man of my hunting skill can do."

As he glared into his father-in-law's disappointed face, Coconino saw Hummingbird running toward them. She had heard their raised voices and had come to intervene. "Father!" she cried out gaily. "Father, did you see the fine, fat duck my clever husband brought home yesterday? It had the prettiest green head; I wanted to make a rattle from it for the baby, but Ironwood Blossom said it wouldn't look very pretty in a few days. So I saved the feathers instead, and I'm going to use them to decorate a shirt for the baby." She caught Coconino's arm and beamed up at him.

Coconino looked down into her shining eyes and round face, and it did, indeed, leach some of the bitterness from him. If only the rest of the People could accept him as Hummingbird did, making only those demands which were reasonable to make. He touched her cheek and gave her a small, reassuring smile.

Then he turned back to his father-in-law, who was still smoldering at the rebuff. The man would never believe him. No matter how many times Coconino explained that he was only human, that he had no mystical powers or undue influence with the Mother Earth, Pine Pitch would continue to think that Coconino was holding back. The older man would return to the Council now and tell them that Coconino had refused to do anything more than pray to the Mother Earth.

"I am sorry, Pine Pitch," he heard himself saying. "I wish I could do more. I wish I could do half the things the legends say I can. But all life still rests in the hand of the Mother Earth, and I cannot tell Her what to do." If I could, he thought miserably, do you not think I would tell Her to bring my Phoenix back to me?

The apology softened his father-in-law's hurt expression somewhat, but still Pine Pitch seemed disinclined to leave. "Perhaps," the older man suggested, "if you would sit with us on the Council . . ."

"I will not sit on the Council," Coconino repeated, as he had repeated each time he was asked. "I am a hunter and a storyteller. Let me be what I am, Pine Pitch."

"Come, I will go back up the hill with you," Hummingbird volunteered, dragging her father away from her moody husband. "I want to speak with Mother about how big I should make the shirt for the baby. I have never sewn for a baby before, you know."

Coconino watched them go, and a small guilt nagged at him as he saw Hummingbird struggle up the steep path to where the rest of the village lay nestled in the shallow caves of the island. It was unfair to his wives to keep his dwelling down here on the canyon bottom, away from the rest of the People. It was especially unfair to Hummingbird in her condition to make her climb so far just to visit her mother or join the other women grinding corn in one of the common areas.

But he could not build a wickiup on the steep slope of the butte; nor was there room on any of the rock shelves to construct such a dwelling. And wickiups were where the People were supposed to live. They were constructed of wood and earth, grasses and leaves; they were round, making the floor a circle as all of life was a circle. They were domed as Father Sky was a dome above their heads. It was *moh-ohnak* to live in such a place.

How had the People come to forget that?

* * *

The solarium was a high-ceilinged room of spacious proportions with tall multipaned windows and rich velvet drapes. It was done up in shades of blue, a cool and relaxing place even on this warm spring day. At first Chelsea thought the room was empty, it was so quiet and still; then a movement near one of the windows caught her eye, and she turned to see a pale slender figure clinging to the drapes.

Camilla. Dressed in robes of warm sky-blue, with her honey-blond hair swept up in soft curls on the crown of her head, she was the epitome of grace and elegance. One hand flitted nervously around her mouth, which was soft and full and painted a gentle rose. As one who had to work at beauty, Chelsea had always envied it in other women. But from the moment she saw Camilla again, Chelsea could not envy her nearly so much as she pitied her.

"Good morning, Camilla," Zachery greeted her softly, as though she were too fragile to bear the full impact of his resonant voice. "Do you remember me?"

The nervous hand flitted from Camilla's mouth to her delicate ear and back again, then came to rest on the blue velvet drape. Was she searching her memory behind those vacant blue eyes? "Zachery," she said finally, and her voice sounded oddly lost in the quietness of the room. "Zachery Zleboton. Your—your mother was on the *Homeward Bound*."

"Yes, and I'm your lawyer," he reminded her.

But Camilla seemed not to notice that he had spoken again. "I'm sorry," Camilla apologized, as though the entire tragedy of the *Homeward Bound* had been her fault.

Zachery ushered Chelsea several steps closer. "Camilla, this is a friend of mine. I think you met her once. Her name is Chelsea Winthrop."

"Winthrop?" A little tremor ran through the ghostly Camilla and her hand began to flit more rapidly. "There was a Captain Winthrop. And a doctor, ship's doctor, Jacqueline Winthrop. They had a son." She looked desperately at Chelsea. "Do you have a brother?"

Chelsea swallowed hard. She began to understand why Zachery had been so moved by this gentle, lost soul. "Yes, Ms. Vanderhoff," she managed, "I have a brother, Cincinnati. You met him once."

"Oh, yes, Cincinnati." A smile broke unexpectedly across Camilla's face and she stepped away from the drape toward them. "What a handsome boy! Like his father. Dark, wavy hair. I liked Cincinnati."

"He liked you, too," Chelsea said.

Then Camilla's features clouded again. "But he made me feel so sad," she said. "So sad. Poor boy. Poor boy."

At that Chelsea stiffened, too well acquainted with people's misplaced pity for Cincinnati. He lives a full life, she thought defensively. He laughs and he loves, and he hurts and he heals, just like the rest of us. We don't pity children, do we? Why pity Cincinnati?

But Zachery was more in tune with Camilla's thoughts. "Why did he make you feel sad, Camilla?" he asked.

"Because he didn't know that his parents were dead," she replied. "He didn't know, and I did. It made me feel sad to know."

Chelsea and Zachery exchanged a startled glance. "You knew?" Chelsea asked. No news of the disaster had been made public until after all family members were notified, nearly a full day after Cincinnati had spoken with Camilla in the museum. "How did you know they were dead?"

"I tapped into the TRC reports as they came in," Camilla told them. "I had . . . passwords. Codes. Dillon needed information, all kinds of information. I got it for him."

Of course, Chelsea realized. You were his information specialist, and you had none of my scruples for how you came by it. So you have seen the original logs. You have seen what I would give my eyeteeth to lay eyes on. "Tell me," Chelsea said earnestly, drawing near the pale woman. "When you read the reports, did it seem—did it seem that there was something wrong? Something the TRC wasn't telling the public?"

Camilla gave her an odd, vacant stare. "Wrong?" Her mouth twisted into a wry smile. "Wrong for who? Wrong for Dillon? Or wrong for the crew?" Then her mind slipped sideways and she began to chant, "Wrong, wrong, wrong for who? Wrong for Dillon? Wrong for the crew?"

Now Zachery stepped in and took hold of Camilla by her arms. It was a firm grip but gentle. "Camilla," he said sternly. "There were problems on the *Homeward Bound*. We know that. There was a navigational error and a probe that malfunctioned. Were those accidents, Camilla? Were they just accidents?"

But like an antique phonograph, Camilla's mind now jumped back into a well-worn groove. "He promised me no one would die," she said plaintively.

"Dillon promised," Chelsea prompted.

"I asked him, and he promised me. He said he paid his agent a great deal of money, and the man would surely come back to spend it."

Chelsea jumped, and Zachery nearly lost his grip on Camilla's arms. "His *agent*?" Zachery pressed. "What agent? Camilla, what was the man's name? Do you know?"

"He asked if I wanted to be Queen of Earth," Camilla whimpered. "Queen of Earth. I didn't want to be queen of anything. I just didn't want people to die. They were good people—did you know Captain Winthrop?" she asked suddenly, gazing up into Zachery's eyes.

"No, I never had the pleasure," Zachery managed.

Camilla's eyes drifted over to Chelsea. "You're his daughter, aren't you?" she asked.

"Yes."

"He was a good man, wasn't he?" Camilla said. "I mean, a truly, truly *good* man."

Chelsea's throat tightened. "One of the best."

"Camilla, what about the agent?" Zachery asked again.

"Dillon . . . wasn't a good man," Camilla said sadly. "I think I knew that all along. I should have known that. But he was so . . ." She waved a hand vaguely, unable to come up with the right word. Then, for just a moment, her eyes lost their vacant stare and there was a glitter of recognition in them. "I killed him, didn't I?" she asked.

Chelsea could see the pain that lanced through Zachery, pain that was more than just one soul grieving for another. "I wasn't there," he whispered.

"Camilla," Chelsea intruded softly. "The agent. Do you mean that Dillon had an agent onboard the *Homeward Bound*? Is that what you meant?"

But Camilla had slipped over the edge again. "He promised me no one would die," she said simply, and twining herself in the velvet drapes, she stared out the window with her soulless eyes and would say no more.